Brimstone Huntress

Book Four of The Royal House of Galadin

By Clair McIntyre

 Cover art by Carley Bylow

ISBN- 9798603366456

Dedication

This book is dedicated to my best friend and cover artist Carley Bylow. Thank you for supporting me in all my crazy schemes and for being the amazing artist that you are. I know how hard it has been for you to put your art on display for the entire world to see, but I'm so proud of you for so doing so. You're a true superstar. :)

Prologue

Yorkshire Moors, 1821

The cool, foggy, desolate evening silence was broken by the sound of shattering wood and glass. Startled by the noise, Lenox stopped dead in his tracks and search the landscape around him with his preternatural senses, in a effort to to determine where the sound was coming from.

Unfortunately for him, these ancient mystical lands were known to play tricks on a person, especially during the evening hours. So after a few moments of hearing nothing more, Lenox continued on his walk unfazed, as he thought in depth of all the things he had learned recently.

Suddenly he was startled again by a strange noise, that sounded like the heavy paws of a large beast running full tilt somewhere very close by. Lenox stopped once more. This time, he closed his eyes and cocked his head in order to listen more carefully to the environment surrounding him, in order to determine the direction that the beast was heading. Regrettably, the answer soon became very clear, when the beast slammed directly into him.

Feeling nothing but the wind rushing past his face, Lenox flew backwards several feet before slamming hard into the ground and rolling ungainly down the rocky terrain. Once he stopped, Lenox took in a shuttering breath and felt the pain of his injuries swamped him. Nearby, he heard a low distinctly canine whine of suffering, that was soon followed by the scratching of animal claws against stone, as if the poor beast were trying to unsuccessfully free itself from a rocky trap.

Lenox sat up and shook off the discomfort of his injuries, before he made his way towards the sounds of the mysterious dog. About ten feet down in a rocky crevice to his left, Lenox spotted the ghostly dark form of a hellhound, who appeared to be the being that hit him moments before.

Bizarrely, Lenox couldn't help but be taken aback by this hound, though for the life of him he couldn't understand why. So instead he took stock of the hellhound and he soon realized two things; one, this hound was definitely female given her scent and look; and two, she was much different from the rest of the hellhounds he had seen before, who had typically been large, dark, sinister-looking shadowy creatures that radiated a soft black or sometimes dark bluish hellfire from their bodies.

Hellhounds were also known to have the ability to automatically strike fear into the hearts of anyone; mortal or immortal alike. However, this hound seemed almost ethereal and gentle in comparison, since she did give off any sense of menace to Lenox. She also had unusual dark fiery golden fur and a very soft reddish hellfire glow.

The hound looked up at him with piercing golden aquamarine eyes that caused Lenox's heart to suddenly stutter in his chest.

"Hi there, I mean you no harm, I so swear it," Lenox said very softly as he held out his hands to show that he didn't have a weapon.

A moment of silence passed between them, before a gentle Northern English female voice mentally whispered, *I know. You're a Vampyr right?*

"Yes I am and my name's Lenox Moregan."

Another moment of silence passed between them before the woman asked, *Why are you out here? Vampyr or no, it's real dangerous, you know.*

Lenox shrugged not wanting to explain the real reason behind why he was out here in the middle of the Yorkshire Moors, so he instead answered with, "I am in no real danger of this place."

Not true, everyone is in danger here, even me. For the Moors know neither friend nor foe.

"That doesn't apply to me," Lenox muttered which caused the hound to cock her head in curiosity before her face belayed a grimace of pain.

Partly deciding to cut of any further lines of questioning and partly unable to stand to see the woman in pain, Lenox made his way down the small crevice towards her. Then he gently freed her and carried her down the rest of the uneven hillside, until he reached a flat boulder very near the bottom.

Once on a firm ground, the female hellhound tried to scramble up into a full standing position, only to let out another soft whine of pain again.

"You can't put any weight on your left rear leg, can you?" Lenox asked as he noticed the large gash on it.

The hound was quiet again before she murmured, *No.*

"Do you have a human form?"

Yeah... came the soft reply.

Lenox said nothing as he waited for her to shift forms. Soon enough, the female hound shifted to her human form. Lenox was dumbstruck by her beauty; She was tall yet willowy, with long fire-tinted golden blonde hair that fell in soft waves down her back. She was also fairly pale, which was not uncommon for hellhounds since they were predominately nocturnal. However far from appearing ghostly, she still maintained the ethereal essence that he had noticed earlier.

Suddenly the baying howl of blood hounds and the shouts from men on horseback, swiftly reminded Lenox of the danger the woman had been escaping from.

Saying nothing more, he scooped her up in his arms and used his own magic to mask their presence from the pursuers. Then wasting no more time, Lenox bolted across the marshy bog land, towards the small cottage he was staying in, that wasn't that far away.

Arriving a short time later, he used his magic again to further hide the cottage from anyone. Then he placed the woman down on a small cot and lit a lamp on a desk nearby.

He turned to face her. "You don't know me from Adam, however I give you my word of honour that you will be safe here tonight."

"I know, for I can see the goodness in your soul Lenox. I'm Penniah by the way. Penniah Hawksley but everyone calls me Penny," Penny said, offering him her hand with a small smile.

"Well met, Penny," Lenox said as he took her hand and kissed the back softly.

Hearing one of the outriders' voices nearby, Lenox focused his magic on the Will o' the Wisps sprites who inhabited the Moors.

"Air sprites hear me," Lenox called out in ancient Gaelic.

"We hear you and obey," the wisps replied in unison.

"Let these men harm no more innocents. Find the source that has caused them to commit such evil and end it," Lenox intoned.

"Aye milord," the wisps said once more.

"Uh…" Penny started to say, when she overheard what he had done.

Lenox turned to her, "I know it is much to ask of you, nonetheless, can you tell no one of that?"

Penny nodded, though she still had a curious look upon her face.

"Sometimes, it is best not to leave the essence of evil to fester," Lenox muttered, hoping that would be enough of an answer for her.

"So the sprites are going to kill them, then?" Penny asked.

Lenox shook his head.

Penny frowned, "I thought that's what you just ordered them to do."

"No, I would never kill those whose will is not their own. Instead, I asked them to deal with the evil force behind it all. Oh here, I'll help you with that," Lenox said, changing the topic while pointing to the wound Penny that had suffered.

Penny nodded gratefully, and Lenox gathered healing herbs that cleansed the wound. Then he carefully cleaned and bound it with a clean cloth as Penny stoically sat still, watching him work.

Giving her a small smile, Lenox said, "I'm sorry I can't heal it instantly for you but it shouldn't need more than one full day of healing with the aid of these herbs."

"Many thanks and I owe you my life," Penny stated gravely.

"You owe me nothing," Lenox instantly replied.

Penny shook her head, "That's not how things work for hellhounds. Everyone knows that."

Lenox sighed and rubbed the back of his neck, "You truly

owe me nothing Penny, though consider my request of silence regarding the Wisps as payment for my aid."

Penny frowned slightly before she sighed and nodded in agreement.

With that sorted, Lenox helped Penny draw up the blankets on the cot to keep herself warm before he took up a spot at the window on the lookout for further danger.

Penny watched him for a time completely befuddled by his kind nature and serious expression. Eventually she dozed off and awoke early the next morning to find him gone. Though in truth, Penny could still feel his presence nearby and she knew that Lenox was still watching out for her.

"Who are you really Lenox?" Penny wondered out aloud in amazement, before shaking her head, "It matters naught, for you will always have my protection from any evil villain that dares to try to harm you, I so swear it."

True to her word, from that day on, Penny constantly watched over the mysterious yet very kind and wise Lenox Moregan. Her vow to fulfill a simple life debt evolved with each passing year as Penny fell in love with him from afar.

Unfortunately for Penny, she knew that if she ever made her feelings known, then there would be far reaching consequences for not only her but her family and her people. Consequences that could cost them everything. However, love is never a simple thing, and Penny also knew that one day she would have to make a choice to either follow her heart or forever live in the shadows.

Chapter One

Present Day

Penny looked at herself in the mirror and took in her appearance with a serious scowl on her face as she ruthlessly checked for anything that would deem her out of place in the 'hallowed' halls of Harvard University.

Hair in a sleek chignon? *Check.*

Blue cable knit sweater covering the shoulders of her plain white dress shirt? *Check.*

Camel coloured dress pants with modest designer boots? *Check.*

Large black tote bag with computer as well as secretly hidden pink notepad and pink pen? *Check.*

Penny grinned briefly at herself, rubbing her hands in glee before she remembered where she was and instantly schooled her features into a 'smart' look.

Wandering out of the bathroom, Penny tried not to skip down the hall as she headed towards the physics lecture halls.

Today's the day! Penny thought excitedly.

It had been a whole three months, two weeks and four days since she had originally overheard the news about this event from the Vampyr king himself in his favour English pub. Though not one to take such news without looking into it first, Penny had ruthlessly researched everything about it and what academic credentials she needed in order to be eligible to attend.

Luckily for her, the only requirement she had to fulfill, was to take one small physics course that ran for six weeks and obtain top honours in it. Which Penny happily completed, since there was a snowball's chance in hell that she'd miss today.

Suddenly her cellphone chirped, alerting her to a text message. Letting out a disappointed huff, Penny checked her surroundings to make sure no one was nearby before she withdrew her flashy, neon pink, rhinestone encrusted phone.

<Penny hon, where are you?> Her dad had texted.

Penny looked down at the words in horror before she let out a small curse.

<About to attend a physics class dad,> Penny texted back, hoping that was vague enough for her father, so that he wouldn't inquire further.

<Oh okay, just wanted to give you a heads up that your mum's looking for you.>

No, no, no, no, Penny thought in mild panic.

<Uh, okay? Why? > Penny texted back instantly.

She could almost hear her father's snort of derision from afar.

<Light, Penny, don't tell me you're attending a certain someone's class today?>

Penny stared at the screen in horror, unsure of what to say or do, before another message popped up.

<Calm down sweetie, I'll take your mum and her reprobate twin out to a double matinee at the cinema this afternoon, which should give you plenty of time to attend the lecture in peace.>

<Um... can you please keep them occupied for three days dad? Pretty, pretty, please?> Penny typed frantically as she inwardly begged him to say yes.

<What!?! >

<Please, please, please, dad! It's a three day workshop on Quantum Physics that I've been waiting over three months for!>

<*SIGH* I've got you covered sweetie, don't worry. Enjoy your workshop and tell me all about it later.>

<Really?>

<Yes hon, really. See ya later :) >

<Thanks dad :) >

Penny nearly jumped for joy before she looked at the time on her phone and realized that the first lecture was about to start very soon.

Ack! I need to get my perfect seat! Penny mentally cried out before she booked it down the hall.

Slowing to a sedate pace when she rounded the last corner, Penny straightened her sweater and patted her hair to make sure it was still ruthlessly in place, before she walked the short distance that led to the right room.

Breezily walking through the open door, Penny nearly let out a whoop of glee when she saw that her perfect spot that she had secretly scoped out a few days before, was still available and made a beeline for it.

Sitting down on a hardwood chair, Penny unpacked her things on the desk in front of her. Though as she did so, she took in the entire room in an effort to calm the butterflies fluttering in her stomach. Unfortunately, they only grew when she saw 'him' enter the classroom and take his position at the front of the room next to Dr. Steven Brant, the head of the physics department.

"Good morning class, I'd like to welcome a very special guest from Cambridge University, Dr. Lenox Moregan. Dr. Moregan is..." Dr. Brant started to go on about Lenox's qualifications, though Penny ignored him as she completely focused her entire attention on Lenox.

He looks so handsome today, she sighed in delight as she fought back the need to mentally squeal at the sight of him.

Lenox was dressed in pressed black dress pants, a clean crisp white dress shirt, a dark red tie and dark grey sweater vest, making him looking every bit the Cambridge professor that he was and it drove Penny wild.

Good gracious, I really do have it bad, Penny mentally tutted herself, though she quickly shrugged that thought off as her mind instantly zeroed in on Lenox again, when he began speaking.

Fighting back a grin, Penny happily wrote down every word he said, intent on taking copious notes, despite the fact that she was also recording his voice with her phone.

Oh what a glorious day today will be, Penny gleefully thought as she continued on in a happy daze.

*****

Lenox had not been looking forward to the Quantum Physics Workshop that he had been talked into giving months ago by the Dean of Cambridge. Since he had originally planned to take a sabbatical year in order to work on all the projects gathering dust in his lab.

However, for some reason he had found himself agreeing to the course and now here, Lenox was rather glad he had, when he spotted a certain 'someone' in the crowded room.

She looks really lovely today, Lenox thought as he took in Penny and her very serious 'student' look.

It lightened his heart to see her in the crowd and he wished a thousand times over, that he could muster up his courage and actually ask her out on a real date.

Maybe, after this course I will finally do so, Lenox thought to himself, though almost instantly he knew the truth.

The rare beauty that was Penny Hawksley, robbed him of the ability to form full coherent sentences and made him very prone to blushing, which was a bit galling since Lenox never blushed otherwise.

Though that didn't stop him from wanting to hear her speak, and midway through the first lecture, Lenox found himself asking the class a complex problem that he knew Penny could solve since she had done so before in one of his other classes.

Unfortunately for Lenox, a young man in the front row, raised his hand and answered his question in a very asinine tone. Adding insult to injury, he even added the obligatory, 'They taught us this, in first year prep school.'

Inwardly grimacing when he saw the 'I'm smarter than you' smirk on the young man's face, Lenox decided to nip this problem in the bud early.

Giving the man a small smile, Lenox wrote an equation on the board that had yet to be answered by anyone.

"Would anyone like to solve this?" Lenox called out, knowing full well that no one generally ever to attempt such an equation.

The class seemed almost taken aback by the question and even the young man who had smirked at him minutes ago, was now frowning.

"No one? Yes Miss..." Lenox almost cursed when he forgot how much hellhounds liked a challenge.

"Uh Penny... my name is Penny and I'd like to give it a try," Penny said with a very seriously earnest expression on her face.

"By all means," Lenox said, unable to deny her as he stepped away from the whiteboard and held out a marker towards her.

*****

Given her absolute love of mathematical problems, Penny was inwardly chomping at the bit to solve this equation, despite the fact that she knew that Lenox was planning to solve it, in order to put the arrogant jerk in front row in his place.

Unable to stop herself, Penny's hand rose in the air when Lenox asked the class if anyone wanted to solve the equation.

"No one? Yes Miss..."

"Uh Penny... my name is Penny and I'd like to try," she said.

"By all means," Lenox said smoothly, holding out the marker to her.

Losing her self-control a second time, Penny nearly ran down the steps, before remembering to play it cool and act like a serious student.

"Give me a break! There's a million dollar reward being offered to anyone who can solve this equation. Like you stand a chance!" The idiot declared.

Penny rolled her eyes at his response before she took the marker from Lenox. Looking at the whiteboard for a long moment, Penny started to see numbers and functions dance together in her head before it prompted her to write... and write ... and write.

So completely intent on her task, Penny didn't hear the mumbles or murmurs behind her as the entire class watched her work in avid fascination. She also didn't seem to notice the department head, Dr. Brant, leave the hall for ten minutes, only to return with the entire Harvard Mathematics faculty.

Lenox noticed though and he felt dread build within him

when he saw people's phones start to rise and record her. Almost instantly, he lashed out with his magic, causing all electronic devices to die but it wasn't enough as he saw the faculty members make copious notes on notepads.

"Uh, Ms. Penny..." Lenox started to say but then stopped.

Penny was so focused on solving the equation, that Lenox knew that nothing would be able to stop her until she was finished. Which was would soon by Lenox's quick mental estimation.

"Dr. Brant, why don't we let Ms. Penny finish in peace and use another lecture hall in meantime? After all, I wouldn't want to trip her up," Lenox suggested, pouring in as much charm magic into his words, as he could.

Though unfortunately for Lenox, he had no idea how to truly use charm magic since he had never put any stock into learning the craft. However he cursed himself fully, when he saw that Dr. Brant easily swatted away his attempt.

"Nonsense, this is the most exciting thing that any of us could have witnessed today..."

Yes, Lenox thought almost bitterly, *I can clearly see that all the prestige, recognition and power you will receive, due to Penny's hard work is exciting to you. Light sake's! Why did I offer her the marker?*

Lenox knew the answer almost immediately. He liked Penny, in fact he more than liked Penny and such a simple fact kept him from using his magic to erase her work since he knew it would upset her.

Lenox also wasn't oblivious to the fact that there were quite a few people eyeing how they could claim this solution as their own, no matter how ridiculous that was. Amoung them, was the well regarded Dr. Brant, who looked on eagerly and was so excited, he unwittingly started to loudly projecting his thoughts.

I'll claim this work as part of a consortium, although, I'll need to do is make sure that my name is all over every report so that the million dollar prize will be all mine.

Lenox shook his head slightly in mild disgust, before he did something that he had never done in his life up until now... he made a very rash decision.

He reversed his earlier magical impulse and restored all the devices to record Penny's work. Then he went a step further and recorded Penny with his own laptop and sent the feed to the head of Cambridge Mathematics department, Dr. Victor Finebeck.

As he did that, he sent a series of texts explaining what was going on as well as the plan that was starting to form in his mind to cover all his bases.

Then, not twenty minutes after she started, Penny stepped back from the board and the room was deathly quiet.

The idiot in the front row spoke up again, "See! I told you that it can't be solved!"

"It can," Penny said as she turned around to face him before adding, "Because I just did so."

With that Penny dropped the marker on the floor like a mic drop.

"That's impossible," the man retorted.

"No it's not since she really did solve it," one of the mathematics professors remarked in stunned disbelief.

"You sure?" Dr. Brant asked the professor.

The professor nodded before his colleagues concurred with the result, although they weren't the only ones as Dr. Finebeck finally spoke up.

"She did indeed and congratulations Ms. Hawksley. I've submitted your answer to Clay Institute as well as the British Mathematical Quantum Society. It'll be a few weeks before they make it official but it looks like you've got yourself some serious accolades and a million dollar prize."

"Say what?" Penny asked, completely confused.

"I'll explain, Dr. Finebeck," Lenox cut in.

"Now wait just a minute!" Dr. Brant sputtered.

"I understand your confusion, Dr. Brant, however Ms. Hawksley is part of our Pure Mathematics and Quantum Physics PhD program at Cambridge. Therefore it our policy to directly submit any astounding student breakthroughs to the proper institutes or societies, so that they may be recognized. Am I right Dr. Finebeck?" Lenox asked, knowing the man's answer.

"Yes that is correct."

"If she's a Cambridge student, why is she here?" Dr. Brant demanded.

"Ms. Hawksley will be working with me at the start of the new term and she took this class..." Lenox started to say but suddenly ran out of words.

"I took this class because I wanted to understand Dr. Moregan's teaching style better. I mean, I've had him before as a professor but I still want to brush up before we started working together," Penny inserted smoothly, instantly coming to his rescue.

"But you never take on PhD candidates Dr. Moregan!" Dr. Brant argued.

"With genius like this, how could I resist?" Lenox stated, finding his voice again.

Dr. Brant looked like he was about to erupt but then, Dr. Finebeck stepped in on behalf of Lenox and started speaking.

Lenox chose that moment to use his magic to stop time so he could speak directly to Penny.

"Light Penny! I'm real sorry. I should have never wrote that blasted equation on the board."

"It's okay, you were about to solve it..."

"I wasn't," Lenox admitted, blowing out a sigh as he shook his head.

"Why'd you write it then?" Penny asked confused.

"To put the idiot in his place."

"Sorry but how?" Penny asked again, feeling her confusion grow even more.

"Penny… the equation on the board for all intents and purposes, was merely a bluff. A way, if you will, of showing the idiot that if he was all smart and knowing then he should be easily able to solve it. Normally when I write something like that, the room goes quiet and I continue on, however this time…you solved it."

"Why does that sound like a bad thing?"

"Since it kind of is. After all, a discovery like this gains a lot of attention and for immortals, that is a bad thing. Though even more so for you given the fact that hellhounds are notorious about keeping to the fringes of the human world and this… well, it puts you front and centre."

"Oh crap," Penny muttered as it started to dawn on her.

"Yeah and I let that happen," Lenox replied feeling very remorseful.

"Why?" Penny blurted out.

"Because I couldn't let Dr. Brant take all the credit for your hard work and trust me, he would have in a heartbeat, since he was projecting his thoughts on the matter loud and clear. Which really, really pissed me off and I acted rashly. I reversed my magical impulse that I used to block people from recording you, so that there would be evidence to prove that you were the one who did this not him. Then I made sure Dr. Finebeck saw it all because I knew he would be more interested in the prestige of having one of 'his' students solving this equation, then the allure of money or other accolades that came with it. Light sake's, what a mess! I'll fix this somehow for you, I promise Penny, I really will!"

"Lenox—" Penny interrupted, reaching out for his hands impulsively. However, Lenox beat her to it and held onto her hands gently as he looked deeply into her eyes.

"I want you to take the credit—" Penny started but Lenox adamantly shook his head, looking appalled by her suggestion.

"I can't do that Penny! This is all you... all wonderful you!"

"You think I'm wonderful?" Penny nearly squeaked out.

"I... I do. I also find you to be very smart, sweet, lovely, kind..." Lenox blurted out, stopping only when Penny's lips touched his.

For a moment the world stopped for both of them, as they shared a brief kiss, both too stunned to allow it to morph into anything more.

"I think you're wonderful too," Penny admitted after she drew back.

Then she let go of Lenox's hands and stepped back before using her own magic to end the time distortion.

Chaos erupted all around them, which gave Penny an ample

excuse to make a hasty exit. Eventually finding a safe place to teleport home, Penny was so dazed that she missed her own living room and ended up in her parents' garden.

Looking around briefly as she realized her mistake, Penny felt the weight of everything that had happened, crash down upon her shoulders and tears started to roll down her cheeks.

As if sensing her emotional turmoil, Penny's father Sebastian teleported in front of her.

"What's wrong, sweetie? Come on you can always tell your ole dad."

"I royally screwed up dad!" Penny wailed, unable to stop the tears from flooding down her cheeks like a torrential rain storm.

Chapter Two

Lenox felt his anxiety and ire rise as chaos erupted all around him. Mentally swearing, he wondered what he should do first.

Brother, what's wrong? Lenox's twin Lulu, mentally asked.

I screwed up, Lenox answered then gave her a brief rundown of what had happened.

I'm sending Freya to take care of everything. Come see me when she arrives, Lulu said calmly.

Lenox instantly breathed a sigh of relief at his twin's response.

A moment later, he watched Freya saunter into the room with her own twin Frey and their best friend Vale.

Don't worry Lenox, we got this, Freya called out.

Once the three of them started taking charge, Lenox quietly slipped from the room and teleported to his sister's home.

Arriving in her living room, Lenox saw Lulu sitting on a couch with their mother. Neither said anything as they got up and hugged him.

"I don't know what to do. All the hellhounds are going to hate me. Our family is going to be upset..." Lenox blurted out in agitation.

"Oh no, no, my son, you have done nothing wrong. Come, let us go see Penny's family at once," his mother Mina murmured.

Lenox dreaded doing so but at the same time, he desperately wanted to see Penny. Nodding slowly, he felt his mother teleport the three of them to the hellhound compound.

"Wait! Who's watching—" Lenox started to ask but his sister finished his sentence.

"Who's watching my children? Dad is, Len and he wanted to come too but Mum put her foot down."

"Huh? Why mum?" Lenox asked her in pure bewilderment.

"Light knows I really love your father but he's super overprotective of all of us and well... it's just for the best if he stays put."

"But how did you—"

"Know? Lenox, my son, I didn't know the details until Lulu briefly told us. However your father and I felt your distress from afar, which was more than enough to cause us to want to move heaven and earth for you. Although it will truly be alright son, I promise."

Lenox's mother continued to smile reassuring as she knocked on the door of Penny's parents' home.

"Go away!" The voice of Ally, Penny's mother, shouted.

"Ally it is I, Mina, and I have come bearing some good news!"

The door flew open and Ally stood in front of them barring the door.

"Mina... goods news or no, now is not the time! My baby is really upset."

Lenox paled instantly at the thought of Penny being upset and he felt his stomach bottom out.

"I understand but so is one of my children and thus, we're here to sort that out. That way everything will be right as rain again."

"I don't see how, Penny won't talk."

"Trust me, Ally, it will be. Now can we please sit down and talk?"

Ally sighed, "Well this goes against my better judgment but... alright, come on in."

Mina nodded before all three of them followed Ally into her living room.

"Ally! Now's not the time for guests! Why'd you invite them in?" Sebastian huffed out in exasperation as he held onto a quietly sobbing Penny.

"Mina said she's here to sort everything out and knowing Mina like we do, that's more than likely true. Therefore I'm willing to hear her and her twins out."

Penny stiffened when she heard the word 'twins' and instantly tried to dash her tears away.

"Penny, I'm so very, very sorry," Lenox said at once in remorse.

"Why the hell are you sorry?" Sebastian erupted like

Krakatoa.

"Shut it, Sebastian. Let the man talk," Alfie, Ally's twin brother said from across the room.

"The hell I will! Penny came home in tears and that alone makes me want to draw blood!"

"Sebastian! I get it but still, it's Lenox for Light sake's."

"What the hell is that suppose to mean?" Sebastian demanded.

"It means just sit there in silence and let him continue on because Penny wants to hear him out. Right sweetie?" Alfie asked her.

Penny nodded her head.

"Right, Lenox, the floor is yours," Alfie stated.

"Uh... I meant every word. I never wanted to upset you and I know my explanation was very brief but I really was pissed when I mentally overheard Dr. Brant think about taking credit for your work. I know it was wrong of me to risk exposing you to the world but, Penny, you deserve the praise for your brilliance and then some."

"Hold up, what happened exactly?" Ally asked curiously.

"Penny was attending a seminar that I was running on Quantum Mechanics at Harvard. There was this idiotic jerk in the front row who intended to cause a ruckus and I decided to put him in his place by writing an equation on the board that no one in the world had solved yet."

"Okay, but why use an equation that no one has solved?" Ally asked, confused.

"It was a bluff, kind of 'if you think you should be the one running this seminar then by all means prove it by solving this'."

"Oh... well, fair play then," Ally stated with a shrug.

"Not really because I actually issued the offer to the entire class, completely forgetting all about the fact that hellhounds like solving complicated puzzles."

"Ah I see now, so you took one look at the equation, Penny sweetie and wanted to solve it, right?" Ally asked.

Penny nodded.

"Okay, so now how did things go sideways?" Ally asked.

"Well... the Head of Mathematics and Physics Department at

Harvard was there and once he saw the breakthrough Penny was making, he gathered every Professor from the Mathematics Department. I know this sounds overblown to you but the equation on the board was so notoriously difficult, that there's a million dollar reward being offered by one of the leading Mathematical Societies in world to anyone who solves it."

"They'll seriously give you a million dollars if you solve a math problem?" Ally asked incredulously, before she briefly swore and remarked, "We've been backing the wrong horse Alfie. Engineering not where it's at, math is."

Alfie snorted, "Royalty rights on patents are far higher Ally."

"True, but only if Sebastian lets us market our stuff, which probably won't happen because so far everything we've created has been banned from human use and confiscated."

"Hey twins are you freaking serious, right now?" Sebastian demanded of them.

"Yes we are and this is actually awesome news, Sebastian! Our smart baby girl has earned a million dollars by being her awesome brilliant self. Go get the champers, let's celebrate!"

"Okay yes, that's great news. However Penny can't claim the money or accept any of the accolades surrounding it. Now I can see why you're upset, hon. You think we'll be mad at you because you've been exposed to the public over this," Sebastian blew out a sigh.

"Hold on, why the hell can't she be rewarded?" Ally demanded.

"For the same reason I confiscate some of your non-lethal inventions. We're hellhounds and our first priority is to protect the world from the forces of evil."

"So? Who says we can't protect the world and have side interests?" Ally demanded.

"We can't have side interests, Ally! End of story."

"Hell yes, we can!" Ally argued right back.

"No, we literally can't. Reggie made it a mandate years upon years ago, that we can't do anything that will potentially expose us to the world at large. Light sake's, Ally! Why do we have to keep having this conversation?" Sebastian demanded.

"Which conversation exactly, Sebastian? The one about having dreams and aspirations that go well beyond the hellhound norm? The one about forcing ourselves to appear like all the other sheep so that, Light forbid, no mortal figures out that we're very different than they are? That one?"

Ally and Alfie both crossed their arms, looking pure mutinous.

"Oh for Light sake's!" Sebastian hissed, knowing full well that there would soon be hell to pay.

"Mina hon, quick question, did Conalai go and erase everything from everyone's memories already?" Alfie asked.

"Not Conalai. Freya, Frey and Vale did or are currently in the process of it."

"Can you tell them to restore it and kind of hold everything in a bubble for the time being," Ally inserted.

"What!" Sebastian shouted but the twins shot him a death glare which temporarily quelled him.

"Mina, Lenox and Lulu, thank you very much for visiting and enlightening us. We're also not mad at you at all, Lenox. In fact, I'm quite happy you protected my baby's girl from some a-hole ripping off her work and I owe you one. However, right now before this all continues, we have to talk amoungst ourselves, you know — a *'Come to Jesus'* talk as humans like to say now. So... not to be a terrible host but could see yourself out? We'd greatly appreciate that," Ally said sweetly.

Mina nodded swiftly in agreement as she and Lulu instantly rose to leave but Lenox didn't want to until he heard Penny speak up.

"Penny, please," Lenox whispered as he saw Ally about to prompt him to leave again.

"Lenox, there's nothing to forgive for I'm not mad at you at all. It's just... it's just that I wish it could all be different, you know?" Penny whispered in return.

Lenox nodded in complete understanding before he bid them all good day and teleported to his sister's home with his family.

Arriving in Lulu's living room, Lenox's mind kept focusing on Penny's whispered words. For he, too, wished everything could be different but for the life of him, Lenox didn't know how he could begin to make the changes in his life that would allow him to make his dreams a reality.

*****

Penny felt lower than low after uttering the words she had held in her heart for so long.

"You wish things could be different, Pen?" Her father asked softly.

Penny sighed, "There's no sense—"

"Penniah?"

"I do, dad."

"You want the accolades?" Penny's dad asked her.

"No and I don't know what I'd do with a million dollars either."

"Oh I know what I would do with a spare million dollars. There's a little black market in—" Penny's mum started.

"Ally!" Alfie snapped.

"What? I can't help it. If I had a million dollars I would use it to buy plutonium."

"You have a million dollars, idiot," Alfie replied, rolling his eyes.

"Okay, we're digressing here but yes, I have that and more in the bank. However, I don't have direct access to because a, I really, really hate money, and b, I spend it all on plutonium in order to have a lot of nuclear based fun. Now shut it because I'm about to go nuclear for a whole 'nother reason."

"Ally..." Sebastian inserted.

"Sebastian, you need to fix this cock-up with her before I go postal," Ally retorted.

Sebastian sighed, nodding wearily in agreement before he focused on his daughter.

"Penniah, what is in your heart? In all seriousness, I want to know what your dream is."

"I want... I want to get a dual PhD in Pure Mathematics and

Quantum Physics. After, I want... I want to use those degrees to teach in a school like Cambridge and solve complex equations all day long."

Sebastian stared into his daughter's face, looking briefly devastated and Penny immediately wanted to take back everything she had said. However her dad shook his head adamantly when she opened her mouth to speak.

"Don't you dare take back what you've said, Penniah. You've done nothing wrong and I only look upset because I realize the grave mistake I have made. A mistake I will fight to fix, though don't you worry about that. Instead go have a wee visit with your Aunt Rika."

"Dad!" Penny started to protest.

"Trust in me and go see her," Sebastian said in a tone brooking no argument.

"Okay but, dad..."

"Honey, remember, *trust in me.* Okay?"

"Okay," Penny said reluctantly.

Sebastian hugged Penny tightly before he let her go. Ally swiftly hugged Penny, too, before Alfie took Penny to see his wife Rika.

*****

The room was quiet for a long moment after Penny had left.

"Sebastian..." Ally started.

"Will you also trust in me?" Sebastian asked her almost immediately.

"Light, don't you start. Of course I will but if you don't think I don't want to have my say after seven hundred years of marriage, then you don't know me," Ally retorted hotly.

Sebastian couldn't help the snort that escaped his lips, "Alright love, the floor is yours as you like to say."

Ally nodded then spoke.

"'Dreams aren't something to fear,' Sebastian. It was something my dad used to say to Alfie and me time and again before he died."

"Having dreams is what makes the Baskervilles different," Sebastian stated with a sigh.

"No hon. Everyone has dreams. It's acting upon them, that what makes the Baskervilles different. It's a need that has been burning in Penny for a long while but she doesn't want to make waves with others. Maybe because she's very different in other ways..."

"Not true, she's exactly like you were years ago, Ally."

Ally snorted this time.

"You don't think so?"

"I'm naturally meaner than Penny and I also have never given a crap about what people think of me."

"Again not completely true. You're not meaner than Penny, love. You're just more unpredictable which is why the hounds give you a wide berth. You are also freer when it comes to not giving a crap about what people think because your twin has pretty much laid down the law with everyone when you were growing up. However, we've failed Penny in doing the same."

"Yeah we have. Damn it all! Why didn't she say anything, Bas?" Ally cried out suddenly, upset that Penny had been suffering in silence for so long.

Sebastian got off the couch and gathered his mate in his arms.

"You know why Ally love. Some damn idiot got it into her head that she can't make waves like the rest of Baskervilles. Then to add to it, stupid overprotective me, accidentally reinforced the idiots words in my attempts to keep her from danger."

"Where was I in all this? Am I so stupidly self-involved that I can't see how sad my own daughter has become? Light! I should have dealt with this nonsense much earlier!"

"Ally, don't blame yourself. You are a damn good mother and you know how idiots talk! Especially the ones who want to keep to the 'old ways'."

"Ugh but don't they know about—" Ally started.

"No one knows my love." Sebastian finished. "We've kept it a secret for a long time for a reason. Besides, the hounds who like to talk aren't actually the old ones but the young ones who think they know everything about the 'old ways' but in truth, know absolutely nothing."

"Reggie needs to do something about that!"

"Ally..."

"Sebastian, I want to make waves, big obscene waves so that this crap never happens again! She was in tears for Light sake's! All because she didn't think she could live a pretty tame dream since some idiot drilled it into her psyche to mind her place in our world? Oh, hell no!"

"Exactly love, which is why I'm going to act."

"Oh?" Ally asked, going eerily calm.

"Yeah."

Ally nodded happily when she realized what he was about to do and chose to said nothing more as she held her husband's hand, waiting for her twin to return.

They didn't have to wait long, since a few moments later Alfie appeared.

"So..." Ally started.

"I've got some names of hounds that we need to deal with." Alfie scowled before he let out a soft curse, "It looks like the a-hole's back trying to cause trouble again."

"Oh no freakin' way!"

"Don't worry sis, I don't know how he's wormed his way back into the packs good graces again but he'll be dealt with permanently once I can freely make a move against him. Though in order to do that, Sebastian I need you to—"

"I know and I'm willing now to do what must be done. Will you two stand in my corner?" Sebastian asked.

"Don't insult me, of course I will," Ally instantly retorted.

"Really why is this a question? Though if it wasn't obvious, the answer is yes and let's get on with it already," Alfie added with a scowl.

"Thanks," Sebastian said before he let out a slow breath and sent out a magical pulse.

Moments later Reggie appeared looking at Sebastian curiously.

"What's up, Bas?"

"I'm issuing you a challenge, Reggie. I want the hellhound leadership role," Sebastian said.

Reggie folded his arms before looking over at Ally and Alfie.

"We back him," the twins said instantly in unison.

Reggie slowly nodded in agreement.

"Alright, though what the hell prompted this?"

"Penny," Sebastian responded.

"Penny?"

"Yeah," Sebastian answered then began to tell Reggie everything that had happened.

Reggie slowly shook his head, "Well can't say I'm surprised but I can see why now's the time to change things. Let's do this."

Chapter Three

Penny sat on her aunt and uncle's couch with her Aunt Rika and her cousin Lucy.

"I made a big deal out of nothing," Penny muttered with a sniff.

"No hon, you didn't," Rika whispered soothingly.

"I did though and now mum is freaking out!"

"Well that's not new. Look Penny, we're Baskervilles," Lucy stated.

"Technically I'm a Hawksley."

"Technically nothing, you're a Baskerville. Hold on, has no one ever explained what that means?"

"Lucy," Rika chided.

"It's important mum, well dad always said it was important."

"It is important, Lucy," Rika reluctantly agreed.

"What are you talking about?" Penny asked, feeling confused.

"Honey, you really need to talk to your mum and dad about this once they come back. However I will tell you that the Baskervilles were the first hellhounds," Rika explained.

"Okay, I've heard that before."

"Yes and that's very significant to the hellhounds."

"Why?" Penny asked confused.

"Just is," Rika said hesitantly.

"Please tell me," Penny pleaded.

Rika sighed, "I really can't say anything beyond the fact that being apart of the first hellhound family isn't what you're thinking, which is something along the lines of one of the first founding families that humans like to go on about."

"What?"

"I mean, it's not an empty title honey. It actually has meaning but that is for your parents to tell you."

Penny was dying to know what her aunt was really talking

about but she knew she couldn't press her. So instead, Penny looked at her aunt and cousin.

"What should we do while we wait?" Penny asked.

Lucy instantly summoned up snacks.

"Lucy sweetie," Aunt Rika chided again, though with a soft laugh this time.

"I need food, mum, I have to pretend that I'm on one of those rabbit food diet like that all the other prima ballerinas are when I'm on tour and it leaves me constantly starving. Seriously Light only knows how they survive," Lucy declared, breaking open a giant bag of jerky and offering it to her mum and Penny.

Both took a piece.

"You still on the road, cuz?" Penny asked her self-described 'diva' cousin.

Though in truth Lucy was no diva. She was mostly super sweet since she had inherited most of her mother Rika's nature and the only thing that hinted otherwise, was her sarcastic streak. Good Light, Lucy could cut any fool down to size in three seconds flat if she was in a mind too. However that was kind of expect since she was the daughter of Alfie Baskerville, who had to be the most sarcastic being on the planet.

"Nah, I'm coming home to roost since I'm sick of the road and the nitty picky idiots. I'm going to start my own dance school and maybe dance with a ballet company during the Christmas holidays since I love the Nutcracker. Either way this is where I stay."

Both Rika and Penny were super pleased by that fact and were quick to hug her.

Lucy snorted as she returned the hug and remarked nonchalantly, "It's not a big deal really."

"Oh course it is, honey. I mean, I know you had to go out and make your mark on the world but I'm so much happier that you're at home," Aunt Rika said.

"It was always in the cards, mum."

"I know but still... wait you're going to live here right?"

"Um… I kind of wanted to have my own home. One super close to you," Lucy said quickly, when she saw her mum's crestfallen look.

"Um... what if you built a cottage here on your parents' land like I did, Luce? You could also build a separate dance studio for your students in Moonlight Valley too since we've magically connected the compound to it," Penny suggested.

"Yes, that's a great idea," Lucy's mum said looking very pleased by that suggestion.

"I dunno. Do you think dad will go for it?" Lucy asked.

"Of course. Why wouldn't he?" Rika asked with a small frown.

"Well, I kind of expect him to argue that I don't need a place of my own and that I can stay here. He's also probably gonna be a little bit… bull-headed about it too," Lucy finished.

Penny understood immediately what Lucy was getting at. After all, Penny had to fight her own mother tooth and nail to have her cottage built when she moved out three hundred years ago. In fact, the only way Penny had won that battle was by allowing 'escape tunnels' that connected her home to her parents' to be part of the design as a 'just in case' measure. Something she hadn't minded then or now, since it was real nice to have her own personal space.

"Don't worry sweetie, I'll talk your father into it," Rika stated firmly.

"Mum..."

"Lucy, dreams are nothing to fear."

"That's the second time that I've heard that today," Penny muttered.

"Well, it is our family motto," Lucy pointed out.

"I know, but still I feel terrible about having dreams."

Lucy looked aghast, "Why?"

"Because my dreams will bring nothing but trouble for everyone."

"Big deal!" Lucy scoffed.

"It is a big deal... to me."

"Penny, I know why you're afraid for real, and I get it too, since I've been in your shoes before. I mean, I love dancing and I hid that from the world for a long time until my dad found out. He supported my dream of being a world class dancer though I didn't want to make waves with the other hounds who'd be against it. However, dad told me, ' Lucylamyla, don't give up on what you want because of ignorant disapproving busybodies. Keep aspiring to do what you love sweetie and let me do what I love doing the most—making trouble for idiots'."

Rika sighed, "Unfortunately that's the truth, however it did work. Alfie deliberately went out like pure thunder and fury until every hellhound agreed with that the fact that Lucy being a dancer was a great decision or at least, no one said anything about it. Though now it's time for your mum to do the exact same for you, Penny and don't start wishing she wouldn't. For one day, when you have a child of your own, you'll become that 'crazed' Baskerville who burn the world down for their child's dream. Mark my words."

"Yeah you will and so will I. Can't wait really to do it either," Lucy stated matter of factly.

Penny laughed, "Well yeah that's true, I'd fight for my future child's dream in a heartbeat."

"And you say you're not a Baskerville. Light sake's, we're the only folks who look forward to being crazed. Oh, speaking of which we need to catch up on our daily dose of drama!" Lucy declared as she turned on the TV to a reality show that both she and Penny were avidly following.

"Um... I'll watch it with you but what's going on so far?" Rika asked hesitantly.

Lucy and Penny both grinned before they gushed over all the juicy details that occurred so far in the show.

"Oh boy..." Rika muttered with a sigh, though she still happily settled in between her niece and daughter on the couch and watched the show that fascinated them so.

An hour later, Penny smiled when she heard the usual chaotic entrance of her mum, dad and uncle in the front hallway.

"Jeez, Ally, what the hell!" Penny's dad demanded.

"*Ceellllabraaaation time, come on!*" Penny's mum sang at the top of her lungs.

A cork popped loudly, causing her mum to squeal in delight and her uncle to laugh. It was soon followed by sounds of them running down the short corridor, probably elbowing each other out of the way as they did their usual, 'one up' routine. All the while, Penny's dad could be heard demanding that they both act like adults.

Suddenly the door swung open with Penny's mum holding onto what had to be the world's biggest bottle of champagne in Penny's opinion.

"*We're baack*!" She cackled.

"Where'd you get that, Aunt Ally?" Lucy asked eyeing the bottle of champagne with delight.

"The liquor store!"

"They sell champagne bottles this size, for real?"

"If you go the right liquor store, hon," Ally replied gleefully.

"Wait... is it safe for consumption?" Lucy asked hesitantly.

"What kind of question is that to ask your aunt, Luce?" Ally laughed.

"An accurate one given the fact that it's you," Alfie retorted.

"Hey!"

"Hey nothing. You buy things in sketchy places Ally. That's a fact," Alfie replied, rolling his eyes.

"Well what can I say? I like great bargains in literal cut-throat markets. It adds a sense of fun to the mundane. Any who, I didn't source this, you dad did Luce, so you're alright. Now let's celebrate already!"

"Mum, sorry to cut into your celebratory mood but what are celebrating exactly?" Penny asked.

"You're awesome smarts, your future acceptance to Cambridge, your dad's new role as Leader of the Hellhounds and your Uncle Regg—"

"Wait, what?" Penny and Lucy shouted at the same time.

"Huh?" Ally asked in confusion.

"Seriously, Ally?" Alfie laughed before shaking his head, "I told you we had to ease them into all this news."

"Why?"

"Because it's shocking for one thing," Alfie pointed out.

"Don't see how—"

"Ally!" Sebastian hissed.

"What?"

Sebastian rolled his eyes, "You know what? It doesn't matter. Come with me, Penny hon, and I'll explain."

"Hey wait a tick! You're just gonna leave me here by myself like I'm chopped liver."

"No," Sebastian said with deliberate patience, "I expect you to put down the bottle and have a proper quiet... *quiet* conversation with our daughter."

"Why'd you emphasize quiet?"

"Because that's what I hope you'll be when I properly explain the bombshells you're dropping so casually."

Ally sighed, "Yes, I'm coming with you but don't expect me to quiet. I've never been quiet a day in my life, so I have. Oh, and the champers stays with me because it's mine."

Sebastian shook his head in fond exasperation, before he beckoned Penny and Ally to follow him. Rising off the couch, Penny followed her dad out the room with her mum trailing behind them.

They walked towards a small settee that was half down the hall. It was a tight squeeze but they all fit, the champagne bottle included. Although it was soon abandoned to a spot on the floor when Ally decided to wrap an arm around her daughter and she realized that she couldn't hold both the bottle and her daughter at the same time. Sebastian snorted briefly before he draped an arm along the backside of the couch so he could reach both of them.

"I really screwed up things didn't I?" Penny mumbled finally.

"No hon, you didn't and it's time to talk about that finally. First off, just to get this out of the way, my becoming Leader of the Hellhounds has been in the cards for a long time now. In fact, Reggie first offered me the role the very day that you were born but I decided to wait until I felt fully ready. Today was that day."

"Why was today the day, dad?" Penny asked quietly.

"Penny, my dear one, you're not the one who fears their own dreams. I've wanted yet feared the role of being the Hellhound Leader from the very beginning. Well, not actually feared it *per se* but more like worried that I'd screw up everything. However, when I saw you in tears today, I realized how very similar we are and that I couldn't encourage you to follow your dreams if I didn't lead by example. Though things might be a bit of a rough for a while but I'll have..."

"Me! What? I'll always back you and so will my reprobate twin, Alfie. Reggie's also going to be on hand too, since he's now officially our pack Elder."

Sebastian snorted, "Thanks, love. I appreciate your support, despite the fact that I kind of worry about it, too. Anyway, back to the matter at hand, it's time you knew about your Baskerville heritage in truth. For the blood in your veins is special, hon, very special."

"I'm only half Baskerville dad," Penny mumbled.

"Nah, sweetie, there's no such thing as half when it comes to being a Baskerville. In fact, if you possess one drop of the blood, then you are one us. Any who, it's time to live up to that name and become a *hellraiser*." Ally said.

"Wait Ally—" Sebastian cautioned.

"You said we need to be open and honest which I'm doing and you're still cautioning me. Jeez, Sebastian, make up your mind!"

"I'm going to regret this, but alright, continue, love."

"Fully planned on it," Ally replied flippantly before continuing, "Anyway, we Baskervilles might be called hellhounds in public, but in truth we're hellraisers."

"Sorry mum, but isn't that a campy eighties horror film about..."

"Oh yes! It's totally the name of a hilarious movie about some freaky stuff but that's not what I'm getting at. A hellraiser is the name given to those of us who carry the blood of the spirit who created the hellhounds. Now our family no longer has the ability to create others, however our bloodline keeps the hellhounds still... well hellhounds and without us, every single one of them would die en mass."

Penny's eyes opened wide with shock.

"Ah, sweetie, don't freak out. It sounds huge I know but it's really kind of not."

"It actually really kind of is," Sebastian sighed.

Penny nodded fervently.

"Jeez, seriously, Sebastian? Look how pale she's gone! Ah Penny hon, you have nothing to worry about. Truly, don't think you have to wrap yourself up in cotton wool because that's my job as your mum," Ally said contritely.

"Ally," Sebastian growled.

"What? I want to protect my baby Bas. Anyway, your uncle and I might seem really off our rocker but we're all business when it comes to protecting you and Lucy. So you don't have to change who you are now that you know the truth. Well this truth... since yeah there's more to find out but I swore to your dad that I'd tell you it in stages since you first you need to learn how to live as a true hellraiser."

"What?" Penny asked.

"Honey stop being afraid of things to start. Since fear in any form, restricts our true abilities. You also need to break out of the safe little box you've created for yourself, and start living your dream."

Penny nodded.

"You aren't alone either hon because your dad and I will also be in corner no matter what. Now that we've sorted that out, let's talk about other news. Tomorrow morning we're going to that big fancy clothing store that Valiant and Anarchy run in Moonlight Valley and buy proper stodgy English clothes before we take a grand guided tour of Cambridge in the afternoon."

"Seriously?" Penny asked in shock.

"Uh huh, your dad, uncle and I arranged it with the head of the whole kit and caboodle, wait... I think he's called a dean? Yeah that's right the dean! Then your we spoke with him. Lenox and Dr. Something or Other—"

"You spoke with the dean, Dr. Finebeck and Lenox. Light Ally, please remember his name tomorrow," Sebastian pleaded.

"I will, for I've got to look good at our baby's new school. Also, your Great Uncle Reggie is currently making sure that you get your big impressive award without too much fallout. Speaking of which, can I keep your trophy, sweetie? Pretty please?" Ally begged.

"What trophy?" Penny asked.

"Oh the one for solving the equation that you solved earlier. Actually they said you get a trophy, an award certificate, a big check and something else. Sorry, I kind of got distracted by the big check remark because it put me in mind of that America advert, where the people knock on other people's doors and give them a big check and balloons... ooh! We needed balloons, Bas! We forgot!"

"I'll sort that, though what do you say, Pen? You ready for all this?"

"Yeah, and I won't let you down, I promise," Penny vowed solemnly.

"Honey, you were never in jeopardy in that, in fact you never stop making us proud. Now come on, let's go celebrate." Sebastian winked.

"Woo hoo! Champers time!"

Penny laughed before following her mother back into her uncle's living room to celebrate. As she did, she couldn't help but feel like Neil Armstrong landing on the unknown surface of the moon.

Well that's one small step for me and hopefully one giant leap for all hellhound kind, Penny thought.

Chapter Four

Lenox sat next to Dr. Finebeck feeling filled with restless energy, despite the fact that he hadn't slept in more than twenty four hours. After all, since yesterday's debacle, Lenox had been doing everything in his power to smooth Penny's transition into Cambridge once her parents had given the go ahead.

However, setting her up for Cambridge wasn't the problem. Actually, it had been the infamy of solving the equation that had set off a firestorm within all the mathematical societies of the world. They had began to contact him almost immediately, in order to confirm the possibility that Penny was also the elusive Ms. H. A mysterious woman who had apparently solved numerous notoriously difficult mathematical problems in her spare time. Lenox had taken one look at the work they sent over and knew it was Penny by the remaining energy he could pick up from the page.

Nonetheless, it had taken him a few hours to confirm it for the eyes of the world and once he had, the societies had once again inundated him with paperwork, only this time it was with offers of grant money and rewards for Penny.

That had opened up a huge can of worms since both Cambridge and Harvard began to claim Penny as one of their students due the grants all together exceeded several hundred million dollars. Though, again there was more...

"She's really a 270! Can you believe it, Dr. Moregan? Another individual with a 270 IQ, here at Cambridge! I never thought I would live to see the day that two rare geniuses would be in these hallowed halls," Dr. Finebeck whispered in awe for the eleventh time that day.

Lenox nodded and inwardly sighed because he worried over the fanfare that the news would bring Penny, given the fact that he had known nothing but grief for being so smart.

"We have to secure her for our program. It's imperative that Harvard not gain her," Dr. Finebeck muttered.

"It still must be Ms. Hawskley's choice," Lenox reminded him, though he was fully ready to fight for Penny to study at Cambridge, albeit for a whole another reason.

"I can't believe that we must both make offers to her! She directly claimed to be a Cambridge student and she's done the majority of her studying here. We have proof of that, which means Harvard must have some sway, somewhere. Good God man, I can't believe we didn't recognize her at the time! We could have saved ourselves a world of grief," Dr. Finebeck sighed.

"I guess so and I also don't like it since I know that after Harvard overhears our pitch, they will offer her a private jet to take her directly to America to see their campus."

Dr. Finebeck cursed and fumed at the reminder.

"Dr. Finebeck, relax. Their offer will not appeal to Penny," Lenox stated calmly.

"How can you be so sure? Harvard's going to offer her the sun, moon and stars to get their paws on that grant money."

Just like you're also willing to do albeit for the prestige not the money, Lenox mentally added, but didn't say the words out loud as he instead said, "Cambridge has a lot more going for it than Harvard does. Especially when it comes to 'special' individuals like myself."

Dr. Finebeck did a double take, "She's a—"

"Yes."

"How do you know for sure?"

"Her family and mine have been allies for a long time."

"Oh... is that why—" Dr. Finebeck started to question before stopping.

"Is that why I contacted you through video chat to keep her away from Harvard? Yes. Penny's family is a very 'special' kind of 'other', one who will need a lot of allowances and I know we will have the ability to apply those here," Lenox replied.

"Er... what kind of 'other', exactly?" Dr. Finebeck asked after a moment.

"Ever read Sherlock Holmes, Dr. Finebeck?"

Dr. Finebeck snorted before he pointed numerous well-worn

copies of the series in his academic library and retorted, "I am a huge fan of Sir Arthur Conan Doyle. This is well known."

"Well... Penny's mother and uncle knew him personally and he was so enchanted by them that Sir Arthur wrote them into one of his novels."

"Which one... oh my God! That cannot be," Dr. Finebeck gasped when he remembered seeing Penny's mother's maiden name.

"It is and I cannot stress how very important that we must do our to meet they're requests, especially when it comes to security because that will be paramount to them. It also goes without saying but what we've talked about, should go no further than this room."

"You have my word," Dr. Finebeck said, affronted that his vow of silence on all things immortal, was in question.

"I know, and don't be offended when they ask for your silence because I can guarantee you that they will, just like my family did. Now come on, Dr. Finebeck, I can feel their presence nearby and we must go meet them before Harvard does."

Dr. Finebeck stood up and walked swiftly to his office door. Lenox joined him and they walked together in silence to the main entrance hall, where the Harvard representatives were already waiting.

"Dr. Brant," Dr. Finebeck greeted coolly.

"Dr. Finebeck," came the response that was equally as cool.

"Terrible weather today in Cambridge must be a sign of things to come," Dr. Brant said moments later, when two vehicles drove up the driveway towards them.

"Contrary to popular belief, rain is a sign of good luck not bad, old chap. Especially to the *English* since we're down right at *home* in it."

Lenox almost snorted at the response because the intent was clear. To the outside world, Penny was considered English, since her parents held genuine English nobility titles as the Lord and Lady of Craven Hollow, a holding that was deep inside the Yorkshire Moors. Ergo Cambridge, one of the most revered English academic institutes, would appeal to them, which it would but again, for a different reason.

Though Lenox also couldn't help but briefly find it kind of bizarrely funny that the story 'the Hounds of Baskerville' was set in the county of Devon not York, given the fact that anyone, who knew anything about the Baskerville family and the English Hellhounds in general, knew that they were proudly from the Yorkshire Moors.

Lenox focused back on the present and heard the animosity between Dr. Finebeck and Dr. Brant escalate.

"Gentlemen..." Lenox interrupted using his quietest yet also deadliest calm tone, "The Hawksley family has arrived."

Lenox then grabbed an umbrella and headed down towards the two cars that had just pulled up without waiting for anyone to follow him.

Almost instantly Sebastian, Reggie and Alfie got out the vehicle, holding their own umbrellas as they scanned the environment around them with their eyes, as if trying to determine the threat level that Cambridge presented.

Lenox knew that this was to be expected, since his Aunt Raven had given him a crash course on hellhound etiquette just after he had sought out her help yesterday. After all, she was the Queen of the Vampyr and had many connections worldwide, including those in the academic field.

"Ah, Lenox Moregan, good to see you," Alfie called out first, greeting Lenox warmly after the threat level had been deemed low by the three male alpha hellhounds.

Lenox was struck by this, since Alfie wasn't one to greet anyone warmly given the fact that he had a very low tolerance for people in any form.

"Well met, Alfie," Lenox replied seconds later as he shook his hand.

"Hey… what's with all the tossers over there?" Alfie asked as his normal scowl started to return when he noticed a group of individuals start to head towards them.

"Uh well... Penny's made quite the mark on the world's academic communities, since she actually solved multiple equations that were deemed unsolvable. Therefore, all of the mathematical and quantum physics societies have pooled their vast resources and have offered up grants that total several hundred million pounds..."

"Wait, say what?" Alfie guffawed.

"Uh... there are several hundred million pounds of grant money that will be awarded to both Penny and any institution that she chooses to work with. It was then determined by the communities at large, that to be fair, both Harvard and Cambridge would make offers to Penny since both schools appear to have a decent claim of Penny being one of their students in the past."

"Ugh really?" Alfie almost whined in disgust.

"Yeah."

"Is there anything you can do about that, Lenox? I mean, no offence to Harvard, I'm sure they're a great school given the fact that my baby girl would only attend the smartest of places but still…we're English, man. Well, you know what I mean," Sebastian stated with a small huff.

"Yeah I do," Lenox said, knowing what Sebastian was really getting at.

Great Britain, Europe and a good deal of East Asia had long established immortal communities built directly into the bedrock of the societies within these place, which made it a lot easier to live a 'normal' life. Case in point, Cambridge had several buildings that were set up to give immortals both a place to relax and live openly as themselves.

"I'll deal with it," Lenox finally said after a long moment.

"Thanks but why didn't you do it before?" Alfie asked.

"My Aunt Raven said that I had to let you make that call. I tried to contact you last night and this morning about it..."

"Oh... shoot, our phones were turned off, sorry mate. We were celebrating into the wee hours of the morning! Though it seems like more celebrating will be done today too," Alfie retorted gleefully.

"That's fair. Hold on," Lenox said as he reached out to his twin telepathically.

Hiya Len, what's up? Lulu asked.

Can Freya come here and give the delegates of Harvard the memory that they've made their pitch and were unsuccessful before sending them home?

Sure but it'll cost you, she teased.

I'm willing to pay anything, sis, Lenox said seriously.

Don't tell her that and don't worry about it. I always have got you covered. You can buy me lunch at our favourite spot in Cambridge tomorrow as payment.

Done deal, Lou.

A moment later, Freya showed up again and led away the American delegates away with a magical compulsion.

"Much better. Thanks Lenox," Reggie said, finally speaking up before he stepped to the side and opened the door of a limo, that everyone else had been travelling in. Ally came tumbling out, though she still managed to land on her feet.

"They're gone? Good!" Ally muttered as she fixed her soft pink Chanel suit and patted her hair to make sure it was in place.

Lenox offered her his umbrella.

"Thank you kindly, Lenox, but I've got one to match my suit today. After all, I've got to look smart to blend into this place!"

"Yes, yes, we know, we know, since apparently nothing less than a full penguin suit was appropriate attire," Alfie sighed as he tugged on his English morning suit cravat. "You'd honestly think that we were attending a function for the Queen."

"No, you're doing one better. You are attending a milestone event for my baby girl, so quit your bellyaching or I will give you something to truly whine about," Ally retorted with a tight smile.

"Mum!" Penny called out from in the car as she moved to get out but her cousin Lucy gently pushed her back and said, "You're the last one to get out of the vehicle Pen because this is your day to shine."

With that Lucy got out with an umbrella in hand, followed closely by her mother Rika and Reggie's wife Yuna. All three were dressed in very smart suits that could be classified as royal ascot attire. In fact all that was missing was the obligatory hat.

Lenox noticed that Penny was dressed in more sombre attire once she was finally able to exit the limo herself. Nonetheless she was breathtakingly beautiful in her modest dark blue dress, that had three quarter length sleeves and a skirt flared out slightly at the knee.

To round off her look, she wore jet black pump heels and two strings of soft pink pearls around her neck.

Noticing that he still held his umbrella since none of the hounds had taken it, Lenox offered it to Penny.

Penny gently shook her head and said softly, “It's pouring out, Lenox. Let’s share it, instead.”

Lenox nodded as he tried to cover his rolling emotions, hoping to the Light that he wasn't about to piss off the other hounds by showing his attraction to Penny.

Don't be stupid, Lenox Moregan, Lenox chided himself.

Luckily for Lenox, Ally, Penny's mother, was already drawing all the hellhounds’ attention away from them with a sudden exclamation.

“Are shi... *kidding me*, several hundred.... woah! What?” Ally exclaimed in stunned amazement.

“Ally!” Alfie hissed, “For Light sakes' stop acting so bloody shocked by it. We’ve got that in the bank and we’re supposed to be part of the stodgy set today. Though not even thirty seconds in and you've already created a *faux pas* by being taken aback by money.”

“Yes we do have that amount in the bank but it took us several ... *generations* of investments to build it to that level, we didn't earn it all at one time.”

“Grants aren't our money. It's the university's money,” Alfie dryly retorted.

“What?” Ally asked with a scowl this time.

“Not fully true in this case, since the money is meant to fund both the school Penny chooses as well as any future research that Penny will conduct. However, there is also a sizable portion that Penny will get outright and we shall go over that soon,” Dr. Finebeck explained, before he fully introduced himself.

“Do you want to do the school tour first or shall we talk about everything?” Lenox asked them after an awkward silence.

“Let's talk, my good man, for I want to know everything up front before we agree to this fully,” Sebastian stated.

Dr. Finebeck nodded before looking to Lenox.

“Please follow me then,” Lenox said calmly as he mentally

preparing himself for well… anything.

After all, when it came to the hounds, it was best to expect the unexpected.

Chapter Five

Lenox sat next to Dr. Finebeck in his office, waiting for the other man to speak. From the looks of mild boredom and irritation building on the faces of Sebastian, Alfie and Reggie, as well as the growing fear emitting from Dr. Finebeck, Lenox knew that wasn't about to happen, so he took over instead.

"Thank you all for joining us here today. Now, Dr. Finebeck, my Aunt Raven and I have gone over Penny's academic history and in truth, you could have a PhD in both Pure Mathematics and Quantum Physics without submitting any dissertation."

Sebastian looked positively gleeful at the remark, though Penny looked more crestfallen. Lenox instantly hated himself for causing that look.

"So coming here today was an utter waste of time then?" Penny asked quietly.

"Absolutely not!" Lenox instantly countered, before he remembered himself and continued on more sedately. "No, what I'm saying, Penny, is that we'd like to bestow a dual PhD in those fields as well as make an offer of a full time professorship here at Cambridge."

"But I want to earn my PhDs. I don't want it handed to me," Penny declared quietly.

"Penny, you have earned them and then some. If you don't agree, look at these," Lenox remarked, pushing the pile of glowing reports towards her.

Sebastian and all the hounds, save Penny, grabbed the reports and started to read them.

"OMG, Penny!" Ally burst out happily.

"I actually second that," Alfie muttered as he switched reports with his twin moments later.

Penny sighed before she looked at Lenox, "I still want to earn a PhD like you did Lenox."

"I didn't earn them the conventional way, Penny," Lenox admitted before he continued, "I'm not lying to you when I say that either. For as far back as when I first received them in the 1800s, I never wrote a single dissertation. Instead, I did very much the same as you, which was taking classes in hodge-podge fashion before making a revolutionary break through. Then once that occurred, Cambridge gave me my PhDs, my professorship and my very own lab."

"Yes, and that offer is well on the table here too," Dr. Finebeck added.

"But still..." Penny started.

"Penny," Lenox stopped and checked himself, not wanting to aggravate the hounds. "Please tell me what you truly want."

"I want to earn my PhD for real!"

Lenox blew out a small sigh before he realized something.

"Penny what do you think earning a PhD is?"

"Hey why are you questioning my baby?" Ally demanded.

"Relax mum, it's okay. Lenox just wants to determine what I want, is all."

"I truly do, I promise and please answer my question Penny. What do you truly think it entails?"

"Obviously studying in class, taking exams, teaching then writing a big final paper..." Penny stated before trailing off when she noticed Lenox gentle shake of his head.

"What?" She asked with a frown.

"A PhD is none of that, Penny. It's a cumulative research degree, whereupon the majority of doctoral candidates spend years researching a hypothesis, finding evidence that proves or disproves their theory and writing the results in a thesis. There are no exams and the only real schoolwork you have to put in, so to speak, is meeting a professor who acts as your guide as it were, to make sure that you are prepared to defend your thesis in front of an academic panel. Any one of these..." Lenox said picking up one of the solutions Penny had solved from a large stack of paper on the desk, "Can be your thesis. They've also been rigorously looked into and proven by numerous panels despite the fact that you've never appeared before them."

"Oh..."

"So tell me Penny, what would make you happy here?"

"I want to research more," Penny admitted, "I also want to write academic papers and have them published in journals like everyone else. I also want to teach and hold my own lectures, though that might be a hard one. Above all, I want to complete a proper PhD and if that means writing another thesis and defending it in front of a panel instead of writing an exam, then that's what I want to do."

Lenox nodded, "Alright then, I will make sure that that's exactly what will occur."

With that, Lenox, began to go over a full written offer that met all of Penny's conditions as well as all the bonuses.

"You're going to be my academic mentor, Lenox?" Penny asked in a stunned amazement.

"Ooh that's a great idea!" Ally said gleefully.

Sebastian frowned, "How?"

"Well I didn't want a human—"

"Ally!" Sebastian hissed.

"It's alright," Dr. Finebeck assured them, "Cambridge has a long been a safe haven for immortal intellectuals and we go to great lengths to protect that."

"Hmm... I really like that, though truly how's the security here?" Alfie asked.

"Alfie!" Sebastian hissed at him this time.

"What security is paramount to us hellhounds."

"So you really are hellhounds?" Dr. Finebeck asked intrigued.

Alfie frowned before nodding warily.

"And you are really two both Baskerville hellhound?" Dr. Finebeck asked Ally and Alfie directly.

The hounds looked even more suspicious.

"What do you know about the Baskervilles?" Reggie asked quietly.

Dr. Finebeck looked alarmed, "Eh? Have I put my foot in it? I was told that you were Hellhounds and that two of you were the real Baskervilles that had met Sir Arthur Conan Doyle and had inspired him to write about you."

Reggie let out a sigh, "He's a Sherlock fan... should have known."

"Oh, are you talking about our friend Artie? Man do I miss him," Ally pouted.

"Me too. He was one odd human being but he was one hell of a drinking buddy and a great fellow overall," Alfie said.

"So it's true then? The Hound of the Baskerville is based on you two?" Dr. Finebeck asked Ally.

"More Alfie than me, though overall it was loosely based on a case that we were working on at the time."

"A case?" Dr. Finebeck asked unable to hold back his question.

"Oh yeah, we pick up cases with a detective agency called Paranormal Investigations, all the time and have done so for centuries now. Any who, at the time that we first ran into Artie, we were hunting down a serial killer, Lord Something or Other, who had picked Artie to be his next victim but we saved him instead."

"Yes, and as a thank you, he went and wrote that freakin' novel based on you two reprobates!" Sebastian snapped.

"Ugh, Sebastian, no one knows that we're real and Artie even killed the fictional hound at the end at your behest, which was mean by the way."

"It kind of makes the story, Ally," Alfie retorted.

"I don't agree. He could have let the fictional doggy live and prove it wasn't real hellhound in the end, another way."

"Hey, twins, we're not here to argue about that damn book. We're here for Penny!" Reggie declared.

"It's fine, Uncle Reggie," Penny said.

"It's not fine, hon. Today is all about you."

"I kind of wish it wasn't," Penny mumbled as she tucked a stray piece of fire tinted blonde hair behind her ear.

Reggie let out a small sigh and gave her a gentle pat on the back, "Is the offer everything you want?"

"More than that," Penny said with a happy smile.

"Right, well we still have some more negotiating to do, since I want to make sure there are enough security measures in place. Not to mention multiple damage control clauses for your mum and Uncle Alfie."

"Hey!" Ally declared.

"Don't hey me. I know for a fact that you two will want to be here at all times and I cannot in good conscience, unleash the two of you upon Cambridge with no safeguards because you are public menaces."

"I may resemble that remark but I won't be jeopardizing my daughter's dream!"

Reggie gave her a small smile, "I know you won't, Ally but still, safeguards are necessary. Now, Penny and Lucy, why don't you two go look over Penny's new office with Lenox?"

Dr. Finebeck looked very alarmed when he realized he was about to be left alone with the hellhounds.

"Uh Reggie—" Lenox started.

"Relax, Lenox, I know our very presence, scares the bejeesus out of the vast majority of humans. However, I also know that your Aunt Raven is actually the one who runs the immortal part of the campus since this place is under her protection."

"Yes, that is correct," Lenox's Aunt Raven said, once she teleported into the room.

"Ah, good to see you, Raven. We have security terms to hash out with you," Reggie stated.

"Yes, we do. Shall we do so over tea?"

"Eh why not," Reggie replied with a shrug.

Raven nodded and telepathically said to Lenox, *do not worry Lenox I shall take it from here.*

Lenox nodded slightly before he stood up and ushered both Penny and Lucy to the door. Lenox then, led them down the corridor towards the departmental offices. As he did so, he explained the layout and history of the building.

"This office is mine and your new office will be located right next door Penny," Lenox said as he showed the door to his office.

"Will I have my own name on the door like you?" Penny asked as her fingertips traced the embossed name embossed on the door.

"Absolutely," Lenox agreed, feeling a blush bloom in his cheeks as he watched the delicate way in which she traced the lettering.

"Um, Lenox?" Penny asked almost breathlessly.

"Yes?" Lenox returned, trying to maintain his composure.

"Can I see your office first? I want to see what a real professor's office looks like."

"Penny, I have absolutely no problem with you seeing my office. However, what your office looks like is completely your choice. There's no obligatory way that it needs to look... hold on," Lenox stopped himself from rambling as he opened the door to his office instead.

It was a relatively spacious room, with a large desk that Lenox's father, Conalai, had crafted for him when he first got his professorship. On the far side of the room, a clutter consisting of small mechanical projects, computers, papers and books lay strewn across a large table that sat next to a whiteboard on an opposite wall. Behind Lenox's desk, was a two story bookcase wall filled to the brim with books and even had a rolling ladder. There a decent size sitting area that was in front of a brick fireplace with four comfy armchairs a coffee table. On either side of the fireplace were two large, floor to ceiling windows and in front of the window that was nearest to Lenox's desk, was an easel for his twin sister Lulu, who was a well-known artist. Lastly there were plants and small mechanic devices on shelves, that were throughout the room which gave it a cozy lived in feel.

"Uh is this a normal office? I expected them to be like half the size of this, at least," Lucy asked.

"This isn't a normal office by human standards. However, it is a normal for an immortal. I mean, we both get the same square footage on paper but a long time ago immortals imbued all the buildings with magic in order to have a lot more space. No one knows the difference though because when a human walks into this room they see what they've come to expect from a professor's office."

"Nice. What's with the chairs?" Lucy asked as she walked

over to the fireplace and noticed that chair was a different colour (green, blue, pink and purple).

"My family visits from time to time so I made a spot for them to sit. They don't appear often though, with the exception of my twin sister, Lulu. She's here daily when I'm teaching, hence the artist nook, which is her space."

"She comes here daily? Doesn't she have young kids?" Lucy asked.

"Yes she does and my niece and nephew are called Brynhildr and Lorcan. Although we called them Bryn and Lore instead."

"Ah, I love those names! They are a mixture or Swedish and Irish, right?" Lucy asked excitedly.

"Yeah," Lenox agreed with a nod.

"Lenox? Are you and Lulu, like my mum and uncle?" Penny suddenly asked.

Lenox froze slightly at the question.

"Sorry… never mind that I asked," Penny said at once.

"Say what?" Lucy asked in complete confusion as her head swung between Lenox and Penny.

"Lucy... it was a stupid question, just forget it."

It's not a stupid question Penny, Lenox murmured mentally and he found himself answering truthfully. *And yes, Lulu and I are very much like your mum and uncle.*

Penny stared at him hard as her eyes widened in surprise. She had never met another set of twins like her mom and uncle, though suddenly it all made a kind of weird sense to her.

Your secret is safe with me, Penny mentally returned.

Lenox bowed his head slightly before he showed Penny next door to an empty room that was nearly a copy of his, layout wise.

"You can decorate this place as you want, Penny since this is your office now."

"But my family is still negotiating," Penny stated.

Lenox shrugged, knowing full well that the hellhounds had already agreed to Penny being here and it was only the security that they were arguing about. Which really boiled down to them wanting to vet every single soul who studied here and his Aunt Raven was currently trying to find a happy medium that would appease that need.

"Aunt Ally just texted me and asked if you had your heart set on this place, Pen. Do you?" Lucy asked looking at her phone then her cousin.

Penny briefly looked up at a blushing Lenox before she tried to act nonchalant.

"Yeah," she finally whispered in a breathy tone, which she immediately cursed herself for.

"Well tell her mentally then."

Penny nodded before she reached out to both her mum and dad at the same time.

Uh mum, dad? I really, really like it here and would dearly love for this place to be my school.

Without skipping a beat Penny's outgoing mum let out a half delight squeal before replying, *It'll be in the bag now, hon! Seriously, Sebastian stop arguing with Raven and start acquiescing to some things. I mean sure, strike a hard bargain, my mate but still, let it be a bargain.*

Yes, Ally, Sebastian declared before adding, *Penny?*

Yeah?

Congrats, sweetie you'd did really well and I'm proud of you.

Thanks, dad, Penny said feeling elated at his words.

"Well, it looks like this is going to be my school," Penny said as she looked up at Lenox.

He gave her a soft smile, "Congratulations and welcome aboard, Penny."

"Thank you... uh Lucy, what are you doing?" Penny asked, frowning when she noticed her cousin had summoned tester paint cans and had started testing various shades of pink on the wall.

"I'm testing shades of your favourite colour on the wall. Come on Pen. I don't know why you hid it but everyone knows you love pink and there's nothing wrong with that."

"Not that I have a say in the matter but I like the soft pale rose pink the most, since it reminds me of you. After all, roses may look fragile but they are a hardy plant that can grow in some of the toughest environment and their thorns can keep the unwary fools at bay." Lenox said.

"Oh wow you know lots about flowers by the sounds of it," Lucy said.

"Lucy! His mum is Mina for goodness sake."

"Oh right! Sorry! I forgot!" Lucy said contritely.

"How can you forget he looks like his mum?" Penny demanded.

"Uh, that's the first I've heard that. Normally I'm told that I look like my dad more than my mum."

"Well to me, I see both your parents in you, especially in your dark purple hair since it's a pretty equal mix of our dad's jet black hair colour and your mum's vibrant purple."

Hair? The best I could come up with is to talk about his hair colour? Not his eyes, his physique? Jeez! Penny inwardly hissed at herself, knowing she put her foot in it.

Luckily for her, her cousin soon took over.

"Hey yeah, it is a dark purple colour. That's awesome and I wish I had purple hair! Man my white blonde hair is so plain in comparison."

"It's not plain and people would kill to have blonde hair," Lenox commented.

Lucy shrugged, "People kill for lots of stupid reasons in general, Lenox."

Lenox nodded, "That's true."

Lucy! Penny called out.

What?

He wasn't talking about people literally killing for your hair colour.

He wasn't?

No, Penny stated before adding, *it's just a saying.*

Lucy cocked her head at Penny and frowned as she replied, *I don't get it.*

The saying 'people would kill for that' *is often used in terms of,* 'you are pretty and there are people envious of your prettiness.'

Lucy cocked her head to the other side, *I still don't get it. How do you get you are pretty, from people would kill for that?*

Because it's a euphemism for envy and we both know that lots of people kill others who they envy.

Oh... I don't like that saying, Lucy said with a shrug.

Penny let out a small sigh, slightly wishing that she had garnered the compliment instead.

Lucy winked at Penny before she held up the soft rose Lenox had chosen and nodded to Penny as if to say, *this is what you're going for, isn't it?*

Penny gave a small furtive nod before cousin let out an equally small chuckle and wandered to the far corner and started painting the room.

With her cousin happily distracted, Penny mustered up her courage and said to Lenox quietly, "Um... so I guess I should start by saying, I'm sorry."

"You're sorry? Why?" Lenox asked in confusion.

"Well I've caused you nothing but a world of trouble these past few days."

"Penny, you've done nothing of the sort and I'm actually elated that you're here."

"You are?" Penny asked, instantly perking up.

"Yeah, I am," Lenox said.

Penny notice the deep blush starting to creep up his neck. *OMG! Did he really say that? He also told me I was wonderful yesterday too! OMG again! I kissed him after he did that and I wonder if he hates me now? Good Light, I need to talk to him about that but if Lucy finds out, I will never hear the end of it. Maybe I should try and ask him telepathically but what if I accidentally project my thoughts outwards?*

Suddenly Lucy gave Penny the perfect opportunity.

"Hey cuz, I need to go to the ladies' room be right back."

"Would you like me to show you where it is?" Lenox offered.

"Nah it's fine, let me prowl… I mean *find it...* on my own, thanks," Lucy declared sweetly before she ran out of the room with a laugh.

Hoping her cousin was far enough away, Penny waited a full

minute before she took her chance.

"Lenox, do you hate me for kissing you?" Penny asked in a rushed whisper.

Lenox looked taken aback by her words and he instantly replied in the exact same tone, "Absolutely not! I meant every single word I said to you before, Penny. Though if I truly wasn't clear... I like you."

Penny's mouth dropped open in shock.

"You like me? Like as in a friend, 'like me'?" Penny asked.

"No Penny, I more than like you," Lenox whispered as he cupped Penny's face with his hands, "I've also liked you from the first day we met, Penniah Hawksley and I just hope..."

Suddenly his hands released her and he stepped back. Penny frowned briefly wondering why he did that, until she felt the presence of her mother and uncle Alfie shortly before they came bursting through the office door.

"Penny, we've done it! School's a go! Oh wow, is this your new office? I love it!" Ally cried out.

"Oh yeah, there's so much we could do with this space," Alfie stated, eyeing it critically.

"Nope!" Penny's father declared at once when he stepped into the room behind them.

"No way Jose! Twins, this is Penny's space and there will be ground rules for you two regarding Penny's new academic domain. Meaning that these spaces are off limits to you two."

"What?" Ally cried out, affronted.

"Not fully off limits, dad, because I really hope that mum and Uncle Alfie will visit."

"Those visits are gonna be daily ones too!" Ally interjected.

"Once every other day visits!" Sebastian retorted.

"Yeah right! Though for Light sake's you are so mean to me! Why did I mate with you again?"

"Because you love me and that's not past tense, Allycen."

Ally scowled and sucked in a breath before stopping as if she was now holding her breath.

"You don't need to breathe as an immortal, love, so holding

your breath until you pass out won't work. Ah! Don't be pissed. I'm doing this for a good reason, which we'll discuss later. Anyway, it looks like Penny's got some paint choices going already. Which one do you like, sweetie?" Sebastian asked.

"Alright, I'll give you the benefit of the doubt, Bas. Anyways, I like the bright fuchsia colour," Ally declared happily when she noticed the colours on the wall. Her outrage quickly forgotten.

"You would," Alfie retorted.

"What the hell does that mean?"

"It means it's a crap colour is what it means and the bubble gum pink is much better."

"Ha! As if! It looks like the colour of stomach medication. What's it called again?"

Sebastian supplied the name Ally was looking for.

"Mmm hmm, that!"

"Well I like the soft rose colour!" Penny said, suddenly making herself known.

Ally, Alfie and Sebastian all looked at Penny, completely startled.

"Honest I like this one the most," Penny said again, this time more firmly as she walked towards the wall and pointed out the shade that Lenox had mentioned. Though in truth, it had been her own secret first choice too.

Almost instantly her parents and uncle became distracted by the paint choice and immediately began to squabble over who was going to paint the room. Not one to look a gift horse in the mouth, Penny use the free moment to finally admit to the truth of her feelings for Lenox, that she had been holding in for years.

Lenox in regards to what you said earlier... me too.

Lenox's eyes opened wide as he realized that Penny liked him, too. Then it dawned on him, that after nearly two hundred years of unrequited love, he had the chance of a lifetime. A chance that he would never, ever pass up, though he knew he was going to need a lot of help in making it a reality.

Time to pull out the big guns, Lenox thought as he knew who he needed to talk to in order to get the ball rolling.

Chapter Six

Earlier the next morning, Lenox arrived at his twin's home and let himself in quietly with his key. Unable settle, he began to make breakfast for Lulu and her family, hoping that she would awaken soon. Although, it wasn't Lulu who made it down the stairs first but rather, her wife Freya.

"Lenox, to what do I owe the pleasure of seeing you so early this morning?" Freya drawled, attempting to rile him.

Lenox said nothing as he gently pushed a cup of coffee in Freya's direction. Freya looked down at the dark liquid in the cup and nodded, as if accepting the bribe to say no more to him for the time being.

Lulu awoke and made her way downstairs with her twin toddlers, Lore and Bryn about five minutes later.

"Uncle Len, Uncle Len!" The toddler twins cried out excitedly.

Lenox smiled at them before taking both out of his sister's arms and hugging them.

"How are you two doing?" He asked them when he set each twin down into their high chair with Freya and Lulu's help.

"We great! And you?" Lore and Bryn said together.

"I'm great too!" Lenox said with a laugh, ruffling their hair.

"You certainly look it, did you finally get enough sleep last night, Len?" Lulu asked as she took over cooking breakfast.

"Yes," Len answered as he sat down next to Bryn.

"So what are you doing today, apart from visiting us?" Freya asked changing the subject.

"I've got no solid plans," Lenox remarked, fidgeting slightly.

Lulu cocked her head curiously at him as she plated up the food. Lenox didn't meet her gaze right away as he instead tucked into the meal, after thanking her.

Lulu seemingly wasn't deterred as she gently tilted up his face with her hands so that he force to look her in the eye. Though considered the gentler twin by all, Lulu still had her days when she was 'all business' as their cousin Anya would say and today appeared to be one of those days.

"Nothing is wrong, I swear," Lenox said at once.

"But..." Lulu prompted.

"I kind of confessed my feelings yesterday," Lenox admitted.

Freya choked, "Light sake's, Len, you sure move fast."

Lulu snorted, ignoring her wife briefly as she remarked, "How did it go? More importantly, why didn't you come over last night?"

"It didn't go bad Lou and in truth, I just wanted some time to think things over."

"Hold up, why do I feel like there's more to this story than you two are letting on. I mean, I didn't even know Len was interested in anyone." Freya stated.

"Ah *min storra*," Lulu said calling Freya my darling in Irish Gaelic, "Len has been head over heels in love for years."

"Say what?" Freya retorted in Swedish, doing a double take.

"She's right Freya, I've liked Penny for years," Len admitted openly.

"So when you say years..." Freya prompted.

"Since 1821."

Freya started to curse in Swedish but then remembered her children and stopped.

Lulu ignored her wife's astonishment again, "So what did she exactly say, when you said it?"

"Well, her parents and uncle walked into the room seconds after I said what I did so she didn't say anything right away. Though a few moments later she mentally told me, 'me, too'."

"Wow..." Freya said, earning a small scowl from both Lou and Len.

Instantly she held up her hands in a self-defense gesture before focusing on helping her children feed themselves.

"Well that's great news," Lulu said warmly.

Lenox gave her a small smile back, feeling quite elated that Penny did feel the same way. Then he frowned, when he remembered his present dilemma.

"I don't know what to do now though, Lou. I mean, we'll be working together at the start of new university term and I've even volunteered to help her with her PhD thesis. However, I'm worried about potential conflicts there. I mean, what if someone says it's an abuse of power or something?"

"Stop right there, Len! You have nothing to worry about, for you are the most conscientious and diligent person I know. Also, surely you're the one who could help her with her thesis since I know you are the smartest professor at Cambridge."

"Not anymore, Penny's got a 270 IQ too," Lenox added.

"Stop downplaying yourself, Len. You are amazing and to be honest, I am glad that she matches you in the brains department," Lulu said without missing a beat.

"Hold up! Who is this mythical Penny?" Freya interjected again.

"Seriously, Freya? I've asked you for two favours regarding her in the past few days and you're telling me that you don't even recognize the name?" Lulu demanded with a laugh.

"Hold on, are we talking about the hellhound Penny Hawksley here?" Freya asked her eyes wide opened in shock.

"Exactly."

Freya let out a mild Swedish oath this time.

"Freya!" Lulu cried.

"Sorry, *min hjartet,* but we're talking about the hellhounds here and I can almost guarantee you, that this isn't going to go well," Freya stated, calling Lulu my heart in Swedish.

"Nothing's a guarantee, Freya and besides, I've known for ages that Penny's been holding a candle for Lenox, which is half the battle right there."

"You have?" Lenox asked her.

"Oh yeah, Len. I mean it's kind of obvious given the fact that she has been going out of her way to protect you, me, mum and even dad and Freya on occasion. She also makes it a point to hang out in Uncle Phoenix's favourite local pub in order to overhear things about you and if that doesn't tell you that someone carries a torch for you, then I don't know what to say."

Lenox smiled brightly this time, feeling more secure in what he planned on doing, which caused Lulu to gain the same bright look.

"Oh no. Oh, no, no, no," Freya said adamantly as she picked up on the plan and then called out to her own twin Frey.

Frey immediately teleported into the room seconds later, "Where's the fire Freya? Jeez, it's the crack of dawn!"

"For the love of the Light! It's seven thirty, dolt! And quit whining, I need you to help talk these two out of getting into trouble with the hellhounds."

"Say what?" Frey asked, sounding completely stunned as he sat down on a stool on Freya's other side and immediately focused on Lenox and Lulu.

Freya briefly explained what she knew so far to Frey in Swedish.

"Oh wow, this isn't gonna go well," he said.

"Yeah, that's what I said but I earned a scowl from Lou and Len."

"Ugh, it'll all be fine," Lulu huffed out.

"It won't, Lou," Frey said nonplussed agreeing with Freya's earlier assessment before adding, "We are talking about the hellhounds here. The same immortal species who make the *Predators* from movies, seem tame."

"OMG you did not compare our hounds to the Predators," Lulu cried out.

"Did you hear that Freya? 'Our hounds,' you're so screwed," Frey said to his twin.

"I know, pray for me," Freya retorted.

"Will do sis," Frey nodded.

"You two are so not helping! That's it! Lenox, we're going to go speak to someone who will help us after breakfast."

"Who's crazy enough to do that?" Freya demanded.

"Our mum is not crazy," Lenox retorted.

"No she's not, though she is totally final boss material in her own sweet way. You know what Frey? Don't pray for me, pray for the hounds."

Frey snorted, "You know, I think I might actually do that."

Freya nodded before saying, "Now who wants to see granny and grandad today?"

Lore and Bryn immediately squealed in delight.

Frey got up and poured himself a cup of coffee while saying, "You are going to have to let me know how this all goes later, Freya."

"Oh no, don't think for one moment that showing concern gets you out of helping me out when push comes to shove. In fact, if you really want to do me a favour here, sharpen my sword."

"Don't you dare, Frey!" Lulu cried out.

Frey held up his hands, "I won't, I swear."

"Freya?" Lulu asked, scowling at her wife.

Freya held up her hands mirroring her brother's innocent look.

"I don't believe those looks and you two are so *on notice* with me," Lulu retorted, using the British slang to let them know they were on her 'crap-list'.

Frey and Freya guffawed at Lulu's remarks.

"Wow, Lou, I've never been *on notice* with you before. That actually sounds real scary," Frey finally said.

"It should because I'm being super serious here. I will allow no one to muck up this chance at happiness for Lenox. Also, sorry my dear sweeties but you won't be visiting granny and grandad today. Instead Mama is going to take you to see Grammy Yuri with Uncle Frey. Mummy needs to have a serious conversation with Granny Mina."

Lore and Bryn happily agreed to the change in plans.

"I guess I'll go home and get my own daughters ready for a play date with mum Freya," Frey remarked, nodding in agreement.

"Sounds like a plan," Freya approved.

About an hour later when everyone had a chance to finish breakfast and ready themselves for the day, Lenox and Lulu teleported to their parents' home and found their mum, Mina, in the garden.

"Lenox! Lulu!" Mina cried out warmly as she ran over and

hugged them.

"Hi mum, where's dad?" Lenox asked.

"Oh, I sent him on an errand because I knew you wanted to talk to me about something important regarding a certain special someone. Right?"

"Oh… yeah," Lenox said at a loss.

Sitting down in the tall grass next to a bed of wildflowers with his sister and mum on either side, Lenox took a moment to collect himself but even then, he still couldn't find the right words to say.

"Lenox sweetie…" Mina gently prompted.

"I love her mum," Lenox blurted out.

"I know, my dear son," Mina responded softly.

"You knew that I love Penny Hawksley?" Lenox asked incredulously.

"Oh yeah," Mina said, nodding with a wide smile.

"Does dad know?"

"Uh yeah but he only found out recently."

Lenox went quiet again for a long while.

"Lenox sweetie, have you said anything to her?" Mina finally asked him.

Lenox nodded.

"Oh me, oh my… did she reject you then?" Mina asked in concern.

Lenox shook his head, "No mum, she actually returns my feelings and I feel really kind of stupid for saying this but I don't know what to do about it now."

Mina let out a relieved breath. "Lenox, my darling son that answer is an easy one — you woo her."

"But what about her family? I mean not to be stupid, but I know I'm about to open a whole can of worms for our family since the hellhounds and vampyrs are close allies. Not to mention, I also want a chance to be with Penny without all the well-meaning interference that is sure to come if, on the off chance, everyone accepts us."

Mina hugged Lenox, choosing to say nothing in response, though she didn't have to as someone else chose to speak instead.

"That is truly what you want son? You want a chance to woo Penny?" Conalai clarified as he made himself know and knelt down in front of them.

"Yeah, Dad, that's exactly what I want."

Conalai nodded, "I know I can be overbearingly protective of you, your mum and your sister, son but there's also a snowball's chance in hell that I'm letting anyone ruin your chance at finding true love and happiness."

"Seriously dad?"

Conalai nodded.

"But truly what about our family? Surely—" Lenox started, before his dad cut him off.

"Surely you wooing the daughter of the new hellhound alpha is bound to cause trouble. So? Who gives a damn, Len? You're the smartest, kindness, most hardworking man I know and I'm not just saying that as your dad. It's all the truth and as much as I loathe sitting on the sidelines watching you ride the emotional roller coaster that is love, I know that Penny will be a great match for you. Therefore, honestly and truly, don't worry about the hounds or any of the other nonsense, for me and your mum will deal that. Just be yourself, Len and everything with work out."

"I'll do that dad… though, do you think that's a good idea?"

"Yes son, I do because you being you, is what she fell for."

"Yes sweetie and by the way, before you even ask, you can have any of the plants you want from my garden. I don't mind at all," Mina said.

Lenox nodded before he looked out into the garden deep in thought. Moments later, Lulu pointed out different flowers that she thought Penny would like. Lenox got up with his twin and started to look over the different options which allowed both Mina and Conalai to slip away from them.

*****

Teleporting to Alfie Baskerville's home, since both Mina and Conalai knew that with Alfie as their ally, they'd have better chance at winning over Ally and Sebastian. They were soon met by someone else instead. For as unpredictable as ever, Ally Hawksley sat on a paddock gate just outside her twin's home, seemingly waiting for Conalai and Mina to appear.

"I was expecting you two today," Ally announced, confirming their suspicions.

"Um, sorry Ally but how did you know we'd come here?" Mina asked.

"Well, I figured that once Lenox came to see you regarding his feelings for my baby girl then you'd come to see Alfie to see if he could either talk some sense into me and Sebastian or at the very least keep us from interfering in their budding romance. Which is kind of mean if you ask me," Ally stated with a slight huff.

"I'm so sorry, Ally," Mina said.

"Ah don't be Mina, I'm not really upset by the fact that you tried to take the diplomatic route. In fact I'm not upset at all, to be honest. I just like giving people a hard time. Anyway, it's well known that I'm overprotective of my daughter just like you both are with your twins."

"Yeah and just like you, we're unapologetic for it," Conalai remarked.

"Which is one of the reasons I like you Conalai Moregan. Any who, let's stop dancing around this. I know my Penny is in love with Lenox and I'm not against it. Honest, if I could have picked anyone for my girl, I would have picked him in a heartbeat. However, their future isn't gonna be a bed of roses, especially over the next few months. However, I can't really tell you why because it's an utter mess, but suffice it to say, stuff is about to hit the fan for all us hounds."

Conalai looked alarmed before he let out his breath and asked seriously, "You need any help? I offer my aid freely with no strings attached."

Ally shook her head before she responded, "Nah man, we're alright for now, though thanks for the offer. Anyway getting back to Penny and Lenox, it would be for the best, if they got to know each other secretly for now."

Mina nodded first, “Sounds like a plan. We’ll tell Lenox that.”

Ally sighed again but nodded, “Thanks, Mina.”

Mina nodded and started to step back before a small vision of the future entered her mind. “It'll be alright, Ally, I mean that.”

Ally's normal happy go lucky expression returned. “Thanks again, Mina, I really needed to hear that. Right see ya!”

With that Ally pushed herself off the paddock fence and teleported away in one swift movement.

Taking their cue, Conalai and Mina teleported to their own living room. Needing a moment before they went back outside to see their children. Mina wrapped her arms around Conalai's waist and he returned the favour.

“I know it'll be difficult for you, *min storr* but you truly have to let him find his own way now. It’s imperative,” Mina whispered to her husband.

“The world is truly one hellish place, Mina and I hate having to step back when I've pretty much just been told the crap is about to hit the fan. Though do you think...?” Conalai stopped.

“Do I think it's time that our children’s true powers and the roles they were truly meant to play int the immortal world, will be made known to everyone? Yeah, Conalai, I do,” Mina agreed.

Both lapsed into silence as the held each other and mulled over their secret worries.

*****

Lenox and Lulu had felt their parents teleport away but neither had said anything about it as they focused on finding the right present for Penny. They were also bound and determined, to not worry about anything until their parents returned from speaking with the hellhounds. However when their parents returned and did not come to see them after ten minutes, both Lenox and Lulu stopped what they were doing and rushed to see them.

“Mum? Dad?” Lenox called out in alarm when he entered their cottage and saw them holding each other.

Mina lifted her head from Conalai’s chest and gave him a

small reassuring smile as she relayed what Ally had said.

Then she added, “The immediate future will hold many treacherous pitfalls for you, Lenox and Lulu. However despite that, I know things will go the way we want them to, if you take up the roles that you were always meant to. Nonetheless, I still fear that roles might cause you great pain later no matter how I wish it weren’t so but I guess we cross that bridge when it comes to it.”

“Mum...” Lenox started to whisper as both he and Lulu walked towards their parents.

Conalai and Mina reached out and hugged their children.

“It will be alright, Len and Lou. It truly will be, I know it,” Conalai said.

Mina nodded in agreement saying, “Yes it will, although it looks like we'll need to sit down and talk in earnest with your Grandad Midir in upcoming weeks, for he will know what to do.”

“I am sorry mum and dad,” Lenox said, feeling bad for causing them so much grief.

“There is nothing to be sorry for, Len, for what’s occurring is not your fault. Honest, my son, this would happen no matter what. Besides, at least we’ve been warned this time since it really sucks to be plunged into a hellish battle against the forces of evil with no forewarning,” Conalai muttered, speaking from experience.

Lenox silently agreed with his dad, though part of him couldn't help but wonder if Penny knew what was coming. Though something told him, she didn't and he truly hoped that wasn't the case. However, it didn’t really matter if she did or didn’t because Lenox determined to secretly do his damnedest to protect her.

I’ve got your back, Lulu mentally reached out to him through their deep twin link.

Thanks Lou, Lenox replied, feeling reassured by the fact that come thick or thin, he always had someone he could entrust everything with; Including his heart’s choice. *Penny.*

Chapter Seven

Three weeks later...

It was a little after six in the morning when Penny arrived at her office in Cambridge University, since she just couldn't wait longer.

Today is the day that everything changes; today is the day that I finally get to be the real Penniah Hawksley.

Unlocking the door with her key, Penny entered the office and immediately stopped. On her desk sat a large potted plant and a note. At first, Penny thought that one of her family members had left the gift but instantly she knew that it couldn't be the case because the plant didn't give off their underlying magical essence.

It took her a moment but she soon realized that the person who left the gift had been Lenox.

Biting her lip, Penny closed the door and walked over towards the plant. She took a deep breath in and picked up the card.

Congratulations, Penny, good luck and all the best –Highest Regards, Lenox.

Penny blushed at the note. Impulsively, she pulled out her phone from her pocket and took a picture of the flowers, then sent it in a text to her cousin Lucy.

<Look what I got!>

< WTF! IT'S SIX IN THE FREAKIN' MORNING PEN!> Her cousin texted back, showing her ire with all caps.

<So now that you're up, please feel free to admire this. >

<WHY! WHY! Wait, is that a potted plant? >

<Yup it's from Lenox! :) >

<Whoa that's nice, did he send a card with them? >

<Yup, yup, yup, check it out>

Penny took a picture of the card and sent it to her cousin.

<Huh. >

< :(Why huh?>

<It's kind of formal Pen and it seems to me that he's friend zoned you or I guess colleague zoned you, would be more accurate terminology.>

Penny frowned, **<What's that mean? >**

< It means he wants to be friends instead of boyfriend/girlfriend, hon.>

<Oh but he said he romantically likes me.> Penny texted back, feeling forlorn.

< HE DID!!! WHY THE HELL DIDN'T YOU SAY???>

A knock at the door distracted Penny from texting her cousin back. Turning around, she walked the short distance to the door and opened it. Penny felt shocked elation course through her veins when she saw who stood in the hallway. It was Lenox.

"Ah... hi," he said shyly.

"Hi," Penny answered in the same way.

"Can I come in?"

"Oh sure, by all means," Penny said as she fumbled to get out his way.

Feeling a bit like an awkward fool, Penny tucked an errant piece of hair behind her ear and said, "Thank you very much for the flowers."

Lenox flashed her a smile that nearly caused her to swoon.

"Ah, you like them then?"

Penny nodded.

"I'm so glad… oh here, I brought some snacks this morning and I was wondering if you would like to share them with me?"

Penny nodded again before making a beeline for her work desk in the corner. Sitting down first, Penny was exceedingly pleased when she saw Lenox take the chair right next to her instead of the one across from her.

"I... uh… ahem, I made some cinnamon rolls and jalapeno poppers. I know it's a weird combination—"

"No it's not! Ack! Sorry! Wait, did you say you made these?" Penny asked in a jumble, cursing herself for acting like a total fool in front of him.

Lenox's cheeks reddened slightly, "Yeah I did, well with the assistance of my twin Lou. Sorry, making spicy food is in my wheelhouse but making sweet stuff is not."

"Well, that's more than what I can do. I can't cook at all... well I've never tried but still," Penny stated with a shrug.

"May I ask why you haven't tried, Penny?" Lenox inquired softly.

"Well, when I was a kid, my mum burnt down our house three times when she tried to make supper and it seemed like a safer endeavour to me to not try."

"Well, if you ever change your mind, I'd be willing to help you learn to cook."

"Really?" Penny asked as her eyebrows shot up.

Lenox nodded earnestly.

Penny said nothing for a moment feeling flustered. Then she decided to reach for a jalapeno popper. Biting into the savoury spicy crust, Penny nearly moaned in delight.

"These are really good. Thank you for sharing, Lenox," Penny said after swallowing her first bite.

"Um... I have a confession to make," Lenox muttered, blushing.

Penny said nothing as she stared at him.

"I made these especially for you."

"For me... really?" Penny asked in stunned amazement.

Lenox nodded.

"But why?" Penny asked, completely confounded.

"Um... well as I've said before, I like you, Penny."

"Like as a friend? Um, sorry. My cousin said that it sounds like you friend-zoned... erm, colleague-zoned me."

"What? No!" Lenox exclaimed.

"No?"

Lenox vehemently shook his head. "No, Penny, I don't know what I've done for her to reach that conclusion but I meant every single word that I said before."

Penny went quiet for a long moment before tears filled her eyes. "Me too, Lenox."

"Oh my! Penny what's wrong?" Lenox asked in alarm.

"I'm so utterly clueless!" Penny wailed as tears began to trickle down her cheek.

"Oh, Penny, you're not!" Lenox said before he leaned over and wrapped both his arms around her.

Penny's near emotional meltdown abruptly came to a screeching halt, which stunned even her.

"Light sake's, what is wrong with me?" Penny asked out loud.

"Nothing. Absolutely nothing. You're perfect, Pen."

"No I'm not. In fact, most hellhounds will tell you that I'm boring, cautious to a fault, quiet, studious. Light sake's, Lenox, I don't even know what a real date entails because I've never been on one."

"Me neither," Lenox admitted before an idea came to mind. "Hey, why don't we make up our own kind of dates?"

Penny pulled back slightly so she could look him in the eye, "What do you mean by that?"

"Well, why don't we write down a list... hold on, do you mind lists? I kind of have a habit of writing things down in this format," Lenox admitted.

"Oh no, I love lists of things."

"Oh that's great news. Anyway, why don't we write out a list of things we want to do and we'll do them together as dates."

Penny smiled at him, "That's a brilliant idea, Lenox. Wait! I don't know if I can. I'm sorry, Lenox but my parents are super overprotective and they're also super, super temperamental too. Well... my dad's the temper, my mum's the mental… uh sorry, family joke but what I'm trying to say is—"

"What you're saying is you're worried that your parents may freak out and try to squash our chance to get to know each other better? I get it, Pen, my dad is also super overprotective and even though my sister is happily married to her soul mate, she dated Freya for sixty years in secret before she told my parents."

"Oh wow..."

"Yeah... do you want to do that?"

"What? Keep our relationship a secret?" Penny asked

"Yeah," Lenox said.

"I don't know, Lenox. Something says this wouldn't be very fair to you. I mean, I like you I really, really, really do and—"

"And I'm willing to chance anything for a shot at being with you, Penny. Honest, I've been waiting nearly two hundred years for this day and now that I know you feel the same. I will not be deterred. Sorry to be so forward but you mean so much to me," Lenox admitted.

Penny's eyes went wide in shock.

"So, will you give it a go? I mean, we call these study sessions instead of dates... wait that sounds like something that belongs in a horribly cheesy movie, sorry."

"Kind of... but you know I don't mind it because it's quite truthful in its own way. I mean, this would be dating study sessions, since we're both new to this. We are both new to this right?"

"Not to be presumptuous but you're my first girlfriend."

"Not presumptuous at all and you're my first boyfriend," Penny eagerly admitted.

"I'm sorry if this sounds terrible but I'm so very glad. Now how about it? Do you want to give our sessions a go?"

Penny hesitated for a moment before she vigorously nodded her head. Seconds later, she found her voice and let out a squeal of delight.

"Yes! Sorry, I'm not normally this dramatic."

"There's nothing to be sorry about," Lenox assured her before letting go of her, so that he could summon up a notebook and a pen.

"How do you feel about amusement parks?" Lenox asked her.

"Don't know, never been," Penny admitted.

"Poetry nights at coffee houses?" Lenox asked.

"Never been to those either."

"How about karaoke?"

Penny bit her lip and shrugged her shoulder as if to say, *I don't know.*

"Hey don't get discouraged, there's lots of stuff I haven't done like... skydiving. I've always wanted to try that."

"Oh that's tons of fun. I've gone skydiving loads of times," Penny admitted.

"I'm a bit jealous," Lenox chuckled, holding onto one of Penny's hands.

Penny shrugged as her free hand picked up another jalapeno popper. "I wouldn't be. The fun was taken out of it once I landed in enemy territory and got shot at."

"Have you ever parachuted just for fun?"

Penny was slightly bewildered by that question.

"No," she finally said. "I only go out into the real world as we hounds say when I've got villains to hunt down. Otherwise, I spend my free time reading, watching trashy telly with my cousin, spending time in my mum and uncles' lab building stuff, helping my dad out, going on the occasional pub crawl... you know homebody stuff."

"There's nothing wrong with that, Penny. Although if you could choose, where would you want to go or what would like to do?"

"Well, I'd like to try the stuff you mentioned. I mean, I think karaoke would be awesome. My cousin Lucy went all the time with her friend Kaoru when she was on tour with a dance company. I'd also really like to try a roller coaster and the coffee pub... and shopping in an flea market... and riding a motorcycle through the countryside without baddies chasing me... and parachuting without being shot at... and..." Penny continued to babble on as she thought about the thousands of things that she secretly wanted to try but had made no attempt to do so.

Why hadn't I tried any of this stuff? Penny wondered.

After all, Penny had always thought she had lived a pretty exciting life but take away her hellhound hunts and there wasn't much excitement left. Though to be honest, hunts weren't exciting anymore either.

Penny sighed, causing Lenox to stop writing. Blinking, Penny realized then that she had rambled on more than she had thought.

"Wow, it's crazy to see all that in black and white so to speak," Penny muttered before sighing, "Light sake's, I think I'm having the hellhound equivalent of a mid-life crisis. One if I'm honest, I've probably been having for the last twenty years."

Penny froze, realizing that she had said too much.

"I doubt that, Penny. I think you've probably wanted the best of both worlds but denied yourself because you didn't want to cause anyone any trouble," Lenox said quietly.

Penny looked at him, cocking her head questioningly.

"Penny, I don't really know hellhounds well. However, I've been told that my parental family is pretty close equivalent and using them as an example, I can tell you that for the longest time my dad, Aunt Raven, Uncle Wulf and Uncle Felix had to hide anything that gave them joy in order to protect themselves and those they cared the most about, from Iberius, my paternal grandfather."

Penny nodded in understanding since stories of Iberius and his wickedness, were well known in immortal circles. In fact, his very name was enough to raise her hackles and make her want to dig up his remains and tear him to shreds for the grave sins he committed against Lenox and his family.

Lenox gave her a brief smile "Thank you for your outraged concern, Penny. It truly does warm my soul."

"Huh?"

"You were growling, love," Lenox murmured with a small smile.

Love? He called me love! Penny thought first, before her brain heard the rest.

"Oh whoops, I do that from time to time when I'm super pissed."

"It's okay. When I'm that mad, my eyes go blood red. It's actually one of the few Vampyr traits I have."

"Do you have many? Vampyr traits I mean? Or are you more Ritana like your mum? Sorry but I'm ever so curious about that."

Lenox smiled again. "I'm considered to be more the vampyric twin to most immortals, especially when they meet my sister, Lou. However, it's actually not accurate at all, since I only drink blood during rare red moons. Also, I'm not a man of violence beyond any need of defending myself or my twin in dire situations. In fact, to be a hundred percent honest, my dad and Freya keeps us safe. Which I know that sounds bad but my dad once told me that he'd die a thousand deaths before he'd ever let me or Lou from needing to become an assassin in order to protect ourselves, like the rest of our family. Therefore, apart from the some common Vampyr senses and being Conalai Moregan's son, I truly can't be called a Vampyr. I also can't be called a Ritana because I rarely get struck with moods, unlike my sister and again, I can physically fight without being swamped by an emotional backlash. Ergo in truth, both Lulu and I have actually inherited the lion's share of my maternal grandparents' magic, which is Omega Clan magic, a long side of a hodgepodge of Vampyr and Ritana traits. Does that make better sense?"

Penny nodded earnestly "Oh yeah. I mean, I'm considered a hellhound and a pure blood one at that, since both my parents are hounds, but in truth, that's not accurate either. I've actually inherited some Fae traits that come from my maternal grandmother and Ritana ones that come from my paternal grandmother. Not to mention I am a Baskerville."

"Okay, sorry to interrupt but I'm dying to know about how the Sherlock Holmes story came to be."

Penny laughed. "Oh goodness, that's still a sore point for my dad. He's kind of stickler for hounds sticking to the shadows to protect humans and to be honest, back then, it really made sense because people thought we were demons. I don't get that though. I mean, sure hellhounds wouldn't be winning any pretty dog contests but just because our full hellhound form is both scary and kind of homely looking—"

"That's not true!" Lenox interrupted her.

"It actually wholly is, Lenox." Penny laughed again before continuing, "We actually take pride in it, too."

"Really?" Lenox asked taken aback.

"Oh yeah and don't tell anyone but the male hounds actually have an ugliest hound competition. It happens after the *Last Hound Standing New Year's Eve Battle Royale* and there's method to the madness, for it's said that the ugliest hound is the strongest fighter. Not always the truth though, since my mum and I are considered to be pretty hounds, yet we have the deadliest stats amoungst all the female hounds. Also over all, after my Uncle Alfie, my Great-Uncle Reggie and my dad, it goes me then mu..."

"Hold on, you're the deadliest after your dad, Uncle Alfie and Reggie?" Lenox asked curiously.

Penny nodded sheepishly. "My Uncle Alfie often makes more kills than my mum does when they hunt together. In fact, Great Uncle Reggie may have the highest villain body count over all but if you stacked age versus kills, Uncle Alfie would actually have him beat since his kill ratio is insane. He has something in the neighbourhood of 200 villains killed for every day he's been alive."

"How is that even possible? Sorry, I'm not doubting you, I'm kind of confuddled by the logistics of it all."

"Oh, it's actually kind of easy to get a kill count that high if the stars align, so to speak. Namely, if you kill demon hordes on a regular basis because those same hordes can have hundreds of thousands of demons within them. Now hellhounds who choose to take on these foes are called Legion Killers by the animalia, though we call them Swarm Hunters."

"That makes sense but how old is your Uncle and mum again? 1500 years old?"

"No, 1748," Penny stated.

"Wow... your Uncle must have a villain body count over the hundred million mark, then."

"Oh yeah, and it's about 127,604,000 or so, though I have to check the tallies," Penny said nonplussed.

"How?" Lenox asked, his jaw dropping.

"A big chunk of them were killed during the dark ages because, as my Uncle tells it, demon hordes were on the upswing during that period and often numbered in the several million. Also, we hounds don't hunt using conventional means either. By which I mean, sometimes our being within five to ten feet is enough to kill a demon because our magic essentially unravels them."

"That's amazing," Lenox marvelled.

"Not really," Penny said dismissively before continuing. "It's kind of a downer, since you work super hard to track down the so called 'wickedest' demon horde to ever exist, only to watch all the blighters literally dissolve away in a puff of smoke or puddle of acid in front of you because you breathed ten feet from them. Worse yet, is when they have the gall to self-explode and you get hit with, well you know, and you end up having to take multiple lemon baths and lye soap showers for days."

"That would suck. Are you Swarm Hunter, too?" Lenox asked unable to stop himself.

"No, I'm actually an all-around hunter/protector and in hellhound terms, we called that being a Brimstone Hunter or in my case Brimstone Huntress since I'm a woman," Penny said, trying to stay deliberately vague.

"How many Brimstone Hunter/Huntresses are there?"

"Um... just me," Penny admitted before switching topics. "My dad and Uncle Reggie are called Apex Alpha Hunters which means they have the qualities to lead hellhounds and they deliberately hunt the biggest demons out there."

"Yeah, I could see it and I know this is a personal question to ask any hellhound but what is your mum classified as then?"

Penny shook her head, " It's not that personal Lenox and mum's an Apex Enigma Huntress, which means outside of her kill count, not much is known about what she hunts and what techniques she uses. In fact, outside of my family and the elite hellhounds, no one else has ever seen my mum kill. Though a kill tally can't be forged, no matter how ludicrous it might seem or sound because the grimoire that records everything has our blood embedded in it, so we can't cheat the system.

"Moving on, my cousin Lucy is what's known as a Maniac Huntress. That means, she hunts serial killers, both immortal and mortal. It's also a rare title and only she and Winston who's one of the elites, carry this distinction among the hellhounds since hunting serial killers is actually heavy work and sometimes it can hurt the soul. Lastly, to round out the elite hellhounds, Rocky is the only true protector, meaning she defends more than she actively hunts. She's a Light-giver Protectress, which means she protects all of the Ritana, Zanthe and White Snakes on Celestial Inlet."

"Oh I've met Rocky before and she's quite..."

"Zen? Yeah, in hound terms she's quite serene which we've all chalked up to the fact that she spends her days with the calmest people out there and it's rubbed off on her. Though in saying that, Rocky wouldn't be elite if she wasn't deadly."

"Say no more. I know firsthand that Rocky is deadly since I've helped her rescue kidnapped Ritana before."

"You've worked with Rocky? But no one's said," Penny muttered frowning slightly at this tidbit.

Lenox looked really sheepish. "I'm not surprised about that since any talk of my hunting forays, shall we say, is purposefully buried by my dad and Uncle Wulf. Though it's not without reason, since the older members of my family don't want the younger ones to become targets nor do they want our true abilities to be known."

Penny nodded in understanding since hellhounds were truly very much the same. After all, hellhounds often played up their unpredictability but downplayed their smarts since being a stupid hound often worked to their advantage. Though Penny was quite tired of hiding that among other things.

Lenox noticed that Penny was lost in thought again, so he decided to distract her.

"So... are you ready for teaching class today?"

Penny focused on him and ducked her head shyly. "I've got all my materials ready but... not really. I mean speaking in front of people is tough, you know?"

"Yeah, I know, though I can help you with that," Lenox said.

Penny looked at him curiously, "Really?"

"Yeah... I could magically tune them out for you."

"What's that mean?"

"I'm a null, Penny, which means I can magically void any and all emotional or magical energy."

"Like unicorns can?" Penny asked, knowing that unicorns had that ability alongside full energy purification.

"I think so but I can't say for certain since I've never met a unicorn before."

Penny shrugged. "It's okay, I only know one; Her name is Elizabeth and it's best to be around her in small doses."

"Alright but why?"

"In short because she's dramatic and granted I really like drama, don't get me wrong, however, only in small doses or if I can watch it from afar. Nonetheless, since Elizabeth is really clingy it's hard to do either, not to mention, she likes to use people as literal shields, even though like you, she's a null."

"I would never, ever use you as a shield," Lenox declared, completely appalled.

"Oh, I know, Lenox and you're also not dramatic either."

"No, I'm not, although my twin's wife totally is," Lenox stated with a small grin.

"Oooh... dish," Penny stated as she started to eat more jalapeno poppers.

"Huh?"

"It means please tell me more about Freya's dramatic escapades. Again, I love personal drama and have a standing nine o'clock appointment with my cousin every Thursday night to watch trashy drama filled shows. So again, dish."

"Alright but... it's really weird to talk about Freya drama with you."

"Lenox, I'm a hellhound. We're like the living embodiment of twilight zone, ergo nothing is ever truly weird to us. Well, except normal run of the mill stuff, like paying taxes, I guess. Any who, *Please. Tell. Me.*" Penny pleaded, enunciating the last three words before adding a puppy dog look for added measure.

Lenox nodded with a laugh, knowing full well that weird was soon going to become his new normal and he was completely alright with that.

Chapter Eight

After sitting through Penny's first round of classes in the morning, Lenox returned to his own office to prepare for the only class he had on that day. Which was unusual for him since he normally taught three to four classes three days a week during regular term. However, he had altered ~~it~~ his normal schedule just in case Penny needed his assistance during her first term.

He had also decided to teach only higher level physics and engineering classes this time, which would give him more free time to complete the projects he wanted to complete as well. Nonetheless, it would be more of a pain in the long run, since most the students finishing degrees liked to hound him for last moment extra academic credit projects to bolster their grades or to give a good impression for future prospective jobs.

Sneaking into his office after dodging some graduate students, Lenox found his sister Lulu painting in front of the window.

"So you're doing higher level classes this semester. Glutton for punishment, are we?" Lulu asked with a soft laugh.

"How'd you know?" Lenox asked with a small sigh as he flung himself into his comfy desk chair, causing it to squeak and grown.

"Four students have already come by and left notes asking for extra credit projects."

"You didn't reply to any of them, did you?" Lenox asked in semi-alarm.

"Nope, they slid their requests under the door after excessively knocking for several minutes and I used my magic to summon up the requests, so I could read them before placing them on your desk. I also read your date list, too, while I was at it."

Lenox let out a small laugh this time, "Goodness you're nosy."

Lulu turned to him smiling brightly, "Of course I am. I'm the younger twin, so I get to be the nosy one. Anyways, by the sounds of it, your breakfast with Penny must have gone well this morning for you to write a list of stuff to do as long as your arm."

Lenox found himself nodding with a small content smile. "Yeah it did."

"So..."

"*Dish*? Sorry it's something Penny said this morning, which apparently is something when you want more details on a specific subject. Also more specifically, it refers to wanting to know about gossip."

"Ooh, I'm going to add that to my vocabulary and yes, dish please."

Lenox freely swapped from openly speaking to his twin to their shared mental connection so he could show her briefly what occurred that morning, since he wanted Lulu's honest perspective. Though as he did so, he found his mind focusing on how tough Penny had been on herself. It wasn't natural to him and Lulu was the first to point out the fact that there was probably a group of hellhounds who was deliberately making her doubt herself but to what end, neither knew.

Lenox also had the feeling that her family didn't know what was going on, given their very supportive stance of Penny. Which made Lenox want to either speak up and make the situation known to them or outright deal with it himself. After all, Penny was too wonderful a person to be dragged down into self-doubt and depression by a group of cowardly curs.

Easy, Lenox, I know you want to protect her but it isn't our place yet to deal with such matters. Though rest assured, when we can act we will. There is no doubt in that.

Thanks, Lou. It just bugs me that such things happen because she's a really wonderful being, you know?

Wow, Len, I've never heard you call someone that before.

Well, it's true. There's just nothing not to like about Penny.

Huh, I want to meet her in person, though it looks like I'm about to since she's standing outside your door. You should also tell her to come right in, mentally, before the next pack of overeager grad students swarm her in the next few minutes.

Lenox let out a mild oath before he quickly wrote a note for his door which stated that he was currently unavailable but a list of extra credit projects would be distributed during the next day's lesson.

Lulu laughed softly as she watched Lenox open the door and hastily stick the note in middle of it before gently yet swiftly, sweeping Penny into his office.

"Sorry Penny but there are grad students who are prowling the halls looking for extra credit assignments and it's best not linger in the halls less they pounce on you," Lenox muttered.

"Oh… makes sense," Penny said with a shrug as if she completely understood.

Looking curiously over Lenox's shoulder, she watched his twin sister Lulu, who she had only seen from afar, pack painting supplies away in a wooden box before standing up and smiling warmly at Penny.

"Ah, Penny, please meet my twin sister, Lulu. Lulu, please meet Penny," Lenox said introducing them, when Lulu approached his side.

"Hi, there," Lulu greeted with an impulsive hug, although she immediately apologized for it. "Oh sorry, I'm a bit of a hugger. Well more than a bit."

"Ah that's okay and I really like your painting though—" Penny stopped herself, not wanting to appear rude.

"Why am I painting a picture of the Irish Sea during a full gale storm while staring out at the Cambridge Quad? Well because the new semester drama is best viewed from this angle and the Irish Sea is my favourite thing to paint, ergo two birds, one stone. Anyway, Lenox tells me you like drama, so I will tell you that so far there have been three break-ups have occurred in the Quad, one of the couples immediately got back together, so I'm leaning to there being some big misunderstanding. Oh then there were seven new relationships started too."

"Lou..." Lenox said, intent on interrupting his sister's musings.

"Ah come on, Len, I like romance and spying on the quad is like getting to watch one of those cheesy yet very satisfying TV romances all day long for free. Oh and by the way, Penny, I'm also Lenox's secretary so if you have any paperwork questions feel free to ask me."

"Self-declared secretary," Lenox corrected with a smile.

"Oh yes, it's a hundred percent self-declared but I like aiding my brother when I can, partly because it's a twin thing and partly because he takes me out to lunch daily as a thank you."

"Um, about that today Lou..." Len started.

"Let me guess— you and Penny are going out alone today, instead?" Lou asked brightly.

Penny choked at her blunt words but Lulu just winked at her.

"Ah sorry, Penny. We twins can't really keep secrets from each other, but don't worry— beyond my wife, Freya, I will say nothing. Any who, lunch is a terrible first date brother."

"It is not," Lenox returned with a small frown.

"Okay, you have me there but still, pick something awesome to do this upcoming Friday night as your first real date and in the meantime, get to know each other through the rest of week through office meetings, coffee and breakfast."

"Ooh, that's a great suggestion," Penny declared.

Lenox let out a small sigh, knowing that his twin was right. Getting to know Penny and ultimately wining her trust were key in winning her heart completely. Lenox also knew that Lulu knew more about dating than he did since she was happily married and he was glad that she was willing to help them both with the preliminary date step up.

"So do you want to join us on our daily lunches then, Penny?" Lulu asked before looking contritely at Lenox, realizing she accidentally put her foot in it.

Sorry really didn't mean to steal that question from you, brother, it's just... I can see why you really like her. She is super sweet and even though we haven't talked much, I want to become the best of friends with her.

It's okay, Lou, you're forgiven.

"If you want you can invite your cousin, Lucy," Lenox said after a few moments of silence.

"You two would be okay with that? I mean, I really love my cousin like a sister but she can be a bit overwhelming when you first meet her."

"Oh, we're used to that since my wife is best described as a pure force of nature, though Light knows I love her for it. Um... that doesn't bother you does it? Me being married to another woman, I mean?"

Penny cocked her head in utter bewilderment. "Why would it?"

"Honestly?" Lulu asked in astonishment.

"Yes, you're happily soul-mated. That's an amazing state of being and I'm truly happy for you Lulu," Penny stated openly.

"But you don't think it's unnatural?" Lulu asked her quietly.

Lenox instantly grasped his twin's hand, knowing the hurt Lulu had felt over the hate hurdled at her and Freya over the years. He also didn't doubt Penny's sincerity and he secretly smiled when he saw an outraged scowl form on Penny's face.

Growling softly, Penny demanded, "People say mean things to you, Lulu, because you're mated to a woman? What the hell is wrong with them? Light sake's, what utter feckless clowns they must be to do that to such a sweet person! Good Light! Sorry for the outburst but I will truly state here and now, I have absolutely no issue with you being married to another woman and I will happily punch anyone in the nose who says anything mean to you about it, Lulu."

"Um… why the nose?" Lulu asked curiously, as a relieved smile crept up on her lips.

"Well, punch someone hard enough in the nose and instant blood and tears will form, which is deeply satisfying. It's a hellhound trick that we use to get our point across to daft folk who run their mouths."

"Ah, Penny, many thanks but please don't break people's noses for me. For I truly don't care what people think about my relationship with Freya. Honest, I don't."

"Hmm… I still reserve the right to break the noses of clowns who are the absolute worst about it, otherwise I will endeavour to do nothing more than rain down verbal fury upon anyone who says anything to you or Freya when in my presence."

"I guess that's as close as I'm going to get a vow of non-violence from you, so I'll take it. Anyway, do you like curry, Penny? There's a little Indian cafe not far from here that has some of the spiciest yet most delicious curries I've ever tasted," Lulu offered.

"They also serve you a large basket of onion rings as a starter, too. I swear most of the restaurants in Cambridge have that on their menu for you alone," Lenox snorted.

"What can I say? I like onion rings, though we both know that you do, too," Lulu retorted sticking her tongue out at him.

"Well, I like curry and onion rings, too, and so does Lucy, so I'll invite her, if that's still okay," Penny said.

Lulu and Lenox nodded in unison.

Penny pulled out her phone and saw a staggering amount of messages from her cousin. Ignoring them all, Penny called Lucy directly.

"OMG Penny! Do you know—" Lucy started shouting.

"Yes, yes, Lucy, I do know," Penny immediately cut in before adding, "though I'm going to lunch with Lenox and his twin Lulu and they want to know if you'll come, too."

"I got invited to lunch?" Lucy squealed, her outrage seemingly completely forgotten.

"Yes."

"And Lenox would be alright with this?" Lucy asked suddenly.

"Yeah he would. Right, Lenox?" Penny asked looking at him.

"May I?" Lenox asked holding out his hand for her phone.

"Oh sure, here," Penny said handing it over to him.

"Hi, Lucy, would you like to join Penny, Lulu and myself for lunch today?... Yes, you can teleport into my office. It's a safe zone, and it has been for..."

Lenox stopped when Lucy teleported in. Handing the phone back to Penny, Lenox watched Penny end the call just before her cousin nearly bowled her over with a hug.

"Hiya, how's your first day going?" Lucy demanded.

"It has been great!"

"I want all the deets but first, I heard the offer of food..." Lucy looked at Lenox and Lulu with a puppy dog look.

"Yes there was and we can teleport there, too. The cafe's run by a Vampyr," Lenox stated before he offered his hand to Penny.

Penny took his hand before offering her other one to her cousin, blushing slightly. Lucy said nothing, though curiosity was obviously stamped all over her face. Shrugging it off briefly, she took Penny and Lulu's hand just before Lenox teleported them to the cafe.

Exiting out from a small backroom, Lulu beckoned the two hellhounds to follow her and Lenox to the second floor of the cafe.

"Hey, Vikram, how are you?" Lulu greeted him warmly when they reached a small private cafe that was separate from the human one downstairs.

"Great, Lulu. Table for two today, hon?" Vikram asked her, not seeing Penny and Lucy.

"Actually, a table for four today and I hope you've got an extra spicy curry available since our friends are hellhounds."

"Oh, I sure do— made some devil sauce curry just this morning."

"Ooh, sounds right up our alley right, Pen?" Lucy declared happily.

"Oh, yes," Penny agreed.

"Right, I'll get the legal waivers for you to sign."

"Legal waivers?" Lucy asked, sounding confused.

"Oh, yeah. We don't want to get sued if you end up in the hospital for gastro distress."

Lucy waved him off. "You don't need that. Penny and I ate an entire bushel of grim reaper pepper only yesterday. Here, I filmed it with my phone because my friend Kaoru doesn't always believe me when I tell him that eating hot things for hounds is no different than eating savoury stuff."

Lucy then dug out her phone and showed Vikram the video.

"Oh wow... you guys are bit crazy, no offence."

"It's not an offence to be called crazy as a hellhound; it's actually a badge of honour."

With that, Lucy sat down next to Penny who took the chair

opposite of Lenox and to round out everything, Lulu sat next to her brother.

"Drinks?" Vikram asked clapping his hands.

"A Mango Lassi for me, thank you Vikram," Lenox said softly.

"Same, please," Penny said almost at once, ducking her head slightly when her cousin eyed her curiously.

"Yeah, sounds good. I'll have that to please," Lucy stated.

"Make that four Mango Lassis and four large bowls of onion rings, too, to start, please Vikram," Lulu ordered happily.

"Coming right up. Oh, and, Lulu hon, Mr. Sweet proposed to Ms. Flower today."

"Shut the front door! No way! They have only been dating for how long now?" Lulu asked excitedly.

"Three hundred years give or take but at least he did it in a big way in the middle of the market. I recorded it on my phone for you. Sorry, I would have called you but it was kind of a spur of the moment thing."

"It's fine. I can't wait to see it and we really need to catch up over a cuppa soon."

"Yes, sounds lovely, my dear. I'll text you later," Vikram said before he saw more customers entering and waved goodbye.

"Who's Mr. Sweet and Ms. Flower?" Penny asked almost immediately.

"Oh, that's Eddie and Angelou. They're the candy and flower vendor who are part of the immortal street flea market that's runs daily. Lenox and I have a stall there that we run off and on, since everyone gets to pick the days we want to work. Oh and in the street market circle, we're called Mrs. Artsy and Mr. Fix-it, respectively."

"Ooh, that's awesome, though how's the gossip grapevine in Cambridge, too? Sorry but we hellhounds are terribly nosy and you'll probably be seeing more of us soon or at the very least, more of our family, Reggie and the other two elites. Speaking of Pen, I've joined the elites." Lucy announced.

Penny sputtered, "Eh? Really?"

"Yeah, Uncle Sebastian made me the offer a couple of weeks

back when I announced that I was home to stay and I've decided to accept it."

"Congrats, cuz, though how's your dad taking it?" Penny asked, remembering how her own mum had been dead set against her becoming an elite hound in the beginning but the choice really wasn't anyone's to make after Penny had earned the distinction of being a Brimstone Huntress.

Something that no one outside the hellhounds knew about until today. Since she had accidentally let it slip to Lenox earlier. Though luckily for her, he hadn't inquired further about what that fully meant.

However she knew that one day she'd have to tell him the significance of it and her *'hellraiser'* legacy but hopefully that day was far off since she needed some time to come to terms with it herself.

"You know surprisingly well, given the fact he was so dead set against it before," Lucy admitted.

"Why was he dead set against it?" Lulu asked her.

"Oh, well, our parents aren't like other hellhound parents who actively encourage their children to make a brutal name for themselves. No, ours are really overprotective, especially Penny's mum and my dad; I mean, we both qualified to become elites when we were young, about a hundred or so, but our parents refused to allow it to happen. Unfortunately, Penny had to join... sorry we can't say why since it's kind of a hellhound secret, though I wasn't forced to and my dad blocked any attempt at me becoming an elite until now."

Lulu nodded in complete understanding. Though Lenox had a different reaction as he looked slightly stricken at the thought of Penny having no other choice but becoming elite, before slowly nodding in agreement.

"Anyway, I pretty much just told my dad that you needed a partner in crime on the elite squad Pen, now that I was home to stay and he reluctantly said it was okay. Well, okay, it wasn't that easy since he did get in a scuffle with your dad, Pen, before declaring that he wanted to approve which cases I got, just like your mum currently does for you. Which your dad totally agreed to by the way," Lucy finished.

"Well, I'm just glad we get to team up more, Luce."

"Me, too, and tell me how did your classes go? No one was super mean to you were they? Your mum and my dad blocked my attempts to come see you this morning when you weren't answering my calls. They said that this is 'your domain'–much like the stage was my domain, and I have to be invited first."

"Classes went really well and no one was mean to me… is that normal, Lenox?" Penny asked, knowing that Lenox himself, had to face off with miserable students before.

Lenox nodded, "Yeah it is for the most part, though you'll probably come across the one or two fools who will want to give you a hard time later on in the semester after things settle down. Honestly, right now, everyone is still focused on getting into a routine."

"Yeah and also, the biggest trouble you'll have with students is the over-eager ones who are constantly looking for extra credit projects," Lulu muttered.

Lenox sighed slightly before he nodded.

"Hey, how do you know that?" Lucy asked Lulu.

"Oh, I'm Lenox's secretary."

"One who never directly interacts with Cambridge students and only responds to them via email or phone."

"Darn right. I don't want them to know what I look like or they'll start hounding me when I venture into the halls, in order to get them more extracurricular assignments. Seriously I don't need that in my life."

Lucy looked curiously at Lulu "What do you do as a secretary?"

"Answer calls for Lenox when he's in teaching or field inquiries from other schools, file paper, sort stuff… you know—office stuff."

"I really don't know but could you teach me?" Lucy asked, perking up.

"What?" Penny asked.

"Ah, come on, Penny, please make me your secretary. I promise to be on my best behaviour. Well, as on my best behaviour as a hellhound can be. Pretty please?" Lucy asked making a puppy dog face.

"Ah…" Penny started looking at her cousin then Lenox then ducked her head slightly.

"I swear I won't interfere with 'romance' time."

"Ah, Lucy!" Penny squealed before adding in a quieter voice, "Alright, you can be my secretary."

"Ah yes! … So Lulu, could you please teach me the role?" Lucy asked Lulu.

"Sure but I generally only work a few hours a day in the office when my kids are out with my wife or napping. In lieu of being in the office, I magically send all Lenox's calls to my phone and I also have other magical auto reply emails that I send out to students. So do you want to go over all that tomorrow afternoon? Say 2 pm?"

"2 pm works great for me… Cheers!" Lucy said holding up her glass.

Lenox, Lulu and Penny lifted their glasses to utter cheers, too, before drinking their Lassi. Lenox winked at Penny over his glass and mentally uttered, *Cheers to new beginnings, too, Penny and...you still up for a Friday date night that starts at seven?*

Penny nearly choked as she mentally declared, *Heck yes, I'll be there with bells on!*

Lenox bit his lip to keep from laughing as he replied, *I'm mentally counting down the hours.*

Chapter Nine

Penny breezed through her parents' door later on that night after school was finished, wanting to tell them all about her first day.

"Mum? Dad?" Penny called out from the hallway.

"Hi, Pen, I'm in here with your Uncle Reggie. Your mum's down in her lab with your Uncle Alfie since we expected you a little later," Penny's dad Sebastian called out from the living room.

Penny bound into the living room happily and immediately hugged her dad tightly. Then she sat down on the couch next to him and looked over at her Uncle Reggie.

"Hi, how you doing, Uncle Reggie?" Penny asked him.

Reggie shrugged with a small smile on his face. "Trying to enjoy the semi-retirement life."

"Oh… sorry, Uncle Reggie," Penny said feeling guilty.

"There's nothing to be sorry about, Pen, I'm quite happy that I'm not the leader of the hounds anymore."

Sebastian looked at Reggie with suspicion. "Why does that sound ominous?"

"It shouldn't, but if it does, it's probably because..." Reggie stopped when a loud bang could be heard from outside. "*They* are no longer my problem. *They* are one hundred percent your problem."

Sebastian let out a small curse before he got up and ran out of the house. Penny moved to follow him but Reggie stopped her.

"It's fine, Pen hon, it's just your mother and uncle being well... your mother and uncle."

"Are you truly not mad at me, Uncle Reggie?" Penny asked him.

"Penny, your dad becoming alpha has been a long time coming. In fact, I'm quite thankful he decided to take on the role because I've been leader of this hellhound circus for over fifteen millennia and I hadn't planned on having that role for more than a single millennium. Anyway, Penny, don't listen to any political pack nonsense. You are a Baskerville, and I'm sure you've heard that numerous times and still really don't have a clue what it means."

"That's right. How did you..."

"How did I know?" Reggie asked with an eye roll. "Because I've known six generations of Baskervilles in my lifetime and not once has the older generation ever fully explained it to the younger generation. Though I have a feeling you're mother and uncle will soon do so soon."

"Uh..." Penny started then stopped, unsure of what to say to that.

Reggie looked at her with a small smile playing on his lips before he changed topics and said, "How were classes today? Have you picked your topic for your thesis yet?"

"My classes were amazing today! Oh, and Lucy's become my secretary!" Penny declared happily before she launched into everything that had happened that day, omitting, of course, that she had breakfast with Lenox alone that morning since she knew it would cause a ruckus.

Reggie sat quietly, listening to every word with a look of contentment on his face. It had been a long time since he'd heard Penny talk so passionately about something and he was glad she was finally coming into her own. For that was something he wasn't sure would ever happen, since unlike her mother, uncle and cousin, Penny never wanted to rock the boat, so to speak and that worried him for a long time.

Reggie also noticed Penny's blushing cheeks every time she mentioned Lenox's name and he was glad of that blossoming romance, too. Nonetheless, he knew she would keep her budding relationship quiet for the time being and Reggie felt that it was for the best. After all, Penny's parents would probably erupt, or at the very least, Sebastian would and Ally would ... well, Light only knows what she would do. For despite the fact that Reggie had partially raised the Baskerville twins, he still couldn't predict their reactions, nor, did he expect, that he ever would.

Reggie, everything alright my love? Yuna, Reggie's mate asked him mentally from afar, sounding sleepy.

Oh yeah, Reggie replied happily, *just catching up with Penny and learning about her first day at Cambridge.*

Oh you... you jerk! Yuna yowled in a cat-like fashion before adding, *why didn't you wake me sooner! I wanted to know how it all went!*

Reggie snorted briefly before watching his mate Yuna teleport into the room and almost immediately fly across the room to hug Penny.

"How was school, Penny sweetie?" Yuna asked, scowling briefly at Reggie, who bit his lip to keep from laughing at his miffed kitty cat mate's angry look.

"Oh, it was great! I was telling Uncle Reggie about it!"

"I know, and he is, as they say now, a complete jerk," Yuna yowled softly.

"What?" Penny asked, taken aback.

"I've been waiting all day to hear about how things went at Cambridge and your Uncle Reggie promised to wake me up from my usual afternoon cat nap when you got home. However he clearly did not do so..."

"Hey, in my defence it's the one time of day where your normal sweet nature does not exist and the threat of being maimed is quite real," Reggie said, holding his hands up.

"When has the threat of being maimed ever bothered you?" Yuna asked, raising an eyebrow.

"Never," Reggie said with honesty as he held out a hand to her.

Yuna let go of Penny and walked over to him, taking his hand. Reggie reeled his mate in and tucked her into his side, seconds after she sat down.

Penny watched the scene, happy that Reggie and Yuna were finally together after being torn apart by the Horseman of Pestilence. Though she also dearly wished that she could sit with Lenox like that.

Maybe... soon.

"Hey, wait just a minute!" Came the sudden shout of Penny's father as the front door banged open.

"Not on your life, Bas. Our baby's back! Penny!" Ally

shouted gleefully as she came bounding into the room.

"Hiya, Mum. Hiya, Uncle Alfie, um..." Penny started when she noticed that both her mother and uncle appeared somewhat singed all over.

"Hi, sweetie," Ally cried out before teleporting across the room and wrapping her arms around her tightly.

Penny hugged her mum back, inhaling her scent which was a mixture of soft roses and acrid smoke; the smoke mostly coming from the fires, accidental or otherwise, that her mum was known to set.

"Right, my turn to hug Penny. Off Ally," Alfie declared as he pulled at the back of Ally's sweater.

Ally gave a snort of derision as her response to his remark.

"Come on, you can have her back in a moment," Alfie said, waving his hand.

Ally let out a peeved sigh before she briefly let go of Penny so that Alfie could hug his niece. Swooping in for a near rib-cracking hug, Alfie let her go 20 seconds after Penny's mum declared his minute over.

"Right you two, go shower. We're going out for supper tonight, so make sure to dress nice," Sebastian called out.

"Ooh, are we going to the Carnivore Cafe in Moonlight Valley?" Ally asked gleefully.

"No. We're going to Mr. Buffet World, which is why you have to dress nice and ..."

"And be on our best behaviour, we know, we know. Light sake's, Sebastian, give me some credit. Ooh, don't forget to call our friends, Callie, Tessi and Asa! I want them to come out with us tonight!" Ally declared.

"I already called Callie and invited her, her siblings and their mates to supper, Ally. Now, where do you want to go afterwards, Pen, out to the pub or..." Penny's dad asked her.

"Uh... could we go to the pictures instead? I mean, I wouldn't mind having a round at a pub but I really want to see that new Godzilla movie."

"OMG is that out already?" Ally asked.

"Not in mainstream theatres but the director sent Callie's mate, Memphis, an early screening of it."

"Nice! Come on, Alfie, let's get our butts in gear!" Ally shouted before she bound over to Sebastian and hugged him tightly, before planting a kiss on his cheek then teleported away.

"Right, I'll be back with Rika and Lucy soon!" Alfie replied as he, too, teleported away.

The room was quiet before Sebastian spoke up.

"You don't want to go to the pub at all, do you, Penny sweetie?"

"Not really, but—"

"But nothing, where do you want to go tonight after supper?" Sebastian asked her.

"I really want to go to the pictures as I said."

"Done, and?" Sebastian prompted.

"It would be nice if we could have a cup of coffee at the Teddy Bear cafe in Moonlight Valley and maybe a few laps at the go-kart and arcade. Hold on, maybe not if we're going out in nice clothes."

"The arcade will be fine afterwards, hon. After all, Luna and Falcon go to the arcade on dates dressed to the nines all the time. So why can't we?" Reggie demanded.

Sebastian agreed before he began chatting to his daughter about her day. Penny glowed as she gave him a more detailed account of her first class. Though suddenly there was a knock on the front door.

Sighing, Sebastian called out for the person to come in and see themselves into the living room. A few moments later, Winston, one of the other elite hounds entered the room, looking grim.

"What's up, Win?" Sebastian asked with concern.

"A fight broke out in the club," Winston grumbled.

"So? That's the whole point of a fight club," Reggie said from behind Sebastian.

"No, not at fight club, the dance club in Moonlight Valley and Falcon's hitting the roof over it." Winston remarked before trailing off when he saw the dark scowl on Sebastian's face.

Sebastian looked briefly at Reggie, "I'll be back. Wait for me."

Reggie nodded as he watched Sebastian teleport away with Winston. He turned to see Penny look at him in mild alarm.

"What's going on exactly?"

"Nothing major, hon, just a bunch of fools causing trouble," Reggie said.

"Oh... does dad need my help?" Penny asked.

Reggie was about to wave her off when Ally and Alfie suddenly teleported back into the room with Lucy and Rika in tow.

"Party time!" Ally shouted in a singsong voice.

"Not yet, Ally," Reggie stated.

"Why effin' not?" Ally demanded with a frown.

"Because your mate has to take care of some pack business at a club in Moonlight Valley," Reggie responded with a sigh.

"Are you freakin' kiddin' me? They're at it again? Oh. Hell. No." Ally declared, emphasizing the last three words.

"Ally, whatever you think on..." Reggie started to say, but it was too late. She and Alfie had already teleported away again, causing him to curse.

Shaking his head, Reggie followed them, leaving Rika, Lucy, Penny and Yuna in the room. Penny looked over and caught her cousin's eye.

Wanna go too? Lucy asked her.

Usually the one to follow the unwritten rules, Penny found herself giving her cousin a swift nod and teleported away. Arriving at a dance club in the middle of Moonlight Valley, Lucy and Penny noticed that all hell had broken loose.

"This is unacceptable!" Penny's mum shouted as she wrung the necks of two female hellhounds at the same time.

"Ally! For Light's sake, don't commit violence here!" Falcon, one of the other protectors of Moonlight Valley and Lenox's cousin, declared.

"Shut it, Falcon! This has got to be settled now because I'm sick of this nonsense!"

"I get that..."

"Then let us work in peace, man!" Ally retorted.

A third hellhound woman came running over to Penny's mum with a chair held over her head intent on hurting her.

"Don't you dare!" Penny shouted, instantly reacting.

However instead of using violence like everyone else had, Penny's anger triggered her magic and caused everyone and everything to become suspended in air, unable to move. Penny did nothing for a few moments as her mind fought her emotions so that she didn't accidentally expose more of her true self. Then, once she felt herself enter a calmer state of mind, Penny used her magic to put the room back together and separate the two sides with a magical barrier. Once that was sorted, she continue to hold the barrier in place, since inevitably it deflected an attack from one of the idiot female hellhounds that her mum had been throttling seconds earlier.

"Um, Penny sweetie?" Ally asked hesitantly, gesturing to the barrier as if to say, *please take it down, I'm not done yet.*

"No!" Penny found herself saying, "No, I won't take this barrier down, mum. This is supposed to be a sanctuary for the people of Moonlight Valley and I will not allow anymore fighting to occur that needlessly harms the innocents in the room."

"I'm sorry that angered you, sweetie. It wasn't intentional—" Ally started, instantly going contrite.

"Why the hell are you placating her? She's your bloody daughter! You should damn well—" one of the male hounds started to shout.

Penny looked over to see that it was Triton who was shouting at her, when her father suddenly cut in, "Say one more bloody word, Triton. Go on, I dare you."

"Dad—" Penny said, but neither he nor Triton paid her any mind as they focused on each other.

"If you continue to spare her from the realities of our world, Sebastian, you will make her weak in everyone's eyes. Though too freakin' late there, given the fact she was a born Omega!"

Penny found her voice and demanded, "And just what the hell does that mean?"

"You know what it means. You're an abomination. A blight in

the eyes of the sight of the rest of the pack! A genetic freak of nature that we all would rather hide," he snarled at her.

His words ripped at Penny's soul as her mind echoed with similar hate-fuelled words from the past.

"She's the reason why no two hounds should breed together."

"What a freak! Her kill ratio is obviously faked. There's no way a weakling like her could kill that many."

"Can you believe they made her elite? It's because she's a bloody Baskerville, though that line should do us all a favour and get neutered. Especially the 'precious' Penny, though fat chance anyone will want to mate with her."

Dark gloom started to overcome Penny until a bright spot entered her line of sight. *Lenox.* Penny's pain started to disappear when she focused on him and his course of action.

He had managed to clear Penny's barrier, grab Triton by the throat and pull him away from everyone. All the while his twin Lulu, stood in protective stance in front of him looking positively feral with glowing red eyes, letting out a low snarl that made the back of the hairs on Penny's neck stand up.

"Uh, Lulu..." Falcon started to say.

"No, Falcon, we're handling personal business and no one is going to interfere with that. Absolutely no one," Lulu hissed out in warning.

Falcon held up his hands to her as if to say, *by all means, do what you want.*

"This isn't *Vampyr. Business.*" Triton choked out as Lenox squeezed his throat tighter.

"No, it's not but your stupidity has caused the woman I love pain and I will make you bleed for the dishonour," Lenox snarled.

With that, Lenox chucked Triton onto the ground, and then swiftly followed him. Penny watched Lenox lay his fists into him with both awe and admiration. Triton tried to fight back but a pissed off Lenox was seemingly an unrivalled opponent. Penny's heart beat rapidly at his actions and if possible, she fell in love with him even more.

Eventually, Lenox stood up over the prone unconscious form of Triton and snarled, “I'd kill you but you're not worth another moment of my time.”

With that, he crossed the room towards Penny, stopping briefly for his sister, who handed him a handkerchief to clean his bloodied hands. Penny noticed then, under a brighter light, that Lenox's eyes were still glowing red much like his sister’s but it wasn't the bright red that Lulu's eyes had shown moments ago. No, it was a softer red, as if his usual ice grey colour had started to bleed back in. Lenox then moved again, stopping in front of Penny. Remaining silent, Lenox let his eyes search hers deeply before he seemingly nodded to himself. Without any warning, he brushed back Penny's hair from her shoulder then started rubbing her ears with the pads of his thumbs.

“Lenox?” Penny called out to him softly, unsure of what he was doing.

“Just trying to get rid of all that lying filth he spewed at you, love. It won't take but a minute,” Lenox murmured in his usual stoic calm fashion, though that was wholly at odds with his red-tinted eyes.

“Lenox...” Penny started, feeling a bit ashamed that he had to bear witness to Triton’s words.

“Lenox nothing. You have absolutely nothing to feel ashamed about, since not a single bloody word of that drivel was true. In fact, he spewed all those terrible words, while wanting you desperately. I can’t even begin to tell you how much it galls me that he thought he had the Light given right to say those things to you so that you’d become so depressed, that you'd mate with him out of desperation. Ugh,what an utter fool, for even upset, you would never stoop that low.”

Penny snorted softly, “Lenox.”

“Everything I’ve said so far, Penny, is the truth for I could hear his intent. I also magically picked up on all the other petty evil words said to you before,” Lenox stopped as the blood-red filled his eyes briefly before fading back to pink, “Light sake's, Penny, you didn't deserve that. You really, really didn’t.”

“Lenox, stop,” Penny said, not wanting her family to know,

but Lenox shook his head.

"They took advantage of your kind, sweet, selfless quiet nature. They said and did things to you that they wouldn't have dared to do anyone else because they knew you'd suffer in silence. Well no more! I can't stand and let that happen, Penniah, I just can't. It breaks my soul to know that you suffer because I truly do love you. I also know you are a strong hellhound but you have my sworn oath to not only defend your back but your heart, too. That is, if you're willing to let me."

"You want to defend my heart?"

Lenox nodded solemnly.

"Well, in that case, I want an even trade since I want to defend yours, too!" Penny burst out before shaking her head. "It's not fair you had to be subjected to all that wickedness from your own... from Iberius and all his cronies, and if he weren't dead already I'd willingly kill him for you. In fact..."

Lenox smiled softly, stopping Penny in her tracks, "The deed is already done, love and despite the pain he inflicted on my family, his own flesh is blood, I care not a whit about him anymore, truly. Though I will accept your even trade if you allow me to know one thing."

"What's that?" Penny asked breathlessly.

Lenox said nothing as he stared at her with a very serious expression on his face and it took a few moments for Penny to realize what he wanted her to say

"Silly me, how I could forget to say something so important to you after you've made yourself known? I love you, Lenox Moregan. I have done so since our first meeting on the Moor and I know quite well that there will never ever be another for me since my soul chose you that day."

"Good. For there will never ever be another for me either, Penniah Hawksley," Lenox said warmly as a sincere smile drew upon his face.

With that, Lenox cupped her face and moved towards her. Their lips met and briefly Penny was afraid she'd mess up, but when she heard Lenox's soft groan, her instinct overtook her. Lenox's own instinct seemed to kick in at the same moment as his tongue invaded her mouth, and began duelling with hers. Penny wrapped her arms around his neck drawing him closer as heat race through her veins.

Suddenly, a loud curse snapped her back into reality.

"Sebastian!" Penny's mum shouted, "Way to go and ruin the bloody moment! Jeez romance killer, calm the hell down!"

"Ca-calm down? You cannot be serious! Our daughter just mated, and you're telling me to calm down... wait," Sebastian turned to face his wife as something seemed to dawn on him and he eyed Ally with suspicion.

She feigned innocence but he wasn't fooled.

"Mated?" Penny exclaimed in shock as her dad's words hit her with the force of a tidal wave.

"Uh huh, congratulations, sweetie, I'm ever so proud, I am," Ally squealed with delight.

"But how?" Penny asked, her mind still reeling in shock.

"Well for hounds as well as the rest of the spirits and animalia, a statement of intent in front of an Elder plus the signs of heat, are all that's needed for a couple to be declared mates."

"Oh," Penny let out when she realized her Uncle Reggie was an Elder for both the hellhounds and the animalia. Not to mention, she had definitely been shown signs of heat since that evidence was still pretty evident.

"Yeah... except it goes a little further with Baskervilles, from the moment you willing let Lenox defend your honour, the mating rite was sealed."

"Oh," Penny let out again, bizarrely accepting that fact wholeheartedly once her shock wore off.

After all, it made sense to her since there was no one else apart from her family, she'd let defend her. No, if it had been anyone else, she would have pulled them away from Triton before she wailed on him herself.

"Yup, yup, yup," her mother, Ally, agreed readily, nodding happily.

Penny's head snapped back to look at Lenox as she stuttered out, "A-a-are you..."

Upset? Happy? Sad? Her mind instantly finished.

"Ecstatic," Lenox assured her, "I truly am ecstatic to be your mate, love."

"Me, too! I'm so very glad that it happened," Lulu declared in a happy bubbly tone, before she pushed her twin aside gently and hugged Penny.

"Welcome to the family, my dear new sister-in-law."

"Thanks, Lou," Penny said bashfully as a deep blush crept up her neck.

"You're welcome though I kind of can't believe these events. I mean, gosh, I kind of figured that you two would eventually mate and marry but not before you at least went on one proper date. Oh well, life just happens, you know," she said sunnily, detonating the equivalent of an emotional nuclear bomb on the room with a soft smile and a shrug of her shoulders.

Penny and Lenox both said nothing, as the roar of outrage, shock and laughter erupted in its wake.

Chapter Ten

Lenox sat on the couch, holding Penny's hand tightly as both their families gathered around them in Lenox's cousin Falcon's living room. Penny was pale, almost deathly so but Lenox didn't think for a moment that Penny was upset at their mating. No, she was more or less still shell-shocked by the sudden turn of events.

"I told you school was a bad idea," Sebastian said to Ally suddenly, causing her to burst out laughing.

"Really, Sebastian? Going to university made our daughter get married to the love of her life?"

"She's... she's too young to be mated!"

Alfie, Ally's twin brother laughed this time, "Penny's 497 years old! Ergo, she's not exactly a young spring chicken, Bas."

"Don't even start! Your daughter, Lucy, is the same age."

"Facts are facts," Alfie said with a shrug of his shoulder.

"So, are we going to talk about this sudden turn of events together?" Lenox's Uncle Phoenix prompted them.

"What's there to talk about, Phoenix? What's done is done," Ally stated.

Phoenix shrugged his shoulders, "That's true, and truth be told apart from understandable fatherly outrage—"

"Thank you! Someone finally understands!" Sebastian shouted.

"Truly do, friend, since there's no greater boogeyman for a father than their daughter bringing home a beau," Phoenix remarked.

"Phoenix!" Raven hissed.

"What? It's the truth."

"Stop commiserating with Sebastian, Phoenix! My son, Lenox, is an amazing catch; he's smart, gentle, understanding..." Lenox's dad Conalai started in,

"Oh, yes!" Ally burst in, "And am I ever glad that Lenox turned out to be my sweet Penny's soulmate. For he truly does tick all the boxes and then some when it comes to being a suitor and when he beat the stuffing Triton... wow that just moved his son-in-law pedestal into the stratosphere for me. Seriously, you can do no wrong in my eyes, Lenox."

"Um, thanks?" Lenox said, unsure if that was a good thing or a bad thing, though he mentally swore that he'd do no wrong when it came to Penny because she meant the world to him.

Turning his head slightly, he caught sight of Sebastian's death glare and nodded politely to him in acknowledgement.

Bizarrely, that small action was enough to cause Penny to start laughing. It was low at first before it roared to a full-on fit of giggles.

"Penny, sweetie, you alright?" Her mother asked gently.

"Is this... is this really my life, or am I dreaming?" Penny asked once she stopped laughing.

"This is real life, love. We're truly mated," Lenox said quietly before turning to her and tilting up her face to look at him. "Though one day I'd still like for you to be my bride in a wedding ceremony, so that I can do things properly."

"Lenox... you want to marry me?" Penny asked in wonder.

"Yes, though I did this wrong and let me rectify that mistake. Penniah Hawksley, would you marry me?" Lenox asked getting down on one knee in front of her and summoning up a ring he had purchased long ago with her in mind.

At the time, he felt like a fool since they hadn't even really spoken more than a handful of words to each other but he couldn't pass it up because the ring was Penny through and through, to him.

"Uh well, hellhounds don't have weddings... but yes, yes I want to be your bride," Penny replied, smiling when Lenox slipped the ring on her finger and kissed her briefly, wishing he could have kissed her deeply again, though he didn't want to test Penny's dad further. Therefore he decided to take up his seat again next to her instead.

"Oh, my Light, you cannot be serious! Though wait a tick! Aren't you supposed to ask me for my permission first? Yes that's the way it's supposed to happen!"

"Ah, Sebastian, Penny's right. We don't have wedding ceremonies as hounds, ergo whatever rules that are set by others don't apply to us," Alfie said dryly.

"Don't you even start," Sebastian scoffed though he was immediately distracted by his mate flying across the room with a delighted cry.

"Let me see! Let me see!" Ally called out, sitting down on the coffee table in front of Penny and seizing upon her daughter's hand to look at the ring.

"OMG! Penny, it so suits you, sweetie. Sebastian, come take a look at this! It's got a pink opal surrounded by pink diamonds that are done up to look like a flower! Oh, look, even the band is made to look like leaves on a vine in different shades of gold. Oh it's pure lovely," Ally cooed.

"Allycen!" Sebastian huffed.

"What?" Ally asked, without taking her eyes off the ring.

"Can you please focus? I'm still pissed here," he stated mildly.

"Tch! Sebastian, eff being pissed at the minor details and just be happy for our baby girl. Light sake's, man, why do I have to be the rational one here?"

Alfie burst out laughing at his twin's remark.

"Why are you laughing?" Sebastian demanded.

"Because it's true, Ally is the rational one between the two of you right now, which means hell must have literally frozen over. Ah damn," Alfie sighed when a thought occurred to him.

"Why 'ah damn'?" Phoenix questioned, sounding thoroughly curious.

"Well, if hell has frozen over, that means that I can't kill demons anymore since they've got to be all dead. I don't like that... smarten up, Sebastian."

"You know hell literally hasn't frozen over," Sebastian retorted.

Alfie looked at him, "It hasn't?"

Sebastian shook his head.

"Ah, good deal then," Alfie replied before he joined his twin on the table to admire Penny's ring.

"Rika, you need one of these. Let's go jewellery shopping tomorrow, my love," Alfie said after a moment.

"You sure, Alfie?" Rika asked him.

Alfie nodded, which caused Ally to turn to her mate with a puppy dog expression.

"I'll buy you a ring if you want..." Sebastian replied.

Ally nodded vigorously in agreement, saying "Yippee! Now can we celebrate?"

"Hold on, we haven't talked about any of this," Sebastian pointed out.

Ally let out a peeved sigh, "Talk, talk, talk. That's all you want do lately, Bas."

"Celebrate, celebrate, celebrate is all you want to do lately," Sebastian returned.

Ally fully turned around and held up her hand and began ticking off fingers. "Well that's all due to the fact that: a, Penny got into a very prestigious school; b, Penny earned a hundred million dollars in grant money for being such a brilliant, brilliant being; c, Penny found love and mated with a man who will always put our baby first, which was clearly evident not but a half-hour ago. Now what kind of mother would I be if I didn't want to celebrate any of that? Don't answer that because I will tell you, a terrible mother, and I will never, ever, ever, ever, be one of those. I love our sweet baby girl from the very deep depths of my soul and have done so since the moment I felt her within my womb, so you can just suck it mister."

Sebastian let out a long sigh as he crossed the room. Saying nothing, he pushed Alfie off the table so he could sit down next his mate. Sebastian then looked at Lenox, then down at their joined hands and back at him. Very reluctantly, Lenox let go of Penny's hand and Sebastian quickly snapped it up alongside her other one from Ally.

Looking deeply into his daughter's eyes, he asked, "Are you happy, sweetheart?"

Penny felt her eyes water with the true depth of her emotions.

"I'm over the moon, dad."

"That's all I've ever wanted for you and I'll make no apologies for that either," Sebastian said, directing that comment to Lenox.

"I'm glad," Lenox said honestly.

Sebastian let out another long sigh, "I don't like you stealing my baby girl..."

"Never that!" Lenox declared, horrified that Sebastian thought that, "I would never steal Penny away from any of her family, ever!"

"Does he not realize that's a figure of speech?" Lenox's uncle Phoenix mumbled in the background before his wife gently shushed him.

Lenox focused on Sebastian determined to be clear, "I will never usurp your position in her life. I have the greatest respect for you, Sebastian, since you have protected her and loved her from the moment she was born. That's also not a lip service said to appease you. In fact, I know I probably will never appease you and I don't want to. I just want to live a long happy life with Penny. I also didn't mean to enter into your fight, but when that... *that idiot* said the things he did, I just couldn't stand seeing the poisonous effects it was having on Penny. I also know that the immortal world will try to make this into some alliance between our families but I will do everything to set the fools right. I've been in love with your daughter for nearly two hundred years from afar and I did so, rightly or wrongly because I thought her way too good for me."

"Lenox!" Penny declared hotly, "I am not! And blast me! I've done the same thing!"

Ally laughed, "It's okay, sweetie, and we Baskervilles do crazy things when we're in love. I had a super big crush on your dad for hundreds of years and I literally stabbed people when they tried to tell him about it."

"She did and I swear I still carry the scars," Alfie muttered from across the room where he sat with his wife again.

"You're one to talk! You wouldn't even appear in your human form in front of poor Rika. No, you pretended to be a stray immortal dog for years!"

"Ah, Ally, I knew the truth the whole time, and it was kind of for the best given everything," Rika said gently, defending her husband.

"Oh, my Light, I want to hear more about this," Phoenix stated gleefully.

"Phoenix," Raven hissed.

Lenox saw his uncle hold up his hands to his wife as if to say, *what?*

Though he didn't see his aunt do it, Lenox knew she rolled her eyes in return.

"This sucks," Sebastian muttered suddenly.

"What?" Ally asked her mate, bewildered by his remark.

"I'm having a hard time holding onto my anger at Lenox since my inner hellhound is currently basking in the pureness of his soul. Seriously, he holds no darkness. How is this possible? Light sake's, he's not the only one either. His mum, sister and dad are the same way."

"I know, isn't it a huge plus?" Ally asked happily.

"Hold on, surely I hold darkness in my heart since I've done a lot of *hard stuff*, shall we say, in the past," Conalai said.

"Nope, you don't!" Ally said cheerfully.

"How?" Conalai started.

"*Min storr*, you purged all that darkness from yourself when you underwent the ritual to become a dream protector," Lenox's mother Mina replied.

"Oh... right."

"Um, don't Lenox and I carry some darkness? After all, isn't it the darkness within us, that triggered the wee episode that we just suffered from?" Lulu asked in her usual bubbly tone.

"I've heard it all now; an incident of near full-on homicidal rage being described as a *wee episode*? Oh, Lou sweetie, that's a cracker and I'm keeping that one for future use," Phoenix laughed.

"Phoenix, for Light sake's this is like watching a romantic movie with you. Ugh! Every time things gets really, really good, you have to make a sarcastic comment and ruin the moment."

"Are you telling me that all the mushy lovey-dovey bits are the good parts of those films?" Phoenix asked, incredulous.

"Duh! Nobody watches romance movies for the backstory. They want the angst, the kissing, the declaration, you jerk."

"Huh... well, this isn't a movie, it's real life..."

"Which makes this all the better, so please shut it, love," Raven stated, with an aggravated frown.

"You know, Phoenix is..." Lenox's Uncle Wulf started.

"You, too," Raven said mini glaring at him.

"*Raven-chan* is right... shh, Wulf," Lenox's Aunt Kitsune, Wulf's soul-mate said before she muttered a few choice words in Japanese about Wulf being an unromantic soul.

"That's not what you said last night," Wulf murmured with a half laugh.

"You know I'm going to plead temporary insanity in court just so you know," Kitsune muttered after a moment.

"In the court of what? Public opinion?" Wulf asked

"No," Kitsune disagreed before saying in Japanese, "In actual court, after I stab you."

"Ah, your bloodthirsty nature does make my blood sing, Sunny," Wulf retorted as he kissed the side of her head, despite receiving an elbow in the midsection seconds before.

"Wow, Kitsune," Phoenix said.

"Don't even start, *baka*," Kitsune said, calling Phoenix an idiot in Japanese, "If he gets stabbed it's a hundred percent your fault because you started this."

"How is this my fault? You're the one going to stab him!" Phoenix asked incredulously again.

"Okay, I'm gonna agree with Kitsune here since you're a pure troublemaker and have been from the moment I first met you, love," Raven pointed out.

"This is so bogus," Phoenix muttered.

"Ah, we're going to get along so well with the Moregans and Galadins, Bas honey," Ally interrupted excitedly.

"True story, we will Ally, and we can even bond over flame throwing a horde of zombies later if you want. In fact, I insist, since I've heard you and your twin make the world's best flamethrowers," Phoenix stated.

"Why the hell do you need a flame thrower, when you're a natural-born firestarter?" Raven demanded.

"Because they're so much fun to play," Phoenix replied readily enough.

Raven rubbed her face with her hand in minor agitation though Ally seemed to understand Phoenix.

"Sounds like a plan, Phoenix and I'll even give you the familial rate of half-price off all weapons of mass destruction. Sorry, no freebies. I've got uranium expenses that Sebastian won't pay for. Which is mean, by the way, for just because it's bad for humans doesn't mean it's bad for us," Ally complained to her mate.

"You cannot be still buying that crap! For Light sake's, Ally!"

"Don't know what you're freaking out about, Bas, I see Shadow Kitty, the animalia healer every month to make sure it doesn't have any adverse effect on me and part from occasionally glowing in the dark as well as setting off Geiger counters, we're good."

"So you make nuclear weapons, too?" Phoenix asked her curiously.

"Oh no, I'm trying to achieve safe nuclear fusion power because nuclear is the true wave of the future when it comes to renewable energy."

"Sounds noble, I'll help you with that endeavour," Phoenix said with a shrug.

"No, no, no, no, no!" Raven and Sebastian vehemently disagreed.

"You can have my nuclear fusion generator, Ally," Lenox spoke up finally.

"Say what?" Sebastian asked him dubiously.

"I have a nuclear fusion generator in my lab. Well, I actually have several of them to be honest, though they all are safe and work quite well, I assure you..."

"Lenox, why didn't you tell us that you made safe nuclear fusion generators?" Raven asked him.

"I did. Well, I told dad and Uncle Wulf, and they tried to sell them for me back in the early seventies. However at that time, the world was pretty anti-nuclear, so instead I kept them and I run a few in a town in Northern England and Southern Scotland with them, just to keep them active. They truly are safe. their only by-product is helium gas and some water, which is safe to put back into the environment, though I don't do that."

"What else are you working on, Lenox?" Raven asked fully curious.

"A NGP train or negative gravity passenger train, if you will. Though I already have a working negative gravity passenger vehicle and truck."

"What does negative gravity do?" Phoenix asked, suddenly also intrigued.

"It… it floats and flies," Lenox finished lamely, cutting himself off from going into a detailed technical explanation since he knew less was more when it came to explaining his inventions.

"Do you have patents for these vehicles?" Raven asked seriously.

"Yes, Raven, he does and before you ask about how I know about that, I will tell you that I'm the one who registers everything with the patent office since they used to give him a hard time. Granted, that was back in the early 1800s but I've been doing it ever since," Conalai said dryly.

"Hold on. You knew about all this nuclear and negative gravity stuff?" Raven asked her youngest brother.

"Obviously, I did since I am his dad, ergo I keep myself well up to date with Lenox's engineering projects and Lulu's art. Though none of that pertains to the here and now. Therefore let's get back to the matter at hand, if you please? Lenox, Penny, congratulations to you both. I am truly happy that you're mated and I know it's a lot to take in right now but don't worry about what anyone thinks about it. Truly, if any punter, and I mean any punter, tries to cause you trouble or grief over this, you let us know," Conalai said indicating Sebastian and himself.

"Hey, wait just a minute!" Sebastian called out, upset that he couldn't take on every punter solo.

"Hey nothing. I might be a dream protector now but my spymaster past is still ingrained within me. Ergo, I know all about that small faction of hellhounds who just splintered off into their own pack."

"So? That's my problem and it'll be dealt with," Sebastian admitted with a soft growl, not bothering to deny the truth since everyone had witnessed it.

"Don't play this off as something frivolous, Sebastian. This is their first humiliating defeat and it will cause them to come back around and have another go. Only it won't be you that they aim for. No, they'll have a go at either Lenox and Lulu or Penny and Lucy, though I'm betting on all four and that they'll be more devious and brutal about the second time." Conalai said.

Sebastian looked pissed off by Conalai's words but Penny knew it wasn't because he doubted Lenox's dad but he was madder at the fact that the idiots were going to target his family again.

"Don't worry, we'll deal with them," Ally said sunnily to her mate with a half shrug.

"Be careful, Ally, they'll harm themselves soon enough. Though when they do, bigger issues will arise. Nonetheless, if that happens, know that we will have your back," Lenox's mum Mina said firmly.

"Mina..." Ally started uncharacteristically hesitant.

"I know hellhounds don't believe in future sight I possess because you believe that the future is never truly set in stone. However please hear me out here because they have already sealed their fate. Which is why I agreed to ask Lenox to keep his budding relationship with Penny a secret for it would have only aggravated them, especially Triton" Mina said. "Though that can no longer be done and we will have our roles to play in the upcoming event. However no one will play a bigger role then Lenox and Penny."

Lenox's mum almost sounded sad, but there was a hopeful note. Something that Lenox knew from past experience, meant a hellish battle was coming and that he and Penny were going to need to fight for their future but it was a fight that his mother believed they could win.

Ally, Alfie and Sebastian started to argue over Mina words. Though ultimately Lenox's dad and Lenox's eldest Uncle Wulf, stepped up and began rationalizing with the mulish hounds. However during the uproar, Lenox's mother focused her mind on Penny.

Mentally reaching out, Mina said, *Earning the title, Brimstone Huntress isn't something to shrug off, Penniah. You need to embrace everything that it means and stop living in the shadows.*

But, a Brimstone Huntress is a living shadow, Penny found herself answering.

Lenox's mum shook her head slightly, *No, a Brimstone Huntress is more than that, especially a Baskerville one and soon, the time will come where you step up and show the world what you are truly made of.*

But— Penny started.

But nothing love, Lenox said, cutting in quietly, *you've got this.*

Lenox, Penny started again.

Lenox caught her eye. *I probably only know a fraction of what you are capable of, Penny but that fraction could take on my Uncle Wulf, an 18,000 year old vampyr assassin and not even break a sweat. You just don't have the confidence in yourself that you should but I hope that if you'll let me, I can be the one to bring that out in you.*

Penny felt herself blush. *Lenox.*

Penny love, sometimes you have put yourself out there and I get how terrifying that is but if you don't, it will cost you something significant.

Lenox, you sound like you're speaking from experience, Penny said.

I am, Lenox admitted sadly, before adding, *I didn't take the chance I should have and it caused my dad to bear a terrible stain upon his soul for centuries. Though I hope from the bottom of my heart that you truly hear the words my mum has said to you and heed them. For I don't want you living with the pain that I have known.*

Hearing the sadness in his voice made Penny want to go out and do someone damage, but beyond that, she found herself genuinely stopping for a moment. She was terrified and uncertain of being a full-realized Brimstone Huntress and she didn't know if she could get over that fear. Though what little Penny realized, was the universe worked in mysterious ways and soon she'd have to face that fear whether she was ready or not.

Chapter Eleven

Penny awoke slowly from a beautiful dream, one where Lenox had mated with her after beating Triton into a pulp. Afterwards, they had then spoken to their families, who had more or less accepted the union, which was followed by a night of celebrating.

Such a wonderful, wonderful dream, Penny mused.

Stretching out in bed, Penny felt an arm contract around her middle and a face rub against the side of her neck, causing her to freeze.

"Mornin' Penny," Lenox rumbled with a small yawn cutting into her name.

Penny scrambled up in shock, "Wait, we're mated? It wasn't a dream?"

Lenox rolled onto his back, looking at her with a serious yet happy expression.

"If it was, then it's a dream I never want to wake from, love. Though I can assure you it was all very real. See," Lenox said pointing to a giant card on the side table.

Without even opening the giant congratulations card, Penny knew who the card was from because her mum had a fondness for giant things. A fondness Penny shared, only because it made her feel dainty. Something that was hard to do when you stood five-ten in your stocking feet, though a thought suddenly occurred to Penny.

"Lenox, how tall are you?"

"6 ft 4 last time I checked, love," Lenox responded, rubbing his eyes and blinking.

"I can wear heels then, yes..." Penny declared in a quiet happy whisper using the small 'yes' arm movement.

"Even if I wasn't taller than you, you could have worn heels, I wouldn't have minded," Lenox said resting a hand on her lower back.

"I would have though and I might as well 'fess up to it now... I have a slight complex about all things dainty and lady-like. Well, I don't even know if that's what to call it but I've always wanted to look dainty and lady-like, despite the fact that I'm built like a Viking giantess."

"You're not one of those, Penny. Trust me on that, for I know Vikings since my sister-in-law Freya is one and she is the twin sister to the current leader of the Norra Stam or Norse Omega Clan."

"If you say so," Penny mumbled as she got up out of bed, despite the fact she didn't want to.

"I do say so, love. You may be tall but you're willowy with curves in all the right places," Lenox replied.

Penny found herself lifting her sleep shirt to expose her mid-drift. "I have a six-pack, Lenox, that's not ladylike at all."

Lenox found himself kneeling up in bed and pulling off his shirt completely. "I'll take your six-pack and raise you an eight-pack."

Penny's eyes went wide at the sight of Lenox's gorgeous body before they rolled into the back of her head and she promptly fainted.

Lenox cursed as he jumped from the bed and landed with a loud thump on the floor, managing to catch Penny before she hit the ground.

Standing up, Lenox watched the door swing wide as his twin appeared, having heard the sudden commotion.

"What's happened? You alright? Wait, is Penny alright?" Lulu asked as she noticed the unconscious form of Penny.

"Penny fainted," Lenox replied in mild alarm at the unexpected turn of events.

"What?" Lulu asked with a frown.

"She fainted, Lou, at the sight of my naked torso no less," Lenox babbled feeling panic creep in.

A faint peel of female laughter rang out from afar and Lenox recognized it to be Lou's wife, Freya.

"Light sake's, Freya's here?" Lenox asked, knowing that she would give him of grief over this situation.

"Well, I am married to her and we crashed here with the kids last night since I didn't have it in me to teleport home after celebrating, so yes. Now put Penny down on the divan and put another shirt on before I use these smelling salts," Lulu said as she summoned up a bottle.

Lenox used his magic to change his clothes to what he planned on wearing for the day. Before watching his twin kneel and wave a smelling salt stick under Penny's nose.

"Wha—" Penny asked, coming awake with a start. Then she looked at Lenox. "Oh good light! I'm so sorry, Lenox!"

"Ah, there's nothing to be sorry for, Penny," Lulu said brightly. "Fainting happens to the best of us."

"Okay," Penny said though she didn't look reassured by Lulu's words.

"It really does and this isn't the most embarrassing faint spell in the family. Oh no, our cousin Skull use to faint at the sight of blood, and he's a vampyr."

"Really?"

"Yup, mind you, it's because of a minor curse that his pissed off wife inflicted upon him before they married but still it was pretty funny. Any who, nice to see you again," Lulu said warmly as she hugged Penny.

"Nice to see you again as well, Lulu," Penny replied before she caught sight of a clock on the bedside table. "Ack! Shoot! I'm super late for school and it's only my second day!"

"Relax, hon, you're not teaching today. You teach Mondays, Wednesdays and every other Friday and I know that because Lenox has the same schedule. Today was set aside as a research day for your thesis," Lulu explained.

"Oh, I best get on that," Penny said as she stood up and got dressed with magic.

"Sorry love but not today. I'm stealing you away from the academic world today," Lenox said with a wink.

Breathless, Penny asked, "You are?"

Lulu answered this time, "He is and I'm helping. We're going to the artisan market today since it's our usual market Tuesday and I can't wait!"

Lenox lightly snorted, "You say that every market Tuesday."

"Because it's very true. Now Frey doesn't want to shop like usual but she's pure willing to hock my paintings and whatever you want to sell brother. So you just need to get some stuff together for her," Lulu said excitedly.

"I've got a cart full of knick-knacks for her in the lab. Come on, Penny, it's time you fully met Lou's reprobate wife," Lenox replied holding out his hand to her.

"I heard that, Lenox!" Freya shouted from downstairs.

"I'm not surprised, Freya," Lenox replied.

"Despite their bickering, Freya and Lenox get along real well." Lulu explained to Penny as they walked downstairs together. "It's just they're a bit of opposites. I mean, my brother is serious and studious, and my wife is boisterous and dramatic."

"Lulu Marguerite Moregan Lindgren, I am not dramatic!" Freya shouted again.

"She so is, though it's way worse when she's with her own twin Frey since they feed off each other," Lenox said.

"Are you calling me dramatic, too, Lenox?" A male voice dryly demanded.

Entering the kitchen, Lenox spotted Frey, his wife, Lydia, their twins Heidi and Elsa, alongside Freya, Lore and Bryn.

"Yes, Frey, because I will not lie to my mate and good morning all," Lenox greeted.

"Good morning, Unca Lenox," Bryn and Lore cried out holding out their arms to him.

Lenox let go of Penny's hand to cross the room and scoop the twins up from their booster seats.

"Morning, Bryn, morning Lore, I want you to meet my soulmate, Penny. Can you say hi Auntie Penny?" Lenox asked as he walked back to introduce the toddlers to Penny.

The twins shyly ducked their heads into their uncle's chest, mumbling hello as they did so. Penny smiled brightly at them as a thought occurred to her. Choosing to act upon it, she shifted and took on her favourite dog form that she liked to sneak around in— a border collie.

Letting out a soft 'woof,' she waited to see the children turn and look down at her.

"Unca Lenox, it's a doggy!" The little girl Bryn cried out.

"You're a doggy shifter like our Uncle Memphis," the two other little girls cried out in unison.

Penny shifted forms again, which earned a small frown from both Bryn and Lore.

"Aw man, we didn't get to pet Auntie Penny," Lore complained.

Penny instantly shifted back, earning a cheer from the younger twins. Lenox bent down and set Bryn and Lore on the floor, who immediately made a beeline for her.

"Can we pet you, too?" One of the other little girls asked.

Oh yes, I'm fine with that, Penny agreed.

With the help of their dad, the little girls got out of their booster seats and made their way over to Penny.

"I'm Elsa," the little girl on the right said shyly.

"And I'm Heidi," the one of the left declared with a bright smile.

"Uh-huh, that's our mummy and daddy over there," Heidi spoke up again.

I'm Penny, Lenox's mate and a hellhound shifter.

"You're a hellhound? But this isn't a hellhound form," Elsa pointed out.

We hellhounds, all have other dog forms that we like to take on from time to time because it lets us blend into the human world and it can be any form we like. For example, my Uncle Alfie likes being a British Bulldog, though my mum prefers being a Skye Terrier, which she calls the 'Honey Badger' *of all dog breeds.*

Penny nearly kicked herself when the last bit more or less fell out of her mental mouth.

All the adults in the room snorted, though the kids were puzzled.

Lore asked, "What's a Honey Badger?"

"A small yet very fierce animal, sweetie," Lydia explained diplomatically.

I'm so sorry, Penny said to her as she shifted back and moved to the breakfast table determined to cause no more kerfuffles.

Ah don't worry about it, Penny. My brother, Memphis, says way worse things around the twins, and there's absolutely nothing wrong with honey badgers, Lydia reassured her.

Besides, your mum isn't the only honey badger because I'm one, too, Lulu said in her usual carefree manner.

As if, Lulu, I'm the honey badger in our relationship, Freya retorted.

More like the Rottweiler, Lulu said sweetly.

"OMG, Lulu!" Freya burst out.

"Mama?" Bryn asked curiously, tilting her head as if wondering what prompted the outburst.

"Nothing, sweetie, just your mama being your mama," Lulu replied sweetly.

"Will you stop! The kids are going to grow up thinking I'm crazy!" Freya sighed in exasperation.

Lulu smiled sweetly at her wife saying nothing

"Lulu…." Freya started to growl.

"Aw, my love, I'll make it up to you later, promise."

Freya instantly smiled, her ire seemingly forgotten. Although, her twins' response was wholly different.

"Lulu!" Frey burst out, knowing what Lulu meant by that.

"What? I said something not nice to my wife and I must make amends, Frey. If you thought something different, that's on you," Lulu said innocently.

"Hmm mmm. Anyway, pancakes, anyone?" Frey snorted, placing a platter on the table.

"Cake! Cake!" Bryn and Lore cried out happily, running back over to the table.

Lenox looked to Penny and whispered, *In Sweden, pancakes are often a desert,not breakfast, though on* 'market Tuesday' *as we call it, we get to eat cake for breakfast because it's a special day.*

Penny grinned. *I like that tradition, and I've always wanted to try pancakes. We usually eat meat, meat and more meat for breakfast. In fact, we only eat bread and veggies when we go over to my Uncle Alfie's place since Aunt Rika is most insistent that we eat something other than meat.*

Oh good. Are you allergic to anything?

Like chocolate? Penny asked knowingly since it was a question often asked of hounds or any canine shifter.

Goodness, sorry if it is an offensive question but truly, are you allergic to it?

Nope, I eat chocolate on occasion and my dad is a secret chocolate fiend. He eats it daily even though my mum kind of hates it.

"Your mum hates chocolate?" Lenox asked out loud, stunned.

"She and my uncle Alfie," Penny laughed.

"Oh, Auntie Penny, say it isn't so," Lore said forlornly.

"It's true, sweetie, though my mum loves strawberries instead. Also chocolate isn't my favourite sweet treat either. I love bananas—well bananas and peanut butter."

"On toast?" Bryn asked.

"I've never tried it that way, I usually just mix them in a bowl and eat it straight."

"Ooh sounds like something to try, are you a fan of smooth or…" Lulu asked.

"Crunchy peanut," Penny declared at once, looking aghast at the mention of smooth peanut butter.

"So smooth peanut butter offends you just as much as it offends Frey, good to know," Lulu replied.

Frey let out a small 'hooray' before adding, "Finally someone else who gets it."

Penny laughed, "Smooth peanut offends all hounds, and you'll be hard-pressed to find any of it at our only local store. Though truth be told, you'll be very hard-pressed to find anything beyond meat, barbecue supplies, hot sauce and peanut butter in that store, too."

Lulu looked at Lydia, "Your brother, Memphis, would lose his mind by the sounds of it."

"Wait! I know Memphis," Penny piped up and added, "And you're right. He's been banned from our store after preaching the health benefits of vegan meat and why we should switch to it."

"Yup, that sounds like my brother, though he never mentioned being banned from a store," Lydia muttered with a sigh.

"That's because he gets himself banned from it once a week."

Frey and Freya looked puzzled. "How on Earth does he get himself banned once a week. Wouldn't being banned the first time be enough?"

Penny shook her head. "No, we hounds like drama and Memphis is well…"

"Chock-full of it?" Lydia supplied.

"Oh yeah," Penny agreed earnestly. "So every Friday his ban gets formally rescinded and then gets it reinstated on Sundays when he picks up his usual order of hot sauce. Sorry Lydia but it's quite hilarious to see. Honest."

"I can see why," Lenox said before he summoned up some extra condiments for Penny.

Penny instantly zeroed in on the peanut butter and banana slices before looking back at Lenox. Lenox winked at her before he opened the peanut butter and liberally slathered the top of a pancake with it then sprinkled banana slices on top. Penny found herself copying him and waited for Lenox to take the first bite before she tried her own.

"Mmm… this is so good," Penny groaned before she happily devoured her first pancake.

"Mummy, mummy," Bryn called out.

"Yes, sweetie?" Lulu answered.

"I want peanut butter and banana on my cake, too, please!"

"Me three, please!" Lore cried.

"Well, me four!" Lulu said with a laugh before looking at Freya, who was already slathering the peanut butter on the twins' pancakes.

Freya just laughed before she, too, nodded and passed the plates over to Lulu, who added the banana slices to make smiley faces.

Soon they were all eating peanut and banana pancakes and talking. Afterwards, the two other couples and their children left the room briefly to prepare for the day, as Penny and Lenox cleaned up the dining room.

"Lenox, what's wrong?" Penny asked when she saw a severe expression on his face.

"Well, this is kind of weird but I kind of wanted to discuss living arrangements. I mean, I didn't expect this so soon but everything feels right, Penny. I loved waking up with you in my arms this morning."

"I do too and I didn't get a chance to say this earlier but I am really sorry for fainting."

"There's nothing to be sorry about, Penny," Lenox said at once, moving a step closer.

"I guess so… though I kind of worry what will happen when we become in-in-in…" Penny stopped and swallowed.

"Intimate?" Lenox finished.

Penny looked down when she felt herself blush furiously, wishing the floor would swallow her up whole then and there.

Lenox tilted her head up so that she was staring into his face before he said, "Penny, love, there's nothing to be embarrassed about. I'm a virgin, too."

Penny looked at him in utter shock.

"B-b-b-but," she stuttered.

"But?" Lenox prompted gently.

"You're really hot and sweet. How is that possible?" Penny blurted out, feeling like she stuck her foot in her mouth immediately afterwards.

Lenox snorted softly, "I'm not the only one who can be described as such, Penny, however as I suspect is the same case with you, I swore to myself that I wouldn't indulge in any carnal activities if my heart wasn't in it because it seemed really empty to have sex for sex sake."

"Any carnal activities? What about kissing?" Penny asked, unable to wonder about how he was so very good at it.

"You're my first there, too, although recently I have read up on techniques after I became smitten with you and I hope I wasn't terrible at it. Was I?" Lenox asked with a small frown.

"Good Light, no! And I have no experience with kissing either but I know enough to know that you literally knocked my socks off!" Penny declared, then she groaned at her admission.

Lenox looked relieved as he gave her his most blinding smile to date then schooled his expression into something more serious, though there was still a playful tilt to his lips.

"I am glad to hear it but we should… *ahem*… conduct more research on the matter, together."

Penny laughed, "We absolutely should and I insist that this research be conducted on a very frequent basis!"

Lenox laughed, too, before he leaned in and cupped the back of her neck, kissing her lips in a teasing manner which earned him a soft growl from Penny. Chuckling softly, Lenox's tongue darted out and traced her lips, teasing her lips to open for him. When Penny obliged him, Lenox's tongue swept inside. Though far from forceful, Lenox seemed rather intent on savouring Penny and he nearly groaned out loud when Penny's tentative responses to his kiss became both bolder and sweeter.

Lenox felt her arms wrap around his back and hold onto him tightly but it wasn't enough for him and Lenox found his arms dropping from her face to sweep her off her feet and pin her against the wall.

Penny let out a soft gasp against his mouth but she just as quickly adapted to the more intimate embrace by wrapping her legs around his waist.

Their kiss intensified then, both spiralling out of control with desire until Lenox heard someone call their names. Penny immediately froze in his arms and Lenox reluctantly pulled back to listen to the voice calling out to him.

"Unca Len, Auntie Penny, you ready?" Lore said from nearby.

"Will be soon, buddy! Just looking for our sweaters," Lenox responded swiftly.

Penny chuckled softly, "Something tells me that someone is going to rib you regarding that one."

"Yeah, and it's probably gonna be Freya or Frey," Lenox agreed.

Penny summoned up a dark blue zip-up hoodie, which caused

Lenox to frown slightly.

"May I?" Lenox asked, holding his hand out for it.

Penny held it out to him and Lenox took it. Penny turned around slowly and let Lenox help her into the sweater. Only this one was no longer dark blue but soft baby pink.

"Pink is your colour, Penny and you should wear more often," Lenox whispered.

Penny turned around, "But, it's a bright colour and I should be wearing dark colours so I can blend into the shadows."

"Don't blend into the shadows when you don't need to, love."

Penny frowned slightly, "What do you mean?"

"You know what I mean, Penny. You don't have to blend into the shadows all the time. You only need to do that when you're hunting, otherwise just be your sweet wonderful self."

"And if I'm afraid to do that?"

"Then know that I will always be in your corner and you are not alone. I've tried my best to always watch over you from afar when I could because I didn't want to see you come to any harm. Sorry if I seemed like a stalker though."

Penny quietly responded, "I don't think that you acted like a stalker, Lenox and you know that I've done the same."

Lenox nodded. Both of them went quiet for a long time.

"We're a right pair, aren't we?" Penny asked him.

"Yeah, we are and Penny, I also like this house, though I wonder if you would be alright with me combining our houses so that we have one house because I don't want to live apart now that we're mates."

Penny nodded her head in shy agreement, unable to say the words and Lenox smiled before he reached to her with his magic. Penny saw a mental floor plan of the two houses and almost instantly she reached out with her own magic and started to combine the two different houses together so that they were one and the same. It was fairly easy to do so since the two homes were almost two halves of the same whole with only the main bedroom, living room and library, needing to be melded together.

"You two ready yet? Goodness gracious warn a body when

you decide to combine homes. Jeez, it was like an episode of the twilight zone there for a moment, that or a bad acid trip, eesh," Freya called from the living room.

"Freya!" Lulu cried out.

"What? It's true. The walls were literally melting a second ago."

"Doesn't matter. Don't talk about acid trips when the kids are within listening range."

"Mummy," Bryn started to ask.

"See?" Lulu pointed out.

Lenox rolled his eyes before shrugging on his sweater and offering his hand to Penny. Penny took it, feeling her heart wanting to burst out of her chest in joy.

"Ready for market Tuesday?" Lenox asked her with a wink.

"Oh heck yes!" Penny replied, ready to have some fun at trying something new.

"Good. Though be prepared for some mayhem," Lenox warned good-naturedly as his hand gripped the doorknob to the living room.

Penny laughed, "Lenox love, I'm a hellhound, we're mayhem incarnate."

Chapter Twelve

Penny felt butterflies flutter in her stomach when she saw the crowds in the marketplace. As her anxiety peaked, she felt Lenox's arm draped over her shoulder.

You okay, love?

Penny nodded, slipping her arm around his waist.

Penny? Lenox asked again in a knowing tone.

There are just too many people here and it's overwhelming, though not in the same way it would be for a Ritana. I mean, all it takes is for me to brush against a person full of either hatred or evil and I'll react. Honestly I have no control over it. Case in point, a few months ago, I tried to buy a pastry from a café and I ended up nearly strangling the server.

What did the server do? Lenox asked softly.

Penny was quiet for a moment. S*he killed two of her husbands with poison, it was awful.*

I hate to ask you this love but do you see their crimes or do you feel their emotions?

Penny was quiet again before she found herself admitting the truth, *It's a rare gift but I see it.*

Well, you have nothing to fear because I am an emotional null and I can't block out your inner sight but I can block out all the emotions you feel with your visions. Also Lulu is my opposite, meaning she can make people feel everything and we kind of figure you had this problem, so we came up with a 'just in case' plan in which Lulu will give your pain to the person who caused it.

"Lenox," Penny whispered out loud.

I don't mean to be highhanded love, honest. It's just not fair on you that you can't enjoy a single day out without dreading running into an evil villain.

"I wasn't about to chide you, Lenox. I was going to say thank you. It means a lot that you and Lou are willing to do that, though I still may need to deal with the villain later, yeah?"

Lenox nodded with a small smile, "Yeah, love and don't worry we've got you covered for that eventuality, too. Freya and Frey are excellent when it comes to creating distractions."

"Len! Penny! Come see this!" Lulu cried out as she turned to them with a giant oversized hat on.

Len groaned softly, causing Penny to look at him questioningly.

"Lulu loves hats, especially big floppy monstrosities and she will buy no less than five today, I swear."

Penny snorted, "I bet you she'll end up with three."

"Oh, you want to bet on it?" Lenox asked mildly.

"Yup and winner's choice on reward," Penny agreed.

"You're on," Lenox said before he gently steered Penny to where his twin and her children were.

Penny noticed that Bryn's and Lore's heads were bent down, looking at a puzzle ball that was in-between them in their wagon.

Penny took a moment to bend down and look at the ball while Lenox eyed his sister's hat.

"Oh, is that new?" Penny asked them.

"Yeah, Aunt Penny," they said in unison, though they were thoroughly distracted.

Penny stood up and looked at Lulu as an idea came to mind. "Where did you buy that puzzle ball?"

"Oh, over there, though don't worry, I picked up ten of them in total. One set of five for me and one set for you; they increase in difficulty from easy to impossibly hard."

"Oh, thanks, Lulu! Those will be great distractions for when my family visits… I mean… well… you know what, I'm not going to sugar coat it; unless distracted, my mum and uncle will get in all sorts of trouble. After all, they've both accidentally burnt down their houses twice and blew up their lab three times with failed experiments."

Lenox shrugged. "I haven't done that yet, but I've had numerous close calls when it comes to blowing up a lab with a botched experiment and it's actually pretty hard to avoid it when you're an inventor."

"Well, when it does happen, I've got you covered. I've taken numerous 'disposing hazardous waste with care' classes," Penny admitted.

Lenox and Lulu laughed.

"Hey, Penny, try this on!" Lulu called out after a moment.

Penny eyed the delicate wispy fabric that Lulu held out to her.

"What's that?"

"It's a silk scarf, hon and I think it'll look amazing with your stodgy Cambridge attire."

"Lulu!" Lenox scolded her with a sigh.

"What! Your Cambridge attire is stodgy too, brother. I mean really, tweed jackets in this century?"

Penny looked at Lenox and declared, "Don't get rid of your tweed jackets, Lenox! I love them! You look so adorably handsome in them."

Lulu laughed this time.

"I don't know if I like being known as adorably handsome." Lenox stated.

"Why not?" Penny asked.

"Well, adorable is normally an adjective reserved for children."

"Ah semantics!" Penny said waving it off. "Look, I'm a firm believer that adorable can apply to adults as well as children. Though more specifically, it truly applies to a certain handsome fellow who looks right proper in his professor gear. Tweed suits you, Lenox, as does this sweater and the leather jackets I've seen you wear before. In fact, does nothing not suit you?"

"No, sweetie, you can put him in one of those male rompers that were all the rage a few years ago and he'd rock that since he's serious male model material," Lulu stated.

"I would not rock the romper, nor would I be caught dead in one of them either," Lenox retorted sounding mildly offended.

"I don't see why not, they're like super comfy onesie pyjamas," Lulu remarked.

"I wouldn't be caught dead in a onesie either."

"Really?" Penny asked before adding, "Onesie pyjamas are my go-to for Halloween costumes. In fact, I've been eyeing a panda one online for this year.'s Halloween"

Lenox had a serious expression on his face as he thought over her words for a moment before he finally said, "I take it back. I'd wear a onesie for Halloween."

"Oh, yay! Me too! I'll look into buying some for our family's annual 'All Hallows Eve' bash."

"Um, that's not actual Halloween is it?" Penny asked her.

"Oh yeah, we Vamps are B-I-G, big on Halloween," Lulu said spelling out the first big.

"Lulu!" Lenox hissed.

"Ah chillax, brother, Sunita is one of us, right hon?" Lulu asked the lady on the other side of the table.

"Yup, and have been for 400 years now. Almost all of the buyers and sellers here are immortals, Lenox, so I don't get your reaction."

Lenox sighed, "Being immortal is still a fact we're not supposed to blurt out."

"I guess that's true but anyways, you got other plans on that day, Penny?" Lulu asked.

"Kind of…" Penny admitted.

"Oh?" Lulu asked, looking crestfallen.

Penny was quick to explain, "I'm sorry but Halloween is the day when the border between the living and dead is at its weakest and well… lots of people play with things they shouldn't like Ouija boards, which cause demons to possess them."

Lulu instantly brightened as she declared, "Oh no way! Don't tell me that you exorcise people on Halloween, Pen? That's super awesome!"

"Lulu," Lenox hissed.

"Okay, I'm with your sister here, Lenox. That is wicked cool, though how do you do it exactly?" Sunita asked as both she and Lulu looked super intrigued.

"Uh…" Penny started.

"Do you use holy water?" Lulu asked excitedly.

"No."

"Holy chants?" Sunita asked this time.

"No."

"Holy artifacts?"

"No."

Lulu and Sunita both eyed her, waiting for a response.

Penny sighed, "None of that's necessary because we hellhounds are able to reach into a person's body and take the demon out before disposing of it."

"Reach in where?" Lulu asked.

"Lulu!" Lenox interjected.

"Shh, brother, I need to know this!" Lulu declared dismissively as she gave Penny big pleading puppy dog eyes.

Penny laughed softly. "It's okay, Lenox and it's really not a secret. Now it depends on the type of demon. However, they all choose one of the seven chakra points. You know—the top of the head, forehead, throat, heart, solar plexus, spleen and the root."

Both Lulu and Sunita chuckled at the last one knowing which 'root' Penny was talking about. "Sorry, Penny, hon, I really am but I guess pulling demons out of someone's privates, even on a metaphysical level is mighty uncomfortable."

"It would be, however, lucky for us we don't remove demons from the front of a person rather only the back since demons can't invade a person from the front because a person's natural defences kick in."

"Hold on. People have natural defences against demons?" Lenox asked finding himself intrigued, too.

Penny nodded, "Oh yeah and it's more complicated than what I am about to say. However, more or less, in a nutshell, your eyes are the gatekeeper of your soul, and when they see a wicked demon they go 'nope' and deny the demon access to you. Therefore, for a demon to possess a person they must first attach themselves to one of the seven points along your back in order appeal to your ears since for some stupid reason, people are willing to hear them out. Don't ask me why— I don't get it but it's also why people often hear evil before they see it."

"Oh wow," Lulu said, looking super interested.

Lenox decided to interrupt before his twin could pester Penny more about demons since he was intent on spending a carefree day with Penny. So, gently taking the scarf out of his twin's hand, he draped it around Penny's shoulders.

"Yup, just as I thought. It suits you," Lenox remarked.

"Really?" Penny asked, touching the scarf, completely focusing on it.

Lenox picked up the hand mirror lying next to the hats and wordlessly handed it to her.

Penny eyed the scarf thoughtfully before saying, "I never thought I'd say this, but it looks pretty on me. I'll take it."

"Penny, everything looks beautiful on you," Lenox declared quietly.

"True story, honey," Lulu agreed before adding, "We'll also take all your pink scarfs Sunita and these ten hats!"

Lenox laughed, "You've already tried on ten hats already?"

"Oh, no I haven't. I tried nine on last month but Freya spotted me about to buy them and interrupted me. Which is why, here you go, Sunita," Lulu said quickly handing Sunita money.

"Lulu! No more hats!" Came a cry from down the street a moment later.

"Too late!" Lulu called out cheerfully.

A mild Swedish oath could clearly be heard in response. Penny snorted when she heard it though she was far from the only one as she listened to a chorus of chuckles from other people around her.

Lenox let out a small sigh, "Better hurry bagging those hats, Sunita or else Hurricane Freya will arrive, demanding you take them back."

"It's too late for that, too!" Lulu called out cheerfully as she magicked her hats away, presumably to her home on Ormeglo.

"Lulu!" Freya cried out when she arrived.

"Yes, my love?" Lulu asked sunnily.

"No more hats!"

"Again, too late, I've bought them."

"Sunita! Take them back!" Freya said forcefully.

Sunita snorted and rolled her eyes, use to this exchange, "I can't do that, Freya, since I don't got 'em anymore."

"What?"

"They're at home, love mixed in with all my other hats so you'll never figure out which ones are new," Lulu laughed almost evilly though it really wasn't possible for her, since she was too nice a person.

"Are you serious, Lulu!" Freya demanded in Swedish.

Lulu leaned in and kissed Freya sweetly as she said contritely, "Yes and I love you."

Freya rolled her eyes though looking happier this time. Turning to look at her two children still engrossed in the puzzle ball and not the least perturbed by her outburst, Freya bent down next to their wagon.

"What do you have *mina älsklingar*?" Freya asked, calling them her darlings in Swedish.

The children finally looked up from their toy and responded in Swedish, "It's a puzzle ball, mama. We're working on it together, see?"

"I see that," Freya said with a smile as she ruffled their hair.

"Huh... mummy, did you get all your new hats?" Bryn asked, looking up at Lulu.

"Oh, yes," Lulu said happily.

Bryn looked at Freya, "Don't be mad mama, mummy's hats are very pretty."

"I'm not upset, sweetie, it's just our house is going to be overrun by hats soon!"

"It's okay, mama, we'll put them in the bottomless trunk like all the others," Lore said almost pragmatically.

"See? Problem solved, love," Lulu laughed.

Freya looked briefly behind her, "No, the problem is not solved, Lulu but it will be if you promise me no more hats!"

"Nope, I can't make that promise because we both know that'll be a lie and I absolutely hate lying to you. Though I do promise you, I will try, *try*, not to buy anymore today."

"I shall accept that promise, now I must go back to our stall. I left Frey in charge and he's probably grossly discounted everything, like he threatened to do."

"Let him," Lulu said with a shrug, not caring a wit about it.

Freya looked absolutely appalled, which caused Penny to burst out laughing. Freya looked at her instantly.

"Sorry," Penny muttered, trying to reign in her mirth but found it to be an impossible task.

"Penniah!" Freya cried out this time.

"I can't help it. The look on your face at a possible fire sale... good gracious, Freya," Penny laughed.

Lenox snorted, "Freya doesn't do sales, everything is always full price. Period."

"Hey, I'm willing to let people negotiate with me!"

"But they don't, love, because you always put on your scary 'Viking Warrioress' face when someone even attempts to," Lulu stated.

"So? It works, doesn't it?"

Lulu nodded with a laugh.

"It wouldn't with a hellhound," Penny remarked casually.

"Oh, really?" Freya said as she stood up to her full height, which was a couple inches taller than Penny and levelled a deep glare at Penny that would strike fear into a sane person.

Though being far from sane, Penny just smiled at her, completely relaxed. Freya's look changed to her absolutely fiercest look but Penny was still truly unfazed.

Freya's face eventually drew back to a mild scowl. "You didn't even blink, Penny! What the hell?"

"I'm a hellhound, Freya and I can't hunt down demons if I was easily scared off by a little menace," Penny shrugged.

"A little menace! Do you know how many fools have fled from my ire!"

"Meh," Penny said with a shrug of her shoulders.

"What do you mean, 'meh'?" Freya demanded.

"No fools have every fled from my ire Freya because I've killed them before they had the chance. After all, as my dad always said, 'if a fool is stupid enough to raise your hackles, Pen, then that person is too stupid to live.'"

"Penny!" Freya cried out.

"Ah, Freya, relax. It's not as bad as you're thinking. For despite their seemingly temperamental ways, the only time a hellhounds hackles are raised is with evil, right, Pen?" Lenox asked.

Penny nodded though she looked at Lenox curiously, "Yes, though how did you know that?"

"I don't know much about the hellhounds but from what I've observed in the past few years since you've amalgamated your home 'Compound' with Moonlight Valley, is that innocent stupidity doesn't bother you, and in fact, is almost encouraged. Besides, you also did say that you really like drama, which would be hard to watch if you were easily driven to ire."

"True, we hellhounds do like drama and you're welcome to come visit us any time, Freya," Penny said serenely, gleefully goading the temperamental Norse Omega Clan warrioress.

"OMG! You did not call me dramatic!" Freya demanded.

"She did, love," Lulu said before adding, "Though she's not wrong, so don't bother denying it because I love your dramatic ways."

"Any who, come on, Penny, let's go check out the jam table over there," Lenox said, finishing purchasing the scarves and moving Penny along before Freya had a chance to escalate further.

Penny pulled a face slightly at the mention of jam.

"You don't like jam?" Lenox asked her.

"Not really. It's too sweet by itself."

"Have you tried red pepper jam or a hot mango chutney?"

Penny looked at him curiously' "No, I haven't tried those, just strawberry jam and it was ages ago, too."

"Well, you're in for a treat. Come on, let's try some."

"Jam!" Came the response from a small chorus in the wagon.

Lenox winked at his niece and nephew. "I'll get some samples for you two, no worries."

A little cheer erupted, causing Freya to groan.

"They're going to be hyped up on sugar by the end of the day,

Lenox!" Freya declared.

"Sure are," Lenox agreed before adding, "But that's half the fun of market day. Besides, that vast majority of the sugar you're going to whine about, Freya, is homemade and predominately all-natural treats from recipes that are still created by ancient means."

"Yeah, yeah," Freya retorted, waving her hand airily, "I know that, since you fix those ancient beasts of machines that the sellers use to make that stuff. Oh hey, Penny, I should tell you that Lenox doesn't take money payment for his work fixing stuff, so you'll end up with a horde of freebies today."

Lenox blushed slightly. "I don't want the freebies either but it's wrong to turn them down."

Penny nodded in agreement. "It is, and don't worry, love, I get it. I began a food delivery service for Ritana in Moonlight Valley to help them out and they often leave small presents for me at the edge of the Compound as a thank you. I didn't want the presents at first but my dad said that everyone deserves to be able to thank someone for an act of kindness if they so choose."

"Oh, I heard about the food delivery business!" Lulu stated, before adding, "You started that, Penny? Man, I'm impressed. I've heard you go above and beyond to deliver food in harsh weather conditions and you'll also eat with someone when they're down or lonely. Which is great since many Ritana never admit to being either until they get overwhelmed and it's nice that you look out for them"

Penny found herself blushing this time and nodding slightly in response.

Lenox wrapped his arm around her waist and bent his head to whisper in her ear, "You are a beautiful, loving soul, Penniah. Well done, love."

Lenox! Penny found herself reaching out to him, *I didn't do it—*

I know you didn't do it to start a business or out of a sense of duty. You did it because you probably saw someone struggling in the snow—

Rain, actually.

Lenox said nothing as he squeezed her waist gently and gently planted a soft kiss on her lips when she turned her face to look at him. Afterwards, Lenox wrapped an arm around her waist and gently guided her in the direction of another booth. Though Penny remembered nothing of her body moving nor ending up in front of the jam table until the scent of sweet and spicy things, woke her mind up from a daze, much like smelling salts did from a fainting spell.

What! Penny asked Lenox, completely bewildered and frazzled.

What? Lenox asked in complete~~ly~~ confusion as he stopped what he was doing, in order to look at her.

Oh my, I'm sorry love, Lenox finally said when he realized what had happened.

Ack! You just kissed me senseless, Lenox! No joke! My mind went completely blank!

Lenox fought back a laugh before he leaned in and said, "Well, I promise you love, we'll find a solution to that problem."

"What?"

"Well I plan on kissing you in public often, Penny, thus, a solution must be found. After all, I have been dreaming of being your soulmate for nearly two hundred years, dreams that have included a lot of kissing, hugging or holding of hands, all of which I plan to act upon."

"Oh... okay," Penny said, blushing completely before she quietly asked, "Can we hold hands for five minutes? I need to regain my senses."

Lenox grinned and let go of her waist to hold her hand. Despite having less direct body contact, Penny still felt in a daze as she held his hand and it took her a few moments of focusing on the products to regain her wits. Although when she did, she finally recognized the women smiling at her from behind the table.

"Caitlyn! Maria! Where's Winston? How are you two?" Penny cried out in a jumble, though her senses immediately told her that the other hellhound, Winston, was napping in a basket hidden by a large table cloth.

"We're good, Penny, and is this your mate?" Caitlyn asked kindly.

"Dear Light above!" Penny exclaimed, realizing she accidentally forgot to introduce Lenox. "I'm so sorry, love. Yes, this is my mate, Lenox Moregan."

"Ah, Penny, it's alright. Winston, come out from the table and meet Penny's mate, Lenox," Maria demanded as she lifted the table cloth.

A large Rottweiler lumbered out from beneath the cloth and headed to the back of the tent to a large stack of crates. Moments later, a tall, massively muscular dark man appeared. Waving at Winston, Penny watched him nod at her and give the general appearance of being unfazed by anything. However that was more than just an appearance, since unlike most hellhounds, Winston rarely did get worked up about anything.

"Ugh, mornings suck," Winston muttered as he wrapped an arm around both of his mates' shoulders.

"It's literally afternoon now," Maria retorted in Spanish.

"Morning, afternoon, it doesn't matter since neither favour you when you're from a nocturnal species," Winston muttered in his lilting West Indies accent before looking at Lenox. "Ah, Lenox, Penny nice to see... wait, did my sleepy brain hear Maria correctly? You're mated, Penny? Do your parents know?"

"Oh, yeah, it happened just after Lenox showed up at the fight last night."

"Man, I missed it! Your dad asked me to oversee the patrols while he handled that hot mess of a situation."

Penny let out a soft sigh when she remembered the fight.

"Ah, Penny, don't worry about it. Those troublemakers have been on the outs with us for centuries now and we're better off without them. Besides, everyone else also deeply respects you."

Lenox found himself snorting at that remark, which caused Winston to frown.

"What?"

"Lenox—" Penny said in a low tone, trying to cut in before he said anything, but Lenox still spoke up.

"I know for a fact that there have been other hounds who have said disrespectful things to her." Lenox replied, cutting himself off before he vented his true feelings regarding all those comments.

Winston looked at Penny and said, "Penny, I know we really don't say this as a species, but I'm sorry. Sorry that you've had to listen to disapproving nay-sayers and elders who think that two hellhounds should have never mated. Especially an alpha and an omega, nor Light forbid, have a child together. However, you just gotta... gotta let it go, hon, because there's always gonna be people out there who will be jealous of you or hate you for a stupid reason, and it's just not worth wasting time or breath on them. I mean look at me. I get grief all the time in the human world regarding the colour of my skin, then I go home to the Compound and I hear about how unnatural it is to be mated with two women. Then those same idiots go on and on about how I'm not worth being an elite when they think I'm not listening. However, they sure as shit say nothing when I'm in the room, do they? No, because they know I can wipe the floor with them in a matter of seconds. You have the same ability, pup and you've just got to show them that sometimes, you know?"

Penny smiled at him. "Yeah and I've got a lot to learn it seems."

"That you do, hon but I hear you're attending a fancy-schmancy university now and surely they'll be able to teach you something useful, no?"

"Attending a fancy university? Oh no, I teach there, thank you very much!" Penny corrected him, causing everyone to laugh.

"It's true and I'm proud of ya, hon. Now go on and properly introduce me to your mate. I need to lord this over Figus later," Winston responded, mentioning his eldest brother, who was known to be very anal retentive about hellhound decorum (as if that existed).

"Ah, Winston, Maria and Caitlyn Halliwell, meet my mate, Lenox Moregan. Lenox, my mate, meet my friends Winston, Maria and Caitlyn Halliwell," Penny said properly introducing her mate as her heart swelled with every word.

"Well met," Lenox said as he shook hands with them all.

"Ah, well met indeed and I'm very glad you're her mate, man. Honestly, there was a brief moment in time where I worried that it would be Triton."

"As if! I'd never mate with that snake in the grass!" Penny exclaimed.

"Yeah, hon, I feel your total dislike for him but unfortunately, there is more than one way to end up mated and some of them are pretty questionable. Also, watch your back, Penny, because he may go quiet for a time, but Triton will return for sure and he'll be gunning for you. Not your mate, not your parents, uncle, aunt or cousin... just you, young huntress. Now that's it for the deep stuff. Buy some jam and goodies from my mates while I go back to my napping basket. Light it is the best thing I have ever bought."

"Lenox, Penny, don't listen to him, your money's no good here. Pick out what you want and Winston will drop it off later tonight," Caitlyn stated happily as Maria nodded in agreement.

"Why aren't you chargin' them, my mates? There's no such thing as a free lunch," Winston retorted.

"Yes, yes, however we're not charging them because Lenox fixes our equipment free of charge Ergo this is not a free lunch situation but rather a fair exchange," Maria responded.

"Oh, well, since you save me both time and grief by me not having to take all the broken copper pots to *frick and frack* I'm for it... sorry Penny, no offence to your mum and uncle. However the one time I took Maria and Caitlyn's pots to them to fix, they talked me into helping them create weaponized jam, which thankfully failed. Nonetheless I ended up in the proverbial dog house that night and I'm super glad that Lenox fixes them now."

"It's okay, though... they did," Penny responded sheepishly.

"Did what?" Winston asked in confusion.

"They perfected a weaponized jam recipe, even though testing it was what caused them to blow up their lab the second time. It also took them a week to heal from the wounds, too. Don't worry though, dad confiscated the recipe, all the ingredients and any remaining batches that they were able to hide away and it's in their weapon 'toy box' now."

"Light, help us if anyone ever mistakenly opens the toy box eons from now," Winston retorted blowing out a sigh.

Penny nodded in fervent agreement.

"Why don't we ship all their dangerous weapons to the sun?" Caitlyn suggested.

Penny shook her head, "Oh no, I'm pretty sure the toy box would take out the sun."

"Light sake's! What the hell did those two create?" Winston exclaimed before holding up a hand. "You know what? It's best not to know. Good day, Penny, good day Lenox."

With that, Winston went behind the crates again and shifted forms before he padded to his spot underneath the table.

Lenox's mind secretly whirled with possibilities of safely disposing of sun-killing weapons while Penny tasted a few spicy jams.

Hmm... a project for another time, Lenox mused as he focused his attention back on Penny when she lifted a cracker to his mouth to try.

While eating the cracker, Lenox's mind suddenly focused on another more pressing issue and he realized, that the only way he could solve it was by seeking out advice from his cousin Skull.

Well, that might be a worse ordeal than accidentally imploding the sun, but what must be done will be done, Lenox thought before he telepathically reached out to his cousin.

Hey Lenox, what's wrong? Skull's voice asked.

I need to talk to you. It's nothing urgent. Just more of a personal matter, Lenox said, not wanting to give anything away since he didn't know who could pick up his thoughts.

Skull was quiet for a long time. *I'm free to speak with you anytime, Len. Just let me know what works for you later.*

Alright then, Lenox answered, inwardly vowing on getting this task over and done with as soon as possible.

Looking at Penny, Lenox knew he made the right decision to speak with his cousin even though it was going to be awkward as hell. Then again, speaking to anyone close to him regarding what he had on his mind was going to be way worse.

Well, we all have our crosses to bear, Lenox thought before he focused back on Penny and enjoying the moment.

Chapter Thirteen

Penny and Lenox strode into their home much later on after eating a late lunch together.

"So, where do you want to go..." Lenox started but he stopped talking when Penny stilled. He frowning slightly as he watched her take off.

"Penny?" Lenox called out, alarmed by her behaviour as he closely followed her.

Using his preternatural senses, he realized that Penny had caught the scent of someone in their house, though he just as quickly recognized who that person was—her mother Ally.

"Mum?" Penny inquired when she entered the living room.

"It's all different, everything is different," Ally sobbed, clutching a pillow.

"Oh, Mum..." Penny said softly before walking across the room and knelt in front of her mother. "I'm mated now and this home is meant to be both mine and Lenox's."

Ally let out a small wail as she launched herself into Penny's arms. Neither said anything for a long moment until Ally's tears started to subside.

"I'm glad you found happiness, sweetheart, I really am and there are no sour grapes on my part. I just… I thought I could accept all the rapid changes but when I saw that your house was different, it hit me. You're not my little girl anymore. You're a grown woman. Silly that, isn't it? I mean, you've been grown for centuries now and I haven't lost you, though why does it feel like I have?"

"You haven't lost me, mum and you never, ever will," Penny said vehemently.

"But now that your home is changed, my spot here is gone," Ally stated sadly.

"Your spot?"

"Yes, my pillow that always sits on the floor in front of the fire."

"Ally, I have an idea. Please tell me, what's your favourite colour?" Lenox asked suddenly.

"Hmm? Teal."

"Be back in a moment," Lenox said, marching out of the room and headed towards his lab.

Arriving there seconds later, Lenox made his way to a mini-warehouse in the back and quickly shifted boxes around until he eventually found what he was looking for. Carrying his prize back to the living room, he immediately saw the stunned looks on Ally's and Penny's faces.

"I know it's quite large but this recliner is meant to sit two people. I've got another one in my lab for us, Penny. What do you say, Ally, will this work for you?"

"Huh?" Ally asked, bewildered.

"I know it's not much but instead of a pillow, why not have a recliner instead? Though, sorry that it's a double one, I don't have any singles in stock right now. Normally, they sell out slower than these but there was a convention on recently..."

"Hold on, is that chair truly meant to be mine?" Ally asked as his words started to dawn on her.

"Well, it's a double one, mum, so maybe you can share with..." Penny replied.

"Your dad! OMG! I gotta call him right now. Wait, forget that! I need to find a spot for it, Penny. I mean, I know it's a lot to ask for..."

"No, it's not. You are my mum and I want you to feel welcome in my home even if it looks different. Now I know you like a spot in front of the fire, though Dad's a fan of corners because he likes to be able to see every angle in a room, so... what about here?" Penny said standing in a corner that wasn't too far away from one of the two fireplaces in the room.

"Where's your spot, Penny? I want to be close to your spot," Ally said suddenly.

"I'll go get another one of these chairs, although I don't have it in full pink, love, however will a floral pink rose pattern with a dark green background do?"

"Lenox!" Penny squealed in delight.

Looking at her with a small smile, he responded with, "I'm glad you're happy about that since I truly wanted to share a spot with you, too."

Penny blushed before she said, "I'd like that, too, and a floral pattern would be nice, so long as you're sure."

Lenox nodded, feeling a blush colour his cheeks. Clearing his throat he remarked, "Right, I'll be back."

"Uh, Lenox, do you have a black one, or better yet, a black and yellow one? Sorry but once my reprobate twin sees my chair he'll want one to share with his mate and he knows how to whine like nobody's business, trust in me."

"I understand and I do have a black one, just not black and yellow. Hold on he likes Batman, right? Hence the black and yellow colour scheme?"

Ally nodded.

"I might have a fix for that," Lenox said as he started to leave the room.

"Hold on, Lenox, before you do that, where do your family prefer to sit? I want everyone to feel comfortable."

"Mum doesn't really have a big preference, for so long as she has a lamplight near her to see her knitting, she's happy. That's also my mum and dad's couch," Lenox said, pointing out a soft lavender love seat that was over by a small bookcase with a lamp that had a small wicker basket next to it.

"They don't share a recliner?" Ally asked.

"Neither my mum nor my sister is a fan of recliners; they prefer couches. Also, Lulu, Freya and the kids like to have the corner by the window. Freya likes to sit near the fire as my twin and her kids like to create things all the time, so that craft table and easel are theirs."

"Okay. Come on, mum let's plan out the living room while we wait for Lenox to return."

"You want my help?" Ally asked shyly.

"Of course I do," Penny reassured her.

"You both aren't mad that I was here... when you weren't?" Ally asked in a small voice.

"Mum, I know you like to sneak me stuff without me knowing. I mean, I haven't bought linens or food for that matter in years since you've been supplying me it. Which truly doesn't bother me."

"Nor me, Ally, because I know how much you like to dote on Penny."

"Thanks, Lenox and I truly want to make sure you're happy, sweetie," Ally said as she cupped Penny's face.

"I am Mum... oh! Sorry, I just remembered that Lenox and I bought you and Dad a couple of presents today."

"Presents?" Ally asked.

Penny nodded.

"Ah, sweetie, you didn't have to," Ally said.

"But I wanted to."

Ally said nothing for a long moment.

"Penniah, my darling one, you're everything I prayed for and more. I love you so very much," she finally said in a serious tone, that was uncharacteristic for her.

"Mum," Penny responded, "I love you so very much, too."

"I know, sweetie I really do but sometimes I can't believe how blessed I am to have both you and your father."

Penny nodded in understanding.

I'm blessed, too, Penny love; you're definitely something super special, Lenox found himself saying to her.

I am not! Penny sputtered.

Oh, you totally are, love, though you're too bashful and nice to admit it. Be right back.

Seconds after Lenox left the room, Ally gave her with a small smile. "I know it's only been a day, but how's everything?"

Being completely open and honest with her mum, Penny blurted out quietly, "It's going great apart from me fainting at the sight of his bare chest this morning. Seriously, I don't think there's much hope for me, mum."

"Oh, Penny," Ally sighed. "That's normal for a Baskerville to have an irrational reaction to seeing our mates unclothed for the first time even if it's only partial nudity. Your Uncle Alfie immediately shifted to dog form when he saw your Aunt Rika, and I'd got so tongue-tied that I wasn't be able to speak at all."

"How does it go away?"

Ally was quiet for a long moment.

"Mum?"

"Light, I hate this part but you must know... it happens after you… you couple hon."

"You mean... you mean b-become intimate?" Penny stuttered.

Ally pulled a face. "Sorry, sweetie, that face wasn't meant for you—it really wasn't. I just hate talking about this with you and I know you're an adult, but Light sake's, you're still my baby girl! Though heaven only knows your dad won't tell you and your stupid uncle would be, as usual, as unhelpful as ever. Rounding out the family, your aunt is too bashful like you and your cousin's still a virgin too, so... I can do this! I so can!"

"Mum, you don't have to; I mean, I could figure it out like you did."

"No, that's a bad idea, for I was an utter mess for 150 years and I wouldn't wish that on my worst enemy. Look, you don't need to go the full nine yards to get over fainting hon... just… just… Light sake's, this is so freakin' hard! Just always touch your mate when you can. I mean hold hands, kiss, hug… stuff, you know? Also don't rush yourselves. Let your instincts, not your brain, decide when you're ready for the next step."

"Why not my brain?" Penny asked, feeling slightly confused.

"Because as a whole we Baskervilles tend to overthink relationships and that makes things a whole bunch worse. Honestly, the best relationship advice I ever got was your Great Uncle Reggie who once told me, ' to keep it simple, stupid.' Also, if you get frustrated or mad at yourself, go out and find a demon to kill. It helps. In fact, during this early stage, sweetie, I suggest you go out looking for a fight daily; it'll make you a little less neurotic. Not that you are neurotic..." Ally started to backtrack.

"It's okay, Mum, I am neurotic or at least I have become that way recently, and I thought it was just me, being well… me."

"Nope, it's hereditary and I'm sorry about that. For once we Baskervilles mate, we need to be in contact with our mates daily and again, I'm not speaking carnally, although that is heightened and from what I can tell, will never go away. Nonetheless, what I'm talking about is that you'll constantly worry over your mate. I mean, you'll be wanting to make sure he's okay; you'll be wanting to protect his family so he's never sad; you'll be wanting to hear his voice at all times; you'll be wanting to rile him if he's become too overprotective; you'll be wanting to bask in his presence... you get my drift. To most that sounds like a curse, but to us... it's who we are, hon. You alright with that?" Ally asked, although that question wasn't directed to Penny.

Penny found herself looking up at Lenox who stood just inside the doorway.

"Yes and I truly wouldn't have it any other way. I most definitely want you in my life, Penny and there's nothing about you I don't love."

"How did I get so lucky?"

Lenox snorted and with a smile he murmured, "That's my question, love, not yours." With that, he crossed the room and stole a quick kiss from her. "Come on, love and come on, Ally, let's sort this living room out to everyone's liking before you two go out and hunt down some demons for a few hours. I'll even make supper for you."

"No, no, no!" Penny said vehemently, resorting to her natural hellhounds instincts when she was flustered, "I'm a hunter and I will hunt supper."

Lenox grimaced a little, "I'm not a huge fan of a recently killed animal. In fact, I grew up mostly vegetarian and I still lean to eating more vegetarian meals than I do meat. Sorry if that sounds a bit weird."

"You're not weird, Lenox, it's understandable given the fact your mum is full-blooded Ritana and can only eat meat that is magically created meat instead of real meat. Now I will admit that I do need to eat real blood meat on occasion. However, I am quite happy to keep it out of this house." Penny stated.

"You don't have to do that. This is your home, too. The only thing I ask is if we could keep it in a separate cupboard so that my mum or sister doesn't stumble across it."

"Lulu is also real meat intolerant?"

Lenox nodded. "Yeah, she inherited most of the Ritana traits from my mum, despite the fact that she isn't fully Ritana."

"I get it, Lenox, no worries."

"That's true, though getting back to supper, what do you feel like, Lenox?" Ally asked.

"Don't even start by saying, whatever you want is fine. I picked lunch, so supper is your choice and I'm completely fine with no meat if that is what you want," Penny added.

"I can do no real meat but not, no meat, sweetie. So whatever you pick, Lenox, can you keep a curried meat kebab or twenty on the table for me?" Ally asked.

"Yeah, I can and if you're sure, I wouldn't mind a Welsh rarebit, a cup of tomato soup, some chips with curry sauce and a kebab."

"That sounds delicious but hold on. What's the difference between a Welsh rabbit and an English one?" Penny asked, confused.

"Not a rabbit sweetie, a rarebit, which you've actually had though we've just never called it that name. Instead, we call it a cheese toastie though toasties are completely different. Anyway, it's a type of cheese on toast that has stout and Worcestershire sauce in it. In fact, the best ones were the ones we used to get at Dougal's Cafe every Friday until his ex-wife burnt the place down for the insurance money. What a witch," Ally hissed.

"What happened?" Lenox asked curiously.

"Dougal was a real nice man who was married to the money-grubbing witch, pardon my English, for five years before she decided to try to do him in and burn down his cafe for money. Though luckily for Dougal, it was Friday night when she enacted her plan and Alfie and I had arrived in time to save Dougal. Suffice to say, I let her live only because Dougal asked me to, since he'd have the satisfaction of divorcing the witch and seeing her sent down for a very long time. He retired shortly after and he married a really nice woman four years later. They moved to Spain and last I heard, he's happy gardening in the Spanish sun."

"Oh... I miss Dougal's café. He was always so warm and friendly," Penny remarked.

"Ah, I forgot to tell you, sweetie, Dougal's youngest son, Danny, just opened up a café in a town over from where Dougal's used to be and I swear to the Light he's the carbon copy of his dad in every way. Well mind you, not in every way since he hasn't attracted a murderous witch. In fact, he's got a kind yet no-nonsense wife who's a great foil for Danny, if you ask me. So we'll go to Danny's new place and order some carryout once we're done hunting."

"Yippee!" Penny squealed before looking contritely at Lenox.

Lenox smiled at her and jokingly shook his head in amusement.

"Well kiddies, stop lollygagging. Let's get this place all sorted out so we can go out and kill some demons already!"

"Here, here mum!" Penny agreed before they all set about fixing up the living room.

About a half-hour later, Penny turned to face Lenox about to speak but he beat her to it.

"Stay safe, love," Lenox murmured as he wrapped his arms around her and placed a brief kiss on her lips.

"I will and I'll be back before you know it! I swear," Penny declared as she shifted her weight from foot to foot, antsy to go out and fight the good fight.

"I know, and you take care, too, Ally. Call out to me if you need anything," Lenox offered.

"Ah, you're sweet, Lenox but demon killing is what we do, so we've got this," Ally reassured him.

Lenox nodded before stealing one last kiss from Penny and whispered, "Don't worry about me either; I plan on an evening in my lab."

Penny nodded this time before she and her mum teleported away.

Lenox let out a slow breath before mumbling to himself, "She'll be okay, she's with her mum. It'll all be okay."

Rubbing the back of his neck, Lenox started to back out of the living room intent on heading to his lab when he heard a knock at the door.

Frowning slightly, Lenox walked towards it. When he opened the door, his frown deepened even more.

"Nice to see you, too, Lenox," the man on the other side said sardonically in Norwegian, noting his look.

"It is nice to see you, Tyr Andraste, just wholly unexpected, hence the frown," Lenox remarked before he sighed when he realized something else.

"What?" Tyr immediately asked him curiously.

"Usually when you showed up at my door without notice it was because you and your twin Annika needed a place to lay low, which means you're gonna bring trouble to my door. Seeing as Annika is not here, I'm assuming you need my help to rescue her."

Tyr waved him off as he slid past Lenox, "Nothing of the sort. Anni is visiting Lulu and Freya at the moment and I decided to come here to see what you are up to."

"Oh," Lenox muttered before continuing, "Well I'm planning on building stuff tonight and I really don't want to go out at all. Especially if it's for a pub crawl, Tyr, sorry."

Tyr waved him off again, "Nah, I'm off pub crawls for the moment since the last one nearly landed me in hot water. Though I wouldn't mind trying my hand at some welding stuff, not that you offered, which is kind of rude. I also would absolutely love to meet your new mate."

Lenox let out a bigger sigh as he realized why Tyr was really here.

"She's out hunting at the moment and I'm glad about that."

"What the hell does that mean?" Tyr asked with a laugh.

"Well, you've never exactly been someone that should be thrust upon another person, especially a hellhound since you're quite abrasive at times, old friend."

Tyr laughed again, "Light, how true that is but I'll be on my best behaviour I swear."

"Somehow, I seriously doubt that."

Tyr gave Lenox an angelic smile, causing Lenox to roll his eyes in response. Saying nothing more, Tyr followed Lenox down the hall to his lab. Though in truth, Lenox spent the entire time guiding his curious friend away from Penny's things.

Suddenly, the outside door banged open behind him when they neared the lab. Spinning around, Lenox saw Lucy, her dad, Alfie, and Sebastian enter the room.

"Ah, Lenox… what the hell are you. . . I mean, who the hell are you?" Lucy demanded as she spotted Tyr Andraste.

"Oh, how you wound me so, my sweet, with such a demand since I heard hellhounds were a friendly bunch," Tyr said genially.

"I don't know who the hell told you that, but we're about as friendly as a school of piranhas. Anyway, I'm not really here to make idle chit chat right now. I'm here for my cousin. Penny! Penny, where are you?" Lucy called out.

"She's not here, Lucy. She's gone out hunting with her mum," Lenox replied instantly.

"Ah, damn it all!" Sebastian growled before turning around and saying, "I told Ally to tell her not to go hunting alone!"

"She's not alone, Bas. She's with Ally. Duh! Good Light, you're a slow one," Alfie retorted as he barrelled past Sebastian on his way back out the door.

"How the hell am I the slow one?" Sebastian demanded as he followed him out.

"You told her not to go alone and the nephew-in-law told you she went out with Penny, ergo she followed your orders to a tee. Though did you not even attempt to ask her instead of demand, a-hole?" Alfie asked before he cussed at Sebastian.

"No, I didn't ask Ally because instead I told her of my concerns and she offered not to go hunting alone until this BS with Triton is sorted. Though I did ask her to come here and speak with Penny and tell her to also not to go out hunting unless she has no less than two hounds at her back."

"I don't see why the hell you're concerned, Bas. Penny could mop the deck with Triton and all his cohorts better than the rest of us could. Have a little faith for eff sake," Alfie chided him, clucking his tongue.

"Have faith? Are you stupid? She's my daughter. I don't care if she could kill every demon on this planet with one swipe of her hand. I will always protect her!"

Alfie let out a slow breath, "I get you Bas and I'm sorry. Now come on, let's go."

With that, the three hounds teleported away leaving Lenox feeling out of sorts. Something was going on and they were deliberately keeping him in the dark about it.

"Well, that's not gonna fly," Lenox muttered.

A hand landed on his shoulder, which caused Lenox to turn and look at Tyr.

You know how you said earlier that I always bring trouble to your door? Tyr asked him.

Yes? Lenox responded.

I'm not the one in trouble Lenox. You and your mate are.

"What?" Lenox asked out loud, stunned.

"Prometheus called me earlier tonight and gave me some news. FYI, it's not good."

Lenox did something then that he very seldom did, he let out a curse word.

"Yup, that about sums everything up," Tyr remarked before he used his magic to close the front door, then spun around to head to Lenox's lab without another word.

Lenox stalked after him before he stopped feeling a sense of sinister dread enter him. Needing to do something, Lenox made a quick decision.

"Hey, Tyr, plans have changed," Lenox called out to him.

"Oh?" Tyr asked before backtracking a few steps.

"Yeah... they have, I've got business to attend to, so I'll be right back."

Tyr shook his head, "You can't fool me, Lenox, and don't even think about getting rid of me neither because I will always have your back. Now let's go."

"But—"

Tyr shook his head. *But nothing. I'll keep your secret like I promised I would, my old friend. So don't bother wasting your breath about going alone; let's just go already.*

Lenox nodded before teleporting away with Tyr, hoping that what he felt was nothing but knowing full well that it was wishful thinking on his part.

Chapter Fourteen

A lone man knelt on the cold, wet ground, with his arms and feet bound by a thick rope behind his back and a cotton rag stuffed in his mouth. The man shook with fear as he looked at the maniac who had kidnapped him in the dead of night and had dragged him out onto the desolate, windy moor.

"I told you not to go to the cops, John. I told you that! But, you didn't listen, did you? Did you!" The maniac screamed at him, waving around a carving knife as he frothed at the mouth in anger.

John cringed backwards but was unable to lean back far enough to get away from the sharp edge of the knife that sliced his face. Bloody trickled down his cheek from the gaping wound, causing John's fear to intensify when a look of pure glee entered the other man's eyes.

"What's wrong, John? You look so scared. Not such a big strong man, after all, are you? You shouldn't have taken me for granted; now I'll make you regret it!"

Oh, God, he's going to torture me first before he murders me! Please, somebody*! John thought, frantic as he watched the maniac dance around him with the knife.*

For a brief moment, he could have sworn he saw two large dog-like shadows appear on the moor a short distance away. Almost instantly they seemed to disappear when his mind focused on his tormentor who stood in front of him again, looking pure evil.

"Eyes on me, John! Always on me!" The man raved as he lunged forward with the knife again.

"Oh, I don't think so, you wee evil troll man," a soft Northern English female voice snarled.

Suddenly, time stood still as John saw the silhouette of a tall woman appear behind his attacker. One of her moonlight pale hands held the maniac's left arm completely immobile.

"I'll kill you, too, you—" the maniac started to say before he

let out a scream of agony when the satisfying sound of snapping bone stopped the attacker's next move.

"Come on," the shadowy woman quietly stated before adding, "I've got business to settle with you."

With one last scream of fury from his attacker, John watched the two of them disappear in an eerie, shadowy mist, leaving no trace of them being there.

***Am I… am I dreaming?** John asked in stunned shock, unable to comprehend what was going on.*

Suddenly, before his mind could react to everything, he felt the tug of someone else untying the ropes around his feet. Terrified since he couldn't see the other person because this figure also seemed to be shrouded in dark mist, John tried to scramble away until he heard another soothing female voice speaking, though this one was louder than the last.

"You're alright, pet; you're alright. This is nothing but a nightmare, a terrible, terrible nightmare."

John felt a sense of calm come over him at the woman's words, and his mind started to drift to sleep with her words.

"In a few seconds, you'll awake in your warm cozy bed, such soft warm—"

Coming awake with a start, John wiped the cold sweat from his face as he took in a deep, shuddering breath. In a panic, he frantically felt the left side of his cheek for the bloody wound that his stalker had inflicted but it… it wasn't there. Scrubbing his face in agitation with hands, John turned on his bedside lamp to look at his wrists to see if there was any rope burn.

"Oh my God, it really was just a dream, but it was so bloody vivid, I could have sworn—" John stopped when he saw his cellphone flicker before it started to ring in earnest.

"Hello?" John answered his phone cautiously, despite knowing this particular number.

"Hello, John? Hi, it's Detective Newlands calling. I just wanted to let you know that it's over John. We found your stalker Danny Barton's body under a bridge an hour ago. He's dead."

John felt a rush of emotion start to build within him. Thank God, the nightmare was truly finally over.

*****

Penny reined in her shadow powers as she looked at the happy face of her mother after she finished making her kill.

"Nice catch with the serial killing stalker, sweetie, though you left his body out in the open to be found, right? Nothing is worse for a stalking victim than living with the knowledge that their stalker is out there. The poor souls need closure so they can heal."

Penny nodded. "I left it under a bridge and made it look like he jumped since it's harder to explain away wild animal attacks in this century."

"Light, too bad we couldn't just leave the wounds because there is always a level of satisfaction in that with these kind of evil idiots. Though I am happy that this victim lives and gets a chance to be free of this episode, though there will probably be years of therapy in his future, poor blighter."

Penny blew out a sigh and nodded in agreement.

Ally wrapped an arm around Penny's waist. "I'm proud of you, sweetie, in more ways than I can count, too."

"Thanks, mum," Penny said, bashfully ducking her head at the compliment and blushing at the same time.

"I mean every word. I truly do, sweetheart. Now come on. The night's still young, and there are plenty of punters—" Ally broke off as the air stirred around them.

"Good gracious. Why?" Penny's mum whined a moment later, when she saw four people teleport into view.

"Nice to see you, too, love," Penny's dad retorted.

"Ugh. I told you that I was going hunting and you asked me not to go alone, so I didn't go alone, and here you show up looking like you're pissed about something. Can I not just win with you? Just once?" Ally asked crossing her arms as a scowl marred her face.

"I'm sorry, Ally, I am but when you told me you were going hunting I assumed it was with the reprobate—"

"Hey!" Alfie cut in, semi-outraged, "The reprobate has got name and it's Batman, thank you very much."

"Nice try, Alfie but I didn't call you Batman in the last century, and I'm not about to start in this one. Now, Ally, love, I'm not pissed at you at all, just worried and not without reason."

Uncharacteristically, Ally's expression softened. "I know, Bas love, I really do and I want to gut them from gullet to gizzard despite knowing the consequences that will befall on us if I do."

"What consequences?" Penny asked, interjecting.

"Penny…" Ally started.

Penny shook her head, "No Mum, I know you and Dad are keeping me from knowing the truth about what's going on."

"We're just trying to protect you!" Penny's dad declared.

"I know that, dad and I just… I just want to know what you're protecting me from. After all, how can I know what to avoid if no one tells me what's going on?"

"Penny, sweetie—" Sebastian started but Ally cut him off.

"Penny's smart and cautious, Sebastian, much like her father." Penny's mum nudged him gently as he rolled his eyes. "She also doesn't take ridiculous risks even when we prod her to."

"We don't prod her to; you do that all on your own."

"Guilty," Ally openly admitted before turning to her daughter. "There are hellhound traitors out to kill us all sweetie and unfortunately said traitors are more dangerous to us than anyone else could ever be. By which I mean they are literally toxic to every hound out there except the Baskervilles and it's my job to hunt them down since my actual hunter classification is not unknown but known only to a select few; I'm a Treachery Huntress."

"Omegas always have a special classification and your mum's crazed yet happy go lucky manner makes traitors believe your mum is a non-threat despite the fact she's beyond brutal," Reggie added looking semi-proud of Ally.

"Well, what can I say? When you tangle with this she-devil, you're gonna get demolished, it's a straight-up fact," Ally stated.

"She-devil? Really, Ally?" Sebastian asked her with a snort.

"Heck, yes— " Ally stopped as she spun around.

Penny felt the hair on the back of her neck start to stand on end in warning as she felt a deep anger well up within her despite no one seeming to be there.

Though she soon realized it was all an illusion, as the dark shapes of hellhounds emerged from the shadows stalking towards them.

"What in the hell are these fools doing here?" Ally demanded.

"Bloody Triton seems to think... oh no freakin' way," Alfie suddenly snarled.

"What?" Penny inquired

"Do you smell that?" Alfie asked no one in particular.

"Smell what?" Penny asked in confusion, sensing nothing unusual.

"Exactly, sweetie, they smell like nothing because they are nothing; they have no soul. Well done, idiots, give yourselves a round of applause," Ally snarled in disgust, when the other hounds stopped in front of her.

Triton shifted forms and instead of his usual tawny coloured skin, he was a pale ghoulish greenish-white.

Penny felt her hackles rise at the sight of him and she itched to tear into him much more than she had before.

"What. Have. You. Done?" Penny snarled, her voice stilted as the need to change into her hellhound form rose within her.

"We've become our true selves..." Triton started to reply.

"Lies. You speak. Lies." Penny bit out with a growl.

"No, I am a true Keeper of the Underworld now just as..."

"Hey, idiot, you can't be the so-called Keeper of the Underworld without a soul, ya dimwit."

"I have a soul."

"No, you don't," Sebastian snarled. "You lost that the moment you killed an innocent person in order to become your true self."

"I don't believe you."

Ally let out a snort, "For goodness gracious sake! Everyone and I mean everyone knows that when a hellhound kills an innocent they lose their soul and it is immediately cast into the Shadow Realm. Therefore, they are no longer a hound."

"If you're so smart, what am I then?" Triton retorted indolently.

"Well, to me, you're lower than muddy sludge on the bottom of my boots, but then again, that's an insult to sludge. However, the folks around here do have a name for you—*Kure*; A soul-sucking leech of a wraith, who hangs around in the moors, looking for unsuspecting people to kill or turn into one of you, if they are of the same ilk. Looks like all you idiots already ran into one and decided to cast your lot in with it. Again. Bravo."

"I'm no leech! I am Lord of the Underworld!" Triton roared.

"You. Killed. An Innocent?" Penny growled as the change started to overcome her as her rage and need for vengeance began to rise to levels that astounded even her.

After all, she had never been a hound that exhibited rage-filled episodes. Evil more or less annoyed her but never really angered her, which always struck her as odd. However, her mum had once told her that the reason she never felt anger at the atrocious acts any villain committed was due to a rare gift that allowed the victim's residual emotions to fill that void instead of her own so that they could get their own justice. However, it seemed that enemies without souls meant that no victim's energy couldn't radiate from them, which allowed Penny's anger to fill the void this time and caused her to see red.

"Sacrifices needed to be made," Triton retorted casually as he shifted into a wraith-like form with the others, igniting the emotional bomb within Penny.

"War!" Penny shouted as she lunged towards him, shifting to hellhound form so fast that she completely changed before her paws hit the ground.

Triton and his cohorts were quick to pull away to a safe distance.

"Penny, wait!" Her dad called after her as she took off after them.

Though Penny couldn't stop if her life depended on it. Her need to kill these wretches gnawed at her from the inside and blocked out any form of reason.

Must destroy, must kill.

Snapping and snarling, Penny felt another change overcome her, though she didn't dwell on it as she focused on charging headlong across the uneven rocky moss-covered ground, towards the betrayers.

Hitting the first Kure with the force of a runaway freight train, Penny felt satisfied when her fangs sank deep into the ghoulish flesh, crushing bone underneath and causing the monster to let out a high pitched wail.

Though that satisfaction was short-lived when the rest of the Kure launched themselves at Penny en masse. However, Penny was far from being alone as the loud familiar snarls came from behind her, alerting Penny to the fact that her mother and uncle had entered the fray. Penny made quick work of killing the Kure in her jaws, and jumped back when the beast exploded into a dark mist.

Suddenly, her mother called out to them, *Sebastian, Reggie, Lucy teleport the hell outta here now!*

"The hell I am!" Sebastian shouted but Reggie was quick on the uptake, grabbing the protesting Lucy and Sebastian before teleporting away.

Penny, you need to get out of here, too, love, her mother said in a highly concerned tone. Penny wasn't having it.

No. Penny growled as she started attacking and killing the Kure with ruthless precision.

Penny stop! As much as it galls me, you gotta let them live! Killing them is about to make things a lot worse for us! Penny's Uncle Alfie shouted mentally.

Penny stopped listening as her hellhound instincts took over after causing her to tear through the remainder of the Kure. Letting out a shuddering rage-filled snort at the ease in which she dispatched her enemies, Penny didn't recognize the encroaching dark mist trap until it was too late.

When the trap sealed itself, a dark form began to emerge but afterwards… Penny saw nothing more as a new surge of power within her began to rise as well.

*****

Ally felt herself being suddenly magically propelled away from Penny with a whispered yet haunting, *Go.*

No! Ally telepathically screamed seconds before she hit the dirt nearly a mile away in her human form.

"Allycen! Allycen! What—" Sebastian started when he teleported next to her with Reggie and immediately pulled her to her feet.

"No!" Ally continued to scream before she started to sob uncontrollably at the sight of the battle in front of her.

"Light, no!" Sebastian shouted when he caught on to what was happening. He immediately lurched forward intent on saving his daughter but Alfie stopped him.

"Alfred Baskerville, you better—" Sebastian started to threaten him.

"You can't save her, Sebastian, the miasma that the demon just released will kill you almost instantly. That is, of course, if you can break through the containment barrier Penny erected, however, if you do... she's dead," Alfie said hollowly.

Ally let out a wail at the words.

"What in hell kind of demon is that?" Sebastian asked as he watched the shadowy billowing dark mass almost dance around Penny.

"In short... pure death," Alfie mumbled as he wrapped his arms around his twin and her husband.

"Say what?" Sebastian demanded in pure horror.

"That is the very demon that has killed every Baskerville before us," Alfie whispered.

"No.... no this can't be..." Sebastian said.

Reggie let out a shuddering breath, "He's right, he's—"

Reggie stopped when he saw Penny's hellhound form burn differently than usual, losing its typical deep bluish-purple as it faded to a yellowish white then it started to burn a deep blood red.

"No bloody way," Reggie muttered as he rubbed his face in shock.

"What?" Sebastian asked, but Reggie focused on Alfie and saw the same shock which confirmed his deep hopeful suspicions.

"Red, she's glowing red... it's, it's only a colour," Alfie muttered, though he still looked he had been knocked back for six.

Then the fire changed colours again when the demon started to take a more solid form and move in closer to her.

"Orange... no yellow... no red again, no blue, no—," Alfie stated.

"It's six colours, Alfie. I see all six colours; blue, green, purple, yellow, red and orange! Yes! Keep burning, Penniah, keep burning!" Reggie encouraged as his heart pounded in his chest.

Suddenly one last colour entered the budding fire whirl that began to form around Penny, which sealed everything for him.

"Pink! There it is! She's done it! Penniah's burning with all seven celestial fires," Reggie shouted happily.

"No, it can't be," Alfie said disbelievingly.

"No Alfie, Penny's definitely got all seven colours and she's controlling them, see?" Reggie pointed out when he noticed something start to form in the bright celestial fires.

The fire whirl lifted Penny off her feet, shifting just as the dark creature began to attack. However, just as soon as the ghostly demon's attack touched the flames, it disappeared.

Suddenly, Penny's form changed from her hellhound main form to a new form that closely resembled her human-like appearance but it wasn't the same. To start, Penny's hair colour had changed from its usual fire-tinted blonde colour to a near bright pinkish-white which matched the last flame colour. The rest of her body seemed to have absorbed the other flame colours, giving her a beautiful yet almost patchwork appearance. Nonetheless it was one last thing that appeared with Penny's changing appearance that floored everyone.

"Is that... is that chains?" Sebastian asked in puzzlement.

Ally's head came up from Sebastian's chest at his words, rubbing her tear-streaked face hard before she looked over at Penny. She let out a delighted squeal. One that was nearly drowned out by Alfie and Reggie's loud whoops of glee.

"Will someone please tell me what's the hell is going on?" Sebastian asked.

"In short... Penny's gonna live, now watch," Alfie said cryptically.

Sebastian's heart lifted at his words and he said no more. He watched his daughter unleash the chains at the dark miasma creature.

The miasma reared up into one large cloud before it, too, changed form and looked like the archetypal demon of Renaissance paints, complete with large dark ghost-like skeleton upper body and head, large crooked horns, beastly bloody yellow and red eyes, and a massive gaping mouthy that exhaled a noxious yellow sulphur mist. Despite the demon's overbearing form, Penny was far from being at a disadvantage as the heavy-looking fiery chains burst forward and immediately wrapped themselves around the demon before it had a chance to attack her.

The chains continued to coil around the beast much like a boa constrictor would until Sebastian could see no more of the demon peeking out from the coil. Then, seconds later, a hellish fiery pit opened up below the demon and Sebastian watched lava-like tentacles emerge. The tentacles went through the coil and effectively took control of binding the demon before dragging it down into the fiery depths. The demon wasn't going without a fight, however suddenly some strange bluish-white wisps, encircled the demon and pushed it away from Penny as Penny's chains shoved the demon down. The tentacles took over and dragged it under, before the portal disappeared, with only one last bloodcurdling, hair raising scream escaping from the demon in its wake.

A few moments later, the barrier around Penny winked out of existence before a massive pulse of pinkish light erupted around her and swept outwards across the moor, much like a sonic boom would.

Briefly blinded, Sebastian blinked furiously, trying to clear his sight so he could see his daughter. He was elated to see her gently float towards the ground. Wasting no more time, Sebastian bolted across the moor at a pace that would have astonished even him, had he been focused on it and caught Penny before she touched the soggy cold wet marsh ground.

The fiery light had nearly faded from her, leaving only the faint traces in her skin. Sebastian watched Penny's eyes fade from the apparent rainbow colour they had been moments before her eyes appeared two-tone, aquamarine and violet purple.

"Dad?" Penny whispered as she focused on him with a small frown.

"Yes, sweetheart?" Sebastian asked softly.

"You alright?" Penny asked with concern.

"Yea Penniah, my dear sweet one, I am," Sebastian replied hoarsely.

Penny frowned, "Why are you crying then?"

"No reason, no reason at all," Sebastian found himself repeating before he continued, "You just rest, sweetheart. All will be well. I promise."

"You sure?"

"Mmm hmm," Sebastian mumbled as he stroked her cheek with his left hand and kissed her forehead.

Penny's eyes fluttered closed and Sebastian let out a deep shuddering breath of relief.

Sebastian felt a hand land on his shoulder but he didn't look up.

"She will be well, Bas. In fact, in a few hours time, Penny will awake and remember nothing," Alfie said.

"How? How do you know this? What the hell was that demon? And don't you damn well give me the last answer you did. I need to know everything now," Sebastian bit out as his elation of knowing his daughter was still alive and relatively well, subsided into a fit of anger at knowing how close Penny had been to death.

That anger somewhat dulled when Sebastian's mate, Ally, knelt in the wet grass. Sebastian said no more as he watched her stroke their daughter's hair and waited for her to speak.

"Sebastian, my love, I will truly explain this all in much more detail to you later. However, to start the Circles of Hell described in Dante's Divine Comedy aren't a fable. Though they aren't exactly how he describes either. Nonetheless, the point I'm really trying to get at is, that there are nine levels of Hell, each housing the darkest most twisted demons ever known to us and when it comes right down to it, most hellhounds would only be able to handle demons that come from Level Five; stronger hounds like you and Reggie would be able to handle demons from Level Seven; As Baskervilles, Lucy, Alfie and I can handle Level Eight demons. Though what we just witnessed was Level Nine Demon and no one has fought one of those and lived to tell the tale since the first hell-raising Baskerville created the hellhounds."

"But—"

Ally looked at him with sadness in her eyes. "Yes, Penny did just take one on and survive. However, that's nothing to be truly happy about because it's going to bring her a world of trouble."

Sebastian said nothing as he looked deeply into Ally's eyes.

"Sebastian, they know she exists. They know that the Brimstone Huntress has truly come into her powers and that it wasn't an empty title given to Penny. Now we're going to need to prepare ourselves for them. But for now, let us say nothing."

"Is that a smart move? All Hallow's Eve approaches and the border between our world and the dead will be weak then. You can almost guarantee that one of them will make an appearance then," Alfie retorted.

"We will speak to her about it later but Penny needs to bond with her mate more. It is very important."

"I don't see how that's important!" Sebastian declared.

Reggie let out a sigh before he finally spoke, "Ally's right, Sebastian, it is very important."

"How?"

Reggie slowly telepathically whispered the answer to Sebastian.

"No way, that's impossible that just a story," Sebastian remarked, shaking his head.

"No, Bas, it's not and I know it to be true because in my very long life, I've kept a lot of secrets to protect our people and this by far is one of the biggest."

Sebastian let out a slow breath. "What now then?"

Everyone shrugged unable to give him a real answer.

Sebastian briefly accepted that knowing that if there was an answer, he would find it later.

Though bizarrely, Ally summoned up a bottle of Fae liquor and dosed Penny's clothes before dosing herself with the bottle's contents.

"Ally!"

"Fae liquor is the only alcohol that is capable of blacking out a hellhound. It also strips the porcelain off a bathtub, too, which has always made me wonder what the hell they put in this delightfully fruity tasting brew. Though any who, I'm going out to dye my hair to match Penny's new pinkish-white locks and get a new tat to match that one." Ally pointed out the new tattoo that appeared on Penny's upper left shoulder above her breast.

Then she continued, "I'm also going to get believably tipsy though not out and out drunk, so I can claim that after hunting, we went for a drink though it turned out to be Fae liquor which led to her blacking out and ending up with us having pink hair and a tattoo, which is not a full lie if I do all of the above. Meanwhile, Alfie, go see to Lucy and explain what's going on. Meanwhile Sebastian, and Reggie, can watch over Penny in our home until she starts to awaken. Oh wait, Reggie can you get us a ton of take-away from Danny's. Penny promised Lenox she'd bring home dinner and I don't want to break a promise."

Reggie snorted, "Yeah sure, just the usual?"

"Yeah... wait no! You need to get chips with curry sauce, a kebab, a Welsh Rarebit and tomato soup for Lenox."

"Light, you're difficult," Reggie snorted.

"Yeah well, that hasn't changed in nearly eighteen hundred years and isn't about to anytime neither, so deal with it," Ally remarked sunnily, even though she looked far from her usual sunny self.

Without saying another word, Reggie and Alfie teleported away leaving Ally and Sebastian alone with their unconscious daughter.

"I know you must hate me for—" Ally started.

"Never!" Sebastian cursed vehemently.

"There is nothing in this world that could make me hate you, Allycen Odelyn Baskerville Hawksley. Absolutely bloody nothing, you hear me? So get that out your mind right now! I'm also not pissed at you over this because I know you. I know you so well that I can clearly say that the only reason that kept you silent about this is that you wanted to protect Penny and me from it ever happening."

"No," Ally whispered, shaking her head. "Not all true Bas, I wanted you to have a life, a real life. I mean hunting demons is truly part of our DNA but hunting this kind of demons... it's all consuming. I know that fact well because it consumed my dad just as it consumed my aunt, granny, great-grandfather and every generation before them. Though it didn't just affect them, it greatly affected their mates, too, which often lead to both partners dying during a fight against a Level Niner and I didn't want that to be our fate nor Penny and Lenox's. Though, for them, that ship is sailing."

Sebastian was quiet for a moment as he swallowed a lump in his throat before he asked, "Do you know more about... the Level Niners?"

Ally looked forlorn. "I know next to nothing except the following three facts: one, Level Niners were originally people that were justly killed for a great act of treachery in life and their souls were sent down into the deepest pit as punishment. Two, despite the amount of treachery in the world, there are surprisingly only a few of them which means the act they committed has to be terribly heinous. In fact, I remember my dad once telling Alfie and me that there were only four full Level Niners and generally only one of them can interact with this plain of existence at a time. Lastly, when the Brimstone Huntress fully comes into her powers, it will bring forth all at them at specific intervals and if all four of them are here on our plain of existence we're doomed. Though in keeping them from this plain, it takes a toll on the Huntress and that toll will be her life."

"Do you think... do you think it'll happen now?" Sebastian asked.

Tears ran down Ally's face as she slowly nodded.

"Light, Ally." Sebastian whispered miserably before looking down at Penny.

Ally said nothing as misery and pain swamped her. She began to sob in earnest again as reality set in. For unless a miracle happened, Penny was now living on borrowed time, and there was absolutely nothing they could do about it.

Chapter Fifteen

Lenox stood in the shadows of a large craggy moor rock with Tyr standing beside him, watching the scene in front of him.

So— Tyr started to say.

Forget what you saw, Tyr, Lenox responded instantly.

Tyr said nothing for a long moment before he finally spoke up once more, *That's the second time you've said that to me in my lifetime, Lenox and I don't know if I can. I mean the first time, I thought I was seeing things. But this…*

Lenox let out a soft sigh. "What can I say? No rest for the wicked."

"What does that even mean?" Tyr asked, crossing his arms.

Though a new voice responded before Lenox had the chance to speak, "You are far from wicked, Lenox."

Lenox looked over to see Reggie appear, though he wasn't alone as Thorn, his cousin Anya's husband, stood next to him.

"That's not what I meant," Lenox finally said.

"What did you mean exactly?" Reggie asked curiously.

"When I said no rest for the wicked, I was not inferring that I was wicked. I was inferring to the fact that more will follow soon, though they won't come alone; they'll have minions that in and of themselves, will be a challenge Reggie."

"Yeah, I kind of figured that but how do you know that and why are you here exactly, Lenox?"

Lenox looked away and briefly shook his head.

"Lenox," Thorn whispered to him calmly.

Lenox lifted his eyes to look at him and saw genuine compassion and concern.

You have my promise of silence as a Secret Keeper, Lenox but you truly cannot keep this to yourself much longer. The forces that will come after you and Penny soon...

I know, Lenox responded before he quietly imparted seven

more words to Thorn.

Thorn's eyes widened in shock before he declared, *Lenox, look at me!*

Lenox waited until he felt Tyr and Reggie get distracted before he looked Thorn clear in the eyes, showing him that his eyes had reverted to their true colour.

Thorn rubbed his face before he nodded and then took over speaking to Reggie and Tyr, giving Lenox the silent option of escape.

Lenox took the chance without a second thought and returned home. Lenox arrived in his bathroom where he dug out a small plastic container from the medicine cabinet. Popping it open, he took out two contact lenses and put them in his eyes. Blinking like mad, Lenox squeezed his eyes shut before opening them and looked in the mirror to see the artificial grey colour stare back at him, almost mockingly.

Lenox felt a brief swirl of air stir behind him as he watched his twin appear.

"So it's begun?" Lulu asked softly as she laid a hand on the back of his left shoulder.

"Yeah, Lou, it has but I won't make the same mistake that our ancestor did."

"It's still going to be a next to impossible battle," Lulu responded sadly.

"I know but still, we'll sort it. Though first things first, we need to set something right. Will you come with me?"

"To hell and back as always," Lulu responded.

"Already done that once, Lou and we swore not to do it a second time," Lenox said dryly.

Lulu let out a small soft snort-laugh, "Light, don't say that out loud. Dad might hear."

"He and mum here?" Lenox asked.

"Yeah but let's go see Penny first; Sebastian has taken her next door to their home. Ally's about to teleport away to enact her plan but I stopped her with magic, so we better get a move on before Ally fully realizes what I've done."

Lenox nodded before both he and Lulu teleported to where

Penny was.

"What the hell—" Sebastian started to snarl.

"Peace," Lulu said calmly as she let her soothing calm nature loose.

Ally looked up at Lulu with dull eyes before they suddenly sharpened.

"You two—"

"Shh, Ally, we will explain as best we can but first we must see to Penny. Lenox," Lulu murmured, while looking at her twin.

Lenox nodded as he crossed the room towards the prone form of Penny. Ignoring the soft growl coming from Sebastian, Lenox knelt beside her and grasped Penny's hand. Closing his eyes, he focused on his full powers.

The still air began to stir and gently swirl around them as the air wisps appeared. Lenox directed them to lift the heavy residual energy of the demon off of Penny. The wisps responded and pulled the darkness away and purified everything.

Once the heavy energy was wholly gone, Lenox looked to his twin and nodded again. Lulu then pulled out a potion contained in a hip flask from her coat pocket. She drank half before handing it to Lenox. Lenox took it with his free hand and watched Lulu step around the stunned Sebastian to gently grasp Penny's free hand.

Lenox downed the remaining potion and carefully tucked the flask into his pocket with his free hand as he felt the liquid start to pulse in his body. Within seconds his magic not only restored him but it also grew exponentially alongside his twin's.

Focusing their surging powers on Penny, Lenox and Lulu slowly and methodically started to funnel it into Penny to replenish her depleted energy levels, while also trying not to overwhelm her with the raw force of the power.

It took several painstaking moments before it began to work and Penny began to stir. Lenox opened his eyes and watched Penny start to move on the divan.

"Lenox... Lulu, what on earth?" Penny asked in confusion.

Lenox said nothing as he and Lulu ended the link. Then, without another word, Lenox helped Penny sit up before he sat down on the divan behind her. Penny scooted back into Lenox's warmth as Lulu sat down in front of her, still holding her hand, though this time in comfort.

"Can someone..." Sebastian started.

"Explain?" Lulu finished before nodding. "I know what we're going to say won't be nearly enough to explain what's going on. However, we truly can't tell you everything right now."

"Why the hell not?" Sebastian demanded hoarsely.

Lulu looked at him with understanding. "I know you are upset and my words bring you no comfort but our secret was bound by two secret keepers. If we tell you everything now, it will cause a lot of things to unravel before everyone can be properly prepared and in effect, doom us all."

"How the hell is that possible?" Sebastian asked, stunned.

"You can't always apply linear logic to the world, Bas. Especially when it comes to magic and demon hunting. I've told you that many times," Ally said as she moved around the divan and sat down next to her mate, leaning into him seeking comfort. Sebastian immediately wrapped his arms tightly around her and rested his chin on top of her head.

"Yeah, that's true and we'll tell you what we can. I promise. To start off with, Lenox and I are like you and Alfie, Ally, meaning we're symbiotic twins. To which I will say that I am sorry if that will drive you crazy in future, Penny." Lulu explained.

"It won't!" Penny said at once.

"It might since it drove my wife Freya crazy at the very beginning of our relationship. Though truth be told, at that time in our lives, Lenox and I had never been apart from each other for more than a few moments. Heck we even shared a room which sounds really weird I know but—"

"Symbiotic twins are not normal twins, they need to be in constant contact even in sleep sometimes, though only when you've suffered a grave injury because you're essentially two halves of the same whole and you cannot replenish your magic or heal without the other," Penny finished, watching her Uncle Alfie suddenly appear next to her mum as if wordlessly sensing her emotional pain and needing to aid her.

"Yes, we also share emotions, pain and thoughts as you see," Lenox murmured.

The room was quiet as everyone let those words sink in before Lenox spoke again, this time in a whisper. "Long.... long ago, Lulu and I had a run-in with a terrible demon, one that almost killed us. However, it didn't because we came into our full true power at the time, much like you did tonight, Penny."

"Um..." Penny started as the evening's events were still very much a jumble in her mind.

"It'll come back to you over the next couple of weeks, love and I know you very much want to know what happened but you can't force yourself to remember since it'll do more harm than good. Please trust me on that," Lenox said quietly.

"Hey, wait just a minute! You haven't explained anything so far!" Sebastian burst in but both Ally and Alfie lay a hand on his shoulder.

"Lenox is right, Bas and I know as a father, you're super mad and upset but you need to put that aside for a moment. Lenox and Lulu aren't keeping things from you by choice; they're doing it because they have to, just as Ally and I have done."

Sebastian let out a hiss, "Light sake's, I hate when you do something like that but I damn well get it! Look, Lenox! Tell me something honestly. What are you damn well going to do about the predicament we're in now? Don't tell me you don't have a plan."

"Oh, I've got a plan alright, though it mainly focuses on protecting and loving your daughter," Lenox said at once as he wrapped his arms around Penny.

"Wait a tick! I can protect myself," Penny said hotly, though she was still pleased by his words.

"I know, love and me wanting to protect you is no slight against your skills as a huntress of evil. I also do not want you ever to feel that you have to change that because you're one hell of a huntress, the best in the world..."

"Hey! I'm the best hellhound hunter," Alfie declared.

"Pfft, as if Alfie! Penny's well got you bloody beat," Ally

retorted.

"How? I've got the most kills by far as a swarm hunter," Alfie snorted, rolling his eyes.

"Killing millions of tadpole demons is nowhere near the same league as lampooning Blue Whale size demons. Therefore, Penny is the best and I'm obviously next," Ally started, causing Sebastian to snort this time.

"I'm not the best. Uncle Reggie's got to have that spot," Penny said, weighing in.

"Nah, honey, again you kill Blue Whale size demons on a fairly frequent basis and none of us can touch that with a ten-foot pole despite your Uncle's whining. Your cousin Lucy is up there, too, because she kills a decent amount of Sperm Whale size demons. Though, obviously I'm..." Sebastian said.

"Nope," Reggie cut in as he appeared carrying a large box of food. "The top three are Penny, me and then a four-way tie between you, Ally, Alfie and Lucy. Now quit bickering and come over to Penny's house to get something to eat. The body doesn't run on air alone, you know."

"I'm not hungry," Ally muttered, blowing out a sigh.

"Ally... whatever fears plague your mind..." Reggie stopped as if thinking on his words some more before he just shook his head briefly. "You've just got to let it go for now because there's no sense worrying yourself sick over something that may not come to pass for many years yet."

"Or it could happen next week!" Ally shouted in response.

"Mum?" Penny whispered as she saw tears start to stream down her face.

Ally shook her head. "I can't tell you, love… I can't, I just can't."

Without another word said between them, Penny moved off the divan and hugged her mother tightly as she began to cry.

"I know what you can't say revolves around me and what happened tonight. I also know you're worried about me dying, right?"

Ally let loose a wailing sob at the words.

"Mum," Penny whispered at a loss for words.

"Ally, I know you think there is no hope but—" Lulu broke off and looked at her twin.

"But there is," Lenox whispered quietly.

"How'd you know that?" Ally wailed.

Lenox was quiet for a moment as he formed his words carefully before he finally telepathically spoke to Ally directly, *Please hear me, Ally. I know you are nearing the brink of despair but please hear me out.*

We're listening, Alfie suddenly responded gruffly.

We cannot say anything beyond this right now, but Penny isn't the only one in this fight okay? We are, too and we have been for a long time and we've been preparing.

Ally stilled as her eyes took in the bent heads of Lenox and Lulu. Lenox briefly lifted his eyes to look back at her earnestly and Ally immediately noticed the glassy sheen.

Fake— Ally started.

Lenox nodded before adding, *Yes and it was for a purpose. For if they don't know about us, they will never see us coming until it is too late.*

Ally let his words sink in as her hopes began to finally rise as she remembered something her dad had said to her and Alfie when they were little.

"Remember to seek out the Wild Ones when the time comes, my dears, for they will never let you down."

I knew I liked you two for a reason. You are good people, Ally responded jubilantly.

Thanks Ally, Lulu said on behalf of both of them.

Lenox nodded as he watched a change overcome Ally as she scrubbed her face with a free hand and gave Penny a hard squeeze.

"We'll be okay, sweetie, and you know what? I am hungry after all," Ally responded, changing on a dime.

"What the—" Sebastian started.

"Ah, Sebastian, don't start. We all know I'm bipolar."

"We don't all know that!" Sebastian declared.

Ally rolled her eyes. "Honey, I'm the legit poster child for that affliction."

"I don't see how..."

Ally whipped out her phone and started reading the symptoms to him from the internet.

"Don't use the internet to self-diagnose!"

"I didn't," Ally chirped before adding, "The psychiatrist at that really nice place in Switzerland that Alfie and I briefly stayed in last year, did."

Sebastian's mouth gaped before he began to sputter in shock.

"Ah, honey relax, we needed an alibi in a hurry in order to get out a rather sticky situation we found ourselves in and you know how prison is really no place for a hound. So we decided to commit ourselves into a fancy yet exclusive mental health retreat in Switzerland for a few days."

"How is that possible? I don't remember you staying away from me for a few days and I certainly don't remember any sticky situation that required an alibi!"

"Ah hell, things happen when you're hunting evil rich jerk faces that the cops feel inclined to look for after you make them disappear and I have no regrets when it comes to doing what needs to be done. Anyway, I also didn't stay away from you, I merely used my magic to turn a few hours into a few days and you know, I wouldn't mind staying there again. I mean, the food was great, the bed was soft and the amenities... oh honey, the amenities were off the chain, especially the private Jacuzzi room."

Penny saw a light enter her mother's eyes as she began pondering something in earnest.

"Whatever it is that you think on doing—" Sebastian started.

"Only you in a hot tub," Ally declared openly.

"Light sake's, Ally, that's an inappropriate thing to say in front of our daughter!" Sebastian hissed.

Alfie sighed, "Gross."

Ally rolled her eyes at both of them, "Ah, for goodness gracious sake, I was only joking, though either way don't get your knickers in a twist. Any who, is that really dinner in that box, Reggie? If so you're the bestest!"

Reggie rolled his eyes this time. "You asked me to pick up dinner and then seem surprised when I do. I really don't know what to say to that, Ally."

"Best response? Absolutely nothing," Ally retorted.

"That is true," Penny agreed, causing Lulu to snort.

You okay, love? I mean are you angry, upset, hurt, sad? Lenox asked in earnest, more preoccupied insuring that Penny was okay.

None of the above, Lenox, honest. I kind of feel like my mind is in a bit of a jumble but beyond that, I'm not really upset at you, Lou or my parents. I mean, if the roles were reversed, I'd be doing the same that you having been doing, so there's no sense getting upset is there?

Doesn't matter. You can still be mad if you want to, Lenox responded.

But that's the thing, Lenox. I don't want to be mad all. If anything, I'm a bit more stunned by how much everyone cares about me.

You're worth caring about, Lenox replied seriously, looking slightly affronted if she felt any differently.

Lenox— Penny started.

Lenox shook his head slightly. *No, Pen, there is nothing you can say against that and we may not have been together as a couple long but I truly count my blessings when it comes to having you in my life. You're also wise beyond your years and you not being mad when you have every right to be because you understand the motives of everyone in this room, proves it.*

I'm not the only one who can be described that way, Lenox, Penny responded.

"Mmm…" Lenox responded noncommittally.

"Hey, what are you two up to?" Ally demanded.

"Nothing much," Lenox responded absently before continuing, "I was hoping to go home and eat dinner with everyone, maybe watch TV or a movie after."

"Or we could do both at the same time?" Penny suggested.

"I'm up for that, what do you want to watch?" Lenox asked

her.

"Something with Godzilla in it. I mean, I want to see the new one soon but I don't think I'm up to going to the pictures so maybe one of the old ones will be just as nice."

"Oh, it so would," Penny's mum readily agreed.

"I guess but why don't we watch the new one in our home?" Lenox asked.

"Uh duh because it's in the pictures," Alfie retorted.

"Hey, be nice to the son-in-law!" Ally immediately scolded him as she cuffed him upside the head.

"I was, I could have been a hundred times more sarcastic to the nephew-in-law but I wasn't."

"You two are so funny but you're totally missing what Lenox is getting at," Lulu said sunnily.

"What'd you mean, Lulu?" Ally asked her.

"Well, Lenox is an inventor, the very same one in fact, who created the movie projector for the in-town cinema from scratch. Though it's no ordinary projector since it's able to convert any film format into a digital media file and then projects it into each theatre or home entertainment system. Ergo, if you have the right set up, you can watch the same movies in the pictures in the comfort of your own home."

"How did we not know about this?" Ally demanded.

"Oh…" Reggie murmured, "Lenox's cousin Falcon might have mentioned it to me a couple of years ago when we connected the Compound to Moonlight Valley but I forgot."

"Reggie!" Ally declared.

"What? I'm over twenty thousand years old, do you really expect me to remember every trivial detail?"

Ally shrugged. "I guess not but this is still awesome news, many thanks, son-in-law."

"No problem," Lenox responded as he leaned forward and scooped up Penny into his arms.

"Lenox!" Penny squealed.

Lenox said nothing in response as he teleported them to their own home and immediately ran into his parents.

"Mum, dad..." Lenox started.

"It's alright, honey, we understand," Lenox's mum responded with a gentle smile.

"We do?" His dad echoed.

"Mmm yes, we do, *min storr*," his mother stated softly yet firmly, calling Conalai my darling in Irish.

Conalai sighed, "I don't like this but alright, though, what are you two going to do?"

"Umm..." Penny floundered, completely not understanding what was going on here.

"Take things one day at a time," Lenox answered.

Lenox's mum nodded. "Yes, my dear son, that is the best plan. For it is best not to worry about what tomorrow will bring when your mind is in a jumble since it could bring catastrophe upon you before you are to deal with it."

"Umm..." Penny started again.

"Thanks, mum… oh, it looks like everyone is coming over now. Can you..." Lenox started.

"Go son, we'll stall them so you can talk to Penny alone for a minute."

"Thank you."

Lenox teleported away again though this time he landed in their bedroom. Sitting Penny down on the edge of the bed, Lenox knelt in front of her and took up both of her hands before looking her deep in the eyes.

"I know this is all confusing love and I've given you nothing but half-answers at best, however please don't lose trust in me."

Penny looked into Lenox's eyes for a long moment before she responded with, "Lenox Moregan, you are the most honest and sincere man I know. Therefore, it stands to reason that whatever you are currently hiding is not because you are trying to keep me in the dark but because you are both cautious and wise. After all, any fool can charge blindly into battle but it takes someone of great personal strength and wisdom to be able to step back and properly assess the situation from all angles before acting. I also know you are from a seer line and you have learned from an early age how to weigh your words and actions before doing anything, no?"

Lenox nodded. "Yes, that's true."

"Well then, I'll heed both your words and your mum's, by taking this all one day at a time then."

Lenox gave her a smile. "Penny love, you are amazingly wise."

"If by that, you're speaking of how pragmatic I am, then my only response to that is I am a northern lass, Lenox."

Lenox snorted. "What does that mean?"

"We northern lasses are a hardy, pragmatic no-nonsense kind of woman, is what that means."

"Huh... you know I don't know if I ever told you this, but I'm a west coast Irish lad."

"Hold up. Your gran Medb was the Queen of Connacht, no?" Penny asked when a sudden random thought accord to her.

"Yeah, in the third century," Lenox replied.

"And Galway is in the Connacht region, no?"

"Yes," Lenox stated, bewildered since he knew Penny would have known that.

"Do you by chance, play fiddle in an Irish band?"

"On occasion," Lenox admitted.

"OMG! You're my Galway Guy!"

"Um..."

Penny started humming the popular song, which caused Lenox to chuckle.

"That song is about a girl, not a guy," Lenox said, knowing the song well since the singer was favoured by his sister.

"Doesn't matter, love, it's us just in reverse. I'm the English lass, and you're the Galway guy."

"But we didn't meet outside a bar."

"Doesn't matter."

"I also don't smoke and don't have a brother," Lenox added.

"Doesn't matter."

"I'm also not little."

Penny pouted "So you won't dance with me either then, like the song says?"

"No, I'd dance with you in a heartbeat!"

"So can I call you my Galway guy, sometimes?" Penny asked, sounding hopeful.

Lenox sighed "I'm not really from Galway, love but you know since I am from Connacht... sure, why not?"

"Yay! Now come on love, movie and food await! I'm starved!" Penny replied, pleased by his answer.

Lenox teleported them back to the living room as Penny hummed the song tune happily.

"Hey, that's one of my favourite songs!" Lulu declared happily.

"Mine, too, especially now that I have my Galway guy! Lenox agreed!"

Lulu let out a happy laugh in understanding, but her wife did not seem to.

"Hold on are you talking about that pop song on the radio? The one that's about the Galway girl, not a guy? Also aren't you two aren't technically from..."

"*Fre-ya!*" Lulu dramatically called out before adding, "Don't kill the romantic vibe. Besides, every couple needs a song that reminds them of their love and I think that's song perfect for Lenox and Penny."

"What's our song, then?"

"Well, since you're Swedish so, *I've Been Waiting for You* by ABBA," Lulu said at once.

"ABBA?" Freya echoed dubiously.

"Yes, ABBA and *Take a Chance on Me*, is a very close second."

"ABBA?" Freya echoed again.

"Yes, Freya, ABBA," Lulu replied sunnily before stealing a quick kiss.

"Fine. ABBA it is but I like *Take a Chance* more— it's catchier."

"Okay, I can live with that. Any who, supper and Godzilla await us!"

"Wait, is Godzilla okay with you, Mrs. Moregan?" Penny

asked Mina, wondering if Godzilla might be too violent for Lenox's mum who was from a tranquil immortal race, known to be incapable to handle real life violence, due to their empathetic powers.

"Mina, my dear, please call me Mina and I love watching Godzilla. In fact, I'm a long-time fan of his and on screen violence does not bother me because I know it is made up," Mina said.

"I love Godzilla too and please also don't call me Mr. Moregan Penny, instead call me Conalai or just Lai is fine."

"Okay," Penny agreed.

Seconds later, she felt the gentle tug on her hand that-clasped Lenox's. Penny looked over at him and saw him nod to the door that led out the living room.

Penny followed him out and into a room that was next door to Lenox's lab. Stepping inside, Penny was astounded by what she saw.

"Lenox... what is this place?" She asked in wonder, looking up at the large movie screen that ran up a concave ceiling and seemed to surround them. Nestled below in staggered stadium-like seating, were large overstuffed recliners like the ones in the living room.

"Oh, this is a prototype movie theatre. I built it to be one third the size of a normal one in order to test this type of screen. It's worked out well and I've been in talks with Falcon and Luna about adding a full-sized one in the movie theatre in town."

"Is this an IMAX screen, Lenox?" a male voice called out behind him.

Penny turned her head in the direction of the voice to see Memphis, the mate of one of Penny's honorary aunts named Callie.

"Similar technology but not the exact same," Lenox answered.

"What does IMAX mean?" Penny's mum asked when she entered the room after Penny and Lenox stepped aside.

"It's more or less a newer type of film and film equipment that produces a higher quality video. Also similar to the original IMAX viewing experience, I've made this theatre to be a more encompassing viewing experience, by using the whole screen."

"Hold up. The movie is going to play on the giant screen that stretches into the roof above us?" Alfie asked.

"Yes, which is why we need the recliners," Lenox answered

"You've design the theatre so that it'll feel like we're in the movie, right?" Alfie asked again.

"Yes."

"Can Batman movies be played on it?"

"Yes, I can adapt almost all movies post-1933 to play here. I just need the film, a digital file, VHS or a DVD of the movie in question, to play it."

Alfie immediately walked up and hugged Lenox. "You are the most amazing nephew-in-law ever. Welcome to the Baskerville family, oh greatly esteemed one."

"Lenox is already an esteemed member of our family, idiot, because he makes my Penny happy, duh."

"Yeah, but he's even more so now. In fact..."

"Don't even Alfie! He's mated to my daughter and my daughter only!" Ally shouted at him.

"Say what?" Penny gasped.

"Nothing, sweetie, just your idiot uncle being your idiot uncle," Ally retorted with a roll of her eyes.

"But I wouldn't mind him being my son-in-law, too!" Alfie near whined.

"Say what?" Lucy gasped this time "You must be joking, dad. I don't like Lenox that way! Honestly, Penny, I harbour..."

Penny snorted with laughter. "Relax, Lucy, I know that and I also know Uncle Alfie means no ill will. He just sees my mate for how awesome he is and I can hardly be upset about that."

"Well, I can be mad at him! What the hell is wrong with you?" Penny's mum retorted.

"Ack! He ticks all the right boxes, Ally," Alfie replied with a sigh.

"Yes, I sure the heck know that, thank you very much."

"What the hell are you two talking about?" Sebastian asked this time.

"Well, when our daughters were born, we created lists of attributes that we wanted their future mates to have."

"For Light sake's, Allycen!"

"Ah, it was only a bit a fun, Bas, though I'm not taking it back neither. I mean I wanted a strong, smart, kind, sweet man who put my daughter first always and I got that with Lenox. Good gracious am I super pleased that my spell worked."

"You used a spell?" Sebastian shouted.

"Ah relax, Bas, it wasn't meant for anyone, in particular, so don't go getting your knickers in a twist again. I just… put out good vibes, shall we say, strong vibes but good ones."

Mina laughed softly, and everyone turned to her.

Blushing at the sudden scrutiny, she responded, "I must confess I have done the same for both my children. Though truth be told, I have yet met a parent who does not want to make sure that when their child seeks out a mate it will be one who will love and cherish them for life. I am doubly blessed in that endeavour and I know in time, you will also be blessed, Alfie for Lucy knows her own mind."

"Uh, Mina..." Alfie started.

Lenox's mom said nothing as she smiled at him instead.

"Right... Godzilla time!" Alfie shouted, deciding to change the subject.

Everyone agreed before settling into the recliners, as the food was magically passed back and forth once the movie began playing.

About a third of the way through the movie, once dinner had been consumed, Lenox felt Penny shift slightly next to him. Looking down at her, Lenox noticed that she was now holding hands with her mother, who sat on the recliner next to them.

Looking back up at the movie, Lenox telepathically reached out to Penny's mother and whispered, *It will be alright, Ally, I swear that to you.*

I don't feel those words yet, Lenox but something tells me that in the near future, I will. Though either way... thank you.

Lenox nodded, saying nothing more as he focused on the movie letting his mind go blank to quell the pending fears and anxieties that started to rise within him.

Don't go borrowing trouble, Len, because it'll soon arrive all in its own time, Lulu whispered to him through their twin link.

I know, Lou and I only hope it arrives later rather than sooner, Lenox replied, hoping against all hope that whatever came for them next was a long way off, but it was also an impossible wish because deep in his mind he felt the stirring of the wisps letting him know that indeed, *they* were coming.

Chapter Sixteen

Midway through the next day, Lenox walked down the long hallway to his office at a spirited pace, planning to obtain his next set of lecture materials and have quick cup of tea with his twin while Penny was still in class. Though when he walked through his office door, he was surprised to see that his sister wasn't there but his four cousins, Mydnyte, Falcon, Skull and Anya were.

"Uh... hello," Lenox said.

"Hey, Lenox, long time no see, jerk face," Anya called almost immediately.

"Anya! We saw him but a few days ago and don't call Lenox a jerk face! He is anything but!" Mydnyte scolded her.

"I can, too, call him a jerk face because not only does he keep from me that he's in love with Penny Hawksley, not Penny du Marais, with whom I thought he was in love, but also because his twin sister Lulu threatened me!"

"I did," Lulu freely admitted when she entered the room behind Lenox.

Why? Lenox asked her through their link, not bothering to scold his twin since Lulu rarely did things like this without good reason.

Well, Anya being well... Anya was probably going to blurt out the fact that she thought you liked a different Penny in front of your Penny by accident. Which in turn, would upset your mate, just like Freya felt all those years ago when Anya blurted out that she thought I liked Frey. So I threatened her not once but twice after I heard from gran that Llyr Tirenagan wanted to know which of his granddaughters you liked. I, then, had Freya set him and the rest of her family straight. Then a few nights ago after you mated, I fully set down the law with her again, which is probably why she's miffed.

Oh thanks, Lou, Lenox said, feeling the relief seep into his veins.

After all, he had heard a rumour that Llyr thought he was in love with one of his granddaughters but he didn't know where it came from. Though he had also hoped like hell that Penny hadn't heard it because he didn't want to upset her. In fact, that was the very last thing he ever wanted to do. However, he knew he had to set the record straight with Penny as soon as he could.

"Ah, Lenox," Lulu whispered in awe.

"What? Wait seriously!" Anya demanded.

Knowing that his cousin had probably heard from her invisible sources of exactly what he had planned, Lenox said out loud for everyone else's benefit, "Yes, I am going to set the record straight with Penny."

"Set the record straight about what?" Penny asked from behind him again.

Lenox immediately whirled and replied in a rush, "I want to make sure that you know that any rumour that I love any other Penny is wrong. I love you and I have always loved you only. I say this because you might hear that I like Penny du Marais since Anya believed that I liked her and accidentally told her grandfather Llyr, though it truly isn't true."

"Ah Lenox, I know that love," Penny said with a smile.

"You do?"

Penny nodded her head

"Seriously?" Lulu asked, sounding slightly incredulous.

"Yes, I heard that rumour long ago but I also heard you set Llyr straight, so I'm not bothered by it. Unless someone's bothering you, in which case, give me a name and I'll sort them out. Any who, now that that is sorted, can I borrow your whiteboard love?"

"Absolutely, though, what's wrong with yours?" Lenox frowned.

"I ran out of room, even writing serial killer tiny. I was about to move onto the one in my classroom but Lucy said it was a bad idea and told me to go borrow yours, so no one copies my work."

"What does that even mean? Serial killer tiny?" Anya asked, sounding completely intrigued.

"Oh, it's something my mum says all the time and if memory

serves, it stems from the fact that a few serial killers back in the seventeen hundreds that she took care of, were compulsive writers and wrote their crimes out, albeit in the tiniest print ever, on their victims."

"Huh… I remember hunting down some idiots like that around the same time or maybe it was a century later," Falcon pondered, trying to place the miscreants in his mind.

"How can you not remember your jobs?" Mydnyte asked her brother.

"If you averaged out my kill count over my entire life, Nyte, I'd have somewhere in the neighbourhood of 5 to10 kills per day. Therefore without consulting my death notes notebooks, I honestly couldn't even begin to tell you about the people I've assassinated, everything blurs together."

"That's kind of understandable and I'm the same way when it comes to demon kills, I can't remember them for the life of me and I also happen to be a fraction of his age."

"Hey now!" Anya bristled.

"Ah, Anya, don't take offence. Penny is nearly 500 years old, whereas, you, Skull and Falcon are all over 3500 years old, making her one-seventh your age. Also, I do not understand why you bristle at being considered older. Your mate is over 35,000 years old, making you one-tenth his age," Lenox pointed out.

"Ha! Thorn's a cradle robber," Falcon snorted.

"Says that man whose wife is only twenty-eight," Anya retorted.

"A very mature twenty-eight," Falcon remarked loftily.

"Well, Thorn's very mature, too!"

"I know that. I called him old already," Falcon stated dryly.

"For the love of the Light Falcon!" Anya shouted but Penny tuned her out as she looked at Lenox, itching to get on with the equation plaguing her mind.

"Go on, love, you can use my whiteboard at any time and you need not ask. Although are you sure my family won't break your concentration?"

"Ah, Lenox, your cousins' squabbling just sounds like home

to me. Besides you should hear it when my mum and uncle get into a heated argument. They erupt like Krakatoa. Well, my mum erupts, whereas my uncle becomes bitingly sarcastic."

"Well, that pretty much sums up Anya and Falcon," Lenox muttered.

"Hey!" Anya shouted.

"True," Falcon countered.

"Okay true, but no one has to say it out loud. I mean can't stuff just be a given and leave it at that?"

"Okay, you two, here's what we're going to do— Falcon, Anya you're coming with me," Lulu interrupted.

"Ooh, where?" Anya asked, intrigued.

"To my favourite paint shop; I ran out of golden meadow yellow paint today and I need more to finish the scene I am working on."

"Lenox and I can go with you," Penny volunteered instantly.

"Thanks, Penny, but Falcon and Anya can help me this time since you need to work. Besides, Skull wanted to talk to Lenox and Mydnyte—"

"Mydnyte needs a little peace before the four of us head to lunch and more mayhem ensues. Mind if I sit in this chair and read a book?" Mydnyte asked Penny.

Penny shook her head at the same time Lenox did.

"I'm going to talk to Skull in your private office and leave you in peace love, if that's alright?" Lenox asked.

"I'm fine with that but sorry about kind of kicking you out of your own office."

"You're not. I was just planning to stop in for a moment anyway. "

"Oh, okay," Penny agreed.

With that, everyone teleported away, leaving Mydnyte and Penny alone in his office.

Looking at Lenox's oldest cousin, Penny murmured, "I know Lenox and my family worry about my safety but it's okay you know, I can defend myself quite well."

"Oh, I know that," Mydnyte said in Japanese before

continuing, "I also know a lot more about you than you realize, Penniah Moregan and I'm not here to defend you, merely warn you if you get lost in your work and don't sense an attack."

"Really?" Penny asked.

"Yes really," a male voice said as two other people teleported into the room.

Immediately Penny recognized them as Reggie and Mydnyte's husband, Trey Andraste. Trey took the chair next to his wife as Reggie took a spot nearest to Penny.

"What's going on, Uncle Reggie?" Penny asked quietly, knowing that he wouldn't appear out of the blue.

Reggie sighed, "To be blunt, Penny, nothing but an abundance of over-caution. Your mother is worried sick about you and your dad asked me for a favour."

"Why? I mean, she is always worried about me."

Reggie nodded in agreement. "That she is, Pen but this time… this time is really justified. Though again, you've got to remember for yourself what happened, pup and really all at this point, the only thing I can say is don't go looking for trouble."

"I know, Uncle Reggie and I swore to mum that I wouldn't act stupidly."

"Penny, hon, that was never in the cards for you. I mean, I probably do more stupid things in a single hour than you do in a month. However, sometimes you can't prevent trouble by being cautious. Therefore, it pays to have people watching your back at all times, especially assassins, hounds and Vikings."

"Vikings?" Penny asked, completely confused by the remark.

"Yes, Vikings. They are the immortal equivalent of tanks, heavily armoured, super strong with the ability to take on large number of foes at once. They also are able to draw most villains away from you because they also have the keen knack to piss everyone off when the mood strikes."

"I thought all of the above was, in essence, hellhounds," Penny said.

"Similar pup but the Vikings or the Norra Stam as they go by now, also have one last ability we don't. They are able to go into a rage frenzy, also called a berserker state which is an extremely strong magical state that is hard to explain but awesome to see in action. Anyway, expect Mydnyte, Trey or Falcon will shadow you when you're not on any of the immortal isles. On top of that, Winston, Lucy or I will also shadow you at any given point too. Also, there is a slight change to your Cambridge study plans. Since you and Lenox have mated, he cannot be your academic mentor now since it would be a direct conflict of interest. Therefore I'm going to take over that role."

"Say what?" Penny asked in completely confusion.

"I said I'm your PhD mentor and here are all my qualifications," Reggie said as he produced a massive stack of papers.

"When did you obtain these?" Penny asked as she walked over and started reading the first few pages.

"Here and there since 1945. I got bored around then and decided to see about obtaining degrees. I also never said you couldn't obtain your PhD, Penny. I said you couldn't take up an academic post, full research post, or publish in a human magazine."

"But you need those for a PhD."

"You actually don't, though most PhD candidates choose to be published, take a professor's position or research post because they want to work in this field. As an immortal, we don't need to hold down a human job to pay our bills, so to speak and for us a PhD is actually strictly a research degree, where you look into a chosen topic and try to prove or disprove it through research. Now I want some researched topics for your thesis by the end of the week."

"Oh, I have a few of those ready already," Penny admitted as she summoned up the research papers she had been working on, ever since she got the okay to attend Cambridge.

"Light sake's, seriously?" Reggie asked when he looked at the mountain of paperwork in front of him.

"Is it not enough?" Penny asked with a frown.

"Not enough? You could write four theses from this!"

"Well, I've gathered all that for one topic in particular," Penny stated before she started giving Reggie the cliff notes version of her work.

Reggie lifted his hand. "Let me read it all pup and I'll get back to you later with some insights. Anyway continue with whatever you were working on. We won't bother you."

Trey looked at his wife as if telepathically speaking to her before he summoned up a crossword puzzle book and a pen. Looking to Penny he briefly nodded to her with a smile then focused on the first puzzle. Mydnyte was the next to pick up a task as she picked up a sizable thick novel and started to read. Penny then turned her attention to Reggie who nodded towards the whiteboard behind her.

Letting out a small sigh, Penny turned around and got to work on the equation that was plaguing her recently. Soon her focus was ensnared once again and she lost all track of time and space. That was, of course, until she felt a warm hand on her shoulder and scented a familiar presence.

Startled slightly, Penny spun around and immediately froze when she spotted Lenox. Blushing, Penny tucked a piece of straight hair that had come loose from her French braid behind her ear.

"Sorry to interrupt, love, but you're next class starts in five minutes. I was going to go teach it for you but Reggie wouldn't let me," Lenox murmured apologetically.

"That's okay. I'll go… wait! Shoot! Five minutes? Ack!" Penny floundered.

Lenox leaned in while Penny was starting to work herself up to a mini panic and stole a kiss. Feeling his soft, warm lips upon her own, Penny let out a moan as her hands drifted upwards, intent on threading themselves through his silky dark locks.

"Ahem!" Reggie's deep voice grumbled interrupting them.

Penny let out an annoyed grumble, "Dang blast it, Reggie!"

"Don't start pup, you're going to be late. Get your tail in gear now!"

Penny huffed as she found herself starting to move out of the room, mildly cursing Reggie under her breath as he smirked the whole time and continued to read her working thesis research.

"Ah, Penny love, real quick. Before you go, is a coffee date okay on Friday? Lulu told me that we should go for a coffee date first because that's the modern convention and I thought that we could go to a local coffee house here that has a poetry reading on that night. Though we could do anything else if that sounds lame," Lenox finished with a small concerned frown.

Penny let out a happy squeal and started towards Lenox, before a growl interrupted her.

"I'm going, I'm going, you old meanie! Light, bless us and save us from me being late for the very first time in my life! See you later, Lenox love and please don't change whatever you're planning because I like it. Ta-ra!" Penny called as she took off in a dead run out the door.

The room was silent.

"*Daito*?" Mydnyte asked, using the Japanese word for date as she reverted to her first language.

"Um… yeah," Lenox answered lamely as he rubbed the back of his neck

"Not to be a jerk here but why not go on a pub date instead of a coffee one since the pub is where most British folks go?" Trey asked him.

"No, I want to take her out on dates from her list," Lenox declared.

"List?" Mydnyte echoed in English this time.

Lenox felt himself clam up, not wanting to talk about Penny's list.

"Lenox…" Mydnyte started again.

"It's not a huge deal. It's just a list of some things Penny wanted to do and let's leave it at that," Lenox said, knowing full well that his oldest cousin wouldn't let up.

"Do you want to do these things, too? I mean, love isn't all about sacrifice, Lenox," Mydnyte stated quietly.

"I'm sacrificing nothing, Nyte, since I know full well that I'll enjoy myself because I've done a lot of these activities before. In fact, I will fully admit that I like going to coffee houses and enjoying a cuppa while listening to people around me."

"Well, it does sound real nice and don't worry about security come date night. Trey and I will watch out for you, so you two can enjoy yourselves."

Lenox wanted to argue against that but knowing the truth of the situation Penny and he were currently in, or more accurately, knowing the evil that would come for them soon, Lenox chose to accept his cousin's offer.

"Thanks, Nyte and Trey, I appreciate that."

Trey snorted, "You're too nice, my man."

"I'm not too nice, Trey. I'm just smart enough to see that there's nothing wrong with having someone have your back when things are… well, are the way they are."

Trey snorted again. "Fair enough. Do you have an address for this coffee house? I want to do some recon on it this afternoon and get a sense of the lay of the land, so to speak."

Lenox nodded and pulled out his phone to look up the address. While he did so, the room was quiet until his cousin Mydnyte suddenly broke the silence.

"I want to make a list of date activities to go," she muttered with a huff.

"Are you serious?" Trey asked his wife, sounding incredulous.

"As deadly as my favourite knives," Mydnyte retorted in Japanese again.

Trey let out a laugh, "Come on, Nyte; your date list would be full of nothing but roller coasters and amusement attractions since we haunt those places when we're not on jobs."

"That's not true!"

"Is so," Trey retorted this time and added, "Okay, tell me one thing you want to do that can't be done in an amusement park."

"I want to have a picnic under a cherry blossom tree!"

"That can only be done in the spring since it's not cherry blossom season."

"So? I still want to do it! I also want to go to the Sapporo Autumn Fest."

"Fair."

"I'm not done!" Mydnyte declared hotly before she started to list off reams of activities.

"Nyte wai—" Trey started, but it was too late as Mydnyte

seemed to be on a roll.

Lenox quietly sent Trey a text of the address before he tried to sneak out the room but was quickly caught.

"Where are you going, Lenox?" Mydnyte suddenly demanded.

Lenox blurted out the first thing that came to mind, "Bathroom."

"Oh, okay," Nyte replied before she continued on her tirade.

Without another word, Lenox made his escape and walked out of the room, though he was soon joined by Reggie.

"You aren't really going to the bathroom, are you?" Reggie asked.

"No, though it was the only excuse I could think of on short notice and as much as I love my cousin when she's on the warpath, it's better to stay clear for a bit. I just hope they don't do anything… er... rash afterwards, in my office."

"Like having sex in it?" Reggie asked bluntly.

"Er yes," Lenox admitted shuddering at the thought.

Reggie snorted in laughter.

"Relax, Lenox, your sister-in-law, Freya, arrived seconds after you left and from the way she was setting down the law with Mydnyte and Trey, I don't think you have anything to worry about."

Lenox blew out a sigh of relief, knowing full well that his twin probably picked up on his mild distress and sent her wife to right the ship, as it were.

"You probably think it's cowardly that I didn't do anything myself," Lenox murmured to Reggie.

"No, Lenox, I don't. In fact, I see you as a man who has more Ritana traits than you let on and would have suffered in silence rather than voice your distress. Also, to be quite honest, had Freya not arrived, I would have dealt with them for you and I have no problem doing so. Though I also do think you should speak up more in general, since you are a lot like your mother and what little you say carries much weight, if you get my meaning."

Lenox nodded. "I do understand and that is why I choose my words and battles with care. Though I still can ramble on from time to time like everyone else but granted, when I do that it tends to be about whatever I recently invented."

"As you should. Your inventions are mind-blowing, Lenox. Anyway, changing the subject, I hear there's a posh lecturer lounge around here, and I want to take full advantage of its amenities."

"Uh… really?" Lenox asked.

"Why do you seem shocked, Lenox? Do you not think I'd fit in?" Reggie demanded with a snort.

"Well, some stodgy foolish professor might feel that way, since you're not wearing the obligatory tweed jacket and tie that people assume all lecturers wear when at Cambridge. However, I was astonished at your wanting to check out the lounge because well, it's not that great. I mean, the left side of the room is drafty since the ventilation system seems to favour that side whereas the right side is stuffy; there's also a faint musty smell of mothball and cigar smoke that you can still pick up as an immortal, despite the fact the room has been rigorously cleaned. Also, Ms. Fairburn, the woman in charge of the room, will make you either a very strong cup of tea or a very weak one, there's no in-between with her and you don't get to choose either."

"Huh... have any suggestions?"

"Yes. Use your magic to regulate your body temperature, sense of smell and tea preference."

Reggie laughed. "I will keep that it in mind, Lenox."

"Good," Lenox returned as he showed Reggie the way to the Lecturer's Lounge. Lenox hoped that by the time he returned to his office, he'd truly have his peace back again. Though knowing his well-meaning yet often overbearing family, he sincerely doubted that.

Though overall, Lenox was just glad that he had the chance of talking to his cousin Skull in private about intimate relations, since it would have been a well and truly awkward conversation if his other cousins had listened in. Although it still had been an embarrassing conversation to have regardless, despite the fact that Skull had plenty of training as a healer who specialized in psychology including sex therapy.

"Nothing to be embarrassed about," Lenox muttered to

himself as he walked back down the hall, intent on focusing on the safe world of mechanics for the time being instead of the unknown world of intimacy and romance.

Chapter Seventeen

Penny had a weird sense of deja vu when she peered into a mirror, trying to make sure her appearance was perfect. However, this time, instead of aiming to look like a no-nonsense university student, she was aiming for a pretty Beatnik look.

Black ballet flats? *Check.*

Soft pink slimming pants? *Check.*

Black turtleneck with three quarter length sleeves? *Check.*

Pink striped scarf tied in appropriate ascot fashion? *Check.*

Black beret? *Check.*

"Are you done checking your appearance yet?" a laughing female voice asked from behind her.

Penny looked up in the mirror and saw her cousin Lucy lying on her bed on her stomach poring over a fashion magazine with her face resting on her palm of her hand and her crossed ankles behind her.

"I guess so... though, why are you here?" Penny asked with a small frown.

"For moral support... *hipster*," Lucy drawled when she briefly looked up.

"I'm not a hipster! I'm dressed up as a beatnik from the late fifties or early sixties! You know the artsy people who attended poetry reading at coffeehouses all the time!"

"Yeah, I know. They were the original hipsters."

"Ugh! I'm not a hipster! I just thought it would be fun to dress as a blast from the past."

"And you look beautiful, cuz," Lucy complimented.

"Aw, thanks!"

"For a hipster!"

"Ugh, seriously!"

"Yes, and don't try to take away my fun! Oh and lose the beret; it takes away from your look. Now this is the first time you've ever gone on a date and I get to be the one who ribs you for it, though expect a lot more hassle from your mum and dad."

"They're here?" Penny asked, carefully taking off the beret and smoothing out her hair, begrudgingly agreeing with her cousin.

"Heck, yes, they are. Your mum wants pictures to commemorate the occasion and your dad is here... well probably to give Lenox a hard time."

"Oh, Light, no!" Penny wailed.

"Relax, cuz, Lenox's own mum dad and twin are here, too, so your dad will probably keep himself in check and not do something over the top."

"You think so?" Penny asked sounding hopeful

Lucy was quiet for a long time before she drawled, "Nah!"

Penny glowered at her cousin, who laughed at her own remark.

"Oh come on, Pen, you'll have a right laugh yourself when you think back on this in later years."

"Hmm, I hope so."

"Anyway, are you ready yet?"

"As I'm ever going to be, I suppose. Light, I'm so nervous."

"Don't be, Pen. He loves you, you love him and this date is more or less a formality at this stage," Lucy said.

"Going on a date is not a formality!"

"Sure it is," Lucy retorted.

"Ugh… nevermind, I'm going downstairs now," Penny muttered.

"Yay!" Lucy cheered before she teleported out of the room, presumably ending up downstairs ahead of Penny.

Penny gathered her courage as she quietly repeated, "I can do this. I can do this."

With that, she left the bedroom and made her way down the stairs. The butterflies in her stomach started to flutter in earnest, causing her to nearly bolt back up the stairs in panic. Though luckily for Penny, it was then that she caught sight of Lenox. Taking in his dark wash fitted boot cut denim jeans, dark emerald green V-neck sweater and black motorcycle jacket, Lenox looked smoking hot in

Penny's mind. Lenox's eyes lit up at the sight of her and he blushed before he held out potted flower to her.

"Sorry it's in a pot, I have issues with cut flowers," Lenox said softly with a small grimace.

"Don't be sorry! I love potted plants! These are really lovely, Lenox. What kind of flower are they?" Penny asked as she made her way to him, nerves completely forgotten.

"Amaryllis," Lenox replied as he handed it to her when she was within reach.

"Thank you, Lenox."

"You're welcome and I know we were going to a coffee house, but are you up for a motorbike ride first?"

"You own a motorbike?" Penny asked in surprise.

"Uh… yes, several," Lenox admitted.

"Any of them Triumphs?"

Lenox laughed softly, "Oh yes, I love their design."

"Me, too, well them and Yamaha," Penny said before she telepathically asked him, *is everyone in the living room?*

Lenox nodded.

Do you want to avoid the awkward kerfuffle that is sure to happen when we go see our families and run away with me instead?

Absolutely, Lenox agreed.

Without saying another word, Penny silently set the plant down on a nearby side table and offered her hand to Lenox. Biting his lip to keep from laughing, Lenox took it and then teleported them away to his office in Cambridge.

"Quick, let's run to the parking before they noticed we've escaped," Lenox laughed as he tugged her hand and they ran down the empty corridor out to the parking lot, using their magic to block any electronic device from registering their presence.

"Ooh nice!" Penny said, admiring the black and chrome motorcycle waiting for them in Lenox's spot in the parking lot.

"Thanks but first, I'm sorry I didn't say this sooner, you look really lovely Penny."

"Are you sure? I mean I don't look over the top or anything? I thought going as a beatnik would be fun but now I think I went a little nuts..." Penny babbled.

Lenox silenced her with a soft kiss.

"Penny, I mean every word. You're a complete stunner."

Blushing mightily, Penny mentally whispered, *Thanks.*

"Here, love, let's take a few quick selfies to send to our mums, so that way yours won't hunt us down later."

"Oh, she totally would!" Penny agreed.

Lenox snorted, "Oh, I know, she said as much when she arrived. Though luckily, I set up a contingency plan with my twin earlier. By which I mean, Lulu is going to distract your mum with every monster movie known to humankind by playing them in our little movie theatre. Hopefully, that should work."

"OMG, you're a criminal mastermind. Well not criminal, but you know what I mean," Penny blurted out as she telepathically face palmed herself.

"I do understand, Penny, no worries. Anyway... smile," Lenox said as he wrapped his arm around Penny's waist and pointed his phone at them.

Penny wrapped her arms around him and smiled.

Lenox took a couple of pictures before sending them to Penny, who immediately downloaded them on her phone and set one as her backdrop before forwarding them to her mum. She smiled even mor,e when she noticed Lenox do the exact same thing.

Without another word, Penny summoned her motorcycle helmet and put it on along with her protective leather jacket, just as Lenox put on his helmet. He got on first and Penny quickly followed suit, making sure her feet her were on the right places before she tightly wrapped her arms around Lenox's waist.

Lenox started the bike and drove out of the car park and Cambridge University itself. Lenox then took them away from town and headed out into the country for a leisurely drive as he began to pepper Penny with questions telepathically.

So since this is our first date, I've got a list of first date questions off the internet, want to play a little game called Getting to Know Me?

Yes!

So, first question is, what is your full name?

Oh good gracious, it's a long one; Penniah Sebastian Olivia Neely Baskerville Hawskley. My mum was determined to make sure my second name was my dad's, despite the fact that everyone wanted to feminize it to something like Sebastina or Sebastine. It's also hellhound tradition to give children their mother's maiden name before their last name.

Could our children also keep Baskerville, too or would it be frowned upon? Lenox asked seriously.

You want to keep the Baskerville name?

Yes, it's part of who you are, Penny and any children we have should have it, too.

I'd like that, Penny admitted before asking, *so what's your full name?*

Lenox Markos Moregan.

Hey, I think this is going to be off-topic but where did your mum and dad come up with the names Lenox and Lulu?

We're named after people my dad knew and greatly respected. I'm directly named after an old Scottish Chieftain, though Lulu's name comes from two different women; Luighseach and Luanna. Luighseach raised my dad until the age of 8 and Luanna was an old friend of my mum's who died not long before we were born. Now next question: What's your favourite genre of music?

Hands down metal, Penny answered at once.

Oh, thank goodness, that's mine, too.

No one ever sees it though, Penny found herself saying before adding, *they think because I like pink and lady-like stuff then I must like pop music. Though I don't see why I can't like pink and like metal.*

I believe you can and I also believe you can like more than one genre of music at the same time, too. I mean I like metal but I also like classical and electronica, too.

True, and to be honest, I completely believe that as beings we're meant to be a mix of contrasting likes because it makes us interesting. Now it's my time to ask a question, what's your favourite sport to watch or play?

I like watching football but when it comes to playing, I prefer baseball despite it not being played much in Britain.

I watch football, too! In fact, I'm a huge Man City fan.

No! Lenox mock whined, *Say it isn't so, Penny!*

It so is. I love Man City though don't tell me you're a United fan, Lenox.

Lenox laughed. *No, I'm an Arsenal Fan.*

Well, so long as you're not a Man United fan, I can respect that but when your team and mine play each other, I will not be responsible for my comments or actions, Penny retorted primly.

Lenox laughed harder at that remark.

After a few minutes, Lenox asked Penny, *so do you have a favourite vacation place?*

Hmm, that's a toughie but I'd have to say the whole country of Iceland. I love running full tilt in my hound form across the glaciers and dormant volcanoes, though I also really enjoy the numerous wonderful hot springs. How about you?

I have to say I like the whole country of Japan, though more specifically the rail system there. I could spend months at a time, hopping on and off every train they have. I guess it's my engineer's mind at work because I'm constantly fascinated by mechanical stuff. My sister Lou jokingly says that I have literal gears in my head that are in constant motion.

Well, if you have gears then I have numbers, Penny stated before asking, *Do you play any instruments?*

I play the guitar, piano, violin, flute, trumpet, bagpipes and drums. You?

I can play the guitar, cello and violin though by far, the violin is my favourite and I have eleven of them.

You have eleven violins? Lenox asked surprised.

Yes, I have seven Stradivarius violins, two violins my mum and uncle made, and two I obtained from others. Nothing nefarious, I swear, one I was gifted by a Romany gypsy in the 1800s and the other, I bought in a music store a few years ago when I was out shopping with my dad.

I know there has to be a story behind the seven Stradivarius violins.

Penny snorted. *There definitely is and the short version is my mum, dad and uncle are to blame. The kerfuffle started when I first showed an avid interest in violins and my dad became determined to find me the best one. So he did his research and eventually bought me my first Strad, though my mum was a bit miffed that he hadn't mentioned it to her, so she went out and bought one, too. Then as part of a practical joke that my uncle loves to play from time to time, he decided to hide them both to piss off my parents. Though unintentionally, he upset me because I couldn't find them and almost instantly, both my parents went out and each bought two more Strad violins as replacements. When they showed up with the four new ones, my Uncle decided to reveal then, that he had the original two. My parents didn't take the joke well and my uncle ended up buying me another Strad as an apology present. So I now have seven and also don't be mad at my uncle Alfie because my mum pulled a similar prank on my cousin Lucy. Which is the reason why she now owns one of the most valuable collections of ballet dance shoes.*

I'm not mad and my family has similarly pranked each other when they were bored. Well not exactly the same way granted, they are more likely to one-up each other by finding the most ridiculous gift, which often means that Lulu and I have both been given rare mechanical journals, artwork,
tool-sets, and paint supplies. Though most items have a dubious history as to where they came from, especially gifts my Uncle Phoenix or Uncle Wulf have given, since they tend to take stuff from villains they kill. Well to be honest, they are actually repossessing stuff that was originally stolen in the first place and they do try to see to it that the victims or their families get their possessions back. Though whatever couldn't be returned or they have really taken a shining to, ends up in our homes.

Oh, I've have received that kind of gift, too, though I often swear it's because my mum and uncle are part magpie, Penny admitted.

Lenox snorted telepathically but said nothing in response as they lapsed into a companionable silence enjoying the beautiful

English countryside surrounding them.

Is this really my life? Penny wondered to herself as she thought about the bizarre yet wonderful turn her life had taken within the past month.

You having fun, Penny? Lenox asked suddenly.

Penny was a bit taken back by that as she answered, *Yes, why wouldn't I be?*

I just wanted to make sure since you seemed really lost in thought, Lenox replied quietly.

I was, how could you tell? Penny mused.

I felt your arms loosen slightly around my waist.

Oh sorry. I was kind of musing about how my life had taken a dramatic yet amazing over this past month. I mean not to sound all creepy but I've been in love with you for years, Lenox and I can't believe that in a blink of an eye, everything just worked out.

I'm also quite thankful for that blessing. Though we'll probably still have to work at being together in a relationship, too, since you may find me overbearing or inconsiderate in the future.

Highly doubtful, you're the most considerate person I have ever met and it might be my crazy behaviour that you'll need to watch out for since this apple did not fall far from a very crazy family tree.

You're not crazy, Penny, eccentric sure...

I prefer crazy. I mean I know they mean the same thing but crazy just seems more honest to me. I also kind of really like being crazy and you truly may need to worry about that.

I'm not bothered by crazy and I really mean it. Besides have you met my Uncle Phoenix as well as my cousins, Mydnyte, Falcon, Skull and Anya? There's seriously no one crazier than them.

Except for my mum and uncle, maybe even my cousin Lucy too, now that I think about it. Anyway, enough of that since no sense scaring you off on the first date.

Fat chance of that happening, Penny, though let's go back to our question game while we meander towards the coffeehouse.

Sounds great, Penny agreed before she started peppering Lenox with questions.

Arriving at the coffeehouse about an hour later, Penny took in the atmosphere and tried not to grimace because there was just something off about this place. Not in an evil twisted way but more like in a 'this place is not for you' way.

Alright, love?

Yeah, Penny remarked before nodding, S*orry yes I'm fine. Let's give this place a fair go.*

Walking up to the counter, Penny was determined to order a cup of coffee instead of tea since when in Rome, you should do what the Romans do.

"I'd like a latte," Penny murmured as she brought out her wallet.

"No love, everything is on me tonight."

"You sure?" Penny asked hesitantly.

Lenox nodded seriously.

"Okay."

With that Lenox ordered a latte and an espresso for them since Penny was hesitant to speak to the barista. After all, given the vibe of the place, the last thing she needed was to pick up on violent past actions as she had done in the previous café she went to and react.

Lenox seemed to understand her motives and guided her to a dark corner that greatly appeased her hellhound nature, before he carried over their drinks.

Lenox sat across from her, holding onto one of her hands as he watched her silently take in their surroundings with an ever-vigilant eye, looking for evil. Almost immediately she spotted their added protection for the night which didn't upset her as she thought it would. Though Penny had a feeling that is was all due to the fact that she wanted to protect Lenox with every fibre of her being and if that meant putting up with assassin help, then so be it.

Penny began to relax and listen to the poetry recital as she stared at Lenox. At first, the poem was more or less like white noise to her, since she was completely distracted by Lenox's sheer utter hotness. However when she saw him grimace at something said, Penny focused on the reading and found it to be utterly terrible.

"Well, that's… no, it's really bad, seriously there's nothing redeemable about it," Penny said to Lenox as she too winced at the screeching voice uttering words that should be thrown out of the English language altogether.

Okay, that might be harsh, since it wasn't the words' fault that they were haphazardly thrown together in the proverbial leaky boat that had been sent out to sea during a massive storm, to face a terrible watery death.

"Yeah, want to hear the other poets up next? They may be not so bad," Lenox remarked but Penny already appeared to be on the verge of running away.

Picking up her coffee cup and downing the latte in three successive gulps, Penny shook her head vehemently in response. Letting out a sigh of relief, Lenox downed his drink before they both got up abruptly and left, feeling the glares of other patrons at the disturbance, though neither cared a whit about it.

Laughing together once they were out in the open, Penny and Lenox linked hands and looked at each other.

"Okay, you can strike poetry readings off my list, Lenox. I can respect art but I wouldn't listen to it again for all the money in the world."

"Fair dues and I will happily strike that one off, love," Lenox agreed readily, ever thankful that another poetry reading was not in his future.

"So, what do you want to do instead?" Lenox asked Penny not willing to call it a night yet.

"I dunno, you want to walk around for a bit and see what's around here?"

Lenox agreed, and they began to walk down the street together, enjoying the cool early evening breeze as they took in the local sights. Eventually, they stumbled across a strangely named pub that peaked both their interest.

"*The Die is Cast*? Ooh! Sounds rather ominous, wanna give it a go?" Penny asked Lenox.

Lenox snorted, "Should I be worried that you like looking for trouble?"

Penny impishly grinned. "What can I say? I don't like being

bored."

"Fair enough," Lenox replied before he opened the door for her.

Penny wandered in and was slightly disappointed to find out that the nearly empty pub wasn't a secret fight club. However, soon the warm atmosphere of the place appealed to her and she eagerly walked in.

"Can I help you?" a man from the bar called out.

"Ah, sorry, is this a private club or something?" Penny asked him while looking around and spotting the numerous board games and memorabilia that lay on the shelves.

"No, this place is a public establishment, though I take it this is your first time here."

Penny and Lenox nodded.

"Well, this place is meant for people to come and enjoy games of the past and present in a pub setting. So we rent tables by the hour and you're welcome to bring your own games or borrow any of the ones on the shelves over there. We also have an assortment of standard pub drinks and food, alongside locally made micro-brew ales."

Want to rent a table love? Lenox telepathically asked.

Sounds like fun! Ooh! I want to try the Lavender mead micro-brew thingy from the ale list, too. Hmm what kind of game are you up for? Battleship, maybe? Penny asked, already looking at the board games with avid interest.

I'm up for a game of Battleship, Lenox agreed before he walked to the bar to purchase a table and a couple of drinks.

Penny picked up the game cautiously, though she was happy to sense no evil residual energy from the game before walking over to a table tucked in a corner and set it up. Lenox soon followed her, sitting down with their drinks and watching Penny take a sip.

"Hmm, that's good!" Penny remarked before she offered Lenox a sip.

Gingerly taking one, Lenox grimaced slightly before saying, "Not for me, I'm afraid love but I bet my sister will like it."

Penny nodded in understanding before taking a few more sips

as they began to play. Eventually she got distracted by a small group of people playing an exciting game from a close by table.

Unable to contain her curiosity, Penny blurted out, "Excuse me, sorry to interrupt you but what are you playing? It sounds like loads of fun."

"Dungeons and Dragons, do you and your boyfriend want to join us? We were just about to start a new adventure tonight but we're short a couple of players. We could teach you how to play as we go."

Penny looked back at Lenox excitedly.

He instantly responded with, "We'd love to join you if you don't mind."

Shifting over a table, Penny listened intently to all the instructions given by the three other players as she sipped a new variety of mead.

Then when they finished, they looked at Penny and Lenox.

"Right, I'm ready! How about you, Lenox?"

"Me, too, now let's pick character names, love," Lenox remarked as he rubbed his hands in anticipation.

Much later on, after the pub had closed for the night, Lenox and Penny teleported home, though they deliberately chose to end up on the street in front of their house since they both knew that their family would be waiting inside, given the fact that Lulu had briefly telepathically warned them.

"They invited us back to play Dungeons and Dragons next week! I can't wait!" Penny enthused.

"Me neither; it was a lot of fun, though I've got a random question for you now that I think about it. Why do all the hellhounds call this place the Compound?" Lenox asked barely able to contain his curiosity.

"Huh? Oh... we couldn't decide on a proper name for our town without triggering a huge verbal war, so we just refer to it in a general sense. For the longest time it was just called the Village, then at some point, it became the Fortress until we changed in during the early 1900s to the Compound. Although there was a brief movement in the sixties to call it the Commune."

"I take it your mum led that charge?"

"How did you know?" Penny asked him and then caught his knowing look and sheepishly laughed, "Okay, yes, my mum did and it was totally just to disturb the relative peace during that time because she and my uncle were bored."

"So, why did you choose the Compound?"

"We're sort of loosely military-ish. Okay, not really since hellhounds are as unruly as they come. However, I can't give you a halfway decent answer, beyond the fact that it just fit and still does. Also most people recognize the Compound as the home of the hellhounds."

"Why not say you're from the Isle of Terriana?" Lenox asked her, interested in knowing why the hounds didn't say that instead because the Compound was part of the Island home of the animalia. Lenox was quite stunned by Penny's answer.

"Because it's not where I'm from since the Compound isn't part of Terriana. It actually inhabits the area between Terriana and it's so-called sister Island Celestial Inlet, the home of the ritana. Though very few people know the truth and it was done on purpose. After all, back when the Animalia first took over Terriana they were mercenaries and we hellhounds set up shop between them and the ritana so that they couldn't be enslaved or exploited."

Lenox nodded, "Wow, I'm very thankful that the hounds protect Celestial Inlet because I know of the peaceful happy lives that the Ritana are able to live there and nowhere else for too many want to exploit them. I'm also very thankful that the hellhounds have kept evil in check for all these years because if not for you lot, this world would have been a vastly different place, and I shudder to think of it."

"The hounds aren't the only species that keep others in check, Lenox. Your father's people, the vampyr, have been doing that as well for a long time."

"Not nearly as long as the hounds because it wasn't until my Aunt and Uncle took the throne and then led a fake civil war against each other in order to rid the vampyrs of the majority of the wicked nobles, that we have been known as protectors, not enslavers."

"Hold on. Fake civil war? Why have I never heard that story?"

"Well, like the hounds, we have our secrets and the fact that the civil war was fake, was a big one. Anyway, as you know, my Aunt Raven was born queen and was supposed to take over the crown when she was two thousand years old since Iberius was suppose to hold the role for her because he was deemed untrustworthy. However, Aunt Raven didn't want the crown, so she dragged her feet for nearly a thousand years before, unfortunately, an entire vampyr village was massacred by Iberius and his subordinates. My aunt was hell-bent on seeking revenge but my eldest uncle Wulf said that if she sought that out without proper support, it would lead to her death. Therefore, he devised a plan where Raven and Phoenix who had been long-time lovers at that point, would marry and take over ruling the vampyrs together. However before their happy united reign began they would wage war against each other because that would force Iberius' followers, the nobles, to openly pick a side, which would then let the opposing royals kill them for going against them. This effectively purged the vampyr kingdom of the most wicked and set themselves up as bloody no-nonsense rulers, which silenced a lot of evil rebellions."

"That still seems like a convoluted plan. I mean, why would the followers pick sides at all? Why not create a third option of seizing power and killing both? It's not something I do but that's what evil villains do all the time."

"I see your point. However weak greedy fools don't look at things in a sensible fashion. They just want power and influence without having to do any hard work. Therefore to that end, the easiest option would be to back one of the two rulers, then wait until one of them died before revolting. Besides, no one liked Iberius as a king, not even the worst of the worst, so seeing him ousted was by no means, a hardship for them."

"Wow, royal life sounds nuts to me," Penny muttered, not understanding why anyone would subject themselves to all of this nonsense.

"Oh, it's completely full on nuts, pet," a male voice said

cheerfully from the dark, and Penny immediately recognized the man as Lenox's Uncle Phoenix, who was the King of the Vampyr.

"Seriously, Phoenix!" Raven, Phoenix's wife scolded from nearby.

"What? Going to vampyr court back then wasn't a thing I would inflict upon my worst enemy, and that's got to say a lot right there. It also didn't get much better when we took over because we still had to pretend to like all those backstabbers and that thought hurts my stomach even now, ugh. Though I much prefer my life these days where I can just do what I want and be damned the consequences."

"Don't listen to him, Penny, we're not that bloodthirsty, really," Raven remarked.

"Sure we are, we're bloody Vampyr Royals, love," Phoenix retorted.

"Says that man who only calls himself king when he wants to piss someone off," Raven muttered, shaking her head at him.

"What? I don't need a fancy title to let people know who I am anymore. Most people know me by name or sight alone, now."

Penny frowned, "But, I thought you were the King and Queen of the Vampyr? Are you no longer?"

Raven sighed.

Lenox was quick to explain everything, "I know this is kind of all confusing, Penny love but my Aunt and Uncle are still King and Queen, though we had to get rid of the whole Vampyr royal court a few year back because we didn't need the support of the nobles to get things done. In fact, we really never needed them, however, we kept them around so we didn't look like we were Iberius."

"I am really confused by the whole royal thing you lot have going on. However, good riddance to all those stupid nobles, no offence, because I never liked them. I also won't lie to you, I killed a few evil Vampyr Courtiers in my lifetime. Though I'm not ashamed and I'll own up to that any day of the week."

"Ah, Penny, we knew when you and any other hellhound did so and we were quite thankful about it. In fact, we just fudged their official death reports by making it known that a wild demon attack or something caused their deaths. Honestly, I can't really recall what I wrote down but it was something to that effect," Raven remarked.

"You covered up the courtiers deaths for us?" Penny asked.

"Oh yeah, otherwise, the idiots would have wanted to wage war on you and we wouldn't have stood for that. However, if we fought against them at the time, then we couldn't have protected the Fae from the evil Wretch and they would have been all murdered. Good Light, everything in the immortal world is an intertwined mess that you have to navigate carefully so not to cause lasting damage," Raven explained.

"True story, though I like that, that stuff is mostly sorted and I now get to hang out openly with the hounds on Friday nights and get into some mischief." Phoenix remarked.

"Um... not to sound like a jerk, Phoenix but why are you here then? I mean, at this hour everyone should still be at our fight club," Penny pointed out.

"Correction, that was where everyone was but plans changed," Phoenix responded cheerfully.

"Plans have changed? What do you mean?" Penny stopped and telepathically reached out to her mum, wondering what was going on.

Almost instantly, her mum appeared with Penny's dad and her uncle Alfie.

"Mum, what's going on?" Penny asked instantly.

"Well, you ran away with Lenox before I could take any pictures, honey and that's not very nice. Not nice at all in fact."

"But it was our first date, mum!"

"I know, sweetie," Ally remarked before adding, "But still there are certain things that we parents get to do. By which I mean, your dad gets to threaten Lenox and I get to be over-emotional about my baby growing up."

"And I get to be amused at their daftness," Alfie added with a shrug.

Ally rolled her eyes at her twin before continuing, "However, none of that occurred. So we decided to wait for you until you returned to talk to you about this. Though your dad had some hellhound pack business to conduct during that time, so he told everyone to come here. As the hounds droned on about daily problems, I got bored and chose to watch movies in the theatre. Unfortunately, after the hounds wondered why I wasn't making any kerfuffles and found me in your awesome personal cinema, word spread. And well... the theatre's packed now with hellhounds and there's no getting rid of anyone until morning."

"Why?" Penny demanded out loud, wondering how this insanity could be her real life.

"It's okay, love," Lenox soothed.

"It's not okay! This is ridiculous! I apparently can't go and enjoy a night out without—" Penny stopped when she felt Lenox lips upon hers. Stunned, she didn't move as he kissed her briefly and cupped her face gently while looking deeply into her eyes.

"It's going to be okay because the night is still young and we can still go out. In fact, I didn't want the night to end and this kind of gives us the opportunity to go to Johnny's cafe and get a cuppa tea before going mini putting at the giant play place."

"I haven't been mini putting in ages," Penny admitted breathless as her ire seemed all but
forgotten. Then it came back, "But what about our overrun home, Lenox?"

Without turning away from Penny, Lenox asked Ally, "Ally will you watch over our home and make sure—"

"Without question! Rest assured, they will also keep your home clean or feel my wrath!" Ally retorted instantly.

"Then we've got nothing to worry about love. Your mum and dad will take care of our home and the hellhounds..."

"And vampyrs! Hey, I want to be invited out, too!" Raven declared when everyone looked at her.

"You are welcome in our home, Aunt Raven, no worries. Anyway, love, they can watch movies in our theatre until morning then we get our house back. How does that sound?"

"Why do you have to be so reasonable," Penny huffed out with an amused expression on her face, no longer mad since her parents had actually done her a favour and prolonged a wonderful night out with Lenox.

"I've always been that way, love. Besides I won't lie, this works out in my favour since I wanted to spend more time with you alone anyway," Lenox admitted with a warm smile.

"See here, you!" Sebastian erupted instantly but stopped when Lenox spoke again.

"Sebastian, I swear to you that I will never do wrong by Penny at all, ever. Though if it makes you happy, I will fully listen to you later on because Penny means the world to me truly."

"Lenox!" Penny squealed in delight at his very open admission though her happy mind couldn't find the proper words to say in response.

Lenox winked at her response to show that he well knew her feelings before offering his hand to her this time. Penny immediately took it and with shouts erupting all around them, they ran off down the street together in a joint blissful daze of true love and happiness.

Chapter Eighteen

The following Monday, Penny curled up on a couch in her office next to Lenox with a cup of tea in hand, staring at the fireplace, enjoying some peace.

"Lulu told me yesterday that we went to the wrong poetry reading. Apparently, the one we attended was given by a woman whose poetry is notoriously bad. However despite that, she has a huge Twitter following, which is why she still gets gigs. … whatever that means," Penny told Lenox.

"You don't know about Twitter?" Lenox asked, amused.

"Is it something to do with the internet? Because if it is, despite being a great lover of drama, I've got no patience for the online kind. Honestly, the only reason I have a Facebook account is because my mum nagged me to have one. To which, I dutiful post a once a month update on my life but otherwise, I'm only on it to farm my farm in one of the game apps."

"You have a Facebook farm?"

"Yeah and I know it's lame but I like feeding and caring for the virtual animals."

"It's not lame, Penny and I only asked because I'm curious about farm games. Lou says I need to stay away from them because bingo is the only game worth playing online, however I've been thinking of building a little virtual farm because I kind of miss tending to a real one."

"You've tended a farm before?" Penny asked, intrigued.

"Yeah, though it was more of a vegetable farm since the only livestock I had was a cow that my mum named Sweet Marie."

"What happened to your farm?"

"I sold it when people started to become suspicious of me. I mean, you can really only keep to yourself for so long before people start thinking you're a hermit or a witch. Though don't be sad, when I get the itch to tend to a farm, I normally go to my parents' home and help my mother with her extensive gardens. Nonetheless, I miss growing vegetables from time to time since mum doesn't like growing them for some reason. I've also tried growing veggies in a conservatory but it's not the same. They need real sunlight, water and good soil to which I will say, I have yet to find a piece of land that contains all three."

"I confess I'm no good with plants in any way, shape or form. However, there is a large plot of mud in the backyard that you are more than welcome to work with. I mean, I've been told the soil is great for growing stuff but grass doesn't even seem to like me, hence the mud."

"I'll give it a go in the springtime then, love, since it's a bit late to plant now. Besides, Falcon has been asking me to start a new project for him, for the past few months."

"Oh?" Penny asked.

"Yeah, he wants to build an amusement park in Moonlight Valley but I'm at a bit of a loss. I mean, I want it to be a fun place that will appeal to everyone but I also want to make sure that it doesn't overwhelm the Ritana, Zanthe and White Snakes."

"Yeah, I understand. It would be hard to be in an amusement park as an empath since you're bound to be overwhelmed by everyone's emotions, though I have an idea regarding that."

"What's that, love?"

"Well… have you ever tried to instill your powers as a null into items?" Penny asked him.

"No…" Lenox admitted as it dawned on him that it would work, but then another thought occurred to him. "It would take a lot of energy and time to instill my magic into enough items for it to work."

"Yes, however, I don't believe it will be a problem for you, Lenox, because I believe you're a lot more powerful than you let on. In fact, I'm pretty sure you dramatically downplay your abilities."

Lenox went quiet.

"You're not alone in that, Lenox, because I do it, too. Hell, we probably have been taught to do so for the same reason— not to attract the attention of others."

Lenox nodded. "Yeah, that's true. My dad was worried that if Iberius or Ateria, my paternal grandmother, knew what Lou and I could really do, then they'd exploit it. In fact, they both tried it to exploit us once albeit for a different reason when they kidnapped me and Lou…"

"Your grandparents kidnapped you?"

"I don't consider them family for a reason, love," Lenox responded, letting out a mirthless laugh.

"But Lenox…"

Lenox shook his head, "Not everyone in the world is nice, Pen and I know you know that. However, in Iberius' and Ateria's case, their evil was driven by greed and madness, which doesn't excuse what they've done by any means. However, it made them predictable in a sense because we knew that they were always out to hurt us. Though speaking of the kidnapping incidents, Ateria was actually the one who had me kidnapped when I was stupidly weak. I had spent a great deal of energy trying to save people caught up in the path of a terrible storm and I forgot to protect myself from being swamped by their emotions when my magic was at its lowest. Luckily for me, my maternal grandfather rescued me and took me to the Ancient Glen to heal. Unfortunately, my dad didn't know that and it cost him dearly. Also, as an unintended consequence, Lulu was weakened, too and about a year later when we thought we were fully healed, she was kidnapped by Iberius which also cost my dad dearly again. After that happened, Lulu and I swore to never be weak again, so we secretly went out to learn how to properly use our powers so that it wouldn't drain us to the point of weakness. We found a way alright but that too nearly didn't go well and it became the incident that I can't fully speak of. Sorry love, I really want to tell you but I can't yet. Please don't be mad."

"I'm not, Lenox, and besides… my memories of what happened last week with the demons are starting to come back to me."

"Good Light, that's too soon!" Lenox whispered in horror.

Penny shrugged. "I think it's because I've faced something similar in my past and I, too, can't speak of it either right now.

However, the only thing I really remember is, brushing against the demon's mind. I mean, I could clearly see a terrible longing within it to annihilate all life; I also saw the wicked choices of others that brought it forth into our world and the echoing pain of millions of people suffered. That was what caused me to throw caution to the win and unleash my true power in order to deal the demon proper justice. Though amoungst my anger I felt something else; this sort of calming influence, for a lack of a better term, that didn't speak any words to me but still its silence tells me volumes. It essentially told me not to let my anger get out of control because it would feed the demon and weaken me; It tells me that the only way to win is to return the monster to the place from whence it came and then… and then, it both showed me and helped me, do exactly that. That influence I felt was you, Lenox, wasn't it?"

Saying nothing, Lenox slowly nodded.

"I'm not guessing at the secret you keep but you and Lulu have dealt with a demon from that level of hell before, haven't you? After all, you couldn't have shown me nor helped me defeat that demon without having done so in the first place, no?"

Lenox said nothing for a long moment before he finally whispered, "You are a very brilliant lady, Penny."

Penny shrugged slightly, "So I've been told but often I just find myself plagued with more questions than answers and doesn't being smart mean that you hold the answer to everything?"

Lenox shook his head, "No, Penny, being smart is the ability to know that answers you seek will never be the easiest to find yet you're still willing to look for them nonetheless."

"Huh… sounds troublesome, well whatever, can't say that I would ever choose to shy away from trouble, now can I?"

Lenox let out a small snort, "No, I doubt you can, love but trouble and I are like old friends, too. Though again, we'll just take this all one day at a time."

Penny nodded as they fell into a comfortable silence, both staring into the fire in front of them. A few minutes later there was a soft knock on the door. Reaching out with her magic to see who it was, Penny smiled, then jumped up from the couch.

"Aunt Callie!" Penny cried out as she raced over to the door and opened it.

Lenox stood up, too, and noticed a tiny woman standing just over five feet in height, enter the room. She had long, naturally golden streaked dark hair that fell nearly to her waist in a single braid. She wore a smart cream coloured business suit that was decorated with a small gold belt around her middle. Slightly behind her stood a man Lenox had met numerous times in the past, Memphis Halsin, Callie's husband, who couldn't be dressed more differently than his wife. He sported dark green hair that was shaved on both sides, though it was long on top and slicked back. He also wore a thick black leather jacket, black jeans, black combat boots and a black T-shirt with a logo on it. Though the pattern was obscured by a bright pink child carrier strapped to his chest, which held a small infant that could barely be seen from the cradle of her father's protective arms.

Memphis strode past his wife towards Lenox and clasped hands with him.

"What's up, Lenox?" Memphis greeted him briefly before going back to holding his daughter.

"Nothing much and you?" Lenox replied.

"Well, I was getting a tiny bit bored and then low and behold, Callie and I heard about some trouble going on with the hounds recently, so—"

"Memphis!" Callie hissed, shaking her head at her husband in mild dismay before she looked back at Penny and continued, "We did hear of a spot of trouble with the hounds, my dear but that is not why we are here. I want to see you and congratulate you for following your dreams."

"Thanks, Aunt Callie, and please meet my mate and fiancée, Lenox Moregan. Lenox, love, meet my aunt, Callie Kalomahaya-Halsin, who is best friends with my mum and dad."

"Hold on! What about me? Am I chopped liver or something?" Memphis demanded at the lack of introductions.

"Yes," Callie instantly retorted with a bright smile as she, too, crossed the room to shake hands with Lenox.

"Thanks for that, kitty cat," Memphis snorted, rolling his eyes.

"You're welcome, doggy," Callie responded in Indonesian.

Lenox shook hands with Callie, who looked at him for a long moment before smiling widely again.

"You've found a great soul mate, Penny and I am truly happy for you," Callie responded in Indonesian again.

"Thank you," Lenox said in the same language.

Callie said nothing as she continued to smile at him, though Memphis was quick to let out a small cough to cover his chuckles.

"So have you two eaten breakfast yet?" Callie asked, pulling a face at her mate who winked at her in response.

"Not yet, we were going to eat at the staff dining room soon. However, there is a nice cafe in town we could eat in."

"Do they have vegetarian options?" Memphis asked immediately.

"Oh yes, my sister doesn't eat meat, so we're known to haunt many vegetarian cafes around Cambridge. Though this one will be a good blend of both meat and vegetarian options since I know Penny's mum and uncle will be probably joining us for breakfast soon."

"Is your mum here often, Penny?" Callie asked in amusement knowing her friend well.

"Every day," Penny confirmed before adding, "She even has her own small lab here now."

"How'd she manage to get a lab here? Don't you have to be a full professor or something?" Memphis demanded.

"Well it's not her own lab. I gave her a small part of my research lab so she and Uncle Alfie can have a place to tinker around in when they come to visit, which does keep incidents down to a bare minimum. They also get this corner in my office," Penny said as she pointed to a five-foot table tucked into the corner that was stacked with books and puzzles.

"Don't they drive you nuts being so close all the time, Penny?" Memphis asked.

Penny shook her head, "No, never. I like how close I am with them and they more or less visit to make sure I'm okay, which is nice.

Mum has also laid down the laws of etiquette for all the hellhounds who happen to come here for whatever reason because she wants to make sure that no one does anything that would jeopardize my position here. Not that any of them would because all the hounds are very supportive of me. "

"That's not surprising, Penny. For despite what any idiot has ever said about you in the past, there are a great many hounds who greatly respect you. Unfortunately, the ones who say positive things are often drowned out by those who say hateful things because the idiots happen to have louder voices, or at the very least that is how it will always sound to us," Callie remarked.

Penny didn't say anything as she could see the wholehearted truth in Callie's words.

"Uh, so what about Ally..." Memphis started to say, breaking the silence before stopping as if trying to find the right words.

"Mum is quite calm here, Memphis," Penny admitted. "She spends most of her time not in the lab but reading scientific journals from the library when I'm lecturing. The puzzle books are Uncle Alfie's. The rest of my family is here, too; my cousin Lucy is my secretary, my Uncle Reggie has taken over as my academic advisor. Meanwhile, my Aunt Yuna uses the computer over in the far corner to familiarize herself with the world. In fact, only my dad doesn't spend much time in my office, for he'll come here from time to time to see my mum or me but the rest of the time, he goes to the main security office to make sure everything is on the up and up."

Callie nodded, "That's a good set up. I like it."

"It is?" Memphis asked, looking stunned.

Callie nodded again. "Yes it is, *tercinta,* and when our little Starla grows up and decides which human university she wants to go to, then I wish to have a similar set up in place to protect her."

"Huh… don't worry, my sweet Starla, daddy is going to make sure your *mami* doesn't go in to full-on overprotective mama kitty mode for the rest of your life," Memphis crooned to the sleeping baby tucked against his chest.

Callie rolled her eyes. "You will be just as bad, doggy, for not even moments ago, you hid our daughter from view with your jacket as soon as we teleported to this place."

"I wasn't hiding her from view. I was merely making sure she was warm since England is super chilly for fall compared to our home on the island of Terriana, which is currently floating somewhere in the South Pacific."

Callie snorted as if to say, *you fool no one.*

"Anyway, breakfast?" Memphis said.

"Ooh, yes! Though can we teleport in near the town centre then walk? Sorry, but I need a bit of fresh air," Penny said.

"Don't be sorry, love, that sounds lovely. Are you two game?"

"Despite the fact that it's probably frigid cold outside, yes," Memphis agreed sarcastically.

"Can't take a little bit of cold?" Callie snorted.

"Hey, kitty cat, I'm from Chicago, I know cold real well. However, I've become acclimatized to the tropics these past few years, so sue me for thinking that England in autumn is going to be frigid cold," Memphis retorted.

"Well, I have lived in those same tropics for many centuries yet a little crispy English morning air has never bothered me because I remember to regulate my body temperature with magic, unlike a certain whiny doggy I know."

Memphis pulled a face in response as he remembered he could do that. Lenox seized on the brief moment to teleport them to a safe spot next to the river a short walk from the café that he had in mind.

"You have all the magic in the known universe and yet, you still forget to regulate your body temperature. Well, that's my husband for you," Callie muttered with a sigh seconds later.

"I, a- do not have all the power in the known universe, and b - can't be the only one who forgets to do so from time to time."

"You, a- do so, and b- are too," Callie retorted sweetly.

"Oh, hey do you smell that? Is that scent Lily of the Valley, Lenox?" Penny asked, cutting in before the bickering Minotaurs could continue further.

"A variety of it, yes. I'm pretty sure that's a Rosea," Lenox said as he identified the scent.

"What's the difference?" Memphis asked.

"Memphis!" Callie hissed softly.

"What?"

"It's okay, Callie, I am not offended by Memphis' question and to answer it, the Rosea Lily of the Valley is pink in colour, which differs from most Lily of the Valleys since they are white."

Penny perked up when she heard the flower was pink, causing Lenox to bite his lip to keep from smiling. Instead he walked towards the scent that was ten feet away and he picked a small bloom and then headed back towards her. Penny started to move towards him but stopped when Lenox cocked his head, frowning.

"Len—" Penny started to say.

Suddenly, Lenox moved at preternatural speed and knocked her to the ground, covering her body with his.

"Wha— No!" Penny screamed when she felt Lenox being pulled away from her into a large cloud of black dust.

"Oh, hell no!" Memphis roared from behind her.

Callie was the first to react. Sprouting wings immediately, she attempted to take to the sky to go after Lenox but the second she lifted off the ground, an unseen force pinned her down. Memphis moved quickly, grasping his wife's hand and used their intertwined magic to break free of the trap.

"How can this be? We are both limitless Minotaurs, yet our magic won't work on this beast. It's feels like it is not real, although I feel it. I am so confused," Callie wondered out loud as she realized that her powers and her mate's, wouldn't be able to take on this foe.

Penny said nothing as she watched Lenox be pulled further and further away from her. Then she suddenly let out a howl of rage and hit the ground in full hound form, taking off after him.

"Not alone, Penny!" Callie cried out before she took her secondary animal form, a griffin and chased after her.

Penny ignored her as she focused intently on Lenox and killing the cloud that had him in its grasp.

Penny love, I will be okay but you need to calm down, Lenox mentally reached out to her.

Be calm? Now? No way!

Please love, things need to be done in a set sequence in order to defeat this beast and to start off, you need to let go of your angry because your fuelling it.

Can't! Penny howled as her hellhound instincts were taking over more and more.

Suddenly Penny felt a wave of calming magic admit from Lenox mentally. Penny first attempted to shrug it off, irritated at the attempt to 'calm' her down but then, her inner hellhound finally reacted to the magic and the rest of the world came into focus again.

As soon as it did, Penny felt Lulu reached out to her.

Penny, please hear me, Lulu pleaded.

Lulu? So. Mad. Penny snarled, too pissed off to form full sentences.

I know, honey but I also know how to defeat the Kulcair and save Lenox, too. Though I need you on side.

How?

Get in the car behind you and I'll explain. Please, Penny, please do this for me.

Penny howled loudly before she leapt backwards much like she had felt her Aunt Callie had, only she purposely landed on top of the car in a half- hound, half-human form, holding onto the roof with one hand.

How? Penny asked again Lulu, still too emotional to fully speak.

Memphis and Callie will take out the invisible tentacles that protect the Kulcair with special made weapons. Once that's done, phase two will begin.

Phase two? Penny questioned.

Lulu told her what phase two entailed.

And that leaves me as phase three, right?

Without question, Lulu answered.

Okay, Penny agreed as she felt her anger and ire rise at being so inactive for the time being.

Penny, love, please calm down. I know your anger is justified, but still— Lenox reached out to her.

How can you say that? Penny declared, interrupting him.

I say it because it needs to be said. You need to stay calm, love, since Kulcair are ghost demons that feed on pain, rage and fear. Right now, I am giving it nothing as an emotional null, however, it still stays ever-powerful because you are mad and Lulu is fearful. Though Lulu's fear is fading as each skull disappear, it will all be for naught if you stay angry.

Penny used her magic to pin herself to the roof of the car as she sat down cross-legged in her full human form. Taking a deep breath in, Penny closed her eyes and focused on the violent anger within herself. In her mind's eye, Penny saw her anger appear as a wild uncontrollable fire twister. Breathing deeply, she focused on slowly extinguishing it by using the pattern of the repeating breaths to calm herself down to the point that she was utterly serene.

"Hold on. I thought you said hellhounds don't meditate, Callie!" Memphis called out to his wife, breaking into Penny's thoughts seconds after the technique worked.

"Most don't but Penny has always been an exceptional hound. Good job, *keponakan*," Callie replied, calling Penny, niece in Indonesian.

"I learned from the best, *bibi*," Penny said calling Callie, her aunt in the same language.

"Good. Now quit slacking, *tercinta. W*e've got three skulls left and I shall bet you ten dollars that I will hit more of them than you," Callie called.

"Pfft as if," Memphis retorted as he fired, though true to form, Callie beat him to it and took out all three remaining skulls.

"Really, Callie?"

"Yes, really. Pay up, *anjing*," Callie retorted, calling her husband doggy instead of darling in Indonesian.

Which wasn't an insult given the fact that Memphis' secondary animal form was a Bull Mastiff.

"Lulu..." Penny called out, wanting to know when phase two would begin but Lenox reached out to her telepathically.

It's okay Penny. It'll be okay, Lenox reassured her.

It's— Penny stopped when she saw a large Viking Warrior

riding on top of a massive white wolf.

Lulu had warned her about his arrival, yet Penny was still stunned to see the man ride towards the demon at speeds she couldn't even muster in full hound form. Suddenly, the Wolf leapt up and did a weird flip, launching the Viking from his back before disappearing in a fine wintry mist.

A loud guttural roar filled the air just as the Viking speared the demon, then slashed the beast with a sword, and freed Lenox from its grasp.

Lenox and the Viking fell towards the ground, as a massive gust of wind that was magically directed by the Minotaurs, caught them and brought them safely to the ground.

Lulu stopped the car and Penny got off the roof. Then for the first time in her life, Penny didn't care about finishing the fight with the beast as she ran to Lenox threw her arms around him, when he was firmly on the ground.

"You alright?" Penny asked immediately.

Lenox nodded earnestly.

"Don't ever do that again! You scared me half to death!" Penny exclaimed before Lenox cut her off with a kiss.

"Please, love, I know you're angry but I had to do it and I'll explain later because we've got to finish it off now."

Penny turned her head back towards the dark miasma-like beast with no distinguishing features.

"I can deal with this as I would normally now, right?" Penny asked him.

Lenox mentally agreed.

Penny snarled as she shifted back into her hellhound form and launched herself at the demon using her claws, fangs and hellfire to get her pound of flesh. While she ripped into the beast, Penny's mind kept focusing on how close she had been to losing Lenox and that fuelled her with different need altogether as she wanted to cement their bond.

Her interest lost in drawing out the fight, Penny killed the demon by shredding it into tiny pieces before she turned her attention back fully to Lenox. Shifting to her human form one last time, Penny single-mindlessly headed in Lenox's direction.

Lenox frowned when he saw the animalistic glint in Penny's eyes but assumed it was due to her recently finishing the fight. So decided to introduce his best friend Tyr Andraste, to her.

"Ah, Penny love, meet Tyr Andraste—" Lenox started but didn't finish when Penny launched herself at him.

Penny knocked him down to the ground and started to rub her upper body against his in a feverish motion. Instantly, Lenox teleported them away since he had a very good idea where this was heading.

Penny? Lenox asked, as he felt her lips on his, kissing him in earnest.

Penny love—

"No, Lenox! Don't reject me! I need to mate with you so bad, it hurts! Oh Light! I've gone feral," Penny growled and whined at him in full-blown need, as her inner hellhound instincts took complete control of her.

"Feral?" Lenox asked.

"I can't say... what that... ugh! Need you, Lenox, please," Penny whined.

"Penny, love, are you in heat?"

"Yes!"

"Penny, I must know with absolute certainty, do you truly want this? "

Penny took a few deep breaths as she fought down her inner beast, before she looked Lenox square in the eye, "I'm not utterly mindless, Lenox. I want you as both the woman who loves you and shifter in full-blown heat for her soulmate."

"Right... I'll take care of you, love but be warned that when we do this, you are mine forever. I want a full soul bond," Lenox replied as his full immortal nature started to come out in response to Penny's heat.

Penny paused before the brightest smile lit up her face, "We can full soul-bond for real? I want that! But how?"

Lenox smiled at her and whispered, "Shh... trust me."

Penny nodded slowly, saying no more when Lenox carried

her off to their bedroom.

*****

Lulu watched her twin disappear with a full-blown in-heat Penny, causing a smile to draw upon
her lips. A few seconds later, Tyr walked up to her looking bemused.

"You know what's coming right?"

Lulu nodded, saying no more as she saw Sebastian, Ally and Alfie appeared.

"What the hell just happened? Where's Penny?" Sebastian demanded instantly.

"Yes where is Penny... wait," Ally muttered as she picked up a scent in the air and looked astounded.

Lulu smiled at her, "Yes, Penny did go into heat."

"No way!" Sebastian snarled.

Ally rolled her eyes as she laid a hand on her mate, "Relax, Bas. We knew this would happen, besides it looks like Lulu got something really important to tell us."

"How'd you know that?"

Ally rolled her eyes again as Alfie retorted, "Shut up and listen Bas. On you go sweetie, we're all ears now."

Lulu briefly looked at Tyr who nodded at her, before she opened her mouth and spoke.

"You may believe that Penny's living on borrowed time now that the Niners have decided to make their move to conquer this realm again but that is not the case."

"How?" Ally whispered, "How can you be so sure Lulu?"

"Simple, the Wild Hunt will rise up before then."

"The what?" Sebastian asked.

"The Wild Hunt? The. Hunt. That one?" Alfie demanded in pure astonishment.

"I don't get it. What is the hunt?" Sebastian asked.

"Bas, the hunt is an army designed to back the Huntress, though more importantly, the Hunt contains two Sentinels who-"

Ally broke off and cursed when she saw Lulu just smile in

response.

"You?"

Lulu nodded.

"And Lenox?"

Lulu nodded again.

Ally let out a sob as she flung her arms around Lulu.

"It's going to be alright now Ally, I promise. Though come, let's go speak in private and I'll explain everything in more detail to you. You two, Callie and Memphis, for you will always have roles to play here."

With that Lulu teleported everyone to her home on Ormeglo. Smiling at her scowling mate who met them in the front hall, Lulu immediately hugged her.

"Everything's going to be right as rain, my love," Lulu said in Irish Gaelic.

"It better be! Or I will unleash pure holy hell on everyone!"

"Please trust in me."

Freya huffed, "I do, you know that and before you even say it, I wholeheartedly trust Lenox too, but is it too much to ask for the apocalypse not to happen every other year?"

Lulu shrugged, "We live in precarious times, love, things are bound to happen."

"Lulu!"

"It's the truth and can you not, stress out the hellhounds anymore? I swear Freya, you can be such a Negative Nancy when it comes to apocalyptic situations. Now everyone sit, the kettle is on and we've got much to discuss."

"Lulu?" Alfie called out.

"Yes?"

"You and Lenox may seem all friendly and serene but you both are pretty badass, aren't you?"

"You don't even know that half of it," Lulu said sunnily before she summoned up a kettle and began pouring cups of tea for everyone.

Chapter Nineteen

Penny awoke slowly in Lenox's arms later on in the day. Yawning, she stretched and then settled against his chest.

"You alright, Penny?" Lenox asked softly, coming awake at the same time.

"Oh yeah… though I can't believe that a few weeks ago, I passed out at the sight of your bare chest and then today, I all but threw myself at you like a hussy," Penny replied.

"You're no hussy, Penniah, not at all."

Penny looked up at Lenox's serious expression, "Thanks, though I am sorry about not warning you about mating heat."

"Well, I'm sorry I didn't mention Kulcairs before, so I believe we're even, love," Lenox reasoned.

Penny gently thumped his chest when he finished speaking.

"What?"

"You know what! You just reminded me you put yourself in grave danger! Never again!" Penny declared.

"I wasn't in great danger, love, though you would have been."

Penny sat up and looked down at Lenox with a scowl, "Explain."

Lenox let out a groan, "Don't think I can focus on that right now, love."

"Why not?" Penny demanded

"Because your natural charms are very arousing, as it were."

"Oh… oops," Penny said as she realized she completely bared her chest to him and crossed her arms to cover herself.

Lenox pouted slightly at her action, but Penny merely shook her head, "No hanky panky until you talk."

Lenox burst out into chuckles. "Alright, love, you win. A Kulcair isn't really a demon or a living entity. Instead, it's the accumulation of wicked energy, particularly rage that is dispelled out into the world when an evil being dies. Kulcairs also don't form on their own, for it takes someone well versed in spells to create it for a singular purpose. In this case, I believe someone summoned it to do you harm because the angrier you became, the more damage the Kulcair could inflict upon you. However, being a null, it couldn't harm me and it more or less just held me captive until the energy could be dispersed properly."

"For future reference, how does one do that?"

Lenox sighed. "There are four things needed. The first is that you have to keep strong emotions like fear or anger to an absolute minimum. Secondly, you need a sharpshooter with a special weapon that I've created, to hit its tether points, which often look like ghost-like skulls, and no, I don't know why they look like that. However, despite their look, the tether points are what keeps the Kulcair bound to whoever created them since they gain energy from the beast and which they often use to fuel it with because it takes quite a lot magic to form the beast. Now once the tether points are gone, you need a curse breaker with berserker traits, to which I will say that Tyr is the only one because no one else has figured out how to combine both traits and that is key. After all, by going into a berserker rage, he can do massive damage with his curse-breaking spell, which often knocks the summoner out and in turn, stops them from recalling the beast to them and reusing it for another purpose at a later point. Lastly, you have to disperse the negative energy with pure energy quickly because often, when a Kulcair is in its death throes it will attract stronger demons."

Penny looked slightly alarmed but Lenox telepathically soothed her. "There was no time for that to happen this time because the summoner must have been extremely overconfident or a complete and utter idiot. I believe it was 50-50 to be quite honest."

"What?"

"It's true, the summoner used a ton of magic and they've got to be desperately weak now."

Penny frowned when she picked up a thought in Lenox's mind, and she thumped his chest again. "You know who it is!" she accused.

Lenox groaned again. "I do and I wasn't going to keep the

answer from you, honest."

"I know that but I also can see in your mind through our bond that you want to send your cousin Falcon after him. I'm a bloody hellhound, Lenox. I know you want to protect me, but it's super bloody galling to have someone else go in for a kill that should be yours."

Lenox sat up so that they were mere inches apart. Penny felt the mating heat rise within her again. Though trying to stay mad, Penny scowled at him but her heart wasn't in it as she could see Lenox's logic.

"Can we compromise love? I know it's a lot to ask, but the key here is to keep anger at a minimum."

"I can keep myself from being pissed off, Lenox!" Penny declared hotly.

Lenox shook his head slightly. "No love, you can't, especially when you're hunting down a villain who is trying to harm those closest to you, which is wholly understandable. I'm also not asking you to not exact justice either; all I'm truly asking is that we get Falcon to find the summoner and cut off any remaining Kulcair energy before you get to go in for the final kill."

Penny pursed her lips. "That's a very reasonable compromise; however, I'm not the only one you're going to have to talk into this. For my parents and all the hounds will want to be part of the hunt since if you attack one of us, you attack us all."

Lenox nodded in understanding before an idea came to him and telepathically posed the question to Penny.

Penny snorted at the idea. "Do you think it'll work?"

Lenox laughed softly. "Honestly… I dunno but it's worth a shot, right?"

Penny wrapped her arms around Lenox's neck and murmured, "What the hell, let's give it go later. Much later, since we have unfinished business between us."

"We definitely do, love," Lenox agreed before he leaned in for a kiss.

*****

A few hours later, Penny sat next to Lenox in the living room when he made a call. After two rings in, the person in question suddenly teleported into their living room alongside Lenox's Aunt Raven, Uncles Wulf and Felix and his father Conalai.

"Good evening, Lenox and Penny, thought I'd save you the trouble of speaking to me over the phone and teleport here. So what can I do for you?" Lenox's Uncle Phoenix grinned, looking like the cat that ate the canary.

"I have a favour to ask of Uncle Phoenix. Though hold on, I have to know, you aren't mad at me for calling him first are you, dad?" Lenox asked.

"A bit but not for the reason you think. I'm mad that you and your sister didn't tell me about the attack and I had to learn about it from a third-party source."

"Oh, crap!" Penny let out as she realized her parents would probably be pissed over the same thing.

"Relax, Penny, your parents already know since they were my source."

"Oh," Penny muttered before shrugging slightly knowing there was very little that her parents didn't know when it came to fights against any evil in this realm.

"I'm really sorry, Dad," Lenox stated quietly.

Conalai let out a soft sigh and shoved his hands through his hair. "Lenox, you're alright, son. I mean, I get that it wasn't truly an intentional slip on your part and you would have told me soon enough. So don't worry about it. Though tell me, why'd you called your Uncle Phoenix instead of me moments ago?"

"Hold on, that's my question," Phoenix demanded.

Conalai rolled his eyes, not bothering to respond as he focused on his son.

"Well, I needed someone who could directly reason with the hellhounds."

Four out of five of the Vampyr royals looked completely dumbfounded over Lenox's remark.

"Phoenix? Reason? With the hounds? Are you crazy?"

Lenox's Aunt Raven asked incredulously.

"Hey, hey, hey! I can reason with people when it's necessary!" Phoenix returned.

"You can?" Wulf asked before shaking his head. "I've never, ever seen you do it."

"That doesn't mean I can't. Besides, I'll have you know I reason with Iona all the time," Phoenix retorted, calling Lenox's aunt by her real name.

"You do? When?" Raven asked incredulously again.

"I reasoned with you yesterday."

"What are you… that wasn't reasoning with me, you ninny! That was a pure hostile negotiation! You hid my entire horde of chocolate until I agreed to your outrageous demands! I'm still mad about that, too."

"Didn't I make that up to you? I really didn't?" Raven shook her head furiously, "Well, it's on my to-do list, Iona, I promise. Anyway, what am I supposed to be reasoning with the hellhounds about, exactly?"

"Well to start off with, I know who the person behind today's incident is," Lenox said.

"Say no more," Phoenix interrupted, ready to set out.

"No! Please, Uncle Phoenix, hear me out fully."

"Okay, fine," Phoenix retorted in an exaggerated drawl.

"I need you to reason with all the hounds in regards to letting Falcon find the culprit behind the attack today and cut off his supply of dark magic before stepping aside so that Penny can have her kill."

"Are you joking? Why is it that when there's a fight to be had lately, I'm always chopped liver?"

"Why Falcon, son?" Lenox's dad Conalai asked, effectively ignoring Phoenix.

"The beast that attacked us today was Kulcair, Dad; therefore it has to be Falcon because he's the only assassin I now who can fully disengage his emotions like me," Lenox responded.

"Okay, it looks like I'm missing a huge piece of today's tale. After all, all Penny's mum said was that a demon had attempted to kidnap you and that Penny killed it. She also threatened me if I interrupted your personal grand-baby making time, which is not relevant to this conversation but I still thought you should know about it."

"Oh, my Light!" Penny groaned.

Lenox looked stunned before a blush crept up his neck.

Conalai shook his head in mild amusement. "You'll be alright, son. It's a natural part of mating after all."

"Thanks dad but I still kind of want the floor to swallow me whole right now," Lenox muttered before telepathically adding, *I truly don't regret anything Penny but…*

Relax, love, I get it. We're shy folk, you and I, and unfortunately we have relatives who aren't. Though I should also mention you should be prepared for my mum to be as subtle as a bull in a china shop when it comes to our mating. I mean, my mum loves babies, though she could only have me because she was poisoned by a demon not that long after I was born. So expect her to have future grand-babies on the brain. Too bad, I can't bring home any more pets for her because that would have temporarily appeased her. Unfortunately, her maternal instincts make her overzealous with pets to the point that she'll become like that human girl from Tiny Toons. Honestly Aunt Rika always ends up rescuing them from her clutches, though in saying that, she never was like that with me as a child but I believe that's because dad always made sure she didn't.

How about we get her one of those electronic puppies? Lenox asked, trying to think of a solution to a potentially overzealous baby minded mother-in-law.

Ooh, good call love, Penny agreed as she dug out her phone and started searching right away.

"Um… Penny, what are you doing?" Lenox's Uncle Felix questioned.

"I'm looking up electronic puppies for my mum, so she doesn't drive both Lenox and me crazy by being baby mad. Sorry but it's super important."

Felix shrugged as if that made perfect sense.

"So?" Raven prompted Lenox, in order to get them all back on topic.

"We still need Uncle Phoenix to talk the hellhounds into letting Falcon find the villain behind the Kulcair because I do truly believe he can actually reason with them when it comes to these kind of circumstances. Though again, Penny gets to kill the villain."

"Damn right I do. Sorry not sorry," Penny muttered, still looking at her phone while scowling.

"Not damn right, Penny. I want to kill the blighter, too," Conalai retorted.

Penny looked up and scowled at him but Conalai returned the look, causing Penny to acknowledge that that was fair.

"I respect you as Lenox's dad, Conalai and if I weren't so pissed at this blighter for nearly harming Lenox, despite the fact that he says the Kulcair wouldn't have, I'd fully step aside and let you have at him." Penny said, letting out an aggravated sigh. "However, I will compromise and let get your proverbial pound of flesh first, so long as I get to rip the blighter's throat out."

Conalai nodded, "That's a fair offer, Penny. Though why do you think Phoenix will be able to talk the hounds into your plan? Also, I still don't see why your cousin Falcon needs to be involved, son."

"Well, Falcon can hunt with little to no information and he's almost a full emotional null like me which will work in his favour if the villain is trying to create another Kulcair on the spot."

"Well, that's stupid. Why on Earth would anyone do that, when the first one didn't work?" Phoenix demanded.

"I don't know for sure but I believe that the villain is unfortunately more powerful than we first thought and he sent this one as a test for us and not as a direct threat, since he would have backed the Kulcair with a demon horde. So it stands to reason that he has the potential to create another one much stronger to see how we fair against it because he doesn't believe we can defeat him."

Wulf tapped the edge of the couch. "That makes sense because everyone mistakes you and Lulu as weak, despite the fact that you are truly far from that. Also based on what you're saying, I think I know who you believe the villain is, though isn't he dead, Lenox?"

"Who?" Raven asked her brother.

"Lenox believes Triton is behind it," Wulf answered.

Lenox nodded in agreement.

Penny let out a low growl at the mention of his name. "He is dead! He and the other betrayers became demon fodder for the Niner I killed weeks ago."

"He isn't dead, love and I don't know everything yet but he isn't what we thought he was. When I was being held by the Kulcair, I sought out the magical link so that we would know who's behind it and I felt him. Only it wasn't him because the evil power he held was immense and it was as if, the Triton I fought and you 'killed' was merely a puppet for an unknown purpose."

"Well wouldn't the Draggenin of Death be a better choice to find him if he's technically dead? After all, my mum said that a hellhound that kills an innocent has no soul."

"Having no soul doesn't mean dead, love and I don't believe Erebrus could track him without a soul."

Wulf nodded. "Lenox is right. Erebrus tracks people living or dead by their soul, thus being without one would damn near make it impossible to hunt. Though you don't need Falcon to find him since I also have null abilities and I can track him in much the same way as my son can, Lenox. I might be a better choice too because Falcon will probably kill him without telling you, since he does that from time to time, which would probably mess up things with the hounds before Phoenix can speak to them."

"It so would," Penny agreed.

Lenox rubbed Penny's shoulder soothingly and asked his uncle, "Would you mind, Uncle Wulf?"

Wulf shook his head before looking to his siblings. "Absolutely not, Len. I will go with your dad, Aunt Raven and Uncle Felix, since we've hunted idiots like this together a few times before and it is always best to hunt in a group because these kind of villains like to surprise the unwary with a ton of minions. Also, no Phoenix, you're not chopped liver and I will clearly state that I'm not tapping you for this job because we all know you will kill the idiot before hellhounds get a crack at him since you have poor impulse control when it comes to real wicked punters. Not that I think that's a bad thing mind you, it's… ah hell, why am I explaining myself?" Wulf demanded suddenly.

"Well, I say it's because you've been best friends with my husband for over ten millennia and are answering all his usual arguments that he throws your way when you don't let him go on a hunt or an assassin job with you. Anyway, Wulf's right, Phoenix and you've got a role in this fight already since you really are the only one of us who could potentially reason with the hounds. Though you're also going to have to go toe to toe with a few of them too, before they hear you out," Raven stated.

"Well, I'm actually not pissed about that or any of this because I know I'll get to enjoy a pint, some carnage and earn a wee bit of dosh by betting on said fights at the Hellhound Fight Club, while you four slug away to get intel."

"I'm not following you, what fights are you betting on?" Wulf asked, bewildered since he knew you couldn't bet on yourself at the Hellhound Fight Club.

"The fights Falcon is gonna to be in since I'm gonna call him in to be my proxy fighter. Got to take it a wee bit easy; I've got into a few too many of them this week and my old bones are feelin' it."

"What? Falcon's not going to the club because he's out with his kids and wife watching a movie at the theatre," Wulf retorted.

"So?"

"What'd you mean so?"

"I mean what part of anything you just said, means that my nephew can't join me for a pint at fight club and also take on any hellhound I happen to piss off ?"

"You're seriously gonna ask my son to take on pissed off hounds that you angered while you bet on him? Are you joking me, Phoenix?" Wulf demanded coldly.

"Aw, your face is pure priceless, Wulf, my man! I'm obviously gonna do most of my own work, duh. I was really just messing with you and I truly can't believe you bought that. Honestly, me? Back down from a fight? Are you nuts? Though I will need to have Falcon at my back tonight because a pissed off hound is both an epic opponent and a brutal one and I can only imagine how a crowd of them will be."

"Well, normally I'd say that hellhounds aren't as bad as you are making us out to be but I also hate to lie and we are that bad, so good luck," Penny muttered with a shrug, adding her own two cents worth.

"Sorry, Uncle Phoenix," Lenox said, feeling bad at asking his Uncle for his help.

"For what, Len? None of this is a hardship for me. Besides, Falcon got some great stats at the fight club and that works out to great betting odds. So I'm pretty much guaranteed to make a wee payday tonight."

Wulf let out a low sigh.

"Don't get into too many fights until we get back, Phoenix."

"Och, why?" Phoenix demanded, looking peeved.

"Because I'm going to kick your ass later; it's a solid promise."

Phoenix rolled his eyes. "You wish, old man. Now come on, Penny and Len, let's get going. I'll call Falcon. Oh and by the way, have you two set a date for your wedding yet?"

"What?" Lenox asked.

"Come on, man. Have you sorted a date yet for the big day?"

"Don't you start on them, Phoenix, I'll be kicking your arse and all," Conalai retorted.

Phoenix waved his hand dismissing him. "Ah relax, Lai, they're already mated in the eyes of the hounds and they also got a fully soul bonded as far as my Fae soul powers tell me. So at this point, a wedding is only a mere formality and an excuse to have an epic shindig."

"Still, Phoenix, they will…" Raven started though Lenox and Penny weren't listening.

When do you want to get married, love? In the new year or sooner than that? Lenox asked her.

The new year is too far away. I want to have it sooner if that's okay.

Lenox smiled at her, *I'd marry you tomorrow if you want,*

Penny love.

No that's too soon. What about October 13th? I know it's not a Friday this year but it would be cool to have our anniversary on the be-all and end-all of Friday the 13ths in the future.

"Done," Lenox agreed out loud.

"What's done?" Phoenix asked.

"We've chosen our wedding date."

"Well, when is it?" Phoenix demanded gleefully.

Don't tell him, son, Conalai said with a hint of humour. *Let him stew on it for the remainder of the night, and tell him in the morning.*

Okay dad but we've picked October 13th.

Good choice, son. I'm thrilled and I know your mum will be, too, when she hears.

"Hey! I know you're telling your dad secretly, so let me know already," Phoenix complained.

"Hey, husband," Raven called out.

"What?"

"Nope."

"What'd you mean, nope?"

"It means, quit pestering the nephew. He hasn't spoken with his twin or mum about it nor has Penny told her own family. Therefore you'll find out when they're good and ready to tell you and not a moment before."

"Are you kidding me?" Phoenix exclaimed.

Raven shook her head. "I'm not, Phoenix, everyone is entitled to a non-ruined surprise and we all know you like to blab things from time to time."

Phoenix sighed. "Fine but you all owe me."

"Do we what!" Wulf retorted. "You're going to bet money on my son in a fight tonight."

"Only because he's a sure thing, Wulf."

"Not against my dad," Penny stated at once.

"He is so," Wulf retorted before sheepishly agreeing, "Alright, maybe no, given the fact that your dad is the leader of the hellhounds. Anyway, on you go, you two and take the reprobate with you."

"The reprobate has a name," Phoenix called out as he pulled out his phone and dialed a number. "Hey, Fal, I know you got plans but postpone them because I need you at the fight club. When? Now obviously. Ack! Don't whine. I need back up obviously. Why? I'm going to cause trouble obviously. Why do I keep saying obviously? Because everything I'm saying should be pretty clear and apparent, though for some strange reason you keep asking me questions like I'm gonna suddenly give you different answers. Now anything you drink is on me and I promise I will also treat you, your wife and your wee ones to the pictures after dinner. What do you mean, why am I being so generous? Clearly, I'm going to be joining you with my own wee ones at both the pictures and dinner."

"Take my wife Meridee and our kids with you," Felix called out.

"What?" Phoenix mocked complained to him.

"You're also taking my Kitsune, too. Quit complaining," Wulf stated.

"Ooh, we should go, along with Lulu, Freya, their kids and your mum, so that we get to have a nice family night out," Penny remarked to Lenox, who nodded.

"What?" Phoenix demanded.

"Great idea, Penny, my dear. Mina will surely love that," Conalai agreed.

"What?"

Raven nudged her husband, "Bring home a couple of boxes of Smarties and a large bag of popcorn while you're at it."

"What?" Phoenix repeated for a fourth time.

Raven nudged him again, rolling her eyes as she responded, "Well, being so generous will clear your slate for yesterday's hostile negotiation and I'll even reward you privately for your efforts."

Phoenix clapped his hands before stealing a kiss from her. "Now we're talkin'."

Raven snorted and rolled her eyes again before she, Conalai, Wulf and Felix teleported away.

Phoenix clapped his hands a second time. "Well, can't say I

envy them since I hate hunting traitors that I can't kill. Though none of that now, it's pub time and hopefully there's a footy match on."

"Of course there is. Man City is playing," Penny said.

"Man City? No, hon, Chelsea, Chelsea."

Penny gave him a long look before shaking her head slowly and getting up off the couch at the same time that Lenox did, nearly blushing when he took her hand in his.

"Aw, young love, how sweet," Phoenix drawled.

Lenox shrugged before he raised their clasped hands and placed a soft kiss on the back of Penny's hand.

"Ack! Gag me!" Phoenix retorted, making soft gagging sounds. The he called out seconds before he teleported away, "Now hurry up, you two! I'm dying for a pint."

Lenox let out a low sigh. "You know, I should probably apologize for him and whatever mayhem he will cause tonight."

"I wouldn't. I mean, I don't apologize for my family, so why should you apologize for yours?" Penny said pragmatically.

Lenox let out a soft laugh. "Well then, in that case, let's quickly stop by the toy store not far from here and pick up that electronic pet you were eyeing before we go to the club."

"Do you think it's a good idea to leave your uncle in the fight club, alone?" Penny asked with a laugh.

Lenox shook his head. "No, but then again, leaving Uncle Phoenix alone anywhere is a bad idea, so I'm really not that bothered."

Penny shrugged. "Well, that's fair."

Lenox snorted before they, too, teleported away, both feeling oddly content and carefree, regardless that his uncle was probably causing chaos in his wake.

Oh well, c'est la vie, Lulu said through their twin link and Lenox couldn't help but agree.

Chapter Twenty

Despite picking up a present for Penny's mum, Lenox and Penny arrived just in time to watch Lenox's Uncle Phoenix and his cousin Falcon saunter into the fight club.

"What's up, wretches? Who wants a piece of this hot action?" Phoenix demanded as he slapped Falcon on the back.

Falcon gave him a dirty look. "I'm not here for your amusement, I'm here—"

"What are you talking about, nephew? Of course you're here to keep me amused because that is how you keep me out of trouble. Now, Alfie, my good man, pour me a pint of your best lager on tap and put twenty pounds down in the betting books on Falcon for any fight he's in. I'm gonna make a killing today," Phoenix responded in a singsong voice as he addressed Penny's uncle, who stood behind the bar.

"As if. Sebastian's in a pissy mood today and he's already KO'd ten opponents… make that thirteen," Alfie whistled when three bodies hit the ground in the ring.

"Oh no," Penny stated in mild alarm.

"Don't worry, sweetheart, nothing's wrong," Alfie assured her when she walked over to him.

"You sure?" Penny asked.

Alfie nodded. "Yeah your dad's just blowing off steam, and it'll all be good soon. Now, Phoenix, Falcon, sit down a spell since Sebastian knows why you're here and wants to talk to you two when he's finished."

"Damn me, how did he find out so fast?" Phoenix asked with a laugh.

"Rika, Ally, Bas and I went to visit Penny about five minutes ago and we heard everything from outside—which is why Bas is pissed. However Rika, Ally and I, understood your reasoning Lenox. In fact, in the grand scheme of things, I don't get why he's pissed because any which way you slice it, the blighter's a dead man. So I'm just chalking his mood up to the fact that it must be his time of the month—" Alfie ducked suddenly, when a blurred objected flew past him and hit the brick wall behind him with a loud crashing sound before exploding into a million tiny pieces.

"You missed me!" Alfie shouted as he stood and brushed off the dust.

A slew of curses followed the response from the boxing ring.

Penny immediately turned and headed that way, intent on speaking to her father.

"Dad!" Penny called out to him when she was close to him.

Sebastian leaned against the ropes as his seriously pissed off expression immediately softened at the sight of her. "Penny, sweetie, I know you may think, but it's not true. I'm not mad at you or him over there, I'm just pissed at a lot of things that have happened recently and I've decided to work it out, so to speak. So don't worry about me, just go order a drink from your uncle and then see your mum and aunt upstairs. Also, take him over there with you but leave his uncle and cousin because I need new opponents."

"Okay, but stop calling Lenox, 'him over there. He's my mate, dad," Penny snorted.

"Not in my eyes yet pet, definitely not yet in my eyes," Sebastian retorted narrowing his eyes on Lenox.

Lenox didn't take offence to Sebastian's words as he silently approached him, which caused a scowl to return to Sebastian's face.

"You are not supposed to agree with me!"

Lenox shrugged. "I don't see why not."

Sebastian shook his head, then spun around and walked away to the other side of the ring. Lenox frowned slightly in confusion but Alfie soon arrived to explain the reaction.

"Don't take it personal, Lenox. Sebastian just can't find a true reason not to like you and it's pissing him off, which is super funny," Alfie responded with a laugh as he clapped Lenox on the back.

A low growl erupted from Sebastian as he turned to face Alfie.

"You—in the ring! Now!"

"If you want to get your butt kicked that bad, Bas, then sure. Though give me ten minutes," Alfie replied nonchalantly.

"You have five!"

Alfie waved him off as if he was swatting a fly, before beckoning Penny and Lenox to follow him.

Penny looked over her shoulder at her dad, who mouthed the words, 'it'll be okay' to her before she turned back and followed her uncle.

Lenox took her cool hand in his warm one and squeezed it gently. Penny looked up at him and give him a small smile before they followed her uncle to a metal staircase that was to the left of the bar and hidden by another brick wall. Making their way to the floor above, Lenox was briefly stunned by what he saw in front of them when they arrived. For where the club downstairs was best described as downright rustic and manly, with a heavy wood and brick accent, dim lighting (with the exception of the boxing ring that was brightly lit and clearly the main attraction) and very little room to move about in since it was packed to the brim with hellhounds, the upstairs was completely different. Up here, the room was large and spacious, with gleaming white marble floors that had intricate golden patterns woven into them. Dotted around the room, with the exception of the middle, were round wooden tables and chairs made out of blue tree wood, a species native to the Vanishing Isle (home of the Fae). On the tables were airy checkered table cloths and lace doilies.

"Ah, Penny, Lenox, welcome, welcome!" Ally called out from her seat at a large rectangular blue wooden table in the middle of the room.

Lenox noticed his mum along with his twin, Penny's cousin Lucy, her Aunt Rika and a few other women sitting at the table, too. Nearby, at what looked like a diner counter sat Lenox's cousin Skull and Thorn, his cousin Anya's husband.

"Hi, Mum, how are you?" Penny asked as she greeted her with a hug before giving her the toy robot dog.

"Excellent, sweetie. This is a very wonderful gift, thank you. Though nice try, trying to distract me because I know what this is for. I'm a woman on a mission, one that sees my daughter happily wed since I've been told that I can't start inquiring about grand-babies until that's happened, which is bogus if you ask me."

Penny went bright red. "Mum!"

"Aw, Penny, you're a woman now—"

Penny let out a gruff growl this time. "Mum!"

"Aw, boo, I can't talk about that either? This is mental—"

Freya snorted, "No, Ally, the correct phrase you are looking for is you're mental."

"Penny's not mental," Ally instantly defended her daughter.

"Not Penny, I was speaking of you directly."

"Well, of course I'm mental. I'm a hellhound, duh."

Lulu frowned. "Okay sorry to question this but by that logic, if you're alluding to the fact that all hounds are crazy then isn't Penny too?"

"Nope, my baby is a unicorn, Lou. She's the only non-crazy hound born in the last millennium."

"Hold up, Aunt Ally. I was born in the last millennium," Lucy interjected.

"I know, honey but I've also seen that horde of shoes you keep in your bedroom first hand; seriously, you must have a million of them and that's pure nuts! Any who, when's the big date, Penny! Please, please, please tell me!" Ally demanded with a hound-like whine and a puppy dog look for extra measure.

"Yes, my dear ones, please tell us when your big date will be," Lenox's mum, Mina, also insisted.

Lenox and Penny shared a brief look before Lenox nodded at her to say it.

"October 13th," Penny murmured, blushing again.

"Woo hoo! That's only a couple of weeks away. Oh, thank the Good Light for that! I thought you'd go for a year from now. Wait! It is this one, not next year's October 13th, right?"

"Yes, Mum," Penny agreed.

"And it will be two days like Lulu's ceremony, right, Lenox, my son?" Mina asked them.

Lenox bit his lip as he looked to Penny.

Don't look at me to say no. I can't refuse my mum let alone yours, too, Penny joked.

Would it upset you if it was a two-day celebration?

Your sister's wedding was the same, right? Well it's a family tradition then and I love traditions, so we're keeping it.

Lenox kissed Penny's temple before he outwardly spoke to everyone.

"Yeah, Mum, we'll have a two-day celebration, too. In fact, I know our theme since I can see that Penny wants a 19th-century style wedding since that was the century we first met. However, if Penny agrees, I'd like to have a cross between burning man and steampunk festival for the second celebration day."

"Ooh, leather and lace! I like the idea, and it will be fun for the whole family!" Ally clapped her hands in glee.

The room was silent for a brief second as Lenox tried to find his voice.

"Wait! I mean, uh—"

"Yes, it does sound wondrous. We can fully work with that theme," Lenox's mum agreed before adding, "I have gathered some samples for you. Sorry to be presumptuous, my son but I've been preparing for this date ever since you gave Penny a ring."

"Aw, I didn't even think about that," Ally replied with a frown.

Mina smiled, "It is okay, my dear friend, Ally, for we will become the best of allies in future when it comes to this wedding."

"Uh…" Lenox started to interrupt them but suddenly an image popped in his mind through his soul bond with Penny.

The image was of Lenox wearing leather biker pants and matching jacket with his chest exposed underneath. Looking briefly at his blushing soulmate, Lenox snorted and rolled his eyes.

"You know what? Leather and lace aren't that bad of an idea after all. Though I leave all the materials and colour schemes for the wedding to you, Penny. Sorry, love but I'm pure hopeless when it comes to that stuff. However I will promise to do my very best to create the venue and entertainment of your dreams."

"It'll be of our dreams, Lenox, and I also wonder if a kind of a Mad Max dystopia theme would be suitable for the second day? After all, we hellhounds are kind of metal heads." Penny started.

"Kind of? More like are. Period," Ally snorted.

Lenox smiled as a plan started to come to mind.

"Right! I'll have preliminary plan drawn up in the morning for your approval, my love," Lenox responded absently as he mentally went over the things that fit the theme that he had in his warehouse.

"Spoken like a true engineer," Penny snorted with a laugh.

Lenox grinned and quickly kissed Penny before he joined his cousin Skull and his other cousin, Anya's husband, Thorn, at the counter as Penny joined her mum and his.

You're mental, cuz, Skull joked.

Lenox shrugged, *I guess, though do you want to help me with this?*

I'm allowed to help you plan what can only be described as the world's coolest wedding? Yup, I'm in. You, Thorn?

Thorn nodded in agreement, more than a little intrigued with the plans Lenox was telepathically sharing with them.

Nearly an hour later, Sebastian came storming into the room with the same scowl on his face as he had on earlier.

"Lenox—" Sebastian started.

"Here, you! We spoke about this, don't you start in on him," Ally hissed.

"I'm not starting in on him, Allycen. Light sake's, I can be mature and besides, I wanted to talk to him about *business*."

Ally frowned, "What kind of business. Oh—."

She let out a soft growl and Lenox knew that Sebastian had told her something telepathically.

"Dad?" Penny called out in concern.

"It's fine, sweetie, I just need your—" He stopped and shook his head before continuing, "I need Lenox to help me on a little job, it'll be fine."

"Who said that you can be mature?" Ally asked dryly.

"Ally, this is not the time love. Lenox, let's go," Sebastian retorted.

Lenox nodded and stood up, though Skull, Lulu and Thorn

did, too.

"Where do you three think you're going?" Sebastian demanded.

"If you need Lenox's help, then you need mine. We're a pair," Lulu retorted sunnily.

Sebastian begrudgingly agreed before looking at Thorn and Skull.

"You believe Triton's a Wendigo, one of those curse spirits that eat either flesh or souls, which is why you need Lenox's help. Right?" Skull asked.

Sebastian growled in response.

"Thought so and we're coming with you because both Thorn and I have the necessary skills as healers to defeat Wendigoes as well."

"Wait," Lenox said, holding up his hand as he tilted his head as he listened to a voice tell him and Lulu something important.

"What?" Sebastian demanded.

"No one is going anywhere," Lulu responded absently as she too, listened to the same voice.

Sebastian scrubbed his face hard. "Why the hell—" he stopped when he saw a scowl appear on Ally's face, before he continued with a milder tone, "Why the *heck*, not Lulu?"

"Our Grandpa Midir said so," Lulu replied with a shrug.

"You can't be serious! Your grandpa said so, therefore—" Sebastian hissed out.

A sudden flash of dark indigo light interrupted everyone as a tall, imposing figure appeared. Everyone in the room save Mina, Lenox and Lulu took in the legendary Midir Daga, who was known as the Cursed Warrior King, who was once cursed to roam the world endless by the Scath Gadai or the Devil himself for all eternity for keeping the Devil from this realm. Though it was the curse that made him legendary but his persistence and strength, for where most would have broken due to the curse, Midir turned his misfortune into a boon and became a curse-breaking warrior. One who took on some of worse evils known to man, including the Wendigoes. Nonetheless, Midir's wandering was at an end after his daughter Mina managed to break the curse when she took on the literal nightmares with her husband. Nonetheless, that hadn't stopped Midir from still being a mostly unknown yet very revered warrior in immortal circles, circles that included the hellhounds.

"Exactly, Sebastian Hawksley because first and foremost, Triton is not a Wendigo and he is one of the four Betrayers. Therefore attempting to take on him or any of the other Betrayers or Niners, as you call them, before All Hallow's Eve or the night before the season of Winter starts, won't do any of us any good. In fact, it would be pure apocalyptic in my estimation."

Sebastian growled fiercely as he fought back the need to swear.

Midir took it in stride as he replied, "I truly understand why you want to be rid of him, Sebastian and if I were in your shoes, I'd feel the same way. However, I wasn't kidding you when I said that Triton is a Betrayer, and I need to confirm a few things. However, I have a hunch that he most ancient of all of them and that is why he can partially appear on our realm for long periods."

"How the hell can something so evil be among us and no one noticed?" Sebastian demanded.

"For the simple reason that for the exception of the Baskerville line, you hunt evil by weight of soul crimes and if his actual soul is in hell you wouldn't notice the difference at first."

"What?"

"Ah, makes perfect sense for we Baskervilles don't hunt by soul crimes, we hunt by evil essence, which is why he would very rarely be in our presence for longer than a minute or two. Damn," Ally whispered.

"He really wouldn't want to attract the attention of hellraisers… hate to say it, but that's smart," Midir murmured.

Sebastian erupted, "Are you kiddin' me!"

"Ah, love, relax, we're speaking to Midir Daga…"

"What the hell does that got to do with blurting out your biggest secret?"

Midir frowned, "Being a hellraiser is a secret?"

"Kind of," Alfie said with a shrug.

"Not kind of, Alfie, it bloody well is. Period." Sebastian retorted.

"It's not a secret to Midir or the vast majority of the people in this room," Alfie pointed out.

Sebastian shook his head, "How?"

"Well Thorn's a secret keeper, so he obviously knows; Mina, Lulu, Lenox are the daughter and grandchildren of Midir respectively, who knows everything there is to know about hellraisers since their ancestors was good friends with ours as the story goes, so I'm pretty sure they've always known. Then there's Skull, a mystic fox who pretty much knows everything about all the animalia clans and I don't really know why that is but I also don't very much care since the foxes are good people. End of. Now where was I, oh right! Rika's my wife…"

"Stop!" Sebastian called, "I get the picture, but let's get back to the matter at hand regarding what to do with Triton. The Vampyr Royals just came back—"

"*To say goodbye,*" Phoenix sang out as he and the rest of the royals entered the room, causing everyone to look at him.

He shrugged. "What? It's a good song. Anyway, Sebastian, stop getting your knickers in a twist, man. Look, Midir is clearly trying to tell you we can't start hunting any of the Betrayers until October 31st when the season of the dead begins because we'll screw up the world otherwise. That's fine, we'll wait and in the meantime, we'll train and research these blighters so we can make sure the job gets done right the first time. After all, the Betrayers seem to have been around since probably close to the dawn of time like our man Thorn here…"

"I'm not that old!" Thorn retorted rolling his eyes.

"Just about, man but I'm digressing. Anyway, what I'm trying to say is that we've got to do this right because beyond the obligatory talk of a pending apocalypse, there are four lives at stake: Penny's, Lenox's Lulu's and Freya's. Now I really like all of them and there's a snowball's chance in hell, I'm going to let this become a cock-up which ends up with them being killed."

The room went quiet before Alfie spoke up.

"I knew I always liked you for a reason, Phoenix."

"Thanks, Alfie man and Midir, the floor is yours."

Midir nodded once at Phoenix in thanks, before he spoke, "By now you've probably heard whispers of the Wild Hunt. The whispers are true; the hunt was created to aid the Brimstone Huntress in binding the Betrayers to the Nine levels of Hell. It's been part of Lenox and Lulu's immortal roles to find each warrior or wildlings as they are known, who has the skills necessary to fight the minions that these kind of demons attract. Now over the years, they brought many names to me and together we've narrow it down to a small group and before All Hallow's Eve I will speak to everyone who is chosen so that they know what is stake, for Lenox and Lulu have another important task to complete which we cannot discuss at this time. However, there is a more pressing fact we must speak of and that is your wedding celebration which must not be postponed Lenox and Penny. For by celebrating your union and other key moments in life will strengthen your bond and that will be key in defeating the Betrayers. Now I must go and make some preparations but I will be back for your wedding grandson and until then worry not. I truly mean that. Now is the time to be happy."

"Thank you, grandfather," Lenox murmured.

"Yes, thank you," Penny added quietly, too.

Midir gave them a small smile before disappearing.

Penny squeezed Lenox's hand before she let go and moved across the room to hug her parents who both looked overwhelmed by everything.

"I know it doesn't seem so but everything will be okay," Penny said.

"How do you—" Sebastian started, but Ally stole a quick kiss from him.

"It will be, my mate. It will be. Though let us focus on the now and our daughter's wedding."

"Wait just a minute," Sebastian started to object before he blew out a sigh when he saw his wife and daughter's hopeful faces.

"Alright, we will and I'm sorry I didn't say this earlier, sweetheart but I am truly glad you've found your soul mate, and I really do want the best for you and Lenox."

"Thanks dad, that means everything to me," Penny stated quietly yet happily.

"Me too and on that note, mind helping Lenox plan the logistics of this event? It's going to be a two-day regency/Mad Max affair."

Sebastian looked at his contrite mate with an, *'are you serious?'* look.

"Ah, come on, you just need you to help find and secure the venue of Penny and Lenox's choosing, get great bands, elegant food, the poshest liquor as well as everything else except the flowers, cake and tablecloths then put it all together, it'll be easy. Oh, come on, stop scowling at me. You'll have help in the form of Conalai, right, Mina?" Ally called out.

"Right, Ally, Conalai would most definitely help in this endeavour, isn't that right *min storr*?" Mina asked called Conalai her love in Irish Gaelic.

Conalai nodded happily in agreement and patted Lenox on the shoulder, then walked over and sat next to Mina at the table.

Sebastian nodded in response before he looked at Alfie who was sitting down at the counter, "You're helping, too."

"Damn right, I am. She is my beloved niece and unlike Ally, I'm not going to be a crazy indecisive ball of maternal anxiety either. You lot in?" Alfie asked Phoenix and the other Vampyr royals.

"In building the set of what's going to be the greatest show on Earth? Hell, yes."

"Phoenix, it's not going to be a spectacle," Raven hissed.

"Never said it would be, love but there will be moments that will be highly entertaining."

"Not on my watch," Conalai swore.

"Not on mine either," Sebastian retorted.

"Good now that everything is settled, let's get drunk Mina," Ally declared.

"Hey, why are you getting my wife drunk?" Conalai demanded in return.

"Well, our babies are moving on to the next happy stage of

their lives, and well, I accept this, however I'm not completely beyond cursing at Fate for not letting me keep my baby as exactly that, a baby. So I feel the need to get blitzed out of my mind, probably have a good cry while I'm at it and I want to commiserate with a fellow mother of a child who is marrying. Then later on I'm going to attempt to accost my mate's virtue before failing miserably since I'll probably be ending up falling asleep midway through ripping his shirt off."

The room went silently still as everyone but Alfie looked at Ally in stunned amusement.

"What?" Ally declared before shrugging, "It's a solid plan."

Sebastian looked to the ceiling above him for divine intervention before muttering, "Eff it."

With that, he scooped up Ally in a fireman's hold over his shoulder before declaring, "We'll see you lot in the morning. Say goodnight, Ally."

"Goodnight Ally… bye-bye Penny, see you in the morning, sweetie!"

With that, he teleported away with Ally, leaving only another stunned silence in his wake.

Penny moved back across the room and telepathically said, *Well, as much as I wanted to rip Triton to shreds, I am much more pleased with this turn of events. We have a free night to do whatever we want, and you know what that means!*

Jokingly, Lenox replied, *Dungeons and Dragons?*

Ooh! Yes.

"Wait a minute!" Lenox sputtered, instantly cursing himself for not offering sexual activities first.

"Oh come on, we're about to enter that cool dangerous tower and I want to know what happens."

Lenox shook his head. "That's not entirely true. The real allure is that the guys we played with at the Die is Cast, said that if you play your cards right your Paladin character can end up with a Griffin mount."

Penny nodded eagerly.

"What is this?" Lenox's Aunt Raven suddenly demanded.

"Dungeons and Dragons— we have a standing appointment with a small group of other players at a pub called the Die is Cast every Friday now. Penny and I quite enjoy the game."

"And you didn't think your poor Aunt would want to play, too?" Raven demanded.

"Uh, we kind of just stumbled upon this during a date, Aunt Raven, though truly you want to play Dungeons and Dragons?"

"Oh, my Light, don't even get her started! She's been on forums and chats looking for the best character traits and aliments or something. I dunno really, I only half-listen to your aunt when she goes on about it because it's beyond my mental stuffing capacity," Phoenix retorted, calling his own grey matter 'mental stuffing', which always amused Lenox.

"Yes, like all those times you half-listen to me plead with you to take me to one of these places where we can play it!"

"Only because I don't want to go, love," Phoenix admitted openly.

"Why the hell not!" Raven demanded again stamping her foot in irritation.

"Since I'd rather be killing evil punters in real life than rolling a dice to determine if my D&D character will have enough HP and hit capacity to do the job on fictional ones," Phoenix retorted, giving away that he had been more than just half-listening to his wife and fully comprehended the game.

"Hey man, don't knock it until you try it, killing make-believe Goblins is pure fun," Alfie admitted as Falcon nodded silently in agreement.

"How do you… you've been playing, too, Falcon!" Raven shouted at him.

"Not yet, Aunt Raven, though I've sat in on a few games as an observer recently because Luna wants to play and I wanted to get a handle on the lay of the land, so to speak."

Alfie looked at Raven and responded with, "I've been playing for years now with Rika and I've got my storyteller credentials. Well the role's called a dungeon master but I much prefer calling myself a storyteller for obvious reasons. Anyway, who wants to play? I've got everything we need to play hidden here underneath the bar downstairs."

Almost everyone put up their hands to play, except Wulf, Conalai and Phoenix.

Though Mina's enthusiasm for a family games night soon won over Conalai, and he shrugged in agreement.

"Aw hell, sure, why not but keep the lager coming, Alfie. I think I'm gonna need it," Phoenix complained as he too, agreed.

"No playing yet, I'm going to go get Luna!" Falcon called as he teleported away.

"Yes, and we're going to go get Nyte, Trey, Anya, Reagan and mum. It'll be nice to have night out together," Skull stated as he and Thorn moved to leave, too.

"Leave your mother, son, for we'll watch over the wee ones tonight," Wulf stated, not wanting to play but his attempts were thwarted by his younger brother Felix.

"Too late, Wulf, Meridee just told me telepathically that Lucky and Erebrus have taken all of the kids to dinner, a movie followed by a sleepover at Falcon's place, which we've all agreed to including Falcon. Kitsune has also told Meridee that she wants to play," Felix stated as Raven, Lulu and Thorn nodded.

Wulf blew out a sigh, "Well, since my mate seems to want to join this family games night, we're in. Though, Raven, you go ahead and set up my character while I go and get my mate. Please, for the love of the Light, pick me a deadly one because there's no sense in changing anything."

With that, he, Skull and Thorn teleported away to get their mates.

"Well, I for one, want my make-believe character to have a little razzle-dazzle, like an epic cool magician or something, what do you got, love?"

"Necromancer?"

"Meh, not shiny enough… what else you got?" Phoenix asked.

"Cleric?"

"Nah."

"Rogue?" Raven asked, throwing a non-magical role.

"Nah."

"Druid?"

"Nah."

"Necromancer?" Raven asked, offering up the first one again.

"Ooh, that the one sounds fancy, I'll take it!"

Everyone laughed.

Still want sexual relations now? Penny asked as she turned to Lenox with a smile on her face.

Without a shadow of a doubt, I do, love; however, I can clearly see we have a snowball's chance in hell at getting out of this family games night. Therefore, I will play and have fun but will totally be plotting pleasurable revenge that I will enact later.

Ooh, I like the sound of that. Oh and Lenox?

Yeah?

I love you.

Penny?

Yeah.

I love you, too, Lenox said as he closed the few feet gap between them and wrapped an around her shoulder as she wrapped one around his waist.

They didn't say anything more then as they let the familial banter wash over them, both completely lost to a happy loving soul bond which

was far removed from the anxiety and fear that would probably soon fill their days.

Chapter Twenty-One

A few days later, Penny tried to keep herself calm as she mentally prepared herself for the ordeal that was to come.

"Ready, cousin?" Lucy asked from beside her as they walked down the streets of Moonlight Valley.

Joining them were Lulu and Freya's sister-in-law, Lydia, a former fashion supermodel who offered to help Penny.

"To dress shop? No. To get married? Yes."

"Why is dress shopping more daunting than getting married?" Lucy asked with a laugh.

Penny sighed, "Dress shopping is complicated."

"And Lenox is not?" Lulu asked.

"Oh, no! He's complicated. Well, okay, he's not. Lenox is straight forward, serious, sweet and kind. It's just that I hate dress shopping because I'm not feminine and dainty and I wish I could be for my wedding day."

"Penny, " Lydia started before she stopped and started scrolling through her phone instead.

Curious, Penny, Lucy and Lulu stopped and waited for her to find what she was looking for.

A few moments later, she straightened and looked Penny directly in the eyes. "Penny, we're very nearly the same size. I mean, you're what? Five foot ten inches?"

Penny nodded.

"I'm five foot nine inches and just like you, I'm willowy yet muscular. Hard not to be when you become the leader of Norra Stam and have to keep squabbling Vikings from stabbing each other on a daily basis. Sorry for digressing a bit but they really like to fight. Anyway what I'm trying to say is we both might not be petite but that doesn't mean we can't look lady-like. I still model clothes on occasion, mainly for charities these days and the last time I did a show, it was a bridal one that benefited the Chicago SPCA a few months ago."

Lydia offered Penny her phone, which showed a picture of Lydia dressed in a white wedding gown.

"You look lovely, Lydia, but I couldn't look like that. My shoulders are too broad."

Lucy quickly pulled out a tape measure of her purse and measured the shoulders of Lydia and then Penny in rapid succession.

"Your shoulders are only about 1.5 cm different, cousin. You really shouldn't be so hard on yourself."

"It's hard not to be," Penny muttered softly.

Lucy nodded sympathetically. "It's a woman's curse. We only see our faults, not our virtues in the mirror. I mean, I always wanted to be tall and more imposing since most people try to rescue me when there's danger about because I look too small and fragile."

"I've wanted to be less curvy," Lulu admitted. "Having big boobs can be a hassle. People stare all the time. It's nuts."

"I also understand wanting to be smaller, Penny, because being model-thin and pretty, makes people think you are just a display rack for clothes, not an actual person in the fashion world. Though you know, all of this stem from what stupid people have said to us in the past and unfortunately as much as we all probably hate to admit it, it all stuck to us like glue," Lydia said.

Lulu nodded. "Yeah, but you know my Freya has always told me that fools will always mock what they envy, so don't go putting any stock in what they say."

Penny smiled. "Freya's a wise woman."

"I know but please don't tell her that to her face," Lulu laughingly pleaded. "Freya is already the most confident woman on the planet and I don't need her becoming even more so."

"I hear you. Frey isn't much better. Honestly, those twins don't give a damn when it comes to people's opinions of them," Lydia laughed.

Penny nodded. "I'd like to be that way someday soon and I know it'll be a hard rocky road to get there but every journey starts with a small step, right?"

The three women nodded as they all stopped in front of a

store in the middle of town.

"Well, this is my small step."

With that said, Penny grasped the handle of the door and opened it. She took in a deep breath, expecting pure chaos to inhabit the store since her mum had texted her an hour ago, saying that she would wait for Penny at the dress shop, which meant her mum was already there. However, Penny was astonished to find her mum almost subdued as she sat with Lenox's mother, Mina, and Penny's aunt Rika, chatting away.

"Hi, sweetie!" Ally waved when she saw Penny.

"Hi, mum. Everything alright?" Penny asked, somewhat confused.

"Oh, yeah, I'm just on my very best behaviour, that's all."

"Mum, you don't have to censor yourself. You are just fine as you are."

Ally stood up and crossed the room taking both of Penny's hands in hers as she looked her deeply in the eyes. "Penny, my dear sweet child, nothing means more to me than you and your dad's happiness and I will always do everything in my power to ensure it. I also know dress shopping stresses you out, so I promise I won't cause a fuss and add to that stress."

Penny hugged her, "Thanks, Mum."

Ally said nothing in response as she smiled freely instead.

"Oh, hello, bride-to-be. Glass of champagne?" Valiant Eleftherios, one of the boutique owners, asked as she appeared.

"Until the bride-to-be chooses her dress, Valiant, we're going to be very English today. So a nice cup of tea would do wonders if you please," Ally stated.

"Ah, you're no fun," Anarchy Andraste, Valiant's twin and the other boutique owner whined from behind a curtain.

"No, I'm super fun, Anarchy, especially when fuelled with champers but I don't think you heard a single word I just said to my daughter."

"Oh no," Anarchy exclaimed, "I heard every single word you said but as my name clearly states, I am Anarchy and can't help stirring the pot when the opportunity presents itself."

Ally rolled her eyes before looking at Valiant.

"Anna, please go fetch the tea you prepared as we get down to business. Now, Penny, do you have anything in mind for what you want your wedding dress to look like?" Valiant asked.

"Well, Lenox and I originally met in the 1820s, and we're having a regency style wedding, so I want a regency style dress with the high waist and flowing skirt. But, I also think the three quarter length sleeves that have lacy ruffling at the end are very pretty. Also, I know white is traditional for wedding dresses but white is a colour of mourning for hounds and I don't want to risk bad luck on my wedding day, so I was thinking a light pink, like an ice baby pink, maybe? Also, Lenox told me there's a tradition that states that wearing something blue is good luck, so I want that incorporated into the dress in the form of a ribbon or a sash or something. Oh, and I want to incorporate the rest of that lucky tradition too, you know—something new, something old, something borrowed, something blue."

Valiant snorted as she looked at her twin briefly. "And you said she wouldn't know what she wanted, Ana."

"I stand by it. Penny's the first hound ever to get married."

"I like what I like," Penny retorted, knowing fully well exactly what she wanted for the wedding dress of her dreams since she had secretly fantasized about it over the years.

"Nothing wrong with that." Valiant replied with a grin.

"Any who, don't we have a dress like the one Penny wants in stock?" Anarchy asked, looking contemplative.

"Yes and we probably have a few similar ones too, to give her some options. Now, go get them since I dare not enter your stockroom after your last dire threat."

"Damn right, you don't," Anarchy replied in Japanese as she got up and headed behind the curtain again. "Nobody messes with my well-organized stockroom. Ugh, worst thing ever is to have items out of place and I know that you did that on purpose, Vali!"

Valiant nodded in full agreement. "I did and it's the best way of getting back at Anna when she's pissed me off. I have zero regrets."

"Oh, I understand. When Alfie pisses me off, I throw mini firecrackers at him. He's like a cat on a scalding hot tin roof. It's too funny," Ally retorted before looking at Lulu. "So what do you do when your twin annoys you, Lou?"

"Huh? Oh, Lenox never gets on my nerves, only my wife Freya's and when she's irate you know it," Lulu said with a chuckle.

Lulu turned to Penny. "Don't worry about that though, she never really yells at him or me for that matter since she says yelling at the two of us, is equivalent to kicking a puppy, so she relies more on sarcasm and scolding, when she's mad. On the flip side, Lenox and I have never really felt real ire and I kind of think we don't know how, so we don't make each other mad. When one of us does something the other doesn't like, we talk it out, which also kind of drives Freya nuts since we're super-rational. Which I don't understand why it drives her crazy but to each their own."

"That's understandable Lou, since I've never been aggravated at Rika and I think it's because she's sweet, calm and rational. Whereas, as my mate is all alpha all the time, which makes me want to mess with him just because," Ally stated with a shrug.

"Yes I completely feel that calm gentleness coming from Rika, Mina and Lulu, though I kind of get that from Penny, Lucy and Lydia too and it's probably since you all have Ritana-like traits. However, in saying that, I know that being surrounded by this amount of sereneness will make me want to aggravate someone later, though in truth I'm too lazy to go outside and deliberately aggravate someone, so I'll probably mess up the stockroom later." Valiant said.

"The hell you will! I will cut you if you mess with it!" Anarchy declared, her threat betrayed by her happy tone.

"You will legit cut me? Your own flesh and blood twin? For messing up your stock room?" Valiant demanded.

"For deliberately messing with my stockroom! In a freaking heartbeat! Though it won't do you any lasting damage since you're immortal, *baka,*" Anarchy retorted, calling her twin an idiot in Japanese.

"Not the point. Oh, never mind. Come along, Penny, my dear. Let's try on some dresses," Valiant beckoned as she got up off the couch.

Penny nodded and followed Valiant into a dressing room that was off to the left side. As Penny tried on the first dress, Valiant deliberately blocked her from fully seeing it, causing Penny to let out a soft whine.

"Not a chance, hellhound pup, you get to see it in the mirror after your family sees it. Don't start whining again. I know you doubt your gorgeous looks, it's written all over your face, and I won't have a bride who doesn't feel pretty, refuse to leave the dressing room. Now let's go out and show your family so we can hear praise and maybe see tears."

Penny scowled then slowly nodded in agreement before she left the room. Stepping out of the room, she secretly marvelled at the feeling of the silk and lace gown, trying desperately not to ruin the surprise, though she still try to catch glimpse of it as she looked downwards, trying to picture it fully in her mind.

"Stop that! You'll see it soon enough," Valiant scolded, catching her looking down.

Penny blew out an exasperated sigh as she continued to walk out towards where her family and friends waited. Bizarrely, instead of a barrage of reactions she had expected, Penny was taken aback by the silence.

Unsure of what was happening, Penny called out to her mum, "Uh, Mum? Does it—"

Ally burst out into tears. "Oh, my Light! You look so lovely, sweetie."

"Really? But you haven't seen it all. I just walked in," Penny replied.

"You truly do, though come in, come in! Do a twirl for us and don't be alarmed by my tears, I'm just really, really happy for you, sweetie." Ally sniffed as Penny's Aunt Rika handed her a box of tissues after taking one to dab her own eyes.

Penny nodded, walking towards the small stage and stepping up before taking a good look at herself in the three-way mirror. She gasped, seeing her reflection. She was beautiful. The dress fit like a glove with the three-quarter length lace ruffled sleeves hiding her muscular upper arms, making her arms look dainty. The sweetheart neckline adorned with lace, accentuated her breasts, making them seem larger than she thought possible since Penny always felt lacking in that category. However, despite the bustier look, she looked feminine and it made her happy. The rest of the dress was a high-waisted Empress cut with a light blue belt made of bluish-white pearls and pale blue opals that were mixed in an intricate pattern that split the top half of the dress with long silk and lace skirt that had an imprinted floral design.

"Is this. . . is this really me?" Penny asked Valiant, amazed at feeling beautiful for the first time in her life.

Anarchy laughed, "Of course, it's you, silly."

Penny's mum threw an empty teacup at Anarchy. "Don't call my baby silly, harpy."

Anarchy caught the cup in her hands and put it down on the counter. "Sorry. I meant no offence, Ally."

"I accept that, Ana and yes, my dear one, that's all you. See! I wasn't lying to you when I told you that you are gorgeous," Ally stated.

"Thanks, mum and I feel it in this dress. Light! I know you have other dresses for me to try on, Valiant but, I don't want to because— Wait, what do you all think?"

"It looks pure lovely on you, Penny!" Lulu cried out.

"Oh yes, you will be a most beautiful bride in this dress," Mina added, dabbing at her eyes.

"I know you're not supposed to like the first one but Penny, this is the dress for you. You look amazing in it," Lydia stated.

"Oh my, Penny, I love it on you," Aunt Rika replied as she gave Penny a happy yet watery smile.

Penny looked at her shell shocked cousin Lucy, who surprisingly hadn't said a single word yet. "Uh Lucy, you okay, hon?" Penny asked her softly.

Lucy let out a small wail before she flew across the room towards Penny with her arms out towards her. Thinking quickly, Penny's mum caught her before she tackled Penny off the small stage.

"Lucy, I know you want to hug the stuffing out of Penny, but please, no snot or tears on the wedding dress. It's not only gross but it has to be unlucky, too. Come on, pup, it'll be okay. Just tell Penny she's pretty."

"But she's more than that!" Lucy sobbed against her mother, who had gently pried Ally off her and held her as she cried.

"I know, honey. Why don't you pick out a tiara for Penny, and I'll pick out a lace veil? Is that okay, Penny?" Ally asked, understanding Lucy's reaction well since she, too, looked close to a full tear meltdown.

Penny fought back tears as she earnestly nodded at her cousin, who gave her a silent yet pleading look, to be allowed to pick out a tiara.

Lucy and Penny's mum said no more as they both made a beeline towards the tiaras and veils that were on display. Surprisingly, it didn't take long for them to pick something as Ally and Lucy returned about ten minutes later, carrying their choices. Penny lowered her head so her mum and cousin could pin the tiara and veil to her hair. When they finished, they took a step back and gulped back their tears as they gazed at Penny.

Penny turned around and looked at herself in the mirror. "This is it— my dress, veil and tiara," Penny declared giddily, feeling every inch the bride.

"Hold on a tick. You're supposed to try on more than one dress," Valiant retorted.

"I'm an Omega Hellhound and a Baskerville. I was never meant to follow the pack. I've decided this is what I want and I will not change my mind," Penny stated firmly, meaning every word.

The room erupted in full cheers at Penny's declaration as even Valiant, and Anarchy joined in. Soon after, everyone took a bunch of pictures on their phones.

"Alright then—" Valiant started.

"Here!" Ally shouted as she thrust a credit card towards Valiant.

"Wait a minute—" Valiant sputtered.

"I will not wait a minute! Penny said that's the one and I will pay for it now," Ally growled.

"We don't charge for dresses here in Moonlight Valley because the residents voted against money and we accepted that because they pay us in a ton of other goods, remember?" Valiant stated.

"I don't care. I want to buy this one, now charge me for it!"

"Fine, how about $1000 for the lot?" Valiant sighed, knowing it was a losing battle to argue with a determined hound.

"What do you take me for? Give me a higher price!" Ally replied, offended at such a low number.

"You want to be charged more?" Valiant echoed, completely stupefied.

"Damn straight. My baby deserves the best and I want a price that matches, Valiant!"

"$2500?"

Penny's mum growled.

"$5000?"

Ally didn't growl this time but she still wore a fierce scowl, still not appeased.

"She's about to throw a mug at you this time, Vali, though don't worry, I've got this. Hey, Ally, this dress retails for ten grand in the human world. Would thirteen grand for everything, appease your need to overpay for a dress, tiara and veil?"

"Why yes, yes it would," Ally replied as she turned her credit card over to Anarchy.

"Want a bill of sale?" Anarchy asked.

"Oh, yes. I want to frame it."

"Of course you do," Valiant muttered.

Ally cut her a lethal glare. "That dress is Penny's now and I won't be allowed to pin it up in Penny's award room so—"

"Penny's what?" Valiant asked curiously.

"It's a room where I get to keep all the physical items that show off my baby's accomplishments; from the skull of her first demon kill to her new mathematical society awards she's getting in June."

"Wow, you kept the skull from her first demon kill?" Valiant asked in amazement.

"Damn straight, I did, and it was lucky that she killed a Kaimber Demon since the only good thing about those jerks is that they don't disintegrate as most demons do."

"Whoa, Penny, those demons are huge. How old were you when you killed it?" Lulu asked.

"Seven. She was seven, Lou. I was so proud. Want to hear all about it over lunch?" Ally asked.

"No one talks about demon kills over lunch, Ally," Valiant returned with a snort.

"I do and what are you two doing just standing there? Valiant, help my baby out of the dress so I can hug her already! Jeez, it's been a whole fifteen minutes since I've been able to do that and Anarchy, don't forget about my sale bill, please. Use extra writing flourish since I want it to look fancy. Oh, and hurry up, too, so we all can go to lunch together."

"Hold on. We're included?" Anarchy asked, completely taken aback by Ally's offer.

"Of course! You sold the dress and put up with me. If that doesn't deserve the world's fanciest meal and finest champagne, then I don't know what does, Anarchy."

"Oh, cool beans. You are serious about real fancy food and champagne, right?"

"My only daughter is getting married. What do you think?" Ally snorted in response.

"Fair dues," Valiant happily replied as she escorted Penny back to the dressing room.

Midway through helping Penny, with her dress, Valiant muttered, "Your mum is truly mental but I absolutely love her for it."

"Yeah, me too and I'm so proud of mum since she doesn't give a damn what people think of her. Oh, and, Valiant?"

"Yeah?"

"When I have a child of my own, I plan to be exactly the same with them, so be prepared," Penny replied sweetly.

"Light, you Baskervilles take all the cake, don't you? Aw hell, I'm just as bad and Light help all of us when my dear Chara or Xan decide to find their soulmates, for I might end up starting World War III to deal with the stress," Valiant stated.

Penny laughed. "Spoken like a true daughter of Chaos."

"Yes, Baskerville hound, that I am. Now come on, let's hustle. I'm in the mood to drink some champers and text my old ball and chain to see if he wants to help make baby afterwards. Light, does he ever have the sweetest chest dimples," Valiant gushed.

"Don't you mean cheek dimples?"

"Oh no, hon," Valiant snorted, "I meant chest dimples and they are a magnificent sight, I must say."

Penny laughed, "Light sake's, Valiant. Really?"

"Oh yes, honey and trust me, being shackled to my lover for as long as I have been, I can tell you that I still like everything about him. Just don't tell him that because I also still like to mess with him from time to time."

"I know what you mean. I love everything about Lenox."

Valiant nodded. "I could see that you two were going to be soulmates. I mean, granted, I only saw the two of you in the same room a handful of times but your auras seem to blend so well that it was hard to tell you apart. It's a great sign, and I wish you a long blessed soul-bonded life."

Penny thanked Valiant though words also stirred a deep emotion in her; *determination.* After all, she'd be damned first before she let any demon keep Lenox and her from having a happy life together.

Hear that, Penny's thoughts directed towards the Niners. *I'm coming for you, and when we meet, I'll be settling this permanently. I mean it!*

With that, Penny went back to being a happily engaged bride-to-be, not willing to give those demons a moment more of her time as she focused on the now.

Chapter Twenty-Two

Waking up mid-morning of her wedding day and Penny was chomping at the bit to get the show on the road. It irked her that she had to spend the night before her wedding day apart from Lenox since apparently this age-old tradition, however it was bogus as far as she was concerned.

Bounding down the stairs of her parents' home, Penny was kind of unsurprised to see her parents up and waiting for her.

Penny took in the scene of her parents sitting side by side at the kitchen table; her dad reading the sports page and her mum filling out a crossword of the same newspaper, completely ignoring a large display of food in front of them.

"Um, mum, dad..." Penny started to say but then faltered.

Ally got to her feet. "You nervous, hon? Can't eat? I'll throw out the food then."

"Wait! Don't! I'm famished."

"Well, that makes one of us," Sebastian muttered.

"Dad?" Penny questioned, causing him to look up.

Sebastian sighed. "Sorry, hon. I know this is your wedding day and it will be a happy event but I'm still your dad and a small part of me irrationally, doesn't want it to be so. I mean okay, Lenox is a great guy, I will begrudgingly admit this. I also admit under duress that he will always love you and put you first. Though still—"

Ally laid a hand on his forearm and said soothingly, "It'll be okay, my love. I mean, look at Penny, she's super happy. See?"

"I am, dad," Penny admitted before she walked over and hugged him tightly.

Sebastian said nothing as he hugged her in return, then he reached out to Ally and included her in the hug. No one said anything for a long time until the front door banged open, startling all three.

"Bloody hell, he has his timing," Sebastian muttered with a snort.

"Who?" Penny asked in confusion.

"Your Uncle Alfie."

"Good morning, all!" Alfie boomed from the front hallway as he made his way to join them.

Penny gasped in amazement when she got a good look at her Uncle Alfie who was dressed from head to toe in a dark cerise pink morning suit that also included a proper top hat and cane sword. She was so taken aback by her uncle's outfit that she couldn't help but wonder if it was indeed him until she noticed the faint imprints of Batman logos in his suit jacket, vest, pants and cravat. Even the top hat and cane displayed his Batman obsession with a light pink bow tied in the Batman logo to the top hat, and the cane with a topper to match.

"Uncle Alfie... uh... you're wearing pink," Penny stammered.

"Like it? Well I do and I wore it for you pet, since pink is your favourite colour."

"Uncle Alfie, you didn't wear pink for me! Did you?" Penny asked in pure delight.

"Absolutely did, hon and I have no regrets at all, I assure you. After all, not many people mean the world to me, Penniah but you are definitely one of them. Besides, this is a very masculine shade of pink."

Penny snorted softly before she readily agreed and she let go of her parents to hug her uncle.

"Morning," Penny's Aunt Rika called out a few moments later.

Penny was instantly delighted again to see her aunt in pink, too, though it was a light cerise pink. Though more surprisingly, Aunt Rika had decided to match her husband by having the same Batman logo pattern faintly imprinted throughout her own regency ball gown dress.

"Aunt Rika!" Penny squealed, completely touched by the gesture of seeing her aunt in pink, too.

"I like this shade of pink and Batman, so I decided to match your uncle as much as I could," Rika admitted.

"Hard not to like Batman when you're married to his biggest

fan," Ally muttered with a snort before replying, "Though your dress looks lovely on you, Rika and I'm really glad you chose it. I also think you look absolutely spiffing, Alfie. Good job, bro."

"Why thank you, Ally, though of course I look spiffing since I'm one hot manly beast."

"I won't go that far but I do like the added touch of Batman logos, so I echo my mate's comment of good job," Sebastian stated with a nod.

"Well, even in the brightest of rooms, I can still hide in the shadows, for I am Batman," Alfie retorted.

Sebastian shook his head, trying desperately to hide his laughter by coughing.

"Come join us for breakfast," Ally beckoned to the couple.

"Nah, I already ate before donning the suit since I couldn't get it messy, you know? Anyways, Lucy needed an extra fifteen minutes this morning, so I thought I'd walk Rika over here before going back for our daughter."

Not wanting to point out that he could simply clean his clothes with magic, Penny's dad shrugged and muttered, "Fair dues."

"Barbecue spare rib, dad?" Penny offered him as she moved back to the table and held out the plate to him.

"Yeah, hon, I think I will have one, thanks."

Penny offered the same plate of ribs to her mother, who also took one but didn't seem to have the same robust appetite Penny had.

Penny chose to say nothing although she couldn't help notice that both of her parents were only eating with one hand as they held hands with the other.

One day that's going to be Lenox and me, Penny thought as she continued to eat breakfast, daydreaming of a happy future.

After breakfast, near pandemonium erupted when the remaining hellhound elite and their spouses arrived, also all dressed in pink, including the fearsome hellhound elder Reggie who wore a full dark fuchsia morning suit to match his wife's light fuchsia ball gown. Penny realized then that the hellhounds had all chosen darker shades of pink while their mates had chosen to wear lighter shades.

"Like it?" Yuna asked Penny excitedly. "Reggie asked me to

pick our pink shade and I was a bit indecisive until I went visiting Lenox's mum, Mina. She showed me a flower called Fuchsia and I thought, that's it! That's the shade I want to wear."

"You're all wearing pink," Penny said softly. "For me."

"Damn right we did, pup," Reggie stated nonplussed. "You are one of our own and we'll proudly wear your favourite colour on your wedding day."

Penny felt overwhelmed, and tears began to trickle down her face.

Penny's mum swore in response, "For bloody goodness gracious sake, Reggie! You made my baby cry!"

"Please relax, Mum. These are happy tears because I'm just happy, really, really happy," Penny assured her as she rubbed her eyes.

Ally reached across the table and stopped her daughter's hands, then dabbed her face gently with a soft tissue.

"Well, I'm really, really glad that you are," Ally replied, echoing her daughter's response as her tears slid down her cheek.

Penny stood up at the same time as her mum and reached for a tissue so she could dry her tears.

"Mum, nothing is going to change. Honest. I mean, married or not, I'm still your daughter and I'll be calling you or visiting you as often as I can, though when I come around, I'll be bringing another person with me when I do."

"He'll always be welcome," Ally said softly, meaning every word.

"Here now—" Sebastian interrupted.

Though Ally wasn't having it as she declared loudly, "I'm about to bawl my face off, Bas. Give me this one concession for Light's sake!"

Sebastian said nothing as he walked up behind Ally and wrapped his arms around her shoulders.

One day that's going to be Lenox and me, Penny thought again.

"You going to be alright, love?" Penny's dad asked her mum gently.

"Nope. I'm gonna be a huge emotional basket-case today and you're going to have to deal with it. Sorry, love," Penny's mum replied, not sounding sorry at all, though Penny's dad shrugged as if he expected nothing less.

"What else is new?" Alfie asked as he entered the room with his daughter Lucy holding the crook of his left arm while he ate a muffin with his right hand.

"I thought you weren't eating because it was going to mess up your suit!" Ally shouted at him.

Alfie waved off his twin with his muffin. "It's fine. I'm eating away from my suit so no crumbs. Besides, this is a snack, one of many I'm going to consume today while we observe proper wedding traditions today."

"No snacking during the wedding photos or ceremony, or I will freakin' cut you!" Ally threatened.

Alfie rolled his eyes at her, "Obviously, I won't be snacking then. Oh, and which side is my better side; left or right?"

"What on Light's green Earth are you prattling on about!" Ally erupted again.

"Well, according to the internet, everyone has a better side of their body for photos and I couldn't determine my better side in the mirror this morning because both my sides are handsome."

Penny giggled when her mum sighed in exasperation.

"For the love of the Light! We're clearly on team bride! Which means, left, left, left!"

"Ah makes sense," Alfie acknowledged with a nod.

"What?" Penny asked, completely confused again.

"Well, when I was speaking with Lenox's Aunt Raven a few weeks ago about immortals' wedding traditions, she told me that immortal brides stand to the left because traditionally that is the side that the heart is on; Whereas grooms stand on the right side because they are seen as warriors and warriors usually always fight with their right side out to protect the heart," Penny's Aunt Rika explained.

"Oh... I like that," Penny stated happily.

"Wait. Shouldn't Penny be—" Winston started before a plate flew past his head and smashed against a brick wall.

"Penny's the bride today, Winston!" Ally snarled.

Winston held up his hand defensively as he nodded in full agreement.

"Good. Glad that's clear and *opa*!" Ally exclaimed

"Um, mum, isn't that a Greek tradition?" Penny asked.

"Yeah and usually reserved for the wedding reception, too. However, your dear ole mum needs a stress reliever today, so—*opa*!" Ally said as she smashed another plate on the floor.

Surprisingly, Penny's dad followed suit and smashed a plate in solidarity before remarking, "Hey, it really does work. I feel a bit less stressed out."

He then smashed three more plates before Rika stopped him. "Sorry Bas but no more plate smashing for a bit. Since Penny needs to go get her hair and makeup done soon and the last thing she needs is a jumpy esthetician."

"Is it that time already?" Penny exclaimed before adding, "But, I don't even have the proper underclothing or my special wedding robe on yet! Oh, goodness gracious, I'm so late!"

Sebastian smashed one more plate.

"Good grief, you can't be stressed because Penny merely mentioned the word underclothing. It's part of the whole attire, Sebastian, for you can't just wear anything under a wedding dress," Ally retorted.

"We're so not having this conversation today, Allycen." Sebastian shook his head in mild annoyance.

"It wasn't a conversation, Bas, facts are facts. End of story. Now come on, sweetie, don't worry about being late because brides are supposed to be late according to the internet."

"Sorry, dad, I wasn't thinking when I spoke."

"You're fine, sweetie. Go with your mum," Sebastian said with a small smile as he stole one more hug from her before her mum guided her out to the hall.

Penny wrapped an arm around her mum's shoulders and said, "Come on, mum, today's going to be a great day no matter what happens."

"How—"

" Because even though we've been mated for a few weeks already, today's the day I get to celebrate finding the love of my life. I've always wanted to find my soulmate just like how you and Dad did."

Ally took in a deep breath, "I'm glad, honey and as much as I like to mess with him, I wouldn't trade your dad for anything."

"Yeah, I know that. What do you think? Hair up or down?"

"Why not both?" Ally responded.

"Ooh, a half updo. I hadn't even thought about that. I like it," Penny agreed.

Ally smiled as she remarked, "You know what? It is going to be a great day."

*****

Ready to walk down the aisle with her dad, Penny hummed happily as she waited at the entrance-way of the Moonlight Valley meeting hall.

"I do like your suit, Dad," Penny whispered quietly to her dad.

"Your mum picked the colour and I thought it was a bit bright at first but then she told me the colour is called royal pink and I knew then, that this was the shade for us. After all, this is your day to be a princess, Penny and what's a princess without her royal king and queen parents to complete the fairy-tale? I'm also thankful she didn't pick bubble gum pink since the last thing I wanted was to wear a colour that matched that monstrosity of a candy."

Penny giggled softly. Suddenly, the wedding march began to play. Penny watched her cousin Lucy, her maid of honour, link arms with Lulu, Lenox's best woman (*who else could it have been?* Penny thought with a smile). In front of them stood Freya and Tyr; Lydia and Frey; And Rocky and Winston who readied themselves to walk behind two flower girls, Heidi and Elsa. In front of them were two little ring bearers, Lore and Bryn, who had been quite adamant about not getting separate wedding roles.

"It's our turn, mummy and mama. We do a good job. You'll

see," Lore and Bryn said in a loud stage whisper.

They slowly pulled their small flower-covered red wagon. Although the red was barely noticeable since Lulu had spent ages with the kids covering every square inch of it with pink silk flowers and green satin pillows. She had even gone so far as to change the handle so the kids pulled a floral vine instead of the wagon's regular black metal handle. Penny's heart melted at the sight of the little children pulling their much-beloved wagon down the aisle since they looked so solemn and focused on their task.

I hope our kids will be like that, Penny thought.

Penny's attention then shifted to the procession of adults in front of her that obscured her line of vision of Lenox.

Dear Light, you are your mother's daughter, Penniah. Please stop growling for you'll see him soon enough, Sebastian teased.

Sorry, dad.

Nothing to be sorry for and if nothing else, it's pretty endearing. Now let's go. It's our turn.

Penny gently squeezed her dad's arm as she took her first step down the aisle and finally got a good look at her mate.

Dressed in a dark jade nineteenth-century morning suit, Lenox looked every inch the breathtakingly handsome man he was and Penny found herself stopping full-on in her tracks in the middle of the aisle so she could take in all of him.

Lenox smiled at her in his sweet reassuring way and Penny found herself returning the smile before continuing her walk towards him, albeit at a much quicker pace.

Slow down, hon. This is supposed to be a traditionally slow walk.

Ah, man! Penny complained.

Seriously, you and your mum, two peas from the very same pod.

Penny changed her pace to meet her father's though she still kept her eyes firmly affixed on Lenox.

Penny noted then that Lenox looked just as relaxed and happy as she was, showing no signs of wedding jitters that brides and grooms were expected to feel.

I'm super glad you're not nervous either, Lenox said, breaking the silence that he had been maintaining since yesterday.

Being separated from you last night was pure bogus, Penny complained to him at once.

Lenox bit his lip to keep from chuckling, though his eyes sparkled.

It was necessary for tradition's sake, Lenox reminded her gently.

Well, whoever is the tradition- master who created all this stuff, needs to change that one because again, it was full-on bogus.

Yes, I agree, love. Though you look so very gorgeous Penniah and I nearly fell over at the sight of you.

You look handsome, too. I love that shade of green on you. You need to wear more of it in the future. Ack! Sorry! Not even wed yet, and I'm already making demands of you!

"And I love you for it, Penniah," Lenox stated openly when she was close enough.

"Well, I love you, too, Lenox, forever and always." Penny smiled.

Suddenly, the guests gave out a loud, "aw," in unison.

"Huh?" Penny asked.

"You were projecting your thoughts aloud, sweetie," Penny's dad replied.

"Oh… *meh*," Penny said as she gave a small shrug in response.

Sebastian shook his head slightly before he gently offered Penny's hand to Lenox. Penny happily took his hand before they moved to stand in front of the officiator, who turned out to be Prometheus, the leader of the Omega Clan.

While holding onto each other's hand, the happy couple stared into each others eyes completely focused on each other as Prometheus spoke. Though managed to say their vows with little prompting.

"I, Penniah Sebastian Olivia Neely Baskerville Hawksley, take you, Lenox Markos Moregan to be my husband; to protect from the forces of evil; to cherish the wonderful man that you are and happily spend the rest of our immortal lives together."

"I Lenox Markos Moregan take you, Penniah Sebastian Olivia Neely Baskerville Hawksley to be my wife; to aid in any battle against the forces of evil; to love the amazing woman you are and to happily spend the rest of our immortal lives together."

"Well, with the blessing of the Light, I now pronounce you husband and wife," Prometheus declared.

Penny couldn't contain her happiness that bubbled up inside her, as she clapped excitedly at the pronouncement and immediately leaned into Lenox for a kiss. Hearing the soft growls coming from her dad at their display, Penny softly laughed. Though she and Lenox tried to keep the kiss appropriate, Penny would freely admit later, it was quite hard to do.

Turning to the crowd of well-wishers, Penny and Lenox raised their clasped hands above their heads.

Unable to contain herself again, Penny declared, "We did it! Yes!"

"We sure have, love!" Lenox agreed with a laugh before he lowered their hands and led Penny up the aisle.

At the end of the hallway, the newlyweds turned to see the crowd of happy well-wishers start to head their way.

Penny and Lenox greeted all the well-wishers. Though as they did so, Penny marvelled at the green and pink clothing choices that everyone wore.

Our mums put the word out that everyone should wear our favourite colours since they thought it would be a nice gesture. Apparently, everyone wholeheartedly agreed, Lenox murmured.

Ugh! I want to cry in joy but must refrain, otherwise, I'll look terrible for pictures later, Penny replied feeling touched.

No, you won't. You'll look lovely because you always look lovely no matter what.

Penny sighed happily. *You're a wee bit biased, my love.*

Who me? Never, Lenox remarked in his most innocent tone.

Penny chuckled.

A few moments later, their parents, who had waited for everyone else to congratulate the happy couple, appeared before them. Both Mina and Ally had clear tear tracks running down their faces but neither seemed to care a wit about it.

"I'm so happy for you, my son and new daughter-in-law, so very, very happy," Lenox's mother cried when she hugged both of them at the same time.

"Thank you," Penny replied as she returned the hug.

Lenox's dad was next to hug the couple. "Congratulations, Mr. and Mrs. Hawksley. I truly wish you both the very best."

"Hold on. What do you mean by Mr. and Mrs. Hawksley? I thought I took Lenox's last name when we got married?" Penny asked.

"Uh, well … I knew that your cousin Lucy was going to keep the Baskerville name when she marries because she's the last one bearing the Baskerville name and I thought, why couldn't we keep the Hawksley name going, too. Sorry, I should have said something but I wanted to surprise you, which now that I think about it, was probably a bad idea… oh, bother," Lenox said, flustered.

"Lenox, that's super sweet of you and I'm not upset. In fact, I'm floored by the surprise. But truly, you want my last name? Won't the rest of your family be upset?"

"Oh no, they fully backed Lenox's choice and truth be told, I'd have changed my name to Mina's long ago if I hadn't been hiding our marriage to protect Mina and our kids from Iberius. In fact—" he stopped, seeing his wife shake her head.

"Oh no, no, I finally have achieved the proper pen flourish when it comes to signing my married name and I do not wish to change this. Though if it still bothers you in a hundred years' time, *min storr*, I am willing to change it back to du Reve then," Mina stated, offering a compromise as many Ritana did, since they had a natural tendency to avoid any arguments, joking or not.

"Nah it's fine, I was only joking, love," Conalai said as he and Mina stepped back to let the other couple in.

Penny's mum seemed to be too overwhelmed to speak, so Penny's dad took the lead.

Sebastian hugged his daughter and shook Lenox's hand as he remarked, "I never thought a wedding ceremony would mean anything to me but seeing how happy my daughter is today and knowing the lengths you are willing to go to make it so, goes the distance with me, Lenox. I'm sorry for any hard time I gave you in the past, present or future, though I will say it's in my nature to be a hard-ass since I am a hellhound alpha. However, don't take it personally, for you are truly family to me now and a member of the hellhound pack, Lenox Hawksley. Therefore we will always have your back as well as the rest of those you call family, for you lot have earned it."

"*Halle- freakin- lujah*!" Lenox's Uncle Phoenix's jubilant shout could be heard from outside.

"Phoenix!" his wife shouted back.

"What? Didn't you hear what Sebastian said? We're honorary hellhounds now, Iona! How epic is that?" Phoenix asked.

"Pretty epic, I agree," Raven mused.

"Truly thanks for that, Sebastian, though you may regret those words since you'll probably be called on to keep Phoenix out of trouble or away from my sister when Raven's on a warpath because he's committed another huge kerfuffle," Conalai said.

"I regret nothing because you do realize that it goes both ways. By which I mean, you're going to have to do the same for us when it comes to my wife and her twin. Which also means you'll be getting two for the price of one," Sebastian retorted dryly.

"Touché," Conalai acknowledged.

Ally finally snapped out of her emotional cloud and said, "As if! There's no way an army of vampyrs is gonna be able to stop me from being ridiculous. Try again, my mate, try, try, again."

Everyone laughed at the remark.

Ally suddenly let out a cry of delight before she wrapped her arms around the happy couple and nearly squeezed the stuffing out of them. "I'm so very happy for you both. The wedding ceremony was beautiful, and as you clearly can tell, I bawled my face off like a champion. Now onto the less stressful bit where we get to party on down. Woo hoo! Oh and Penny hon, don't forget to throw your bouquet when you go outside. Since according to Raven, immortal tradition dictates that the bouquet gets thrown over your left shoulder once you exit the ceremonial marriage grounds."

"Okay," Penny agreed.

With that, Penny and Lenox's parents left the hallway, followed closely by the newly married couple.

"It's bouquet time! Everyone who's in it to win it, get ready!" Ally shouted before she moved out of Penny's way.

"Penny hon, don't forget you have to turn around so you can't look at the crowd 'cause that's traditional, too," Ally told her.

"Got it. Want to count me down, love?" Penny asked Lenox.

"I'd love to. You ready, love?" Penny nodded. "Right, three… two… one!"

Penny chucked the bouquet over her shoulder then spun around to watch the melee in front of her.

"Ta da!" a familiar voice suddenly announced from the middle of the crowd of women.

Penny covered her mouth to keep from letting out a shocked laugh as she watched her cousin Lucy step forward and preen gleefully with the bouquet.

"No!" Alfie wailed.

"It's okay, dad," Lucy called out absently as she admired the flowers. "My secret boyfriend's not gonna propose anytime soon, so you got nothing— ah whoops! Looks like I let that cat out of the bag."

"What?" Alfie roared this time.

So I know there's a movie out called <u>Four Weddings and a Funeral,</u> but really, Lenox said to Penny as he tried to hold in his laughter.

In excitement, Penny turned her gaze to look at her husband. *OMG! This is like icing on the proverbial cake! Best day ever!*

Lenox lost his battle and full-on erupted into laughter as chaos suddenly exploded in front of him.

Chapter Twenty-Three

"Penny, love," Lenox called softly, gently trying to wake his wife who's back was nestled against his chest.

My wife and my soulmate, Lenox thought lovingly, grinning like a fool since it hadn't been that long ago that he had dearly wished for it.

"Hmmph," Penny softly grunted against his chest as she lay on her side in Lenox's arms.

"Penny, love, we need to get up," Lenox coaxed again.

"Nooo," Penny whined as she burrowed deeper into his chest.

"Come on, love."

"What? Wait! Are we late for school? Ack no!" Penny cried out as she came awake with a start, ready to bolt in a panic.

Lenox held onto Penny, keeping her from scrambling out of bed in a blind frenzy. Waiting until Penny started to relax, Lenox rolled onto his back taking Penny with him as she happily shifted herself until she ended up draped across his left side.

"There's no school today despite it being a Monday and we need to get up now, so we can continue to celebrate our wedding. Honestly, today's gonna be a great day," Lenox murmured before he stole a quick kiss.

Penny pouted. "It most definitely is though do we really need to go out? Can't we just stay in?"

Lenox groaned. "Any other day, I would wholeheartedly agree, love, though we both know that if we don't join the revellers, our family is going to come looking for us."

Penny sighed. "Yeah and knowing my luck, my dad will be the one to find us in the buff and have an apoplectic fit over the fact."

" Yeah, I could see that happening, though there's a greater chance my twin sister would come across us first and it'll be mightily awkward. Since Lulu has no boundaries and will cheerfully sit at the edge of the bed and wait for us to get up and get dressed."

Penny snorted. "I love the fact that we both have a very close-knit family, though I'm also not thrilled that they have privacy issues."

Lenox shrugged. "I'm sure there will come a time that neither of us will truly care about that but for the moment, we should get dressed.

Penny pouted again at the thought.

"After a shared shower?" Lenox suggested with a grin.

"Now you are speaking my language, my mate. Besides, aren't the bride and groom traditionally allowed to be late to their reception?"

"I don't know the proper etiquette for a two-day wedding event but that seems pretty reasonable to me."

"Good deal. Now up, up, up," Penny said with a playful nudge.

Lenox winked at Penny as he rolled out of bed and sauntered towards the bathroom.

Penny admired the view, muttering, "Well, I must say that I really love being married and mated. What a lovely view to wake up to."

"I heard that!" Lenox laughed.

"Good!" Penny retorted before she happily followed Lenox into the shower.

Nearly an hour later, Penny and Lenox made their way out of the house to find her cousin Lucy sitting on the top of the garden wall with Tyr Andraste sitting next to her.

"About time you two showed up. Your mum was going to wake you up but I stopped her."

"Thanks, Lucy. Though speaking of parents…" Penny started before stopping to look at her cousin expectantly.

Lucy shrugged. "I told you, Penny, I'm coming home to roost and I meant roost. My boyfriend and I want to settle down and live happily together."

"So when do we get to meet your mysterious boyfriend?" Penny asked.

Lucy shrugged nonchalantly before giving Tyr the side-eye who smirked in response while staring at Penny. Penny was about to let out a happy exclamation but Lucy mentally cut in.

Don't say anything out loud, Pen, please!

I won't but why don't you want to say anything? This is great news!

It's stupid but I just… I don't think my dad's ready yet. I mean, you should see how forlorn and mopey he was this morning. Not to mention, he badgered me for a few hours yesterday about it until mum put her foot down.

Ah, Lucy, Penny replied as she walked over and hugged her cousin.

"Again, it's really stupid," Lucy mumbled.

"It's really not and we're a unique pair, Luce. I mean, we both have well-meaning yet ridiculously overprotective parents, who are so unpredictable that an entire species of badasses gives them a wide berth."

"Do they ever!" Penny's mum called out cheerfully as she dragged her twin by the forearm.

"Ah, dad, please don't be mad at me anymore," Lucy cried when she saw his expression.

Alfie's expression changed from forlorn to mildly outrage in a heartbeat.

"Mad at you? For being in love? No, my dear one, never! I just wish I knew who this rapscallion was so I could put the proper fear of Alfred Baskerville into him. For that would show him! *Humph!* Stealing my baby girl away without stating that he has proper intentions upfront, that'll be right!"

"Oh, dad. He—"

"The rapscallion you speak of does have the very best intentions at heart and has for a long while now," Tyr murmured before jumping down from the garden wall. "Though to be clear, I'm the man you're looking for, Alfie, I'm Lucy's boyfriend."

"No Tyr!" Lucy shouted.

"You!" Alfie snarled.

Before he could react, Ally summoned up a small lit

firecracker and threw it in the direction of her twin.

"Damn it, Ally!" Alfie shouted as he jumped back from it.

"I told you to behave earlier! This is still my baby girl's wedding and there will be no bloodshed at it! End of story! Besides, I don't see why you're so pissed. Tyr Andraste is everything you asked for in a potential mate for your daughter when we did that little ceremony, remember?"

"Why'd you have to go and throw that in my face?" Alfie whined.

"Because, idiot, we wanted happy children who would find real true love with their soulmates. Now, you look at them and tell me that I'm wrong." Ally declared.

"Mum's not wrong," Penny readily agreed as she squeezed Lenox's hand.

"Yeah, Aunt Ally's not wrong at all, " Lucy replied, blushing deeply.

"And that love is returned, no?" Ally asked Lenox and Tyr this time.

"Without question," Lenox answered gravely.

"Yes, I do love Lucy," Tyr admitted.

"See, Alfie? Our girls have grown up and they are both ready for the next step in their lives. Don't get upset about it. Instead, think of the future blessings."

"What's that?"

"Grandchildren," Ally replied happily.

Alfie pursed his lips before he muttered, "Only after she's properly mated."

"Of course, brother, of course. Now, will you stop being a total jerk face and join me in celebrating?"

Alfie slowly nodded before he glared at Tyr and remarked, "You, me, fight club tomorrow."

Tyr shrugged "I have no problem with that. Though I also do have a gift for you."

"I cannot be bribed!" Alfie shouted at him.

"It's not a bribe. It's a gift that I intended to give you out of respect after stating my intentions."

Alfie's eyebrow raised.

"It's true," Tyr said.

"Hmmph," Alfie muttered as he crossed his arms in front of his chest.

Lenox watched Tyr keep his eyes trained on Alfie as he summoned up his gift with magic.

"No freakin' way!" Alfie shouted again, although this time, it was done in happiness, not anger.

Ah... it all makes sense to me now, Lenox thought as he realized he had helped Tyr build the present not that long ago.

In front of Alfie, there appeared a golf cart sized Batmobile, styled after the original 1960s version. Lenox had wondered why his friend had wanted to build one when he had come to him but he hadn't openly questioned it since they had built many of these smaller personal vehicles before. In fact, Lenox had helped Tyr make his twin Annika one that looked like her old Viking raiding ship for a birthday present.

Alfie eyed him warily. "Mine? To keep?"

"Yes," Tyr acknowledged.

Alfie bounded over to Tyr and wrapped him up in a bear hug, lifting Tyr clean off his feet. Something that Lenox thought to be an impossible task since Tyr was built like a solid mountain and stood at six-foot-five inches in height.

"Welcome to the family!" Alfie declared.

"Dad!" Lucy shouted.

Alfie set Tyr down and scowled. "What? You're not playing me, are you? You do have the best intentions at heart, don't you?"

"The very best," Tyr agreed solemnly.

"Tyr!"

" It is true, *elskling*," Tyr replied, calling Lucy sweetheart in Norwegian.

"He really must have," Lenox found himself muttering.

"Huh?" Penny asked her husband.

"It's just that Norwegians don't use terms of endearments like everyone else. Generally speaking, those words are reserved for only the nearest and dearest to a Norwegian and only said after knowing said nearest and dearest, for years."

"Really?" Penny asked him.

Lenox nodded. "Yes. Norwegians rely more on meaningful looks than words."

"Oh. I'm so glad you are Irish, Len," Penny stated.

"What's that supposed to mean?" Lucy demanded.

Before Penny could respond, Lucy added, "Tyr is also super awesome, I'll have you know! He can even fish a Greenland Shark from a depth of 2500 feet with only a large chain and bait! No sonar or anything!"

"Ah, man, why did you fish the shark, Tyr?" Penny's mum asked with a frown.

"I didn't do it to harm the shark, Ally. It was part of a research study run by the government of Norway. The study was to see how offshore drilling in the North Sea was affecting the sharks It all sounded like a good cause to me and my sister, Anni, so we pitched our expertise to those running the study and were chosen to join the expedition."

"Ah, good deal then, oh and PS, Team Shark" Ally said while pointing to herself.

"That's not a proper sentence," Alfie said, rolling his eyes.

"It wasn't meant to be, jerk. I'm merely stating my stance on being a shark lover! Though I'm also a huge animal lover, too."

"One who still eats meat," Alfie pointed out.

Ally shrugged her shoulders. "I'm from an immortal race that has carnivore leanings. I can't help that fact."

"So," Penny cut in smoothly, interrupting the argument, "Which band is playing in the concert grounds, Mum?"

Ally instantly gushed about a well-known metal band who was currently playing a set.

"Nice," Penny nodded in appreciation before she looked over her shoulder to Lenox to see if he wanted to see them.

Lenox snapped his fingers and another golf cart sized two-seater vehicle appeared. This one was done up to look like a cloud with an angry facial expression made of the radiator and headlamps, as well as red highlights throughout its fluffy cloud-like body.

"OMG, it's so cute!" Penny declared.

"Thanks, Lou and I created seven different emotional cloud vehicle that were part of a joint special art exhibit a few years back. This one is my favourite since it's the fastest, and to be quiet frank, I'm a bit of a speed junkie."

"Me, too, and can I drive it?" Penny asked him.

Lenox nodded before he showed Penny how to work it.

"Hey, Lenox, you said there were seven of them altogether?" Lucy asked.

"Yes; happy, sad, angry, loathing, fear, contempt and surprise," Lenox answered.

"Ooh! I want to try surprise," Lucy declared.

Tyr snorted. "It's a good choice but it also highly unpredictable since sometimes it flies and sometimes—"

Lucy interrupted him, "Shh, I wanna be surprised."

Tyr laughed as he summoned it up before Lenox could.

Lucy danced to the car and got in. Doing up her seat-belt as she waited for Tyr to join her, though she didn't have long to wait as Tyr got into the driver's seat.

"You sure?" he asked her one last time with his hand hovering over the start button.

Lucy nodded eagerly.

"Alright."

With that, he pressed the button and a high pitch delighted sound came from the engine before it started to rumble and change.

Penny watched in avid interest as the vehicle changed from a cloud car to a cloud drill that quickly burrowed itself into the ground and disappeared.

"OMG, that's so awesome. I want to try it later!" Penny's mum cried out

"Cool beans, since that means I don't have to give you lifts in my Batmobile."

"Hell, yes, you do," Ally retorted nonplussed."Though don't start whining because I want to go to the concert grounds right now and that's where your mate is, ergo two birds one stone."

Alfie rolled his eyes but didn't disagree. Then without a word,

Penny, Lenox, Alfie and Ally hopped into their vehicles and made their way to the concert grounds that were a step up just outside of Moonlight Valley.

Penny was astounded when the car took off like a bat out of hell without any further prompting after she started it up. Keeping her wits about her, Penny expertly steered around obstacles at breakneck speed, unable to break or stop since the car seemed to have a mind of its own. Then seconds before she was ready to bail out of the car, it stopped all on its own just outside of the festival grounds, which was precisely the place that she had wanted to go.

"How?" Penny started to question Lenox but she could see the sheepish look form on his face.

"I told it where to go. Sorry, I forgot to mention that. All the cars need to be told their destination beforehand and I hope Tyr remembers that otherwise we're gonna have to go look for him," Lenox said.

Penny shrugged. "Don't worry about it. They will eventually turn up on their own once the car stops. After all, Lucy takes chances by teleporting at random to see where she'll end up. Which, by the way, Tyr is probably familiar with because she does it that often. In fact, my Aunt Rika gave her an invisibility pendant so she would stop scaring the bejeesus out of humans when she pops into view."

"Well, okay then… wanna get something to eat?" Lenox asked Penny.

"Ooh, sounds like a plan! I'm famished. What's on offer?"

"Hmm, by the smell of it a little bit of everything. Though I'm kind of interested in the waffles," Lenox remarked, pointing to a waffle stand which wasn't far away.

"Ooh, never had them, but I'm always up for new things. Though, do you think we can get ribs, too? I'm a huge fan of those."

"Without question, love," Lenox replied as he wrapped his left arm around Penny's shoulder and guided her towards the food stands.

"Hey, Lenox. Hey, Penny. How's married life treatin' ya?" Lenox's Uncle Phoenix called out as he headed towards them, holding hands with his son Dante and daughter Aislyn.

"Great," Penny declared happily.

"Oh Penny, I wanted to tell you this yesterday but I really, really liked your wedding dress, it was so pretty," Aislyn murmured shyly.

Penny bent down so that she was eye level. "Ah, thanks, sweetie. How are you enjoying the celebration?"

"Oh, it's so much fun! Daddy, Dante and I just had a turn on the bouncy castle over there," Aislyn replied, pointing behind her before continuing, "But then we got hungry, so we came over here to get a snack. Then we're gonna find mummy since she was having a go on the whirligig machines."

"Whirligig machines?" Penny asked Lenox, knowing full well it was probably one of his inventions.

"It's a flying machine that looks similar to one of Da Vinci's design."

"Only it actually flies and Da Vinci based his work off of Lenox's, not the other way around," Phoenix said.

"Of all the rotten…" Penny stopped herself before she ended up cursing in front of the children.

"It's okay, love, he didn't directly copy my work. He was just inspired by it, which is something that I find to be very flattering, to be quite honest. Besides, Leo was also a dear friend to me," Lenox replied.

Penny nodded in understanding.

"Speaking of which, dear nephew…" Phoenix started.

"Um… yes?" Lenox asked.

"So my Iona 'fessed up today and told me that you're the one she bought all my dirigibles from," Phoenix said, calling Lenox's aunt by her real name not her preferred nickname.

"I didn't want to sell them to Aunt Raven, I wanted to gift them to her but she insisted on buying them," Lenox admitted.

"So she should, Len. We might be magical beings but we've still got expenses and I'm sure you can always summon up whatever you need with magic, but that's just dull. Nah man, I wasn't gonna harass you over the expense. Instead, I want to order more. Say, five more exactly," Phoenix stated.

"Uh… sure. Though, don't you have a fleet of twenty-five of them already?" Lenox asked.

"That's not a fleet, nephew. Well, okay, it's not a full fleet. More like a starter fleet for my future enterprise as an airship pirate."

"Uh… what?" Lenox asked, completely confused.

"You heard me, nephew. I'm gonna be an airship pirate once all these silly humans destroy themselves with nuclear weapons. Since I figure the sky is probably going to be the only safe place on this planet."

Penny shook her head. "Very doubtful since the prevailing winds will carry the nuclear debris through the sky, too. After all, the atomic blast at Hiroshima reached 60,000 feet into the air which would put the dust into the mesospheric level of the atmosphere, well above normal dirigible flying altitude."

"So… I really can't just fly above it?" Phoenix asked.

"Again, even if the dirigible could be modified to fly in the mesosphere, I doubt that would solve the problem since modern nuclear bombs would release particles far higher than that. Though, don't ask me how high since the last nuclear weapon was detonated in 1992, so I can't give you current numbers."

"Oh… what do you suggest then?"

"Talk the silly people into getting rid of their nuclear weapons or do what my dad did, which is create an indestructible toy box that can hold all the deadliest weapons known to man and safeguard the crude out of it," Penny stated.

"That sounds less fun that a future as an airship pirate."

"Phoenix!" Raven cried out in a half-laugh, half groan, "Please, for the love of the Light, tell me that you aren't trying to talk Lenox into building more airships for your crazed future endeavour? For goodness gracious sake love, even if the world ends up doomed to a nuclear apocalypse, you won't have time to be an airship pirate captain, since you're gonna have to set the world to rights as a Wasteland Warlord. After all, humans get one shot to be top dog on this planet and if they screw it up, then tough luck, we're taking over."

"How do you know we're gonna survive?" Phoenix asked her.

"Because I'm clearly awesome, duh," Raven responded dryly.

"How's that even an answer?" Phoenix demanded with a laugh.

"Because it just is. Anyway, Lenox and Penny, I must say that this is the most fun I've ever had at a wedding celebration. Thank you for inviting us."

"How can they not? We're family," Phoenix retorted.

Raven didn't even bother to give a verbal response as she instead rolled her eyes at him.

"Well, thank you for attending and it's really nice to be surrounded by family and friends," Penny said, feeling happy.

"Yeah, it truly is, though I will also say that you can always count on us to have not only your back not in the upcoming fights but with anything since you have our greatest respect," Raven said.

"How?" Penny blurted out, unable to keep herself from asking the question.

"Come on, Penny, I know you have gone to bat secretly for our family for years. In fact, I know you and all the other hellhounds kept evil in check when most of us needed to focus on cleaning our own houses of wickedness before we could join the fight properly. Speaking of which, tomorrow, Phoenix, Epimetheus and Prometheus are going to teach you how to use your the divine fire that comes with your hell chains."

"Sorry…what?" Penny asked at the unexpected offer.

"Penny, I know no one's explained this to you yet but those chains are part of the divine fire which Phoenix, Prometheus and Epimetheus all protect and use like you do. Sorry, it's hard to give you a simple explanation though I promise that we'll go over it tomorrow, right Phoenix?"

"Like I'd cock this up," Phoenix retorted with an eye roll.

"Phoenix!" Raven hissed, looking meaningfully at their children.

"What love? I'm just being honest, though anyway, don't worry about it today, Pen because I know you have managed to figure them out more or less. However, you're going to need to be an expert at it before you crack on against these big toughies."

"Oh, my Light! Only you would call ninth level hell demons, big toughies. Good gracious, Phoenix!" Raven exclaimed.

"Tch. No sense in swelling their demonic egos, love, by buying into their titles. Anyway, less demon talk since I'm hungry. Who wants to go grab something to eat and take another wee go at the bouncy castles?" Phoenix asked his children.

"Yay! Sorry, daddy but I swear my belly was ready to gnaw on my backbone," Aislyn admitted.

Phoenix snorted as his wife shook her head at him.

"I feel your pain, my sweet one, I really do. How about you, baby boy?" Phoenix asked his toddler son.

"So hungry," Dante said with a dramatic sigh.

Lenox and Penny laughed as Raven shook her head again.

"I swear I made sure all three of you were fed before we came here," Raven muttered.

"But that was ages ago, mummy," Dante retorted with a forlorn look.

"It wasn't ages ago, my son, more like an hour and a half tops but you two are your father's children, there's no doubt there. Come on, let's feed you lot again before you become ornery."

"Oh thank the Light, I was like ten minutes away from becoming full-blown hangry," Phoenix replied.

Penny and Lenox laughed before they bid Phoenix, Raven and their children a good day.

Getting into line for food, Lenox mentally reached out to Penny. *Are you worried, my love?*

About the demons? Yes and no. I mean, I know that we'll be in for a hell of a fight, but at the same time, I am hellhound and I kind of relish the thought. Also, we've just got to do our damndest to defeat them since I refuse to give up all future happiness with you because of those a-holes.

Lenox nodded in full agreement as he mentally started to prepare for the upcoming battles ahead since Penny was right. They had a future well worth fighting for.

Chapter Twenty-Four

Early the next morning, Penny found herself pacing the living room floor while Lenox sat on a nearby chair, sipping a cup of tea and staring into the fire. Earlier he had tried to get Penny to join him but she was too keyed up and nervous.

"It'll be alright, love," Lenox murmured finally, breaking the silence.

"I'm not so sure about that, Lenox. I mean, I know these battles are going to come and I've been chomping at the bit to be done with it all before today. So, why now do I suddenly feel nervous? Why am I so worried about failing so bad?"

"You won't fail," Lenox reassured her.

"How can you be so sure, Lenox? I'm a young hellhound. I mean among us, you're considered a seasoned warrior when your over fifteen hundred years old."

"Yet your kill count well and truly surpasses the vast majority of the other hounds, doesn't it? Come on, Penny love, I know that you've gone toe to toe with some of the biggest baddest villains out there. Hell, you even went into the leader of the Horsemen of Apocalypse, Pestilence's home realm and owned him with the other elite hounds."

"Owned?" Penny repeated curiously, completely unfamiliar with the term.

"Oh, sorry, it's a video game term which refers to dominating an opponent. Although in video games they spell it 'pwned', which was a popularized misspelling that arose from World of Warcraft."

"Huh? I still don't feel very confident, Lenox, despite your sweet words," Penny murmured.

"Are you truly worried about the fight, love? Or are you more worried about exposing your true self to others?" Lenox finally asked the real question dwelling on his mind all morning.

"Wow, Lenox, you've just managed to knock me for six with

one sentence," Penny said as she stopped pacing and dropped to the floor to sit in a cross-legged fashion.

"I didn't mean to, love," Lenox said as he set his teacup down.

"I know, Lenox. I really do and to be honest, I just realized you're right. I am scared for people to find out what I can do. I mean, everyone knows I'm part of the Hellhound Elite, I've never hidden that fact but very few know what that really means and even fewer know how we obtain that. For it's more than just earning a reputation in blood by killing demons. You earn it by virtue of your strength, both inner and outer."

Penny paused, causing Lenox to take up a spot on the floor in front of her. Taking hold of her hands, Lenox rubbed slow circles on the back of her hands while waiting patiently for her to find her voice again.

"I've witnessed dark things, Lenox. I mean who hasn't, especially when you are were born in the Renaissance Age?" Penny asked with a mirthless laugh. "Light, I never knew how dark the world was though until much later when I had to fight my first solo fight. It's something that every hound has to do eventually, though try telling that to my mum and dad. They were against it and fought Reggie tooth and nail for decades. But then... but then, I acted on my own. I know it's stupid now but I wanted all the hateful whispers I heard to stop, so I decided to go out into the world without anyone knowing. That was harder than you think because we hounds, can literally track anyone anywhere if we know their scent, though luckily for me, I had my Uncle Alfie on my side. I truly don't know how Uncle Alfie managed to stop them, though I'm digressing here. Getting back to my tale, instead of hunting on our usual patch which at the time was mainly England, Scotland, Wales, Ireland and sometimes France, I went as far away as I could and I ended up in the American Colonies. Light! I remember it so well. I was elated to arrive in a place that was so far from home because I was filled with a sense of adventure, you know? Though not knowing the lay of the land, I was at a considerable disadvantage. Then to add to it, as soon as I stepped ashore, I felt something so wickedly evil that even now it still sends a shiver up my spine. Unable to let the wicked demon be, I hunted for it, though being so young, I could have lost scent of it early on. However, unluckily for me, just as I was about to loose its trail, I stumbled across an Omega Clan protector who mistook me for my mum. I laugh about it now since I don't look that much like my mum with my fire tinted blonde hair even less so with my light pink locks. However, the man knew little of hellhounds and when he asked me for my family name, I told him it was Hawksley, not knowing that he thought that my mum was the only female hound to bear that name."

Penny stopped and took a deep breath as she remembered her past. Even now, years later, Penny could still remember everything about her first encounter with the demon— the bitterly cold winds biting into her hellhound form, the acrid smoke coming from the burned-out buildings and the scent of death and decay that was abound.

"It was a stupid decision. I'll admit that now but it was also the first time that I had ever been asked to help out and I didn't want to disappoint. So I followed the clues the man had gathered and went hunting for what I thought would be another run of the mill demon despite knowing deep down that it was more than that, Lenox. For ultimately, I would find out that the demon I was hunting was called a gatekeeper demon, which are the precursor demons to the Level Nine demons that are arising now. However they are best described as having enough evil in their heart to exist on that level, just not enough power to rule it. Nonetheless from what I witnessed from being in the demon's proximity and they have more than enough power to annihilate the world if left unchecked. What, wicked, wicked fools.

"Anyway, it took me a while to find it, even though the demon wasn't hiding by any means. For it was killing people left, right and centre, all the while stealing their souls to further its evil. However, every time I got close to finding it, it would disappear. Eventually, I learned from the ancient spirits of the land that gatekeepers have to constantly return to the place that they were summoned in order to maintain the link that keeps them on this plain, which eventually led me to a small burned out colony in present-day Virginia, I think. I'm sorry. I'm not really sure since I've avoided the states of Maryland, Virginia, North Carolina and South Carolina because I didn't want to revisit that place again. Sorry but it just... hurts, you know? The even without the reminder, I still remember everything about that fight, so vividly.

"It was snowing, with thick white droplets that reminded me of a snow globe. Though, a demented one since everyone was dead. Their bodies littered the town with still smouldering buildings around them as the demon set the remains ablaze every time it returned. I was so mad at the devastation that it had created. And, rightly or wrongly, I took it on without calling in any aid.

"It was a hard battle, Lenox. One that kept me thinking that I would die at any moment but at the same time, I cared not a whit because I was determined to see the demon off to hell first. Though even with my stubborn determination, I was losing the fight... until something happened. It's kind of hard to describe but I remember a voice so soft yet so melodious speaking to me and saying, 'This is not your end.' Nothing more, nothing less and part of me wonders if I was hallucinating it. However, the pain that came next was very real. Light, did it ever hurt! It felt like getting hit by a thousand bolts of lightning all at once and I thought I was done for this time. But, when the pain subsided, I had
them— the hell-link chains.

"These chains are what truly makes me a Brimstone Huntress because I can bind any evil entity to hell forever. However, I also knew that by possessing these chains, I would now attract the very worst demons out there who would want to keep me from putting them back where they belong and effectively seal my fate.

"However in that moment, I didn't care for I had the means to defeat the gatekeeper demon and I went to work, ripping it apart with the chains since the chains amplify a demon's evil actions and inflicted its own pain back on it tenfold. Then, when the demon was literally in pieces, the gate to hell appeared to take it to where it belonged. I quickly freed the demon's victims from its clutches so that it took no innocent souls into that terrible place before I... well saw it off, so to speak. Light, Lenox! I have never been more satisfied as a hound than when I said good riddance to that piece of rubbish.

"Unfortunately, reality set back in, for my mum and uncle Alfie had chose to appeared at that very moment. Both of them saw the chains and burst out in low keeling wails. Light, for the first time in my life, I saw them cry for me and my fate. I didn't understand it at the time but seeing them like that, I felt lower than low, Lenox. I declared that I'd find a way to remove them but my Uncle Alfie just shook his head and told me it couldn't be undone since the very Light from above had chosen me to be the next Brimstone Huntress, the only being who had the power to bind the four Level Nine demons to their rightful place for all of eternity. Though in doing so, it would cost me my life." Penny sighed and shook her head. "Trust the demons to show up now when I'm truly happy, Lenox. Light sake's, I'm not ready to die."

"Penny, your fate is not sealed. I know we haven't spoken in length about it yet, nor has anyone really told you the truth about the Wild Hunt. However, it was a hunting party that your ancestor created to hunt these Level Nine demons. During your ancestor's lifetime, there were more than four Level Nine demons, there were thirteen. Each had a domain in hell but like all evil fools, they wanted more. They wanted all the souls in this realm under their command and so they created the first hell vents where demons could escape to fulfill their wicked mandates.

"Nonetheless, our ancestors, both yours and mine, did not take it lying down. No, at first, they fought the hordes of demons separately but when more and more powerful ones arrived, they saw the writing on the wall. To in order to win against the forces of evil, they would need more power. My ancestor Altus and yours, Fironyi, took two different approaches to obtain what they needed. Altus first sought to strengthen himself with the knowledge of what these demons were and more importantly, what their weaknesses were so that everyone would have a better chance at defeating them. Whereas Fironyi decided to find the strongest warrior souls on this plane of existence and split her magic with them, thereby creating the magically strong race of hellhounds we know today. It worked for a time, with the hounds pretty much decimating the demon hordes to the point that the hell vents weakened and nearly disappeared altogether. Though it would take my cousin Anya's husband Thorn sacrificing himself for the first time, to close these vents for good.

"However, I'm getting a bit ahead of myself here and getting back to the story of Altus and Fironyi, when the hell vents started to disappear, it angered the Level Nine demons and they chose to enter the world themselves. These demons were beyond powerful and even breathing the foul air around them could kill humans in droves. They could kill more than just mortals as their power seemed unmatched in this realm. Though that didn't stop Fironyi, who wasn't one to give up and had chosen to lead one final stand against these demons. Luckily, Altus stopped her from doing something so foolish. He told her that to defeat these demons, they would first need something to bind the demons back to their hellish homes for all eternity and the only way that would work was if they had something made out of the divine flames.

"So, they sought out the divine fire keepers—guardians tasked to keep the flame of life burning and out of the hands of evil. The keepers denied their request because they believed that if the demons were exposed to the flame for long enough they would be able to corrupt it and thus doom the world. However, an idea came to Altus and he asked them if he could have the burnt ash that remained at the bottom of the fire pit. The keepers agreed, since they did not believe that the ash was of any use to anyone. Little did they know that the embers were imbued with the same essence the fire had. Though when this ash was combined with other life elements such as leaves from the tree of life or droplets from the water of life, it would form a new life element—metal. It was also determined that whoever wielded the metal would have the ability to take on the demons and bind them.

"Fironyi was elated and wanted to create swords and armour for her soldiers out of the metal. However, there wasn't enough for that, there wasn't even enough to make a sword large enough to pierce the demon bodies. Nonetheless, Altus could see that there was enough to create thick chains that could hold the demon. So it was decided that they'd use the chains to bind the demons, weakening them to the point that another weapon could kill them. However, when they went to use the chains for the first time during battle, the actual properties of the hell-link chains revealed themselves.

"For once combined with Fironyi's magical essence, the chains grew exponentially and were able to not only fully bind the demon but to also send it back to hell. Though it was also discovered that weaker Level Nine demons were killed outright with the chains, leaving only the most wicked to be bound and returned to their place in hell. However, two important things about how to keep the demons bound soon became apparent. The first being, that the binding was temporary unless the demon was bound on a certain day during the winter season that was specific to each demon and they also had to be lulled with a special rite that Altus had learned of. The second thing that came to be known, was that Fironyi weakened herself every time she held a demon in place for the permanent bonding and thus would be more vulnerable to attack. Since she needed to hold a demon in place until dawn when the sun's light would activated the rite. However by holding a demon bound for so long, their wickedness would drain the goodness from the huntress. However, all is not lost. For if others share in your burden, you will not be vulnerable. You also need to trust in the Wild Hunt and let them take on the hordes of minions that the demon will summon up to kill you and in effect, free it."

"How do you know this?" Penny asked.

Lenox gave her a small smile."Altus wrote everything down because he knew the demons would emerge again despite being permanently bound because others would take their role. I know that sounds strange. However, the Ninth Level of Hell is for betrayers, those who have committed the gravest sin and it's not beyond them to betray each other to become the most powerful.

"However, it's not something that happens right away from what I can tell. For the emergence of these demons seems to take anywhere from 5000 to 50,000 years to occur, though on average it's close to the 20,000 year mark. Now, when these demons last appeared on this realm, they combined their powers with the

Horseman of the Apocalypse to kill the last known Huntress who was not a hellhound but rather a Fae since the gift isn't directly bound to your line Penny. No, the Light chooses only someone who it believes is worthy of carrying the burden. Now in speaking of the last guardian Andrika Andraste, she and her husband were able to bind all the demons and the horsemen before succumbing to their wounds.

"Though, from the research Lulu and I have done, the demons Andrika bound are all gone and we will face new ones who have been gaining power through the wicked acts of their minions. However, right now, we must focus on preparing ourselves by honing our skills. Though most importantly, we both must hone our ability to keep our mind free of emotion because that will play a key role in these battles."

"No wonder my mum insisted I learn to meditate when I was young," Penny mused. "It wasn't a hardship though and keeping myself calm in battle is something I pride myself on. Honestly, it wasn't until I met you, Lenox, that I started to feel more out of sorts."

"I believe that out of sorts feeling you are describing is what love is and it might feel like a weakness, but it is actually a strength. After all, being soul-mated means you are truly no longer alone, Penniah, since we are meant to face every hardship together. Please remember that as well, for I know that you will want to face things alone to protect me, especially during these upcoming demon fights but without our true soul-bond, love, we will be weak. For together, I will be able to maintain all the goodness you have in your heart when the demon bombards you with never-ending evil."

Penny was quiet for a time before she whispered, "Is that how my ancestor Fironyi died?"

Lenox nodded. "She knew who her soulmate was but refused to bond with them, for fear that the demon would kill them, too. Now that did happen but only because they were not bound together and with her true mate dead, Fironyi lost the will to live. After Fironyi, the next leader of the Wild Hunt was meant to be Thorn, though from my research, when he made his self-sacrifice to close all the hell-vents he gained a new role as a Keeper of Secrets, which is the ability to keep the most deadliest knowledge of this realm away from those who would use it to destroy everything.

"Afterwards, the Light granted Andrika the ability to lead the Hunt. I truly don't know much about her as a person, unlike Thorn whom I have actually met. I have been told by my grandfather Midir that Andrika's biggest weakness was being too bold as a warrior, for she would plunge headlong into any battle without any stratagem. She was also determined to be the bloodiest warrior in existence and her mate Taliscus encouraged this for he,too, was equally determined to create a name for himself as a warrior and not just the Draggenin of Wind."

"That is true but I can tell you more," a strong female voice said as a woman and man teleported into the room.

Penny tensed but then relaxed when she recognized the couple as Arikadelia and Prometheus Eleftherios.

"My mother and father grew up in an age of war and when everyone else around them began to tire of it, they thrived in the bloodshed and would scoff at any talk of peace. I don't know what that says of them as people."

"Nothing," Penny stated, "Just because some people are happy to fight wars against evil and won't settle for peace, it doesn't make them bad people. Heck, that's all we hellhounds know and I would be extremely bothered if all the demons disappeared tomorrow and I had nothing to kill. Wait that does sound bad."

"It truly doesn't, love," Lenox replied shaking his head. "You know such a thing would never happen. It is also why you can't entertain the idea of there suddenly being nothing but peace. However, to others, knowing that there will always be evil in the world makes them wonder why they fight when there's no gain."

"Lenox, you are so wise and that's super hot," Penny replied making a '*mmm hmm*' noise of appreciation.

"Penny—" Arikadelia started to scold her.

"What? My mate's got brains, which I find to be very attractive along with the rest of his hotness. However I will promise to not act upon that attraction in front of you despite maybe a few moments of affection. However, please allow me appreciate him verbally. I mean, wouldn't you?"

Arikadelia nodded. "Oh, I get you, sweetie and I appreciate my mate every day of our lives."

"I know it and return the sentiment," Prometheus admitted with a small smile.

"So—" Arikadelia looked at Penny and Lenox.

"I'm ready to train whenever you are," Penny said.

"Penny, I know Phoenix mentioned that we had much to teach you but in truth, I know there is much you could teach us. How long have you been perfecting the use of your chains?" Prometheus asked her.

"Ever since I got them. I was scared at first that they could overpower me but Oswin the Spirit Elder told me that was not possible since my heart was pure. He also spoke in length about the different uses that the chains have and he told me that the key was learning to be a more well-rounded warrior. He and my Aunt Callie taught me how to meditate, practice yoga and tai chi to achieve clarity and a calm mind. Though I've always done those activities in secret because I didn't want anyone finding out."

"Well, I practice both yoga and tai chi and have done so since the sixties. It all started with my sister Lulu talking Freya and me into travelling the hippie trail, since she wanted to try a modern-day spiritual quest. Though we didn't do any of the drugs or alternative medicines that the humans were, since we were both more interested in immersing ourselves in different cultural outlooks. It was definitely a great experience and once this is all over, we could try it, love. Sorry, I'm digressing."

"Don't be sorry for being you, Lenox. I'm up for that, but right now, do you want to start practicing yoga and tai chi together, love?"

"I would be delighted."

"I'm a bit jealous," Arikadelia muttered. "I tried yoga with my sister-in-law Mydnyte but I'm too high strung for it."

"I found it hard at first, too, since it was really hard to clear my mind and truly focus without the overabundance of hyperactivity that inflicts us Baskerville hounds. However, my Aunt Callie taught me that the best way to start meditating first and the easiest what to achieve clarity of the mind, was to picture a room and slowly remove all objects until nothing remains. I also found aromatherapy and listening to the peaceful sounds of waves lapping against the beach helps."

"Does being able to meditate help you control the chains better?" Prometheus asked.

Penny nodded.

"Do you mind showing us?"

Penny led them down into the basement of her home where she had set up a practice area a long time ago. There were also very few things in the basement since Penny had feared that the chains would set fires all over the place. Something that had happened in the beginning because she feared the chains which caused her to lose control. However, once Penny learned to not fear them, it had gotten a lot easier.

The basement training area was a large well-lit cave that was lit by bio-luminescent mushrooms that happened to be fire-resistant. Around the practice area, a natural underground spring ran, though the channels weren't natural since Penny had dug them as part of her fire protection measures.

Arikadelia and Lenox sat down on a large boulder that overlooked the practice area while Prometheus and Penny walked into onto the area.

Penny took up a fighter's stance facing him. Prometheus let loose his inner fire ability and became a near blinding golden orange figure so that he could protect himself from the flames that Penny would soon unleash. Penny closed her eyes to clear her mind before taking in a deep breath and released the hell-link chains. They first appeared as a deep molten lava red before burning brighter to a near whitish pink colour. Penny directed the chains in a circular pattern around her body. They whipped around in fiery tornadic fashion before she tightened her fists to cause the chains to become invisible.

Suddenly, Prometheus lobbed small orbs of divine fire at her and a ghostly form of an invisible chain cocoon appeared surrounding Penny like a protective shield.

"Nice," Prometheus commented.

Penny threw her arms up and out, causing dark ghostly chains to appear in a spider web fashion, although the web didn't touch Arikadelia, Lenox or Prometheus. Instead, they seemed to weave themselves around them in a protective manner.

"So in this form, the chains can both defend allies against demon swarms and repel the same swarms. Am I right?"

Penny nodded.

"Impressive, Penny. That is some control you have on them. What about when in your hound and alternative forms, can you control them, as well?"

Penny shifted to her hellhound form and the chains retracted to accommodate her. She then ran a circle around Prometheus creating near-invisible anchor points on the ground as she ducked and dodged, mimicking what she would be doing on a battlefield. Then, when she seemed to complete the circle, she slid to a stop and let out a snarling growl.

Suddenly, a flash of light erupted, and a chain trap ensnared Prometheus. Penny gave a short howl and the trap dissolved. Penny then went through a gauntlet of tests that Prometheus guided her through, switching forms breezily as she did so.

Lenox watched mesmerized by Penny's skill and focus.

Uh, Lenox. How's Penny training going? Ally reached out mentally to him for the first time.

Lenox didn't verbally answer as he instead allowed Ally to see what he was witnessing using his magic. Ally thanked him then silently watched Penny.

After what seemed like about an hour and a half in Lenox's estimation, Lenox felt the magical pulse that let him know that his Uncle Phoenix and Aunt Raven had arrived.

"Prometheus, Penny love, come take a small break. My Uncle Phoenix and Aunt Raven have arrived bearing food. They're setting it up in the dining room."

"Oh, sounds great. Are you alright with that, Prometheus and Arikadelia?"

"Call me Arika, Penny, and food sounds wonderful right now," Arika replied as Prometheus nodded.

"Okay. Oh, hey, my mum and dad have also arrived with food, too," Penny called out.

Lenox chuckled at the thought of the mountain of food that awaited them. When they made their way upstairs, Lenox saw the feast of food piled nearly a foot and a half high on the table.

"Now, Iona love, this is what I truly call brekkie," Phoenix said to Raven.

"This isn't breakfast. This is a feast of epic portions, Phoenix."

"Nah, this is brekkie for a hound. Well a small group of hounds at least," Sebastian disagreed.

Ally wasn't focused on the food but rather Prometheus. "So how did it go?"

Prometheus smiled at her. "Penny is well in control of the hell-link chains and if we were enemies, I have no doubt that Penny could truly take me in a fight."

"Shit, seriously?" Phoenix asked doing a double-take.

"Phoenix! Language!" Raven hissed at him.

"Relax love, our children aren't around right now and I've heard way more colourful words coming from the hounds before. Anyway, truly Prometheus, she could take you?"

Prometheus nodded. "In all seriousness, she could."

"She could also take me in a fight by the looks of it, too. Penny is one hell of a calm, focused fighter, and when you combine that with her hellhound war traits it makes her an insane opponent to go up against. Who taught you to fight like that, Penny?" Arika asked her.

"Well. My mum and dad, I suppose," Penny said after she thought about it for a moment.

"Hell no, not us," Ally said adamantly.

"But you did though, mum. I mean, you taught me never to let my crazy out fully because an enemy would know how mad they were making me and that would have me at a disadvantage. Then you, dad, taught me to always see through my opponents, not letting their outward actions bother me but instead search for inner weaknesses while they prattle on or attacked first."

"Shit, really?" Ally remarked, completely dumbfounded.

"See?" Phoenix said, turning to Raven, who sighed in response.

"Well, blast me! I have to say that turned out to be a case of doing as I say, not as I do. I mean Light sake's, I take on my enemies with a psychotic zeal that I will own up to every day of my life and I truly can't say that I am a calm fighter," Ally remarked.

"True," Sebastian agreed readily before looking at his daughter. "I'm proud of you, Penny. I knew you were one hell of a warrior but knowing that you fight smartly not stupidly like the rest of us seem to do, eases my mind greatly. After all, these demons will try to push every button you have."

Penny stopped eating and reached out to take her dad's hand in hers, much like Lenox had done earlier with her.

"Dad, I might not be the most confident hellhound but when it comes to fighting, I will not back down. I want to live and no wicked, decrepit jerk-face of a demon is gonna take that away from me. They can go eff themselves for all I care."

Sebastian smiled proudly. "You're right, baby girl, eff 'em."

Penny looked at Prometheus and Phoenix. "Do you two mind continuing to train with me? Along with my mum and dad? Though now that I think about it, my uncles Reggie and Alfie will want to be in on it, too."

"Hell, yes, sweetie, we'll train hard so that we can make these blighters pay tenfold for all dishonours they have bestowed upon our family," Ally agreed.

"Speaking of which, Aunt Raven will you help me research the demons more?" Lenox asked as an idea came to mind.

"I'm up for that, Lenox, though you know your dad will be, too. How about you, Arika? Do you want to help us?"

"It's not normally my role since Prometheus is the one people seek out to answer all their questions," Arika replied dryly, causing her husband to roll his eyes with a smile before she continued, "but I'll see what info I can rustle up for you."

"Good. Now eat up, folks. We've got training to do, to make some pesky Niners cry. Do you want a rib, love?" Phoenix asked, offering one to Raven.

Lenox couldn't help but feel happy that he was surrounded by people who would go to hell and back with them. For he knew that it might just come down to that.

<u>Chapter Twenty- Five</u>

A few days after Penny had begun her training regime, Lenox began his own regime as he focused on pouring over divination texts and intricate puzzles that held all the information he needed. All of which were courtesy of a few rare moods or divination trances, that had struck Lenox centuries before; trances that coincided with an intense battle with a gatekeeper demon that Lenox had yet to tell Penny about fully.

I need to change that, Lenox thought.

"Change what?" Penny asked as she wandered into the room, picking up on Lenox's thoughts.

Lenox blew out a sigh and looked over at his twin, who was lost in a mood, too, though it wasn't a true mood but rather Lulu's way of solving Lenox's puzzles since his sister was a visual learner and often painted the visions that they shared.

"A few centuries ago, Lulu and I fought a demon gatekeeper.. Her name was Caoranach."

"Why does that ring a bell?" Penny asked.

"She was an Irish demon queen who is said to be the mother of demons in Ireland and legend say she was first banished to the bottom of Loch Dearg by Saint Patrick. Well again, was," Lenox said.

"Yup, she's completely gone now. We banished her right off this plane of existence," Lulu added.

"Yes, and rightly or wrongly, we had searched her out after Lulu and I shared a vision that showed us that by battling her, it would awaken our true powers as the Sentinels of the Wild Hunt. For as sentinels, it would be our role to find those who were meant to be wildlings and also to directly aid the Brimstone Huntress when the battle against the Niners or Betrayers began."

"Wow… I kind of wish I was there to help you. I mean, not that I don't believe you could take her since I can tell that you and

Lulu are like a huge treasure trove of ancient Light Magic that you hide so deeply so that no one picks it up. Hell, I didn't even notice it myself until after our soul-bond formed," Penny said as she wrapped her arms around Lenox's shoulders.

"Yay! Glad that happened and PS, I love being a mongoose in the immortal world. After all, all those stupid demon cobras never saw us coming, which is super awesome," Lulu replied as she got up and stretched her back.

"Lou, you've finished your mood?" Lenox asked, noticing the clouded air of divination disappeared from his sister.

"For now," Lulu replied, yawning before adding, "The wisps told me that we have all the available answers for the first battle and more will come at a later time."

"Huh… that might be, that might be," Lenox mumbled as he eyed the complex puzzle cube in front of him.

"Light, Lenox, I know you are a genius but these puzzles truly take the cake!" Lenox's Aunt Raven declared in slight exasperation after she entered the room with Lenox's dad a few seconds later.

"Raven," Conalai admonished.

"Sorry, brother but it is true. After all, I have attempted many impossible riddles in my lifetime, but these take the cake. Honestly, you're going to need an army of puzzle-solvers to complete these over the next few months."

"Which are also known as hellhounds," Penny piped up.

Raven let out an oath as she realized that she had forgotten all about the fact that hellhounds were avid puzzle solvers, while Conalai chose to laugh instead.

"Honest to the Light, how did we forget that the hellhounds are puzzle fiends? Well fiends in the good sense, sorry, Pen," Conalai remarked.

"I'm not offended by being called a puzzle fiend."

"Ah, good deal then, do you mind calling in some hounds to help us with this? We'll wait for them, since I need a short break anyway," Raven remarked.

"Sorry, Aunt Raven," Lenox said.

"Don't be sorry, Len. Puzzles aren't my forte since I really don't have the patience for them. Though they are your uncle

Phoenix's, bizarrely enough and he'll be around later this afternoon to help out after he finishes a small job. Anyway, I thought you were training Penny?"

"Dad, let me have an hour tea break from training and I made a beeline to see Lenox."

"Have you eaten?" Lenox asked her in concern.

"I ate a muffin on the way here but I wanted to see your face more," Penny remarked happily.

"You really should eat love, for you need to keep your energy up," Lenox said.

"I will, I will, Mum's gone for takeout anyway and she should be back in the next five to ten minutes," Penny said before she stole a small kiss from Lenox.

The small kiss wasn't enough for Lenox, who got up from his seat and kissed Penny properly.

"Ahem," Lenox's dad cleared his throat.

Lenox pulled away from Penny and looked over his shoulder guiltily, "Sorry, dad. I forgot you were there."

Lulu snorted. "Of all the things to forget, brother… wow."

Conalai shook his head in response. "It's alright, son and speaking of lunch, you should take a break, too. In fact, I came over to see if you two had eaten."

Lulu shook her head. "We haven't yet, dad."

"Oh! That was another reason I came over here. Mum said to invite you all to join us. She bought all your favourites, Len and Lou," Penny said.

"Oh, your mum is a gem!" Lulu cried out happily.

"Hold on, how does Ally know what Lulu's and Lenox's favourite foods are?" Raven asked.

"Well, we have alternating dinner nights. Meaning one night Freya and I host supper, then the next night Lenox and Penny host it, then Mum and Dad, and so on. This system works out well for us because as much as I don't mind cooking, I prefer eating at someone else's house and being in good company while doing so."

"I'd like to join this arrangement, though I know Phoenix would eat everyone out of house and home, so I guess it's just better if I cook," Raven said with a sigh.

"Well, if you change your mind, you're welcome to join us, Aunt Raven," Lulu said linking arms with her.

"Oh, yeah and I doubt he could eat us out of house and home. After all, my family is notorious for getting kicked out of buffets in the human world for nearly cleaning out places," Penny said.

"Phoenix is so hellhound in half Vampyr/half Fae form," Raven said.

"That's exactly what I've been saying," Phoenix replied as he teleported in carrying his daughter and son in his arms.

Aislyn rubbed her eyes as if fighting the need for a nap but Dante was out for the count.

"So, I hear that there's food on offer?" Phoenix asked everyone.

"No, daddy! No more food. I need a nap," Aislyn whined.

"No worries, sweetie, I'm getting you to bed in just a moment, I promise but I just wanted to stop by to let your mummy know that we're back. Iona count me in when it comes to more food, though do you mind asking whomever's making it to bring it here, so our little ones can nap in there own beds?" Phoenix asked Raven before he leaned in for a quick kiss.

Raven didn't have time to respond as Penny whipped out her phone.

She texted, ***< Hey, mum and dad, I'm sorry this is short notice but do you mind if we had lunch at Raven and Phoenix's home instead of the Fight Club? Their two wee mites need some nap time.>***

<Say no more, sweetie. That's fine and it's also a good thing that I doubled our order.> Penny's mum texted.

<Yeah, be there in a few moments. Just packing up these behemoth food boxes into a manageable magic crate.> Her dad added to the group chat.

Penny snorted as she could vividly see her dad grouse as he had one of the Minotaurs (probably Callie or Yuna) stop time so he could pack the horde of food her mum bought into a food crate. All the while Penny's mum and her twin watched on, since they had been banned long ago from helping. Though of course, that wouldn't have stopped them bickering the whole time about whether or not they had enough food or if they should order more.

As if right on time, Penny felt a magical pulse coming from her mum a few moments later. Ushering everyone out of the living room and into the dining room, Penny found it full of her family, friends and a mountain of food.

"Lunch is served!" Ally called from her spot in front of a pile of spare ribs.

"Oh, and don't worry. We put all the real meat at this end of the table and left the other end for magically made meat or full vegetarian meals."

"Thanks, Ally," Lenox's mum called out to her happily before she spooned some potato salad onto her plate.

Ally cheerfully waved at her in response, since her mouth was full of food.

Dig in Len and Lou, for this will all be gone soon, I swear it. Penny warned the twins, intent on looking out for them and Lenox's mum before the food free-for-all.

"Not on your life," Penny's mum said around a mouthful of food when she caught Lenox's Uncle Phoenix eye up the plate of ribs she was eating.

"Give me a couple," Phoenix retorted.

Penny's mum and Lenox's uncle began to bicker and Penny used the distraction to quickly scoop up what she wanted to eat before she turned her attention to Lenox and Lulu. Surprisingly the twins, alongside their mother, father and Aunt Raven, had all managed to gather large plates of food and find a place to sit and watch the pending melee.

"This isn't the first time we've been part of a pending food brawl over barbecue, love. Though this is nothing compared to pizza nights," Lenox said as he patted a chair next to him.

"You sure you're not hounds?" Penny asked as she sat down next to him and began eating.

"I'm pretty sure," Lenox chuckled before adding, "Though I've been told that there's not much of a difference between hellhounds and vampyrs."

After lunch, Lenox, Lulu, Conalai and Mina returned to Raven and Phoenix's study. Instead of returning to actual studying, Lulu and Lenox decided to broach the subject that they had been dreading to speak of for a while. Since it was bound to greatly upset their aunt and uncle, though Lenox had a feeling it would affect his uncle more.

"So Lenox… should we tell them now?"Lulu asked Lenox.

"Tell them what?" Phoenix asked, automatically taking the bait.

Lenox sighed and rubbed his face in mild agitation.

"Well, there's no easy way to say this, but we know who the first Betrayer demon is. It's Balor of the Fallin," Lenox stated upfront deciding to rip this band-aid off in one quick fluid motion.

Phoenix did something strange in response—he laughed.

"I wasn't kidding Uncle Phoenix. Balor is one of the demons or at least his essence is and we'll be facing him in Ireland."

Phoenix's laughter stopped and he cursed.

"That's impossible. I killed him, then for good measure, I did it again and made sure to send his soul to the shadow realm or hell directly. Him coming back from hell should be bloody impossible."

"No, who you sent to the Shadow Realm was the demon spirit who had merged with Balor during the dark ritual that extended his life. Sorry, Uncle Phoenix, I know this is hard to take in but the Balor you knew and justly killed with was never one entity but two, a demon and a sickly evil human. When you first killed him, you sent his dark soul to the ninth level of hell but it didn't undo the curse that gave him immortal powers and thus the demon split from him and became a demonic spirit that couldn't leave Kilderheeth, the place where the ritual was held. Though when you cleansed Kilderheeth, just after Aislyn was born, to return the Isle of Kilderheeth to its rightful place as one of the seven immortal isles, you sent the demon back where it belonged. Nonetheless, since his original death, Balor has in been in hell and somehow has managed to beat out all the other Level Nine demons to become a full Betrayer."

"For the love of the Light, you can't be serious!" Phoenix exclaimed.

"I am sorry Phoenix, but Lenox is very serious and I can show you truth through my cauldron if you still don't believe his words to be truthful," Mina offered.

"Mina hon, I don't doubt you, but—" Phoenix broke off and let out a mild oath before he placed his hands on his head, trying to keep himself from unleashing his emotions which would greatly affect Lenox's mother. Though luckily enough, Lenox's Aunt Raven appeared to soothing things over.

"Will you be alright, love?" Raven asked Phoenix, using an uncharacteristic calming tone.

Uncharacteristic to Lenox's ears anyway since he knew that his aunt felt deeply for her soulmate but she had been long conditioned to never show her emotions outwardly, for Lenox's paternal grandparents would have used it against her.

Lenox, my son, how are you feeling? Lenox's mother asked him as his dad and twin focused on him, effectively giving Raven and Phoenix some privacy, by tuning them out.

I really can't say. I mean part of me is worried about how things will go during these upcoming battles but at the same time, another part of me is not willing to accept anything less than victory. Am I being overconfident? Am I not thinking this through? Lenox asked them.

Lenox, you think everything through in great detail and I know you've made sure that nothing has been overlooked. What I really want to know is, are you scared at all? Lenox's dad asked.

That's what worries me the most. I don't believe I know what fear is having not experienced it in life and now I wonder if this emotion would strike me for the first time during the demon fight, and I will react wrongly.

I don't know what to say, brother. I mean, I can cause an overload of emotion in someone but because we're twins, I'm pretty sure that it wouldn't work because your powers can become mine or vice versa. Do you have any ideas? Lulu asked their parents.

I wouldn't worry about feeling fear, my son for I don't believe this will be your biggest issue in battle. No, your greatest issue will be swaying others to listen to you and your battle plans, especially when it comes to the hellhounds, for they seldom listen to reason in regards to anything.

Lenox was quiet for a long moment. *What do you suggest, mum?*

That you always keep this in mind when you speak to them—hellhounds naturally respect the strongest, whether that be warrior or sage. Therefore, do not defer to anyone when you speak up, for the slight display of weakness will cause the hounds to ignore you. This will end in disaster because their base instinct will be to take on the demon themselves. You must also keep this in mind, Lulu because you and Lenox are two halves of the same whole and if they don't respect you, then they will not respect your brother.

So no more Mrs. Happy Go Lucky, then? Lulu asked her mum.

No, my dear. Being Mr. Seriously Quiet or Mrs. Happy Go Lucky as you like to refer to yourselves, will get everyone killed. You need to go into this battle as confident and commanding as you can be. This will be something you both will find hard since you've never done it before but I know you have the ability because you are very much your father's children, Lenox's mum said, smiling at her husband.

Conalai snorted. *I never thought I'd receive a backwards compliment from you, my love but it's still apt nonetheless. Also, I want it stated here and now that I might have gone the overprotective route with you two ever since you were born. Even going so far as to let Iberius unforgivably claim you as his children instead of mine outwardly, which wasn't something that I ever and I mean ever, wanted to do.*

Dad ,we understand why you did what you needed to do. The world was a brutal place for a long time. Though you are our father and we never once saw you as anything else. Even if there was the remote possibility that we could have been his children due to Iberius vile action in hurting mum... sorry mum, Lenox replied not wanting to bring up the evil rape that Iberius inflicted upon his mum so many years ago..

You have nothing to be sorry for, my son, for I have long come to terms with what Iberius did and the lasting consequences it had for all of us. I will not lie. Those consequences anger me even to this day for you were always children created in love but his wicked action in forcing himself upon me tainted that. Nonetheless, it is a testament to the greatness of your character that you always knew the truth and never let his evilness affect your hearts. Truly, I count my blessings when it comes to having you as my own and there's not a day that goes by that I don't wish that we fought to clear this up ages ago.

Lenox's father nodded in agreement.

Mum, if you and dad are looking for forgiveness from us, then I will clearly state this here and now there is absolutely nothing to forgive, Lulu replied earnestly.

Lenox and Lulu let their parents feel the deep well of love they held in their hearts for them.

Mina crossed the small space between them and hugged them fiercely, and was soon joined by Conalai.

"Uh…" Phoenix started to voice in bewilderment.

"The Light answered our prayers when it gave us the two of you," Mina whispered.

"We're equally just as blessed that you are our parents, Mum," Lulu replied.

No one said anything for a moment until Mina and Conalai reluctantly pulled away several minutes later.

"I don't doubt for a moment that the demons will try to use Iberius' vileness against you two."

"I don't doubt it either since Caoranach tried it too and found out the hard way, that by bringing it up, it brought about her doom," Lulu replied.

"What about the Nightmares?" Mina asked, remembering how those wretches tried to do the same thing.

"It hurts to admit that we were vulnerable to their wickedness because of the smallest seed of subconscious doubt. However, after the blood test proved without a shadow of a doubt of who our true father was, Lulu and I decided to bury it once and for all. We sought out Aether in the Ancient Glen and asked him if he'd help rid us of our past pain and fears. He took in all as a secret keeper then burned them away in a sacred ceremony. We did this when dad faced his trials because we never wanted to be weak against those doubts ever again," Lenox explained.

"Light sake's, you're smart," Conalai said in stunned amazement.

"They both have a massive IQs, Lai," Phoenix pointed out.

"Shh… Lenox is the smart one. I am the creative one," Lulu replied, shushing her uncle.

"So not true, sweetie. You both are equally as smart and creative as each other," Phoenix pointed out again.

"Yeah, but no one needs to know that," Lulu replied sunnily.

"You know you are ruthless in your own way, Lou," Phoenix remarked.

"You know I'm part vampyr, so it sort of goes with the territory, Uncle Phoenix."

Phoenix burst out laughing at that. "Hoisted by my own petard. Well done, Lou."

"I guess so. Though, Uncle Phoenix?" Lulu asked.

"Yes?"

"We know you're mad that Balor's soul was able to become a demon and come back as a Betrayer. However, don't believe for one moment that he's going be able to harm Aunt Raven or our cousins or any of our family for that matter," Lenox stated matter of factly.

"Why's that?" Phoenix inquired curiously.

"Because if you think for one gosh darn second, that we don't have a game plan to put the snivelling conniving, skivvy jerk face back in his rightful place permanently, then I truly don't know what to say," Lulu replied as Lenox nodded in full agreement.

Phoenix looked from one determined twin to the other and back again."How?" he finally asked them.

"As you said, we're kind of ruthless though I prefer the term relentless. Nonetheless, we have a confession to make," Lulu said.

"You know the whole deciphering scrolls and painting that

we've all been doing lately?" Lenox asked them.

"Yeah?"

"Well… that was a hundred percent for show since the demons were watching us," Lenox admitted.

"Are they still?" Phoenix demanded.

"Oh yeah, they've been spying on us ever since Penny and Lenox mated. Too bad for them that we've done all the true legwork in secret, centuries ago."

Lenox nodded in agreement.

"Are you going to tell us what you've got planned?" Phoenix asked.

Lenox and Lulu both shook their heads.

"Ah hell, I guess I'll what I've done before in battle, go in bold as brass and kill any idiot that tries to get in your way."

Lenox nodded again, knowing full well it was best for his Uncle to go into battle without a solid plan since he was quite quick on the uptake, especially during ~~a~~ battle, and could adapt to anything.

"So how do you plan on telling everyone else that's there's not gonna be a plan?" Phoenix asked them.

"We tell them that we're doing this Hellhound Viking style right now before we tell them the real plan later," Lenox replied.

"What does that mean, Hellhound Viking style?" Raven asked this time.

"Well, hellhounds like to take on enemies as brutally as they can, with extra points garnered for creativity. Whereas, Vikings like to just kill them all."

"Ooh, I hear a points system in there, Iona love and you know what that means. Anyone with the lowest body count or the least creative dispatch method has to buy the first three rounds of pints at the pub. Man, we're going to have to spread the word because I want this system well established for later when I—"

"End up buying my first three rounds of ale," Raven finished for him with a laugh.

"Them's fighting words, wife," Phoenix retorted before he and Raven teleported out of the room to go speak to the other warriors of the Wild Hunt.

"Well, that's one problem solved, though you two still need to prepare yourselves for the rest," Conalai said while he hugged them both tightly before teleporting away to speak with other key players.

Lenox and Lulu looked at their mum who sat down on the floor in a meditation pose. She hadn't bothered to enter into a trance yet as she waited for Lenox and Lulu. Both of the twins moved from the couch to the floor to take up similar positions. A moment later, Lenox's grandfather Midir and Galen, the former Nightmare of Horror, appeared.

"We've got the circle covered from the demon's influence. Go on,my daughter. You may begin."

With that, Mina led her children into the other plane where they could practice their true powers and go over the rituals they'd need to complete, in peace.

Chapter Twenty-Six

The day of Halloween was a near sombre one, and it would have been a utterly sombre one if not for Lenox's sister Lulu who was determined to see that no demon was going to ruin Halloween for anyone. Something that made Penny happy because she could tell that Lulu's sweet actions were lifting everyone's spirits.

Currently, Penny was following Lulu's antics through her phone as Lulu sent her regular videos and pictures of her, her wife Freya and their kids trick or treating around Moonlight Valley, the Compound and the Norra Stam village over the past few days, leading up to Halloween.

"Only my twin makes Halloween a three-day event," Lenox said, shaking his head as he watched the latest video over Penny's shoulder.

"So she should. Lulu is a ray of light in a dreary world, just like you are, love," Penny remarked, as she wrapped her arm around Lenox's waist.

"I've never been called a ray of light before. Normally, I've always been described as the serious one."

"You might be seriously minded Lenox but I know the truth. You are sweet and kind as the day is long," Penny retorted.

Lenox laughed again. "Ah, Penny, really?"

"Yes, really and I don't care how that sounds. You are amazing, Lenox Hawksley."

"You are pretty awesome, Len," Tyr said as he, Lucy and Annika entered the room dressed in full armour.

In Lenox's opinion, Lucy's armour looked deceptively light since it appeared to be made of ~~a~~ leather and almost looked like a futuristic space suit compared to the chain mail, leather and metal Annika and Tyr wore. However, from what Penny told him earlier, all hellhounds wore special armour made of dragon scales (no dragons were hurt, they shed scales as they grow) not leather, which was

actually far stronger than anything metal. When Lenox heard that, he asked Penny where he could obtain some. Little did he know Penny had commissioned Figus, the hellhound armourer, to make Lenox's and Lulu's suits to protect them from the upcoming battles and they had arrived yesterday.

"Where'd you get the armour?" Tyr asked when he noticed Lenox wearing full armour for the first time in his life.

"Penny had it made for Lulu and me," Lenox remarked, distracted as his mind started to go over their battle plan.

"Looks pretty epic the more I see it. Can I get some?" Annika asked Lucy.

"Sure. We'll get you measured on Monday and you'll be suited up before the next battle. You want any Tyr?"

"Nah, I've been fighting with this gear for thousands of years and it feels like an extension of myself now."

"Fair... oh hey, Lulu, hey Freya," Lucy called out when she saw them teleport in.

"Hey, Lucy, good to see you!" Lulu called out in delight as she made her rounds and hugged everyone in the room, as a very amused Freya sat down in a recliner and watched.

"So I have to ask, Lulu, how did the trick or treating go?" Penny asked.

"Super well! We've got tons of treats for you, Penny, since the kids filled up an extra few sacks for you and Lenox."

"What?" Penny asked, completely stunned.

Freya laughed. "Our kids really take after Lulu I swear and while they were trick or treating, Bryn and Lore each brought up their pumpkin baskets to be filled before lifting a third together for their uncle Lenox and Aunt Penny. It was the kids' idea since they were a bit upset that you couldn't trick or treat with them this year since you had to prepare for this fight. Now I will say, a lot of it's candy but most of the hellhounds and vampyrs also threw in a ton of packaged beef jerky for you, Penny.

"Ah, that's so sweet of them. Lenox, tomorrow we're going to go get them a present," Penny said.

Lenox smiled and gave her a small nod of agreement.

"So, Penny..." Lucy started.

"Yes, I'm going to share the jerky and candy with you for *mi casa et su casa* when it comes to snacks," Penny responded rolling her eyes.

"Good deal; I love jerky," Lucy called out as she ran over and hugged Penny.

"Hey!" Tyr declared, looking amusingly affronted.

"Obviously, I like you more than jerky, though to be honest, just barely because you aren't a chewy delicious beef snack that can go everywhere with me and keep me from hangrily hurting people. In fact—"

Tyr snagged Lucy when she moved away from Penny and crushed his mouth against hers, effectively kissing the stuffing out of her and leaving her breathless a few moments later.

"You were saying?" Tyr asked her arrogantly.

"I still love jerky. Nothing changed but thanks for the kiss, honey. Now you want some?" Lucy returned as she summoned up a bag of barbecue flavoured beef jerky and offered it to him.

Tyr let out an aggrieved sigh before he nodded.

Lucy then offered her snack to everyone before a few other snacks joined the rounds as they all ate and waited for the others to arrive.

Within the next fifteen minutes, the Wild Hunt trickled in, with the hellhounds arriving first in the form of Alfie, Ally, Sebastian, Reggie, Yuna, Winston and Rocky who appeared moments after Lulu and Freya. About five minutes later Lenox's family arrived with: Raven, Phoenix, Wulf, Conalai, Felix, his wife Meri, Mydnyte, Trey, Falcon and Skull; Then came the Omega Clan ten minutes after with Prometheus, Arika twin sister of Trey, their son Keiran, Thorn, Llyr Tiregnan leader of the Celtic Omega Clan, Lenox's grandfather Midir and grandmother Medb, Lenox's Uncle Markos and Morpheus (Maeva's husband) Aunts Marguerite and Maeva, Galen, Lydia, Frey, Vale and his wife Emi (best friends of Freya and Frey). Then to round off everything the Draggenin of death Erebrus and his wife Lucky the Draggenin of Life, along with the Fae King and Queen Aidan and Nia Halsin, followed by Memphis and

Penny's Aunt Callie at the very end.

"Blessed Light, Memphis! I told you we were running late!" Callie scolded him when she saw everyone.

"What can I say, honey? I'm always the last one to a meeting but the first one to a party," Memphis drawled, looking unapologetic.

"As if, kiddo. I'm gonna kill more minions than you will," Phoenix called out.

"Care to put a friendly pint wager on it, Phoenix?" Memphis asked him.

"Damn straight, I do!"

"I'm in," Alfie called out, earning a growl from Sebastian.

"Ah, Sebastian, I know you are worried as any father would be but if you think for one moment I'm not going to kill every demon to protect my niece, then you don't know me."

Sebastian laid a hand on Alfie's shoulder. "I know you will, Alfie, I really do, and I do thank you for it."

"No need to thank me, old friend and we've got this. Speaking of which, Lenox, Lulu, I know you've got a plan so tell us what to expect and so forth."

"Well, the Betrayers are going to start emerging from hell today, October 31st all Hallow's Eve and the night before *Samhain*, which is the beginning of winter to the Celts and when the boundary between life and death is at is weakest. However, all four cannot emerge at once since with the hell vents permanently sealed, there is limited energy for them to use to cross into our world. However, All Hallow's Eve is not the only day during the Winter Season in which they can emerge, for they can also cross at *Yule*, the Winter Solstice; *Imbolc* or St. Brigid's Day which is the first Day of Celtic Spring; and lastly, *Ostara* the Spring Equinox. From what Lulu and I have determined, the order in which they will emerge in our realm will revolve around the date of their original death for the anger they hold regarding this act gives them enough strength to beat out the other Betrayers to come across the boundary. They can also emerge only in the stone circle closest to the place of their death in the human world. Meaning, if they died on one of the immortal isles, then we had to calculate the closest stone circle to the point that immortal isle would have been at the exact moment of death. I know this all sounds very confusing but Lulu and I have been researching the Betrayers as best we can and also making all the necessary calculations to determine where these demons will emerge.

"Now, it is time to tell you of the identity of the first Betrayer. It is going to be Balor the original King of the Fallin, arch-nemesis of the Vampyr. His crime of murdering his mother during the dark ritual that bonded him to the demon that gave him his blood curse, not to mention betraying the remainder of his family to seize the throne of Kilderheeth, has well earned him his spot in the Ninth Level of Hell. Now I know some of you wonder how it can be him when Uncle Phoenix banished his ghost from this plane of existence nearly five years ago, however, essentially his human spirit has been in Hell since the day Uncle Phoenix killed him and the ghost was the remains of the original demon I mentioned. Thus, from what Lulu and I both calculated and foresaw, the closest point to where he died would be the Giant's Causeway in Northern Ireland and we have located the ancient stone circle that will become the gate—"

"Hold on, sorry to interrupt, but what do you mean by that, Lenox? I'm not familiar with Celtic history but I thought the stone circles were ancient druid ritual stones to practice rites and stuff, though they are actually demon gates?" Memphis asked.

"The humans might have used it for that during the past but that was never their true intention. The stone circles were set up by immortals long ago so that we could know where the boundary weakness between the realm of the living and the realm of the dead was. It's not something widely known. In fact, for the longest time, it was considered to be a secret of the Celtic Omega Clan since the Celtic lands have more boundary weaknesses than anywhere else in the world due to the largest hell vent in existence was sealed here and some of its power still remains. Anyway, if you are worried that humans are accidentally summoning the demons forth from the gates or attempting something else nefarious with these gates, then rest assured they can't. For only the Sentinels of the Wild Hunt know how to activate or close them," Llyr explained.

"Yes, and during this battle they will act as the gatekeepers of the stone circles, meaning that they will set up the circles for Penny who will activate the portal once the demon is entrapped. Then she will keep them in place until dawn when they will be sent back to hell permanently. On that note, Penny, do not worry about what you must do and not being prepared, for when the time comes, you will know what to do because is imprinted in Brimstone Huntress DNA. Though if there is anything I can tell you, it is trust in the sentinels and we will all survive the night," Midir said cryptically.

Penny looked to Lenox and Lulu. "Oh, don't you worry. I trust them to literal hell and back."

"I trust you two and Penny to hell and back, too. Also, don't you worry about me, for I will keep my head and kill all those stupid demon minions who dare attack any of you," Freya vowed as she hugged all four fiercely.

"Yeah, we've got this," Penny agreed before she looked around the room and noticed the steely determination in everyone's eyes.

Looking back at Lenox, who had taken up her hand again, Penny waited for him to speak but this time, Lulu did.

"It's time for us to go, for dusk draws near and that is when the demon will emerge."

Everyone nodded and went over their basic battle plan before Lenox teleported them to the Giant's Causeway, which had been cleared of people by Llyr Tirenagan earlier that morning in preparation.

Lenox eyed the stone circle that blended in with the other stone monoliths, feeling a brief moment of trepidation. Taking a deep breath to calm his nerves and turned his head to watch the sun start to slip beneath the calm ocean waves.

"Not to be miserable, Len but you sure the Niner is gonna appear here? I mean, I killed him ten thousand years ago and even I'm a little fuzzy on the exact details of where Kilderheeth is in relation to the human world," Phoenix stated.

Lenox nodded, "This is the spot. I am sure."

"You really sure?"

"Phoenix!" Conalai hissed.

"It's alright, Dad, and I'm sure, Uncle Phoenix, because he's already beginning to emerge," Lenox replied turning to the stone circle.

Within the ancient stone monoliths, Lenox could see a large swirling dark mass brewing in the centre, growing in size as the sun sunk lower and lower on the horizon.

Lenox held Penny's hand as they watched the demon emerge from the stone circle and head towards them. *Patience, love, he's not gonna attack us first. Instead, he's going to summon up a ghoul army because he is a coward at heart.*

Penny briefly nodded one single time before she squeezed his hand tightly. *Stay safe, my love and I'll be seeing you real soon.*

I will and you too, Lenox said as he turned towards his twin who was standing on his other side.

Releasing Penny's hand, Lenox grasped Lulu's and drew her back behind the other members of the wild hunt, waiting for the ghouls who were forming out of the demon's mist to rush them all.

Ready, Lou? Lenox asked his sister, knowing that it was time to act when the ghouls started heading their way.

I was born ready, Lenox, Lulu replied cheerfully despite the severity of the situation.

Moving together smoothly, they darted through the hordes of ghouls, wraiths, minions and other warriors, making their way to the Betrayer who was hovering around the stones seemingly waiting for them.

Lenox magically reached for his connection to the wisps and commanded them to rise up from the sea, which immediately drew the Betrayer's attention since the wisps were full of magic the Betrayer was intent on stealing.

My turn, Lulu said as she released Lenox's hand and headed for the stone circle. The wisps followed her, instantly drawing the Betrayer her way.

Lenox felt Penny and Freya itch to protect Lulu from the Betrayer.

Don't act. It will bring her harm, Lenox warned them before he drew in all his null magic to the core of his being and effectively 'winked' himself out of existence or at least that was how it appeared to everyone except Penny, Lulu, Freya and his dad.

In a non-corporal almost ghost-like form, Lenox floated to the outside of the stone circle and began to draw the ancient runes that he had long committed to memory upon the first stone with a particular type of chalk that he and Lulu had created for this endeavour. Knowing that time was of the essence, Lenox quickly moved from stone to stone, making sure they all bore their proper markings while Lulu kept the demon distracted.

Then without saying a single word to her, Lenox made his way to Lulu and grabbed his sister, pulling her into a tight hug, all the while combining their magical gifts to make her disappear, too. The wisps went into a wild rage the moment they disappeared and took vengeance on the Betrayer by swirling around him and effectively bestowing an ethereal glow upon him that not only weakened his dark magic but also made it impossible for him to attempt to hide his presence from Penny or anyone else. The demon let out a howl of frustration before it swept around furiously looking for Lenox and Lulu but they were safe from his rage since the wisps' fury kept him blind to them.

Right, Penny love, go for it, Lenox urged her.

Penny let out an unearthly snarl before she shifted forms and hit the ground in full hound form, making a beeline for the Betrayer. The Betrayer spun around in her direction and the wisps immediately took off into the elements now that their job was complete. This allowed Lulu and Lenox to finish up with the final preparation as Penny drove hard at the demon, though she still held herself in check, not wanting to tip her hand just yet.

The webbing is in place, love. Drive him into this stone circle now, Lenox called out.

Inwardly grinning, Penny unleashed her hell chains and instantly, the Betrayer drew back in apparent fear as Penny advanced towards him.

Incoming! We've got more demons coming up the stone steps towards you, Phoenix called out suddenly.

What are you standing there for, then? Let's kill these

blighters already, Alfie shouted back.

Now, here's what I've been waiting for all night, Phoenix cackled before he lit his form on fire and was seconds from jumping off the cliff to take on the demon head-on.

"I'll kill him," the demon shouted suddenly forgetting all about Penny as it instantly headed for Phoenix instead.

"Good Light! Phoenix, put your flames out, you're attracting him!" Sebastian shouted out loud breaking the silence they all had been maintaining.

Phoenix instantly doused his flames but it didn't seem to matter as the demon still focused on him, and Penny realized then why. Phoenix was the one who killed Balor in life and the demon was intent on having its revenge by dragging Phoenix down into the same level of hell when it went.

I can protect him from the demon, love but I'm gonna need some help first, Lenox called out as he and Lulu slowly made their way to their Uncle Phoenix.

Penny understood what he was meaning and instantly went on the offensive by switching to her half hellhound/ half human hybrid form and summoning up two long swords. Then she raced towards the demon and slashed its back, immediately causing it to roar in rage.

The demon turned towards Penny again and made a swiping motion with its long ghostly arms at her but Penny was already long gone as she danced out of the way, swirling and slashing until she was able to get right up in front of Phoenix.

"Move with me," Penny ordered him as she dodged a quick attack and slashed the demon in return.

Penny felt Phoenix move with her and together they seemingly inched their way across the short distance to the standing stones while the demon's attacks became furiously strong in its determination to get its claws on Phoenix. The demon seemed to smarten up as it realized that Penny was driving it back to the stones and dug in mere feet from Penny's goal.

Penny let out a small growl of annoyance before she unleashed hell-link chains again, not intending to give up. Then an idea came to mind, and she drew the hell-link chains close to her before she unleashed them in one fiery celestial attack. Penny maintained a constant stream of power which surprised her since she thought that she would be draining herself but that didn't appear to be the case. However, it soon became apparent from the tired huffs behind her that Phoenix was lending his celestial fire magic to her.

How?

Shh, hon, do what you got to do, I'll be okay, Phoenix replied.

Penny said no more as she drove the demon back to the stone circle and then prepared herself for one last magic blast.

Then a thought occurred to her, *Quick before I do this, everyone, tell me you're clear.*

I'm clear, her mother answered.

Me, too, her dad answered next, followed by the rest of the hunt.

We've got Uncle Phoenix, Lenox answered, indicating himself and Lulu.

Penny briefly doubted that response, wondering if the demon was playing with her but when she felt Lenox's ghostly hand lay on her shoulder, Penny knew he was alright.

Nodding to herself, she used a combination of the hell-link chains and one last celestial blast to heave the demon into the circle, which ultimately ignited the chalk markings and stunned the demon. Without a second thought, Penny weaved her chains through the columns creating a perimetre around the demon to make sure he was completely entrapped within before she sat down in wet grass.

Immediately, she saw the demon pull out its trump card by creating a realistic version of three people trapped within its grasp.

"Penny, wait! Don't do it! He's got us trapped," Lulu wailed.

"Penny love, you've got to stop! We'll end up in hell with him!" Lenox cried out next.

A vision of Phoenix looking frightened and on the verge of tears was next.

"Wow, you must really hate Phoenix if you think that's an accurate interpretation of him," Penny retorted acidly.

The demon seemingly huffed as it made the unbelievable

form of Phoenix disappear since it seemed to know that it didn't have Penny fooled, though still it clung to the wailing forms of Lenox and Lulu.

Penny rolled her eyes at the caterwauling. "I don't know how you think that those figures are an accurate form of Lenox or Lulu either. For Light's sake, you're kind of really pathetic."

The demon wasn't giving up and Penny knew then it wasn't aiming the fake twins at her but rather Freya, Conalai and the rest of Lenox's family behind her, however they weren't fooled either.

Knowing she had a brief reprieve, Penny focused on her task of binding the demon. Slowly clearing her mind of all distractions, Penny breathed in deeply and evenly until there was nothing but a clean slate in her mind.

Then she added the scenery around her, starting with the vibrant, lush dark green sea moss, the hard grey granite of the stone surrounding them, the vast dark ocean. She stopped at that one and in her mind's eye, she felt compelled to change it from a dark inky colour to a bright celestial blue. When she did that, she started picturing sea creatures within it, the likes she had never seen before although she felt as if they had always been there.

That's because they have, Penny thought as she realized their significance.

Penny watched the guardians slowly emerged from the crystalline depths of the sea and start to swirl around above her as though hey were dancing but there was no tune. Moving as if she were in a trance, Penny summoned her favourite violin and started to play a song for them, one that she had known all of her life.

The sea guardians let out deep low hums of happiness as they sang along in their own way. However, as they did so, the sea level rose dramatically though not in a violent way, as instead, it merely drew up and up, covering the granite stone steps of the Giants' Causeway and headed towards her. Then when the water began to rise under Penny's feet, the guardians seemed to draw her and the rest of the hunt up from the ground and into the protective bubble in the sky, as the guardians continued to dance and sing all around them as Penny played.

The Betrayer let out a fierce howl and began yanking on Penny's chains, which in turn impacted her directly.

Penny mentally tightened her hold on the chains as she continued to play her violin, still not willing to give an inch.

Then, as if by some divine miracle, the first guardian made its move and infused its essence with one of the stone pillars of the circle which weakened the demon and stopped him from attacking the chains further. Slowly one by one, the other guardians followed suit and entered the other pillars until all of them were alight with their essence.

Suddenly, Penny's chains dissolved through the pillars and wrapped themselves around the demon directly igniting the watery landscape and wiping the remaining Betrayer's energy and his minions from this plane.

Once the evil was vanquished and only the enchained Betrayer remained, completely locked in place as a hell portal formed beneath him ready to take it back when dawn broke, were Penny and the wild hunt safely returned to the ground by the magic of the guardians.

Blinking, Penny focused her mind on the present and felt her mind reel at first, as it struggled to grasp that everything that had happened in the trance was real. However, soon the surrealness of what had happened left her and Penny knew what they needed to do now.

"So..." Phoenix started, eyeing the unmoving demon cautiously as he stood away from the stone circle.

"Now we wait until dawn," Lulu said. She took her position near one of the pillars before directing everyone else to stand near one of the pillars with their backs towards the demon in a protective stance.

"Isn't it dangerous to have our backs to the demon?" Raven asked.

"No, the demon is completely locked in place unless it manages to get enough energy from other evil beings. Therefore we must hold this perimeter and kill any demon before they have a chance to break through the circle and sacrifice themselves," Lulu explained.

"Oh, okay," Phoenix said taking up his position cautiously.

Penny focused her hellhound instincts on the area and the presence of anything evil. Though surprisingly, for the remainder of the night, very few demons made their way towards them and they were easily dispatched. Penny wasn't fooled as she knew that evil minions were waiting to the very end before they launched one last attack.

As the sun began to rise, Penny was proven right. A large horde of demons appeared on the rocks surrounding them but it was too late for them. For even with the weak sunlight beams, the portal beneath the demon triggered. Suddenly, blue fiery lava tentacles burst from the portal before wrapping themselves around the Betrayer and dragging it down, taking all the minions with it. Penny watched them all disappear as the sun rose higher and higher into the sky until it fully emerged and there was no trace of evil left in the area.

Then she watched the sea guardians depart from the stones in a flash of blue light, leaving the stone circle appearing as if nothing had happened.

"Is it really over?" Phoenix asked hesitantly a few moments later.

"Yes, it is over, Phoenix. The demon's spirit is re-bound to hell, where it truly belongs and it will never be free to roam this plane again. Well done, Penny, Lenox and Lulu. I am quite impressed with the three of you," Erebrus the Draggenin of Death spoke for the first time.

"Thanks," Penny replied as she looked over at Lenox.

I like your real eyes, Penny mentally whispered as she noted the glowing and swirling grey, purple, green colours.

Thanks, love and I'm sorry I hid it, Lenox replied, sheepishly.

Penny reached up and touched his face. *Don't be. I get it. Eyes this colour would have brought trouble to your door, especially when your parental grandfather lived. Though, please stop using the contact lens you made because I don't want you to hide anymore.*

I promise I'll keep them as is, love. Though you should speak to your parents, they look worried now.

Penny nodded, walking over to her mum and dad.

"You alright?" Penny asked them.

"Yes and no. I mean, I know you're strong, sweetie but I really wish you didn't have to be," her dad murmured.

Penny had no reassuring words to say but then something caught her eye and she walked towards the cliff's edge.

Looking back, she smiled at her parents and said, "A new day has begun."

Her dad gave her a small smile of understanding. "Yeah, hon, it has."

With that, he walked to the cliff's edge and took in the serenity of life returning to the area, as the sea birds let out loud caws as they flew across the sea intent on coming home. Penny felt her mum step up beside her and they quietly watched whales breach the water far off in the distance.

Suddenly Penny felt Lenox wrap his arms around her shoulders and draw her back against his chest. "So, what do you wish to do now love?"

"Well, I hear Irish hospitality is like nothing else and I feel like seeing it for myself."

"Well, I do happen to know of a place not far away that has some of the tastiest scones full of clotted cream and jam that go really well with a cuppa."

"Ooh, sounds like a breakfast for champions. I'm in."

Lenox laughed softly. "It is, my love. It truly is."

Lenox kissed the top of her head, feeling truly happy that for now, this battle was over.

Chapter Twenty- Seven

By the end of November, Lenox noticed how visibly withdrawn the hellhounds were becoming. At first, he had thought them trying to be subdued around him since he believed that they were kind of unsure of him still and thus less exuberant. However Penny quickly assured him that wasn't the case.

"There's no halves with us love, we either like you or don't and if we don't, you'd know," Penny responded with a laugh.

"Then why do all the hounds seem less boisterous and mayhem-causing then usual?"

"They're just really worried love," Penny mumbled with a sigh before adding, "It's a real shame too because Christmas is coming up and even though we're not Christian, we're super festive."

Lenox said nothing for a moment as he digested Penny's words before suddenly reaching out to his twin and started relaying what Penny had said, knowing full well how his twin would react.

Penny felt him do so and immediately inquired, "Lenox love, what are you thinking of doing?"

"No cowardly two-bit demon is going rob the hounds of their Christmas joy, not on my watch!" Lenox declared, feeling irritated that such a thing would happen.

Instead of cautioning him, Penny openly agreed with Lenox, "Wouldn't call a Niner a two-bit demon love since it's a gargantuan monstrosity but still, you're right, Christmas is special and we should celebrate our blessings. So how can I help?"

"Well we're going to need Lulu on board..."

"Say no more I am here!" Lulu called out gleefully as she arrived with her wife and children almost instantly.

"We're also going to need in reinforcements Lou because we're going to decorate the stuffing out of the compound," Lenox stated.

"I'll call my twin Frey and his wife Lydia in, for that's bound to draw the rest of *Norra Stam* to aid in our cause," Freya said texting her twin.

"We've also got to call in mum and dad," Lulu stated excitedly.

"Hold on before we do any of that, let's go talk to my mum and uncle first," Penny interrupted.

Everyone looked at her.

"As you probably can tell my mum and uncle are kind of the heart of the hellhounds. I mean sure, a lot of hounds call them a pain in the neck or worse. However that doesn't matter because they are upset... well everyone else is and that's why it seemed so subdued around here."

Lenox and Lulu shared a look as they both mentally reached for each other.

This won't do brother, Lulu muttered, her heart going out to Alfie and Ally.

No it won't and besides, the worse they worry, the more of a chance something bad happening during the next battle. Besides I don't like the thought of them suffering anything and I wish to deal with all this right now, Lenox replied.

Lulu nodded firmly in full agreement. Suddenly Penny threw her arms around both of them.

"What?" Lenox asked utterly bewildered.

"You two are amazing, don't both hiding it, Freya and I clearly heard you—"

"True, though I still tune you two out from time to time. Not for any reason in particular mind you but mainly because you two talk a lot mentally, especially about stuff that I can't make heads or tails of until I see the final product. So hence, most things go in one ear out the other and I suggest you do the same Pen, for it will save you all the headaches that I have suffered in the past."

"Sorry Freya but I can't tune them out because I find them to be utterly fascinating," Penny replied.

"I do too but not before my first cup of coffee in the morning. Oh speaking of, be careful when they hand you a coffee for Lulu and Lenox like to experiment with stuff and that includes making weird cups of coffee, like cheese coffee..."

"Cheese coffee is a Scandinavian treat!" Lulu retorted with a snort.

Freya looked at her for a long moment, "I'm still on the fence when it comes to it."

"Ooh I want to try it," Penny muttered.

"We will Penny hon, along with another Swedish delicacy, Banana Curry Pizza."

"On the fence with that one too," Freya replied.

"I don't see how, it's very Swedish," Lulu pointed out.

"Hey just because it's Swedish and I'm technically Swedish, doesn't mean I'm going to like it."

"Not true, you so do!"

Freya crossed her arms and retorted, "Prove it. Name something Swedish I like."

"*Jannssons Fratelese*?" Lulu inquired and Lenox mentally whispered to Penny that it was a fish scallop potato dish.

"Okay I like that."

"*Toast Skagen*?" Lulu mentally showed Penny a piece of toast with a shrimp concoction on the top.

"Okay, I like that too."

"Pickled Herring."

Freya grudgingly nodded.

"Swedish Meatballs."

Freya nodded again.

"Ligonberry jam."

"Okay, okay—"

"Abba," Lulu interrupted.

Freya's eyes narrowed on Lulu's before cocking an eyebrow.

"Worth a shot but I did prove my point which mean you now you owe me and by extension, Lenox, Penny and the kids lunch!"

"Ooh, here's hoping it's a Swedish one, I want to try that stuff now," Penny said.

"Yeah alright, I'll buy you all lunch and I'll even include Penny's mum and uncle if they're up for it. Though let's go see them now since there's no sense in delaying. They're in their lab no?"

Freya asked Penny.

"Yeah, come on, let's go see them."

Everyone followed Penny out of the house and towards the Frankie Lab which was what Ally and Alfie liked to refer to it as and Lenox didn't know if the name fit but then ago the large massive dome structure with hundreds of warning labels plastered to the side looked like it need, a name of some sort. So Frankie lab thus became very applicable in Lenox's opinion.

Though bizarrely when they arrived, it appeared that someone else seemed to have the same idea since Penny's cousin Lucy and her boyfriend Tyr were sitting on a blanket untangling what looked like Christmas lights. Well in truth, Tyr was untangling Lucy who managed to get herself at all wrapped up in them.

"Uh Luce, are you okay?" Lulu inquired

"I will be once I get out of this mess, for come hell or high water we will have lights up for Christmas."

Lulu's twins start to toddled over to the couple before stopping and looking behind them.

"Um… mama, mummy…" The twins started to call in unison.

"You can help them if Tyr and Lucy say it's okay," Lulu agreed.

The twins looked at the couple quietly.

"We're okay with you help, besides Tyr here has only managed to get me more tangled."

"If only you wouldn't struggle so much," Tyr huffed out in both exasperation and laughter.

The children both let out a small dramatic sigh at the adults' antics before Lore picked up a free end of one of the sets of lights and his twin grasped the line it was attached to and they began to work in tandem to unravel it.

"Well let's go talk to your mum and uncle, for that'll keep our kids occupied for the next twenty minutes."

"Twenty minutes, I've been at this for an hour Lou," Tyr retorted.

"Yes but my kids are… well...nevermind," Lulu said with a small shrug, leaving it unfinished.

Tyr stopped and looked at her with a cocked eyebrow, “Really Lou?”

Lulu smiled at him for a brief moment and waited for her children to speak.

“Let's lay this one down here,” Lore said to his sister as they had already got one light string untangled and had laid it down in a straight line away from Lucy.

“Yes Tyr, *really*,” Lulu said sweetly this time before she grabbed her wife's hand and swung it gently.

Freya snorted at exchange before she tugged on Lulu's hand and gesturing with her head to follow Penny and Lenox who had already began to head towards the lab.

Even outside the large metal dome building, Penny could hear her mum and uncle bicker as she approached the building with her preternatural hearing. Breathing a small sigh of relief since they seemed to be in a 'normal' mood, Penny knocked hard on the large submarine style blast door that was three feet thick and could survive a nuclear blast, (a prerequisite for the lab since Penny's mum did have a fondness for both plutonium and explosives).

“Penny's at the door! Penny's at the door! Alfie make sure you've got pants on for Light sake’s!” Ally cackled.

“I forget to wear clothes one time after shifting a long time ago and you still don't let me live it down.”

“Ha, ha, nope! It was bloody golden!” Ally laughed as she breezily spun the locking wheel and opened the door.

“Hiya sweetie! Lenox! Lou! Freya! Nice to see you all!” Ally called out hugging Penny before shouting behind her, “Alfie break out the good snacks!”

“Hold on, you've got snacks in there?” Lucy demanded from her spot on the ground.

Still holding Penny, Ally snorted when she saw her niece and responded, “Ah jeez, Alfie get the pliers too while you’re at it, Lucy has gotten herself stuck in Christmas lights again. Pup, how many times have I told you that diving into a massive mess of lights is a bad idea?”

“Couldn't help it and besides it was fun Aunt Ally. Though

don't worry about me, Lore and Bryn are making good headway so we don't need any pliers this time but I wouldn't mind some snacks if you have them on offer," Lucy pouted.

Alfie nudged by his twin and looked at his daughter assessing the situation before shrugging, "Yeah the wee ones are making good headway I must admit, though you alright sweetie?"

"Oh yeah dad thanks for asking, though still… snacks?"

Alfie waved his hand as snacks appeared next too Tyr who dutifully picked up a cupcake and unwrapped the bottom then placed it in Lucy's tied hands that she had brought up just far enough to eat said cupcake.

Lucy thanked her dad as she gestured for Lore and Bryn to have a cupcake.

Ally shook her head and ushered everyone else into the lab, muttering, "Every year, she does that, Alfie, every year."

Alfie rolled his eyes at Ally, "So? Lucy's part white snake, it's something they do, what's the problem?"

"What?" Freya asked in pure bewilderment.

"White snakes are pretty social beings and they like to group together in living nests when they're in their snake form, especially when it's cold out because they can pool warmth. However a tangle of power cords kind of looks like a nest and sometimes when a white snake is lonely, bored or looking for warmth they get themselves tangled up in a bunch of power cords and can't untangle themselves with magic because electrical current sometimes mess up their powers. It's honest a bit of a trial to untangle them too, let me tell you because their snakey bodies are super bendy and detangling them without pliers can sometimes take days. It also sucks because you sometimes don't know their stuck until someone reports them missing. Luckily for us, the white snakes like to stay together and they happen to like Alfie's home during winter, which is the season they're mostly likely to get stuck since it's so bloomin' cold out, thus making it easy to find them."

"All of them stay at your house for the winter, Alfie?" Lulu asked curiously.

Alfie nodded, "Yeah, Rika is actually one of their leaders,

though she really hates the term and actually prefers the term sage. Though anyway, the white snakes actually come to stay with us throughout the year too, since they constantly move between our house and two other Sages, not because they have to, given the fact they are always welcome to stay with us but because it's natural for them to be migratory. Nonetheless Rika doesn't actually like to migrate like the others, however she does need to constantly see them, so she often spends her days with them which is why I'm here in the lab since the other snakes kind of find me a bit intimidating and at nights, we spend our time together. Now, now that you all know my business, why are you four here for a visit?"

Ally growled at her twin, "Light sake's Alfie! They're welcome to come see us!"

"Didn't say they weren't twit but you can clearly see that they came to see us for a purpose. Hell that should have been super clear from the start, since most people don't willing to knock on the Frankie Lab door because they believe they're risking life and limb, by doing so."

"How'd that happen?" Ally demanded.

"What'd you mean, 'how'd that happen'? We've bloody well blown the literal top off this place three times!?"

"Oh… right," Ally begrudgingly admitted before looking at her daughter with a happy yet curious look.

"We came because... you're not doing up the Compound for Christmas, mum and Uncle Alfie. I mean, normally at this time of year you are very rarely in your lab yet now... your here all the time."

Ally's face fell to a near unreadable one and surprisingly, Alfie became the more expressive one as he laid a hand on Ally's shoulder and squeezed in full support.

"I don't want to celebrate what could be... what could be your last Christmas," Ally whispered.

"Like hell that's going to happen!" Lenox burst out, which was completely uncharacteristic of him.

"It—" Ally started but Lenox vehemently shook his head.

"No, it won't! Lou and I have damn well at this for years Ally, ever since Caoranach though in truth, probably before that since we both knew that one day this we would have to fight tooth and bloomin' nail to keep the huntress alive. Though it goes beyond that now because I love your daughter wholeheartedly Ally and no two-bit rat fink jerk face of a demon is going to take away our happy future. They can all… they can all suck it for all I care! However if that wasn't clear I'll be more precise, I will rip out there spineless spine substitutes and shove it down their throats if they so much as harm one single hair on Penny's head! So don't you start on about this being her last Christmas, for this will be our first Christmas of many! One that's going to be fun, demon or no demon!" Lenox erupted.

Penny instantly reached out for Lenox, "Damn you're super hot Lenox but that's also very correct because my fate's not sealed mum. For it's always going to be what I make it and right now, I aim to shape it into a long happily mated life. I also plan on getting a bloody dual doctorate and you know, I might aim for a Nobel peace prize in either the physics or math field in future. I mean I don't really want the award but I would laugh myself silly for years over it, for come on, a hellhound getting a world peace prize? Epic. I also really, really want my own wee ones with Lenox because something says they'll inherit their dad's super sweet yet serious nature though I also want them to have some real hellhound mischief in them too.

"Though more importantly I don't want to put my life on hold because of these demons and that starts with spending the next few weeks decorating the crap out of the compound in-between training and school. Not to mention, I want to spend Friday nights at the Die is Cast with Lenox levelling up my paladin character before coming home to watch monster movies with all the hellhounds because you've taken over our theatre again. Then after we face this next betrayer, I want your help to work out blueprints of an amusement park Lenox's going to build, that will probably have five hundred changes from his super picky cousin Falcon which will also probably drive you, me and Uncle Alfie nuts. Whereas, I know Lenox will calmly take it all in and then seek out Lou's help into finding into to getting Falcon to agree with what we want. Don't bother denying it Lulu, I know you like being known a happy go-lucky but you can come down on people like a lead balloon which is awesome. Though wow is my speech getting off track. Anyway, mum and Uncle Alfie what I want to hammer home is I have plans for a life, a very, very happy one, that doesn't begin and end with demons battles. After all, demon fighting is something we hounds do but it shouldn't be all that we are. In fact I have a feeling that in future, the immortal world will come looking for our help for more than just demon fights. Seriously if I have my way, we're going to corner the market on engineering, construction and quantum physics since we're all pretty much have hobbies in that field anyway."

"Uh Penny sweetie, our Uncle Phoenix might fight you for the construction market, since building things back up after he's destroyed them is kind of his shtick now," Lulu pointed out when Penny finished.

"I'm not concerned, I can take him," Penny muttered confidently.

Lenox burst out laughing at that remark, "You so could love but please don't he'll whine."

"Fine, he can have 30% of the market and like it. Otherwise he's just going to have to just lump his lot in with us and also like it," Alfie retorted before nudging his sister.

"Ah for Light sake's!" Ally hissed before she let out a stream of inventive curses.

Everyone waited her out before she finally spoke again.

"Dag nab it! I've managed to piss off my son-in-law and daughter in fall swoop! Light, how stupid I've been? Damn right you're gonna live Penny and eff everyone who says different. Also Falcon's not getting five hundred vetoes over this future amusement park either, he gets one because as if I'd let that fox drive me mental. Granted I am already mental, so what would be proper term Alfie?"

"They haven't made a word up for your level of madness Ally."

Ally shook her head, "Didn't think that they did, though it should be named after me when they get there!"

"The hell it should, you got a book named after you even though the author spelt your name wrong."

"So? You've got a butler character named after you in your

favourite comic book."

Alfie grinned, "Which was an epic Christmas present from my baby girl. Speaking of which, I should go see how's she's doing. Hope she saved me a cupcake because those we're the last of the good treats."

"What the—! You were supposed to only give her half the snacks, you numpty! Penny was supposed to get the other half!"

"It's okay mum, we're going to go out and have some Swedish Pizza after we've done some decorating," Penny said linking her arm with her mothers.

"Ooh what! I saw something on the internet about that! Isn't it something weird like banana curry pizza or something? Sounds pure mental, I wanna try it! By the way, Nobel Peace Prize, Penniah? Do it!"

"Oh yeah and we'll help since your dad will probably blow an internal gasket or something when he finds out your nominated. It'll be so worth it," Alfie laughed.

"How?" Ally demanded again.

"Because he'll want to be all supportive and the like, however at the same time the thought of a hellhound getting a bloomin' peace prize will not compute with him or something. Seriously, just watch what happens when we mention it, he'll get all eye twitchy and that big vein in his forehead will pop out for sure," Alfie laughed.

"Not that I wasn't already but I'm also totally helping you both," Lulu said to her brother and sister-in-law.

"Since I love living dangerously, I'm in too," Freya laughed.

Lenox kissed Penny's temple and murmured, "I'll start looking what you need for the Nobel committee when we go home."

Then he turned to look at Ally, "I'm sorry and are we... erm... *good*?"

Ally let go of Penny and hugged Lenox, "Lenox my dear son-in-law, we more than are. In fact, I owe you again, for you getting mad at me, made me first realize how stupid I was becoming. Then when Penny started to tell me her dreams for the future, I realized how far she came out of her shell. After all, the last time we discuss your dreams, sweetie, it was like water torture for you but now, you're ready to fight for what you want and that is a sign of person who will never lay down at the feet of the Fates and die. So now I've just got to stop being stupid and I know that if I act without thinking during these battles you will all get hurt or worse. Besides, I'm also all for scheming right along you, in order to make sure that all your dreams come true. Now come along you four, you can help me tug out the five hundred plastic bins of decorations that are in the Compound warehouse and once that part's done it'll be lunch feast time, which will be on Alfie."

"What?" Alfie demanded.

"I don't carry a wallet jerk face and Bas bought the last round of takeout. Besides if banana curry pizza turns out to be terrible it's all on you."

"Oh no it won't, it's utterly amazing," Lulu declared.

Ally nonchalantly agreed before she moved to wrap an arm around the waists of Lenox and Penny.

Seriously sorry for being stupid but we've got this now, I swear, Ally said mentally.

I know mum, I really do, though in the meantime let's go scatter tinsel around the compound until dad gets slightly eye twitchy.

You are so my daughter! Oh and when are you planning on having my future grand-babies? Ally demanded gleefully as she remembered what Penny had said.

Lenox laughed, happy that everything was now sorted out and the right inroads had been made for the second Betrayer. After all, both Lenox and Lulu knew this one would be more devious than the rest, given the fact that they're share visions had shown them that much. However the Betrayer had nothing on the notorious Baskerville twins and they would be the catalysts of his downfall.

So when are we going to tell them? Lulu asked Lenox.

Soon, Lenox replied.

Solid plan, Penny agreed through their soul link, mentally rubbing her hands together as a cartoon villain would.

Betrayer Number Two, you are going to be so messed up when my mum and uncle get a hold of you, Penny thought happily, knowing every word to be true.

Chapter Twenty-Eight

The night before the second Betrayer battle, Lenox had called Prometheus and requested to speak with him, Epimetheus and Arika. Prometheus had agreed to meet Penny and Lenox at their home. Though true to form, Lulu had shown up before the planned meeting with her wife Freya.

"Hope you don't mind—" Lulu started saying to Penny but Penny waved her off with a happy smile.

"Lulu, I'm the child of a symbiotic twin, I get it," Penny responded.

"Right and for some reason I keep forgetting that," Lulu muttered before she sat down on the couch next to her brother. Penny sat perched on the arm of the chair on the left (Lenox's side) and Freya had decided to do the same on the right (Lulu's side).

A few moments later, Prometheus arrived with his wife, his twin Epimetheus, his wife's twin Trey and his wife Mydnyte.

"Wow," Freya said when she saw everyone teleport into the room.

"Nah, not wow Freya, we were going out to supper together anyway and Prometheus said we should make this little detour together. Sounds like there's a purpose behind that, so what's up?" Epimetheus asked.

Lenox looked briefly at Lulu out of habit before then looking back at Prometheus.

"It's about the identity of the second Betrayer and although I doubt you won't recognize him in his demon form, he'll recognize you much like the first one did with our Uncle Phoenix."

Prometheus blew out a sigh, "Since he's someone I've killed in the past? Who is it Lenox? Zeus?"

Lenox shook his head, "No Cronus."

Prometheus and Epimetheus shared a look this time, which clearly said to Lenox, that this was actually wholly unexpected. Soon after Prometheus sighed and rubbed his face.

"I would have been angrier at the thought of it being Zeus than Cronus, However this actually worries me more than anything else. For he was a devious being from what I remember. Hell, the last battle was a huge test of endurance for both me and Epimetheus, since we had to go head to head with a seemingly never ending waves of minions for weeks before we got close enough to finally finish him off. So you're going to have a hard fight ahead, I can almost guarantee that."

"Um... we might not," Penny muttered.

Prometheus frowned in confusion before it dawned on him, "You have a well thought out battle plan, don't you?"

"Courtesy of Lenox and Lulu, yes," Penny agreed.

"I've never seen someone just openly admit that Pen," Trey laughed.

Penny shrugged, "Well it's honest since they've been at this for years and kept everything between the two of them and Freya, so nothing got out before it should. Though on that note, I will say that you'll find out the rest in the morning which sucks I know but we just didn't want you to be super surprised when you found out who the Betrayer was because we didn't want to put either Prometheus or Epimetheus off your game."

"Prometheus or me?" Epimetheus asked "What are you talking about? I didn't join the hunt."

"The first hunt wasn't really meant to be one where the full force of the Wild Hunt was meant to be shown. In fact, even this one isn't meant to be that way, since the more power we show the more we tip our hands to the demons. However this battle is not only ours," Lenox said gesturing to Penny, Lulu and Freya, "but also yours and Prometheus'. For he will be gunning for you two first, though it should be known, that he will probably aim for Keiran and Arika too, which is why I say to you now, please don't get angry."

"You want me not to get angry when he comes after family? Are you nuts?" Epimetheus asked in Greek.

"No brother he's not and you know as much as I do, that anger messes you up in a battle," Freya replied.

"You die in battle one time then come back to life and nobody ever let's you live it down," Epimetheus muttered.

"No that wasn't what I was talking about and the 'you' in the previous sentence was actually general and not directed at well, *you*. Anyway don't think about this too much tonight and I realize that's a lot to ask but when you find out the rest of our plan tomorrow, this request will make a whole bunch more sense," Freya said.

"Huh, surprisingly I'm reassured by that. Well either that or I just don't give a flying fig," Epimetheus said.

"Light sake's I never thought I'd ever say this but take this situation seriously Epimetheus. A lot of lives are at stake man!" Trey snapped at him.

"Trey, I am actually taking this seriously and right now my flippant attitude is due to the fact that I can clearly see the hard work Lenox and Lulu have done in order to make sure that this fight has the best possible ending and I fully believe in their plan."

"What are you taking about? See the hard work they've done? How's that possible?" Trey asked in confusion.

Epimetheus rolled his eyes, "Prometheus sees the future and I see the past. Ergo, just being in the room with them, I can see all the past actions they've taken to get to this point. Also again goes without saying but you truly have an ally in us, Betrayer or not."

Lenox smiled, "Thank you."

Prometheus spoke this time, "No Lenox, thank you."

With that everyone but Lenox, Freya, Lulu and Penny disappeared in a puff of smoke, leaving everyone in quiet contemplation.

"So..." Freya started.

"That went well," Penny supplied.

"How can you say that? I mean, they just up and left in a puff of smoke, probably to speak amoungst themselves without us there which could back fire tomorrow because they could decide to change our game plan without telling us," Freya pointed out.

Penny shook her head, "No they won't, for although they didn't speak at all, I eyed up Mydnyte and Arika, who clearly backed us in our secret plans. Seriously it was etched all over their faces.

Also although it didn't sound like it since they both had some small reservations both Prometheus and Trey are willing to give us the benefit of the doubt and not interfere. Whereas you can clearly tell that Epimetheus backed us, so we're good."

"Truly?" Freya asked.

"Yes."

"Alright then, we'll see what tomorrow brings, though in the meantime, come on you three. Frey's going to cook dinner tonight and you three need to eat and rest up."

Penny nodded in agreement, though the thought of the next battle didn't fill her with trepidation but rather with a deep sense of calm readiness.

Lenox reached out and squeezed her hand before he teleported them away this time, in order to enjoy a night away from their troubles.

*****

By mid-morning, all the Wild Hunt gathered in the living room and the atmosphere was thick with tension.

"I know everyone is worried for I know that you've probably heard that Cronus is our next opponent and he was a man in life who relied heavily on minions which wouldn't have changed in death. So this is going to be a hell of a battle to put it mildly with seemingly endless waves of minions on the longest night of the years. However don't be discouraged, we actually have a large advantage to combat them," Lenox started.

"Lenox what are you talking about?" Trey asked.

"The advantage I'm taking about comes in the form of Ally, Alfie... and me."

"Say what?" Ally asked, pretending to play stupid.

"The advantage I speak of is weapons, specifically the horde weapons we've created."

"Ooh! Our toy box has got loads of those! Right Alfie?" Ally declared in delight.

"Hell yeah it does and it saves us on spending weeks at a time in the shower trying to get demon gunk off. Gah! Learned that lesson the hard way back in the dark ages so we did," Alfie muttered.

"Okay just so everyone is on the same page, what the hell are you too talking about? I mean toy box? Horde weapons?" Phoenix asked.

"Ooh, our toy box is both an amazing and infuriating marvel, since it is a large bottomless trunk that Sebastian had specially made ages ago, whereupon he keeps all the weapons that Alfie and I have made under lock and key. Which is totally the infuriating part since we could really do some damage if we had full access to it."

"Which is why they're in the bloomin' box, Ally!" Sebastian retorted.

Alfie waved him off, "Still a dick move if you ask me but continuing on, horde weapons are kind of like rapid fire weapons but way better. Since you can literally kill a thousand small demons with a single trigger press. Though for those of you who are about to get all 'super concerned' over their own personal safety, all of our weapons are calibrated to killing demons, ghouls, dreads and the like, which means if you get hit accidentally with the blast of friendly gunfire, you'll feel a mild tickling sensation but others wise you'll be unaffected. Also we know this because we've rigorously tested them against ourselves and other immortal species."

"With or without their knowledge?" Sebastian demanded.

"Both, though it's fair because the people we shot with the ray without their knowledge were annoying the every loving crap out of us at the time. The others got paid the equivalent of fifty bucks in the currency of their choosing, which is a decent going rate for a guinea pig," Ally replied.

Sebastian let out a harsh sigh, "Looks like we're going to have another long discussion on ethics tomorrow, twins."

"That's nothing new, in fact I'll save you the trouble and just play the voice record of the last conversation we had on that topic when Alfie and I return to our lab. Anyway, not against using the horde weapons despite them being under lock and key right now but I know you have something else in mind for us, Lenox?" Alfie asked.

"Yes I do, Cronus is going to be a crafty scheming opponent

who will focus all this energy on attempting to kill Penny, Lou and I. All the while he will be directing his minions to attack everyone else in order to keep them from aiding us. However, the best way to out fox a schemer is to match them against another schemer. Therefore, Alfie, Ally, would you do the honours tonight and *'run with scissors'* as it were?"

The room when quiet as everyone puzzled out the meaning of Lenox words since they knew he was speaking in code, given the fact that there was a decent chance that the Betrayers could find a way to listen in. However the phrase *'run with scissors'* was a well-known code phrase amoungst the elite hellhounds and instantly there was a flashes of near utter joy and pure hellhound satisfaction appeared on every single one of their faces.

Ally and Alfie turn their own nearly demonic look of glee towards Sebastian.

"Will you back us?"

"Without a single iota of remorse," Sebastian responded automatically, also speaking in code.

"And the toy box?"

"It's your to do with as you will. Need anything else?" Sebastian asked them.

"A metric ton of rusty knives, blunt screwdrivers, not the star ones the square ones, and broken glass bottles, for this mama hellhound is aiming not play nice in anyway shape or form," Ally replied gleefully.

"It's all yours," Sebastian happily acquiesced.

Suddenly there was a general sense of understanding that whatever *'run with scissors'* meant to the hellhounds, whomever was asked to do so, became in charge and was given a *carte blanche* to demand what they wanted.

"Right now that, that's sorted, Alfie you better at explaining our weapons, so make sure everyone is given a brief run down on how they work, especially for those with additional pyro tendencies."

"Do your guns have additional pyro benefits for us pyro maniacs, then?" Phoenix asked.

"Phoenix!" Raven hissed

"What? Just being honest," Phoenix responded.

"Of course they do, Phoenix since we're both pyro maniacs too," Alfie responded.

"Good deal though what do your weapons come with Lenox?" Phoenix questioned.

"No pyro tendencies I'm afraid but they all have explosive fallout."

"English please," Phoenix said dryly.

"My weapons make wicked fools explode but before they do, there's a small window of time about forty-five seconds if I remember correctly, where they can infect other wicked entities because it acts kind of like an explosive demon virus. Though this also will not infect you or any other member of the Wild Hunt because it is calibrated only for evil just like Ally and Alfie's weapons. Oh and though I should say it won't cause bigger demons like the Betrayer to explode but it can temporarily stun him if needed. Though with Penny's hell-link chains, I think we should be good on that end."

"Damn, both kind of weapons sound right up my alley."

"Who says you can't use both Pyro King?" Ally asked dryly, this time.

"Freakin' A! That sounds like an epically solid idea! You got any of weapons now Lenox?"

Lenox nodded and summoned his cache of weapons from deep within his warehouse.

"Nothing much to mention with these, except that the RPG style weapons for large demon hordes, there is a recoil effect but I was fully able to null that effect with the rapid fire pulse beams weapons. You also don't need to select any settings, just safety off, point and squeeze the trigger.'

"Wow Lenox, we really need to work together on building weapons together. We haven't been able to make an RPG style weapons yet," Alfie commented.

Sebastian sucked in a breath ready to immediately rebut that but Penny spoke up.

"Uh dad, it might be a real good idea, Lenox is cautious and thoroughly serious when it comes to making weapons which means that there's a greater chance that mum and Uncle Alfie's weapons would be easier to use and less solar system ending."

"Solar system ending?" Raven echoed.

"Everyone can relax the horde weapons are actually completely safe to use and are only in the toy box since the twins like to run around and shoot everyone with them until it drives the whole Compound completely insane. The solar system ones Penny are talking about are buried deep and the twins don't get access to them… ever."

"Fun killer," Ally muttered.

Sebastian rolled his eyes as he summoned the weapons they needed out of the toy box, not bothering to respond as Alfie and Ally became instantly distracted by their own weapons and Lenox's.

A few hours later as dusk approached, Lenox and Lulu teleported everyone to a hidden stone circle near the top of Pen Y Fan, Wales.

"Hold on, shouldn't we be in Greece or something? I mean wasn't Cronus a Greek god or am I just losing the plot here," Phoenix pointed.

Prometheus shook his head, "Cronus actually wasn't a Greek god because during his time, since the gods weren't divided and were all of the same house as it were. He also preferred what would be roughly Russia and Eastern Europe today versus the Mediterranean area. However Epimetheus and I lured him out here because at the time because this area was unpopulated and we were trying to protect him from killing innocents since he would have used them to protect his own skin if he could."

"Makes sense, though Light does he sound like an oily eel, slippery and always leaving an uncomfortable slimy feeling to remember him by."

"Yup that's a pretty apt expression," Epimetheus agreed.

"Heads up," Penny growled suddenly as she felt the growing evil in the the circle.

"Yeah heads up again!" Phoenix added as he nodded to the second growing dark mass, though this one was growing at the bottom of the mountain.

Penny felt both Lenox and Lulu lay a hand on their shoulder before they disappeared from view using the wisps power to hide their presence from the emerging Betrayer.

Suddenly a large blast erupted seconds after the sun fully disappeared, although this blast didn't come from the Betrayer or the demon horde but rather Penny's mum and uncle who had become to cause mayhem.

“Come get a piece of this hot action!” Penny's mum yelled as she and Alfie, loaded up a smallish looking mortar gun that fired multiple demon mortars at one time that targeted the demon horde, though one flew and hit the betrayer.

Realizing that it was time to act, Penny instantly switched to her hellhound form and used the precious few moments that she knew the demon would be stunned and got between the wild hunt and the demon.

The demon let out a howl when it realized what she had done and attacked her instantly but Penny wasn't having that as she fought the demon with all the vicious gleeful relish that her little hellhound heart possessed.

As Penny fought, she caught a very brief glimpse of the Wild Hunt plunging down the mountain and fighting the minion hordes with the weapons that Penny's mum, uncle and Lenox had created, to maximum effect.

The Betrayer let out a snarl of frustration as it realized that whatever it's plan was, had spiralled out of control and had turned away from Penny desperately searching for something that would stop them all in their tracks.

Not something, someone or more accurately someones, Penny thought as she realized that the demon was looking for Lenox and Lulu, who were busy preparing the ancient stones.

Penny drove hard at the Betrayer who still attempting to search for Lenox and Lulu, when suddenly, a bright flash erupted, encompassing the standing stone circle in a blinding light.

At first Penny's heart leapt up into her throat as she briefly thought that something disastrous had just befallen Lenox and Lulu.

However Penny soon realized what had happened; her mum and uncle had lit a bunch of ensorcelled flares, which were designed to keep demons away with pure light magic so that they couldn't get to a specific area while the flare burned, though it also blinded everyone from looking in the direction that the flares were lit in, which was why Penny couldn't see where Lenox and Lulu had gone.

Genius, Penny thought as she realized that Lenox and Lulu could work on prepping the stones without demon interference.

The Betrayer seemed to realize what had happened at the same time as he let out a demon howl of rage before it turned his sights on Prometheus and Epimetheus, who were in the middle of battle.

Not on my watch, Penny snarled but again, her mother and uncle were once step ahead of them all.

Burst of gold green magical waves seem to emit from every direction around Penny and the demon, which caused the demon to go mad and lash out in every direction.

What's this? Penny thought.

Suddenly Lenox mentally whispered through their link, *your uncle, mum, Lulu and I have been working on a secret pet project for the past few weeks love. It's a decoy device that magically makes imitations of a demon's most hate foe appear to distract them from the real person.*

Genius, Penny thought again before she focused on fighting the demon again.

We're done love, so as soon as the flares fade out, start driving him into the portal, Lenox said.

Penny silently agreed as she carefully watched the flailing betrayer while keeping the side of her eye on the light of the flare. Then with bated breath, she saw the light flicker then go out.

The demon seem to notice as it turned it's attention immediately to the stone circle and head that way.

Penny followed closely in pursuit as the demon all but ignored her, completely focused on finding Lenox and Lulu. Though Penny felt both of them brush her back with ghostly hands letting her know that they were okay.

Then, like flashes of lightning, she felt everyone else let her know that they were a safe distance from the portal too.

Penny watched the demon suddenly spin around to face her as he finally recognized its fatal mistake. However by then, it was too late as Penny unleashed a magical blast of divine fire that Prometheus and Phoenix had taught her to use months ago and shoved the demon clear into the middle of stone circle and effectively ignited the stones at the exact same time.

Penny briefly saw that the blast had also had another effect as it had essentially created a hell- link chain bomb, that had which had cause her chains to wrap around themselves around the pillars and fully ensnare the demon within, without her actually summoning them up or directly using them.

Penny briefly shook her head to clear her mind of the distraction before she sat down facing the demon in hellhound form and began to mediate like the last time.

When her mind was clear, Penny added the scenery back into her mental picture, though this time, instead of cold, wet snowy mountainous land, she saw the ground glow a deep dark russet brown and bright vibrant forest green, before a slow thumping sound of rock began to echo in her mind causing her to remember another song that she had heard long ago.

Penny switched forms and began to play the song on her favourite violin as the earth and stone guardians of the mountain stirred and moved beneath her feet in tune with the song, despite not appearing yet.

Penny could feel the Betrayer try to fight against the chains but the guardians shook the ground around the circle, effectively quelling the demon before they burst from the ground and stood still. The demon seemed to seize up too at the sight of the guardians, however Penny didn't, as she played on despite the fact that guardians weren't moving.

However the long she played, Penny began to worry that something was wrong but she knew not to give into her fear for she knew the demon would win and she was soon rewarded, when the guardians did finally move.

The guardians very slowly almost at a snail's pace and they didn't dance like the water guardians had but more swayed slightly as if soothed by the music as they moved into their proper position. Though once in place, they touched the pillars one by one, infusing their essence into them.

The circle ignited again though with earth magic this time and entrapped the second Betrayer in thick chains.

Penny slowly finished the song before she came to her senses once more. Though this time the demon howled and roared in rage unlike the first, as he seemed to summon up more minions in replacement of the ones it had already lost in both battle and when the earth guardians cleansed the area. However when the minions arrived, Penny noticed that their number were considerably less than endless horde the demon once had access to.

Though Penny noticed something else then too, for as the demons moved towards them they triggered secret traps that killed them instantly with light magic.

"What on Earth..." Lenox's Aunt Raven murmured in wonder.

"Not on Earth.... wait yes on Earth but it wasn't caused by Earth. Jeez I'm confusing the ever loving stuffing out of myself..." Penny's mum muttered.

Alfie laughed, "Wow Ally... anyway what my twin is currently trying to find the right words to say is that when you lot were busy preparing to fight the blighters earlier this morning, Lenox used the wisps to create pretend versions of us, while he took us here so we could lay a rather bogus amount of traps. In fact it was more than just this morning, we've been laying these traps since end of November in secret with no one the wiser. To which I will say that you are an awesome nephew-in-law, Lenox."

"Thanks," Lenox murmured quietly.

"Whoa... hold on, is this what *'run with scissors'* truly means?" Phoenix asked.

"No, well not exactly, *'run with scissors'* simply means 'do what you want'," Alfie answered.

"Why did every hellhound elite look like their Christmas had came early, then?"

"Just look at the mind boggling number of traps and mischief that they laid while we were all pretty much none the wiser and you tell me that this isn't awesome thing?" Sebastian pointed out.

"Yeah I get it now, giving a *carte blanche* to the Baskerville twins is a very epic thing," Phoenix replied.

Then everyone went quiet as they prepared themselves to kill any demon that managed to get past the traps. Though despite the intense waiting and dread they felt, Ally and Alfie's traps held the hordes at bay until dawn rose gloriously the next day.

Penny felt the earth stir one more time beneath her feet and she briefly turned her head when the final pulse of earth magic erupted triggering the portal. Large green fiery tentacles emerged and took the demon back to where it belonged permanently. Though it also cleansed the plain fully of both traps and evil minions in one fell-swoop.

Penny let out a huge relieved breath when the stone circle returned to normal and the sun rose higher in the sky, truly letting her know it was all over.

Suddenly she felt two hands rest on her shoulder and Penny turned her head to look over both shoulders only to see both Epimetheus and Prometheus behind her.

"Penny... thank you," they said at the same time before they both stepped away.

Penny nodded once, feeling both tired and really elated that this battle was over. Though she didn't seem to be the only one.

"Wow I'm tired," Penny's uncle declared.

"No really Sherlock? I think just about everyone is tired and ready for bed. Which is a shame because a celebratory breakfast seemed in order but you know, there's also nothing wrong with a late celebratory dinner either. So call me when you're up sweetie and I'll order food for us, okay?" Penny's mum said, giving Penny a chance to escape.

"Yeah mum I will, I promise," Penny yawned before adding sheepishly, "Er... thanks."

"You're alright Penny hon, we'll see you at dinner tonight," Lenox's dad added.

Penny nodded once before she felt Lenox wrap his arms around her gently and teleport them to home.

Feeling beyond tired, Penny sagged back against him.

"I don't know why I feel this way, I mean I didn't feel this tired the last time," Penny said to Lenox worriedly.

"Your not draining yourself anymore this time compare to the last time, however you were running on more adrenaline during the first battle which is why you didn't feel so tired after. Though if you recall, you did pass out just after you ate your first bite of scone."

"Yeah that's right and thank you for saving all my scones for me when that happen so I could eat them later, they were delicious. You know, we should get more scones from that place tomorrow," Penny yawned again as sleep started to encroach her vision.

Lenox swept Penny up into his arms and carried her the short distance to bed. Undressing them both with magic, Lenox pulled up the covers around them as Penny snuggled into his chest.

"Hey Lenox," Penny said out loud just before she started to nod off.

"Yeah?"

"We're really half way done, aren't we? I mean, I'm not dreaming this am I?"

"No love your not, we are half way."

"Great news.... love you," Penny said before she fully fell asleep.

"Love you too Penniah," Lenox replied before he too fell into a deep content sleep, happy that this battle was over.

Chapter Twenty-Nine

A few weeks before the third Betrayer fight, Penny and Lenox had gone to see Aidan and Nia, the King and Queen of the Fae so they could talk about the third betrayer. Though just before they had left, Memphis and Callie had appeared, wanting to go with them since Aidan was Memphis' older brother.

Though all thoughts of the upcoming talk fell away when Penny saw the Vanishing Isle for the first time since the Fae war had ended less than a decade before. After all, when Penny had secretly fought for Fae Independence, the island had been a virtual desert wasteland since the evil Fae Wretch had drained all the magic and life from this place. Though looking at it now, Penny could see that was no longer the case because lush plant life was everywhere and she loved the fact that the Fae had gone so far as to build a sleek futuristic city around it, that was built upwards not outwards to give the plants room to grown.

"Whoa it's like night and day isn't it?" Penny murmured to Lenox finally.

"It is," Lenox agreed.

"Hey Lenox did you design those trains?" Penny asked as she motioned to the vertical trains that ran up and down building or connected to a secondary network .

Blushing slightly Lenox murmured, "I helped, love."

Penny snorted.

"Light Lenox, are you ever bashful," Memphis responded with a laugh.

"Well I have to say that, that is refreshing and *someone* could learn from him," Callie responded dryly.

"Love you too kitty cat," Memphis said not missing a beat.

"I love you as well," Callie replied, "Just wish you were sometimes bashful, well not with me directly because I do like your bold ways. However I wish you a bit more bashful with human officials since a little modesty would cost us less in fines when you get in trouble with the human law. "

"Oh! On that note Lenox, I forgot to tell you earlier but I very seldom get arrested. Sorry seems important to say now that Aunt Callie is on the topic. However the few times I have been arrest was for bogus reasons by crackpot dictators or corrupt officials that I was actually hunting down at the time. Surprisingly it's actually easier to make a kill when they arrest me because they always come to gloat about having me in jail. Seriously like iron bars and cement walls are an effective deterrent for a hellhound, as if!"

"Well... if you ever do need help being sprung from jail, I am a mechanical engineer and I'd help you out in a heartbeat love, no questions asked."

"You serious Lenox," Memphis asked.

"Always Memphis," Lenox responded instantly.

"Hold on are we talking about the same thing here?"

A new voice laughed, "Jeez Memphis! Yes he was being serious and you can clearly see Lenox would spring Penny from jail in a heartbeat. Though that should be a prerequisite in any immortal marriage."

Everyone turned to see Aidan and Nia just to their left. Nia, the one who had spoke, cheerfully waved at them as Aidan snorted.

Walking towards them, the couple were first greeted by Memphis and Callie who then stepped aside to make way for Lenox and Penny.

"Long time no see Lenox," Aidan greeted him as they shook hands then added, "You need to stop by after this is all sorted and we'll have a cards night or something."

"Sure but I didn't think it was wise for a King of the Fae to lose all his money," Lenox responded with a small smile.

"Hold on, you play poker with Aidan, Lenox?" Penny asked astounded.

"Once in a blue moon, yeah, otherwise we just hang out, go to the pub for a pint, build stuff, that sort of thing."

Aidan sighed, "Yeah those nights out are rare thanks to council business but still am I glad to get out and about with a friend.

Especially one who doesn't like to set bar on fire or play with firecrackers around excitable elephants..."

"Hey that was one time," Memphis inserted.

"One time too many, the council nearly had an apoplectic fit!" Nia declared.

"Why do you let the Fae council rule your life?" Memphis complained to Aidan.

"I don't let them rule my life..."

"No he doesn't and they don't interfere with many things of day to day life. However when it comes to dangerous stunts they become real ornery since they like Aidan and don't want to see him injured. Which never happens when Lenox hangs out with him."

"Well I am bit boring—" Lenox started to self-depreciate.

"Your not boring Lenox!" Penny interjected before continuing, "No one who spends his time making flying mag-lev cars, vertical trains and blinding super fast go karts could ever be considered boring!"

"Jeez Lenox you're working on mag-lev cars now?" Memphis asked with a low whistle.

"What's mag-lev?" Nia added.

"Magnetic levitation," Aidan responded to his wife at once before adding to his brother, "And yes Lenox is working on mag-lev. Since we've gone out in a small tour in his prototype and I'm helping him, into ways he can bring it to market."

Memphis turned to look at Lenox, "What else are you working on man?"

"Loads of stuff," Lenox respond with a shrug before adding, "Though as much as I like to talk about it all, unfortunately that's not why we're here. Sorry Aidan my friend but we truly need to talk."

Aidan gave him a small sad smile, "Yeah I know and I have a feeling I know what this is about too. Though promise me tonight, we'll hang out together, sorry but Nia and I both need the night out and I think it'll be fun if we had a double date."

Lenox looked at Penny who instantly nodded eagerly in agreement.

"Yeah we're up for a night out."

"Hold on, are Callie and I invited as well?"

"Memphis, wait a minute who is going to watch Starla?"

"Your brother Asa and before you call me heavy handed I spoke with already about babysitting for the night since I was going to take you out tonight on for a surprise date night when we're done. He agreed, though your sister Tessi wants us to go out next weekend and leave Starla with her and Kei since she also wanted to babysit. So how about next weekend we'll do date night and tonight will be a night out with everyone?"

Callie nodded with a smile.

"Right, now let's go talk about in private," Memphis said.

Aidan nodded this time before he showed everyone to an awaiting elevator train that was very close by.

Penny marvelled at the inside, taking multiple picture with her phone before Lenox gently guided her to a seat.

The train took off, upwards and heading for the top of the building, where Aidan and Na lived. Then when they arrived, Nia and Aidan showed everyone into their living room where they all sat down together on couches.

Penny looked to Lenox and squeezed his hand gently before he spoke up.

"We're here to talk to you about the next Betrayer and there is no easy way to say this but it's going to be the *Fae Wretch*, Guinevere who you led a revolt against in order to take back your kingdom from her. I know you're probably wondering how she became a Betrayer so fast, since it hasn't been many years since the war ended and the best answer I can give you is that almost all of her soul was already in hell before she died."

"How do you know that Lenox?" Aidan quietly asked as he wrapped an arm around Nia, who looked utterly shell-shocked.

"Lulu and I have been researching that old wicked pretender to the thrown for years. Mostly in order to aid the Fae in killing her prior to the end of the war but also partly because we believed she'd become a Betrayer. I know that doesn't sound like much of an answer, however Lulu and I were able to full see the identity of the Betrayers through visions.

"Anyway from what my sister and I have found out is at... well, Guinevere has always been planning to return to this world as a Betrayer and part of the evil acts she committed when she was 'queen' was to give her evil soul enough power to kill the Betrayer who had the role before her as soon as she entered hell. I know this is a shocking thing to hear but her aim in life was never really to become the Queen of the Fae, she always aimed to be one of the most evil demons ever."

"And she bloody got her wish," Nia hissed.

"Not really," Penny shook her head.

Nia frowned.

"You took a great chunk of her power away when you killed her Nia, not to mention, you've been dealing her blow after blow as you seek out and destroy all of her evil cult followers which weakens her even further. In fact because of you, this will be her one and only chance as a Betrayer."

"Will that not make life more difficult for you since once you bind her and another demon kills her then they take her place and you'll have another Betrayer to content with?" Nia asked

Penny shrugged, "If that's what happens then it happens but from what I've learned from the ancient spirits. There aren't as many evil beings in the betrayer realm of hell as we like to think there are and of those bound there, only very few have the capability or will to become a full on Betrayer. In fact, Oswin, the Great Spirit leader believes if we manage to rebind all four for eternity, the four betrayers will act like different pillar that will keep everyone else bound in place for a very long time, if not also eternity."

"Well that kind of makes me feel better. I mean, I can't stand that evil woman and all that she did not only to my people but my family. Though knowing that she bound to the Nine Circle of Hell for all eternity and will pay for crimes, makes me exceedingly happy. It's just... knowing that any part of her has returned to this realm, will be galling and I know I'll have to keep myself in check during battle."

Penny crossed the small gap and took Nia's hands in her as she sat down on the coffee table so that she could look the other woman in the eye.

"I promise you that for every foolish step that the Betrayer takes upon this world, will be filled with pure regret because I will make her feel a world of hurt for messing with you. Though will you let be your champion in this fight?"

Nia was quiet for a very long time before she spoke, "I don't have to like that she's now a Betrayer but I do like the fact that you will make her regret becoming one, Penny. In fact, I've seen you go toe to toe with two other betrayers and I know that you will show her no quarter. Therefore I will gladly accept you as my champion, though what do you think, Aidan?"

"I'll gladly accept Penny as my champion against this Betrayer, too. Don't go looking so surprised Penny, your one hell of a hound, no pun intended."

"That is she my friend that she is and I love her every day for it. Though should we go see the council now?" Lenox asked.

Aidan shook his head, "No Guinevere is truly dead in our eyes and thus no longer a Fae problem. Sorry but it is true."

"Don't be sorry, for we, hellhounds stop seeing people as people once they become pure wicked."

"Aidan we need to hang out with hellhounds more often," Nia sighed.

"Don't worry we will in the near future," Aidan said.

"Damn straight, now is it too early for the pub?" Penny asked as she stood up, though she looked directly at Lenox.

"Nah love and I hope you don't mind but Penny and I have recently adopted a gaming pub in Cambridge as our own local."

"Ooh is that the place where we can play board games and stuff?," Memphis asked.

"Yes."

"Ally told us about it and we want to give it a go," Memphis said as Callie nodded.

"I want to go too!" Nia declared, her mood instantly changing from pissed off to happy in a heartbeat.

"You sure you're not a hound?" Penny asked her with a smile.

"As far as I'm aware but then again Phoenix is my cousin and he's declared himself honorary part hellhound so I don't see why I can't be one too."

"You totally can," Penny agreed before Lenox teleported them to a safe spot near their favourite pub.

Stepping out of the shadows into the sunlight and the brisk cold snowy day. Penny felt relieved that the conversation had gone better than she had ever hoped, though only time would tell if everything would go their plan.

Don't worry love, I've got a tricks up my sleeve yet, Lenox mentally assured her.

Well that does do a soul good to hear, Penny laughed as she wrapped an arm around his waist and decided to focus on the now.

Chapter Thirty

When the day of the battle against the third Betrayer arrived, Penny found her mum and uncle in a more jovial mood than they had been during the last two battles as they busily polished weapons in Penny and Lenox's living room, trading insults like they did every other day.

"Um... mum... Uncle Alfie..." Penny started, confused by their good mood.

Penny's dad sighed from his spot in front of the fire and remarked, "Leave them be in their demented happy bubble, sweetie."

"It's not demented happiness, it's excited hellhound glee Bas," Ally corrected before adding, "Cultists, there are going to be real live wicked cultists according to Lenox. That I get to kill! What fun!"

"Don't say it that way! You sound like a serial killer about to go on a spree, Allycen."

"I'm not a serial killer... wait, does killing demons and wicked entities count when it comes to that title?" Ally asked her twin.

"No they don't count nor do I think that all the evil humans you've killed do, either. Since in my books evil is evil, is evil, who cares if it's in the form of a human, ghoul or demon?"

"That actually seems wise… coming from you," Ally muttered.

"Can't help that I'm the smarter twin," Alfie returned with a shrug.

"Pfft! As if."

"Twins," Sebastian called out.

"Yes boss?" Alfie asked dryly.

"Nothing," Sebastian said with a sigh, deciding to let it go.

"Aw lighten up Bas things will be okay," Alfie said.

"How do you know that?"

"Because this battle is gonna be in Scotland."

"How does that make a difference?"

Alfie stopped shiny his weapon and retorted, "How does it not? Scotland is an awesome place for a hellhound, since it has been our training ground for eons now and we know the lay of the land like the back of our paw."

"Not the Orkney Islands," Sebastian pointed out before continuing, "We've keep our training to the highlands mostly, sometimes the borders."

"Says you, Ally and I go there all the time," Alfie retorted

"Yes we do, it's the best place to fish, fish right out of the sea," Ally agreed.

"What?" Sebastian asked them.

"Mum and Uncle Alfie like fishing in Orkney because they've caught their biggest fish there. I know about it since Lucy and I sometimes join them, though not to fish We go to see the wee baby goats on North Rothesay Isle, they are so cute," Penny answered first.

"How did I not know this?" Sebastian asked Penny's mother directly.

"Don't ask me I talk about it all the time but it appears you've tuned me. Wow Sebastian I feel so very loved at this moment," Ally retorted in a deadpan tone.

"What! Of course I love you and I also listen to you all the time I do but if you think—"

"Bah ha ha! You thought I was being serious! Classic. Relax Bas, I was joking and of course I haven't told you about my favourite fishing spot because you'd go with us and find the world's biggest fish there which would piss me off."

"Allycen—"

"Oh come on, you were being all broody over there, so of course I'm gonna do something to goad you."

"Why?" Sebastian demanded.

"Cause when you enter a fight all broody, one of two things happen; you become a worried mother hen or you become impulsive, both of which is—"

"An utter hassle!" Alfie declared before cursing as he remembered instances when that happened.

"He said it, I didn't but it's true for either outcome cause you plunge headlong in the thick of things in order to prevent us from getting hurt or because you want to take the battle to our enemy first. Which then causes Alfie and I to launch an offensive to get you back. Though in truth, we just want you to fight side by side with us and kill evil *non-human* cultists or at least I'm pretty sure they're non-human because they'd followed a dead dark Faerie who turned into Niner. Though if there's one human among the idiots then – oops."

Penny's dad sucked in a deep breath before he did something wholly unexpected, he burst out laughing.

"Really Allycen?"

"Yes really, when you back a Niner against our baby girl in battle, then it's given that your bum is going to be on the line and I don't care which species they are."

"Fair dues love, though after this is all over, you're so taking me to your favourite fishing spot."

"Noo!" Penny's mum cried out dramatically though she didn't appear to be upset at all.

"Is everything alright?" Lenox asked then when he entered the room with his family.

"Yup, my dad is gonna steal my mum's favourite fishing spot in future," Penny remarked.

"Ooh where's that?" Lenox's uncle Phoenix asked.

"None of your bloomin' business, is where," Ally retorted hotly.

"Wow, territorial over your favourite fishing spot, are you? I get that though and I've kept mine hidden from Phoenix for at least a few hundred years," Raven, Phoenix's wife replied.

"Which is mean by the way," Phoenix retorted.

"Not really, it's where I go to calm down when you've burn down another forest or building block 'on accident'."

"By all means my love, keep fishing," Phoenix said openly.

"Thought you'd see it that way," Raven responded sweetly.

Penny turned to see that behind Phoenix stood his cousin Nia and her husband Aidan. Almost instantly Penny made her way towards them.

"I know you're upset to hear that the Wretch, Guinevere has become a Betrayer but you shouldn't be Nia—"

"Damn right you shouldn't be!" Penny's mum growled before turning contrite, "Sorry sweetie, floor is yours."

"It's okay mum but what I want to say is the Wretch who tormented you is dead, Nia. For this demon isn't her anymore and you never ever have to worry that she's coming back to get you or your family."

"Penny—" Nia started.

"No Nia, truly you have nothing to worry about I promise you on my honour, I will see her back to the place where she belongs and in fact, she'll be begging to be returned there when I'm through with her."

Nia said nothing as she searched Penny's face and then suddenly threw herself into Penny's arms.

"Penny I can't even begin to tell you the relief I feel at your words. Light... it is over, isn't Aidan?" Nia asked her husband as she turned her head to look at him.

"Before it even began sweetheart, hell look at all the weapons Ally and Alfie accumulated—"

"These are all necessary, for we heard there will be cultists!"

"Oh… are you talking about the Dark Fae Cult of the Wretched One?" Nia asked them.

"Yeah that's them, Lenox heard that they're planning to go against us to help the Wretch and we're gonna kill them all, human or no."

Aidan snorted, "They aren't human, they are all dark Fae and they would have killed any human who attempted to join them because they are purists."

"Ah good deal then, now I can't sound like a serial killer when I talk about doing them in."

"Ally!" Sebastian hissed.

"What? The jerk faces made Nia upset and they need to go for that offence alone," Ally retorted.

"But you barely know me," Nia sputtered as she stepped back.

Penny looked at her, "Maybe but we, hellhounds, can clearly

see the goodness in your heart and that alone makes us want to help you as best as we can. Besides I know how good friends our mates are and I wish for us to be the same in future."

"Penny Hawksley, you've got a friend in me for life, not because you're going to see this bloody Betrayer back to the place she belongs but because I think you're an amazing person. I would so go to hell and back for you."

"You don't have to go that far, just maybe take on some evil betrayer cultist minions and maybe, just maybe kept my mum and uncle out of trouble."

"Ha as if! Besides don't worry about me and your reprobate uncle, that's always gonna be your dad's job sweetie," Ally called out.

"Is it?" Sebastian asked dryly

"Yeah..."

"... Well not tonight it's not, for you to can go nuts. I'm also issuing a challenge, hound with the lowest body count buys a round of drinks at the pub tomorrow night, Penny excluded because see the Betrayer off already makes her top dog among us," Sebastian wagered.

"Ooh now who sounds like a serial killer? Though I'm totally in on that wager, sounds right up my alley."

Sebastian looked at Alfie who scowled in return, "Duh... how is that even a question?"

"Count me in since I'm also in as an honorary hound," Phoenix declared.

"Self-described," Lenox's Uncle Wulf added.

Phoenix looked at his best friend and brother-in-law and retorted, "You not in on this?"

"Hell no, I'm an honorary hound too."

"Good deal then, now come on suit up, the rest of the Wild Hunt just arrived and we'll need to be on the move shortly," Sebastian said.

Penny nodded feeling calmly ready for the night ahead, though she knew she wasn't the only one as Lulu and Lenox seemed to be in the same state.

Both twins look at her and winked in acknowledgement

before they turned their attention back to preparing themselves for the night ahead.

Later on that day when dusk slowly approached, Penny, Lenox and the Wild Hunt arrived on a small island in the Northern tip of Orkney Isle chain in Scotland. Though when they did, Penny mentally keyed herself up for battle as she watched the sun slowly sink in the sky.

"Was the Vanishing Isle really near here where we took on the Wretch? Sorry Lenox I'm not doubting you but it's almost like night and day from what I remember the Vanishing Isle was bright, dry and oppressive hot that day not cold, windy and wet," Nia remarked.

"Magical isles are different from their real world counterparts, for no matter where they move to on the real world plain they will keep what they always had. Meaning, the Vanishing Isle is actually considered a tropical immortal island and is completely unaffected by the polar cold that is affecting the rest of Greenlandic coast that it's currently hovering near at this time."

"Whoa, our home isle is near Greenland right now? How do we not know this? We're the heirs to the islands power after all," Nia cursed.

"Does it matter love?" Aidan asked with a shrug.

"No... yes... no," Nia sighed with a pout.

Aidan stole a quick kiss from his wife, "There's actually not a direct way of magically knowing where the isle is at any given point, love. Though there is a looking glass in the Grand Library for each of the seven immortal isles where you can look out and see where the island is exactly in the human world at that exact moment. I've been told by the head librarian, that every morning she looks out of them and charts the location down in a book. These log books have kept the exact location of the isles for over thirty thousand years and are kept secure but Lenox did obtain permission to look up the locations on specific dates for these fights."

Nia seemed stunned before she found her voice and said, "You know there was a time where I wanted to be the head librarian but now that I think about it, it seems like too much work."

"And being a Fae Queen is easier?" Aidan asked her.

"Not really but being mated to you is a huge plus so I guess that balances the books."

Aidan snorted and was about to say something when they all felt evil stirring. Looking to the standing stones, Penny watched a dark mist grow and take shape as the sun sank lower and lower in the sky.

Then seeing night time near upon them, she watched the demon hover at the edge of the circle ready to break free but Penny knew it wouldn't be that simple as the portal wouldn't release that quickly from what she seen before.

Penny briefly caught Lenox's hand gently and squeeze it, in reassurance before she focused everything on the demon in front on her. Then a minute before the barrier around the stone gave way, Penny let go of Lenox's hand and felt him move off to the left slightly.

Penny watched the demon begin to emerge from the dark portal and almost instantly focus on Lenox and Lulu as if the Betrayer knew that they would be the first catalysts of its doom.

Go, Penny directed as she saw the demon make its move towards them.

Not yet love, trust in us, Lenox said as he and Lulu linked hands and looked determinedly at the demon.

Suddenly as the demon approached them was met by a near invisible wall of wisps that had rose up out of the ground to defend Lenox and Lulu.

Penny couldn't help but let out a small snort at the display but she also knew why they chose to do what they did. So far they hadn't engaged in any fighting and they didn't want all of the other hellhounds to choose to defend them which would interfere in their work and ultimately doom them all.

Penny gave a brief nod before she switched to her hellhound form and made a beeline to the demon more than ready to take it on. Suddenly a loud horn sounded and Penny fought to keep herself from getting distracted and lose sight of the demon who was searching for the twins.

Not today Betrayer, Penny thought as she her hell chains loose, *all eyes of me.*

Penny used her chains in a tornadic fashion, whipping them around her as she felt the demon rear back to let loose a sudden magic blast.

Well this is new, Penny thought.

Which it was, as the last two demons had chosen to rely on more physical attacks then magical ones, however part of her was unsurprised because from what she remembered, the Fae Wretch wasn't known to be physically strong and relied more on evil magical attacks and the strength she pulled from her willing minions or unwilling victims.

Speaking of minions, it looks like those cultists that Aidan was talking about just showed up, though Light sake's what do they think this is, the middle ages or something? Penny's mum commented and in her mind Penny felt her mum show her a picture of a large battle troop that were dressed in metal plated magic armour on top of demonic beasts, looking very much like an advancing medieval army.

Hold on, I think they're a bit more modern than I first thought, they brought cannons. That could be bad, Penny's mum responded.

"Yeah friggin' right! Eat lead you mindless cult lackeys!" Penny's uncle suddenly shouted before Penny heard the telltale sound of one their new home made rocket launchers being fired.

At the same time Penny dodged the Betrayers magical attack, using her chains to entrap the magic and diffuse it before it could fly into the Wild Hunt.

Penny felt the fallout of evil energy attempt to infect her and she briefly felt herself weaken, before the energy washed off her much like water would on a duck's back as the hell-link chains seem to purify the evil.

Penny ducked and dodged the magical blast as she attempted to get closer to the demon.

Lock down her magic Penny, Prometheus whispered in her mind.

How? Penny asked in return.

You know how if you only think about it, came his response.

Frowning inwardly Penny stayed focus on her opponent before suddenly an idea came to mind. Penny waited for the next attack and jumped towards it. Spinning in the air, in a gravity defying move, Penny used her natural hell fire to purify the attack before she wrapped the chain around the blast, keeping it intact.

Hitting the ground running, Penny waited for the demon to rear back with a second attack before she whipped the first blast of magic back at the demon. It connected seconds before another magical blast erupted and Penny watched it briefly stun the demon. Wasting no time, she rammed the demon with her body though at the same time she let loose a large blast of hellfire and rendered the demons attacks null.

The demon shrieked and out of the battlefield, Penny could hear whispers coming from the cultists and minions.

"What has she done?"

"It cannot be our Lady's magic has been rendered useless by hellhound hellfire!"

"No! We're doomed! Retreat!"

"The hell we're going to let that happen!" Penny's mum shouted loud.

"That's bloody right! You idiots made your bed when you sided with the bloomin' demon and we're going to make you lie in it, permanently!" Penny's uncle added.

The Betrayer suddenly turned from Penny and seemed to head off in the direction of the battle.

Nope, Penny thought, you're not getting anywhere near them.

Then in pure hellhound fashion, Penny went on the offensive again.

In the thick of things, Lenox and Lulu diligently worked on preparing the stone for the ritual but suddenly, Lenox noticed a large shadow that moving towards him on the ground out of the corner of his eye.

Lulu, Lenox reacted as he grabbed his sister and pulled her away from the stones just before the shadow could touch her.

What is that? Lulu asked as the slowly made their away from the shadow creature.

It's a Fae shadow beasts... dark creatures created by the inner evil of dark Fae in order to do their bidding. Well it looks like the cultists are using the battle as a distraction to allow these creatures to find and kill us.

Lulu let out a mild mental oath

Of all the stop rotten things to do! Do they really think we're that weak? Lulu demanded.

It appears that way, though you do realize that the only way to take on these creatures...

... Is to give up our veil of invisibility and take them on directly. Yup I do, though it must be done Lenox because we're not the only ones in danger here.

Lenox felt a burst of anger well in him at the thought of these evil getting anywhere near his soul mate.

No quarter, Lenox vowed.

No mercy, Lulu vowed as well, before they released their magical protection and chose to burn brightly with Light magic.

Lenox! Lulu! What are you doing! Penny cried out, when she noticed the change.

Dealing with a shadow roach problem, won't be but a minute, Lulu said in her usual bubbly carefree manner despite the fact that neither twin actually felt bubbly or carefree.

Lenox and Lulu both summoned staffs and struck the ground where the shadows were, effectively drawing them up from the ground since the staff were made of ancient magic that instantly made the hidden evil visible. Then once visible both Lenox and Lulu took turns using Ritana healing magic to purify the creatures and render them harmless wisps.

Hold on bad time to ask this but are the wisps that follow you, evil creatures that you've purified? Penny asked incredulously.

Kind of and not really, the wisps are purified dark energy that take the form of sprites not the dark creatures themselves, Lulu explained.

I feel Ritana magic, won't using that do you two harm? Penny demanded.

No love, I'm a null remember.

Right then, carry on, Penny said as she fought to keep the Betrayer from Lenox and Lulu. Though bizarrely she really didn't need to as the demon was more focused in joining the battle against the rest of the Wild Hunt then taking on any of the three.

Penny soon realized why as she could clearly see that the Betrayer was currently on the losing end of battle. As Lenox and Lulu were not the weak links that the demon had thought they were since their little 'roach problem' was nearly completely. In fact, the twins were taking turns dispatching the shadow creatures and finishing the ritual with such breathtaking ease, Penny herself found herself astounded by them.

Eyes on the prize love, we're finished here, Lenox murmured, reminded Penny to focus fully on the task at hand.

I'm focused, Penny said as she wrapped her hell- link chains around the weakened demon who seemed to have put her eggs in one magical basket and was now physically weak. Which pretty much allowed Penny to drag the near comical 'kicking and shrieking' demon towards the stone circle. Though despite the demon being weakened, it still tried everything it could to break free of Penny chains which was taking a toll on Penny's magic reserves.

Feeling the equivalent of a human nearing the end of running a marathon. Penny gathered herself together for one last push.

"Enough!" Penny roared as she whipped the hell-link chains in one solid movement and sent the demon spiralling into the centre of the standing stones.

Without skipping a beat Penny felt her chains immediately lock themselves around the stones and trigger the large trap that kept the demon ensnared within them.

Stopping, Penny shifted forms feeling shaky at using so much magic but she knew that it wasn't over yet. Taking in a deep calming breath, Penny focused on clearing her mind and connecting with the stones guardians.

It was harder this time though, as with each deep calming breath she took, she could feel waves of evil malice pour out from the demon in an attempt to weaken her even more.

You've got this love, Lenox mentally whispered as he opened up their soul bond and poured out love and support in her direction.

Feeling the boost come from the bond, Penny's mind was able to shove away all the wickedness as she focused on the calming sea around her. Though this time the spiritual tune did not come from the sea but from the air above her as a melodious tune began to make itself known through the wind.

Penny first hummed the song to herself before she smiled and summoned up her violin and began to play.

Unlike the previous spirits, the air guardians were much livelier as they made themselves known almost immediately by swirling around Penny and pulling her up into the starry night sky alongside them. Though as they danced all around her, they seemed to push away all the negative demon energy.

Suddenly a large burst of air blew down from the skies and flatten all the cultists to the ground, sparing only the Wild Hunt from its fury.

Afterwards the spirit became gently again, slowly entering the stone pillars one by one as they gently returned Penny to the ground. Though bizarrely before the last spirit entered the pillar it went right through Penny and she felt all the evil that she was unknowing infected with enter the stone circle with the last spirit. Penny felt the spirit attempt to return the evil to the Betrayer, though that was when the Betrayer lashed out against the spirit.

Penny nearly froze up and stopped playing.

Penny play! Don't stop! It'll weaken the guardians, Lenox commanded.

Instantly Penny started playing again but she felt frantic would she realized the last spirit was slowly being infected by the Betrayer's evil.

I've got this love, trust in me, Lenox said before he began to chant.

Lulu joined in and suddenly the sky lit up with vibrant blue, green and violet lightning, though unlike normal lightning it didn't crack or rumble. Instead it zigzagged across the sky in almost peaceful fashion and Penny secretly wondered what this was all about.

Though that soon became apparently when the stone pulsed with a power as the spirits seemed to react and the hell-link chains that kept the demon pinned glowed, weakening the demon. This gave the last spirit the chance to return the evil to the demon before briefly flying up into the sky to be cleansed of anything that remained with itself.

Then it fly down from the sky and entered the last pillar. When the circle was sealed, the stone flashed, cementing the chains before a large pulse erupted and destroyed the demons minions.

Penny finished the song before she took up her defensive position in front of the circle. The demon behind her let out whiny growls as it weakly fought to free itself but it was too drained to move.

"Not on my watch," Penny said as she saw a new wave of cultists and minions appear.

Tired of them, Penny felt a new power rise up in her.

"Take this gift, you will need it to finish this battle and give a strength for the next," a disembodied voice whispered.

Penny felt the new power simmer and pulse within her as she felt her body literally pulse with magic. Then without warning a blinding pinkish golden light erupted from her and Penny watched a wave of ethereal hell-link chains move in an almost tsunami-like fashion across the plain, sweeping up minions and cultists and immediately destroying them.

"What the hell was that?" Penny's mum gasped.

"A new gift from the Light," Penny replied as she felt great satisfaction that the plain was swept completely cleaning and blocked any others from teleporting in to aid the Betrayer.

No one said anything in response as they all held their position until, the first grey light of dawn appeared.

Penny heard the demon let out a loud screaming howl and she briefly turned to keep one eye on the horizon and another on the demon.

The Betrayer fought like a mad fiend trying to escape the

chains one last time but it was much too late as bright golden tentacles burst from the ground and dragged it down into the fiery depths of hell with aid of Penny's chains.

Penny felt deeply satisfied when the stones returned to normal, though soon after her satisfaction gave way to a deep bone weary tiredness.

"Well that was a hell of a battle," Penny yawned.

"Yeah but we owned it!" Her mother piped up and then added, "Did we get all the dark Fae cultists do you think, Sebastian?"

Penny's dad seemed to cock his head in contemplation, "They're might be a few cowards left who didn't show up tonight. Why do you ask? Do you want to hunt them now?"

"Does the world always spin clockwise? Of course I do! You up for it my mate?"

"I am but are you freakin' tired?" Sebastian asked with concern.

"Sure I am but that's nothing five double shot espressos can't fix. Come on, I can't just leave them, those cowardly idiots could join up with the last Betrayer in revenge!"

"Agreed, let's go then," Sebastian agreed.

"Count me in too," Alfie called out before they took off in a wisp of smoke intent on hunting down their remaining quarries.

"Well Aidan and Nia, it looks like all your problems are sorted. For anyone with any fringe leanings towards backing the Wretch in anyway shape or form, is going to dealt with by the hellhounds and if there's one thing you can count on the hounds to be, it's pure relentless," Phoenix spoke up.

Nia smiled brightly at him before bursting into tears, causing it to rain all around them since Fae emotions had effect on the weather. Aidan drew her into a hug and no one said anything as they realized the weight of what they had just done.

One more betrayer was gone, an evil cult had been routed and dealt with and a kingdom was well and truly free of past wickedness.

You did that Penny love, Lenox mentally whispered to her.

No Lenox, we did it and we will face this last fight together, Penny returned, knowing full well that the worst was yet to come.

Chapter Thirty-One

Lenox, Penny and Lulu sat with Lenox's mum, dad and grandfather Midir around the kitchen table as they waited for the hellhound elite to arrive. The final battle would be upon them in a matter of days and they knew they had to have one last conversation about the demon they were to face.

"Do you think we have enough snacks?" Lenox's mum said, fretting as she looked over all the food in front of them.

"We have enough, love," Lenox's dad reassured her.

Though Mina still looked doubtful, causing Conalai to smile.

"Add more cupcakes if you feel it's appropriate, love," he replied.

Instantly, Mina summoned up a near mountain more.

"Hmmm... I've never had one of these before," Midir murmured as he picked up a cupcake.

"You've never had a cupcake, grandad?" Lulu asked.

Midir shook his head. "No, hon, I have what your gran calls a warrior's constitution, which mainly revolves around me eating bannock, dried meats, fruit like apples, porridge and cheese."

"Really? Oh, grandad," Lulu said sadly.

Midir reached out with his free hand."Don't feel bad for me, sweet Lou, it's not a bad thing, I just prefer to eat food that can be consumed quickly or eaten with one hand so my sword hand is free."

Penny and Conalai both nodded as if that made total sense.

"Yeah, I've done that, too," Conalai admitted.

"Me, three, though it's also why hellhounds eat so fast. After all, in the olden days, demons used to try sneaking up on us during mealtimes or when we slept in order to kill us. So, as a species, we started eating quickly and napping in intervals or staying awake completely until we reached a safe place to sleep. Though, unfortunately, those places have been infiltrated once or twice."

"Oh, Penny—" Lulu started looking sad.

Penny smiled. "You are a sweet soul, Lou but don't feel bad for us. Every species has its betrayers in them. Well, maybe not the Ritana."

Mina thought for a moment. "Ritana have been betrayed by one of their own, though you are right, Penny, in thinking it is a rare occurrence just like the hellhounds."

"Truly?"

Mina let out a sigh. "The few that have done so were helping out a devious lover. Though nonetheless, betrayal is betrayal whether one knowingly or unknowingly commits it. However, our outlook regarding the event can look different in everyone's eyes."

"Um, what does that mean?" Penny asked.

"For Ritana, when we are betrayed, we often try to look at the event and determine if the betrayal was intended. Then, we try to determine why the act was committed in the first place and if redemption can be found."

"Er... why? Sorry... but still—" Penny stopped when the other elite arrived.

Mina smiled at Penny. "Ah, Penny, to a hellhound betrayal is betrayal even when done for a good reason, and you seldom forgive as a species."

"Correction. We have forgiven exactly once that I know of," Penny replied.

True to form Penny's mum spoke up and said, "You're right, sweetie. We have only forgiven once, though that was well deserved."

"It was still a hard choice," Reggie said, "I mean, I absolutely love my soul mate and there will never be any doubt in that but forgiving her for faking to fall in love with another to take on the Horseman of Pestilence by herself was hard to overcome. I mean, it sounds like it wouldn't be a big deal but we were together for millennia in secret before she publicly shunned me."

"Aren't you glad you still did forgive her?" Ally demanded.

Reggie smiled. "I am, Ally, and I'm glad you and Alfie stuck to your guns and demanded that I do so."

"Hold on. Why did you listen to them?" Conalai asked.

"Outside the hellhounds, this is not known but Alfie, Ally, Lucy and Penny aren't truly hellhounds. They are hell raisers. For not only are they descended from the first Brimstone Huntress, but within their bloodline are special Light given blessings that make them very powerful and special."

"Yes, that's true but it's more of a curse than a blessing most days," Alfie said.

"Alfie!" Sebastian hissed.

Penny blew out a sigh. "No dad, Uncle Alfie is right. Some days it is a curse, especially on days when you go out with the intention of getting a cup of tea and a pastry, only to end up with your hands around a server's neck because you caught a glimpse of her murdering her past lovers with poison to get their money."

"Or when you want to run free in a nice park, only to run into a wall of visions of being raped and murdered by a footpath serial killer who is still on the loose," Ally said.

"Or when you're dancing in front of a crowd, knowing that they're all about to be murdered by a crazed terrorist," Lucy added.

"Or when you are looking for a group of innocents who have suffered greatly and you have to choose between finding them and making sure they're safe or going out to kill all wicked fools who hurt them. Sounds like a no brainer but still, there's always the little voice in the back of my head that says, 'go on, you can step away from this hunt for five minutes and kill the sucker, he's not that far away.' However when you do, you often let the innocents be killed by another wicked fool."

Sebastian, Reggie, Winston and Rocky were silent as they took in the four other Baskervilles' secret confessions.

"Not to sound like an idiot but why didn't you say anything?" Sebastian asked them.

"Sebastian, do you think our crazy behaviour is normal? No, it is our vent. We do off the wall stuff to blow off steam and not only for us but for Penny and Lucy because Ally and I routinely take the wicked energy that our kids have accumulated within them and vent it for them, so they can live normal-ish lives. I mean, it's not something we discuss or talk about for we don't want sympathy or any of that nonsense. It's just. . . it is what is it is. We live with it and we move on. Though getting back to what we were discussing before, forgiveness is something we need to learn to do as a species because we have alienated a crap ton of people who have gone out and done bigger and badder things. However had we kept them close then I don't believe it would have gotten so bad or at least we would have had a better chance at killing them quietly. One of whom, I know Lenox and Lulu want to talk about but the truth is, we already know all about him," Alfie said.

The room went deathly still as everyone took in his words. Alfie and Ally exchanged a quick glance before Ally nodded for Alfie to go on.

"I know you want to talk about Triton and his role in defeating the first Niners, however the story you've learned of Lenox and Lulu is the garbage one. It's also the one retold over and over by I don't know who. Though that doesn't matter for when the demon appears, everyone listens to that story and then they doubt their actions and when they do the huntress dies every time."

"However, the other version of the story that our family tells isn't the full real version either, though the truth has been lost to us. So without being able to know what to believe in, it causes confusion and doubt. However, our family has determined that the huntress must hear both stories, one is from Fironyi's point of view and the other from Triton's in order to choose her path in the upcoming battle.

"Now both stories start the same; long ago, Fironyi came across two men who offered her a solution to ridding the world of the Betrayer demons, one of them was Altus and the other was Triton. Altus was a brilliant man who had thought that by finding ways to seal the demons away forever by creating the wild hunt and the rituals was best for us all. However Triton had another plan was completely different and it all revolved around convincing a willing person to sacrifice themselves in a battle thereby nullifying the evil and 'destroying' the demon."

Alfie stopped for a moment as Ally spoke up.

"This is where we need to pause and tell you that story diverges from here into two different point of views, however really doesn't matter because it all boils down to two choices; Does one sacrifice themselves for the greater good for a chance to end the demon or does one bind all the demons away for eternity, knowing that the other demons will take their place at a later date?"

"Kill the demon no matter what," Sebastian muttered right away, then swore, "But is that how the Huntress dies in the past? They sacrifice themselves to kill the last one. Well, it doesn't seem to work because they still keep coming back."

"Yes, exactly," Ally nodded.

"So binding the demon is the right answer?" Reggie asked.

"Is it? Could such a thing be the right answer here? I mean it seems simple enough— kill the demon kill yourself or bind the demon and live with the knowledge that another will take its place years down the line. However, as hellhounds, tell me that you'd be happy knowing that all the demons still lives in a sense?"

"But again, the demons still come back either way!" Sebastian pointed out.

"No, Bas, they actually don't. For once there was thirteen of them and now there are four. How do you think that happened? Don't answer for I will tell you. When you make the sacrifice, you actually do kill a demon but that gives the others a chance to overcome the bound ones and for the Niners to return years later."

"Hold on, I thought there were only three Huntresses. I mean, there was Fironyi, Andrika and now Penny, though by the sounds of it, there were more," Sebastian pointed out.

"No Andrika wasn't the huntress, her best friend Lorelei Baskerville was, though much like Ally and I were willing to do before Penny was found out by the other hellhounds, Lorelei's father attempted to hide the fact that she her as the huntress. Therefore he asked Andrika to take the title. However Lorelei could not avoid her fate much like nine other Huntresses from our family including Fironyi, as she chose to sacrifice herself to kill one of the demons."

"No," Lenox inserted, "That's not what happened, for they may have believed that they were sacrificing themselves in order to kill a Betrayer but in truth another Betrayer used them for his own gain."

"Lenox—" Alfie started.

"No, he's right and you must hear him out completely for this is a matter of life and death," Midir warned them.

Alfie was the first to move as he guided Ally to sit down next to Penny before he left space for Sebastian next to Ally and took the next chair. Then one by one the hellhound elite sat down and look at Lenox directly.

"The story first must be told both sides first. In Fironyi's story she mated with a man named Pryor and they had a son and a daughter before Pryor sacrificed himself to protect his mate and child from a demon. Though in her grief, Fironyi learns that it is Triton who has told Pryor what to do in order to kill the demon and she banishes him from the pack. Triton goes out with a group of loyal followers in order to kill the demons on his own, only to accidentally plunge into hell when attempting to kill one of the Betrayers. Though he still sacrifices himself and atone for his sins. Lost without her mate, Fironyi then takes on all the remaining betrayers by herself, binding them all to hell with her chains, though she drains herself of too much magic and dies from grave wounds that she cannot heal from. Now in Triton's tale, it is said that he is Fironyi's secret lover and she chooses her long time best friend Pryor to be the father her children since Triton is said to be unable to father any. Though in doing so, he feels betrayed. So he sets out to first kill himself during a demon battle only for Pryor to sacrifice himself to save Triton's life. Fironyi gets upset at Triton's foolishness and banishes him, only to lose him in another battle. Though when news of his death reaches her, she decides to sacrifice herself in battle to kill all the Betrayers. However you are right Alfie neither are true," Lenox said stopping to look at his grandfather.

"No neither tale are true even if you piece the two of them together and I will tell you the truth of it all, having witnessed everything with my own eyes," Midir stated clearly.

"My father was Altus and I was born to his first wife, Midiria whom I was named after. For while giving birth to me, she was murdered by a Betrayer which is set my father on his course to end their evil, once and for all. As I grew up, he raised me, my father taught me everything he had come to learn about them which was much. Though as wise as my father was, he was careful with words for he knew that by saying the wrong thing could lead to being misinterpreted and that would lead to death of many. So he chose to say very little, which ultimately caused a different problem, for many thought him simple for not speaking and thus did not take his warnings to heart. However Fironyi was not one of them and when he saved the lives of the children of her first mate, Pryor during an errant demon attack, she came to rely on him greatly. Though there were those among the newly created race of hellhounds, who did not like him and of them all Triton's hatred was most evident.

"Triton was an out and out braggart who use to claim a powerful position amoung the hounds of time, by using his position as Fironyi's lover. For he was the one she sought comfort in after her first mate died. Though I must say that her first mate wasn't her true soulmate, my father Altus was and the moment they first met, they fell in love. However Fironyi had made a fatal mistake by allowing Triton free reign to take over leadership of the hellhound pack while she pursued a relationship with my dad. For Triton had long abandoned their creed of protecting innocents from the Betrayers and had chose instead, to make living sacrifices for power.

"When Fironyi learned of what Triton had been doing, she was appalled but at first she refused to believe Altus when he told her that the people had been innocents, for she could not fathom that a warrior she had handpicked to become a hellhound would willing to side with the very thing that they were fighting against, for power. No it was much easier to believe Triton's claim that the person had sacrificed themselves willing to protect them. Though Fironyi knew that that she couldn't trust Triton anymore and had chosen to accept Altus' suggestion, which was to see Triton pay for his crimes. So she outwardly banished him, all the while Altus quietly killed him, as well as his loyal followers quietly. However it backfired, for in killing Triton, it gave him all the power he could have dreamed of, for he was made a Betrayer nearly instantly because of his wicked deeds.

" Unfortunately neither Fironyi nor Altus knew that and they thought that everything was settled. Though it truly wasn't because there were hellhounds who had believed Triton's story that he done everything to save them and they were angry when they heard of his 'accidental' death. Therefore Fironyi sowed the seeds within the hellhounds, that a betrayal in any form was a betrayal no matter if it was for the greater good or not and the only atonement one could seek out was in death. Thus in their eyes, Triton was fully redeemed and he could receive his due as a great warrior. However, when Altus found out what Fironyi had done, he was horrified, for singing the praises of a demon strengthens them and often helps them find sympathetic people who will become their minions.

"However Fironyi didn't believe that, until the last battle against the betrayers when she ran into Triton again. During that battle Altus was killed by Triton and unable to live without her soulmate Fironyi sacrificed herself to 'kill' Triton. Though she was magical weak when she did so and Triton ended up bound in hell, though the binding was weak and eventually he would be able rise up again.

"Nonetheless, after that last battle, Triton's followers were punished by the Light and became skin-walking ravenous wraiths called Wendigoes, doomed to wander this realm.

"At that time, I chose to focus on dispatching the Wendigoes then the Betrayers for I did not believe them capable in returning to this realm. However Triton's name was still revered within the hellhound pack which gave him plenty of powers, alongside all the evil powers the Wendigoes collected for him by feasting on innocents.

"Eventually when I caught wind of what was truly going on during the next battle against the betrayers with the new Brimstone Huntress, I was unprepared and Triton was able to cursed me, for he thought that eventually I'd kill myself to escape this fate. However eventually I was able to learn that I could take breaks from hunting on a special rare 'blue moon' that occurrence for one month every five hundred years until my daughter Mina broke my curse a few years ago.

" Now this is very important to know, since this information has been lost to immortals, however blue moons are very special to us and it has the ability to amplify the power of the Light and weaken demons dramatically. Now one such event is coming up soon and will occur in the month of March."

Everyone gasped.

Midir grinned, "That's right, in his effort to be the 'last' demon to emerge in our realm since he believes you will be at your most vulnerable, he has made numerous fatal mistakes. The first being that his name is dirt to the hellhounds and thus he has lost any power that comes from reverence, which is how a shade of himself was able to walk among you without anyone knowing for so long. Second, he weakened himself further because he sacrificed the only minions he had in an attempt to kill you earlier then used a large chunk of his evil energy to create a Kulcair that failed too. Next, by forcing the other demons to go ahead of him, he will not be able to steal evil energy from them nor other minions because they are fully bound now. Not to mention, you have killed all of their minions too. Which means he will be forced to face you alone.

"Then he hasn't take it into account that Penny has grown in strength not weakened and you only need to remember seeing the new gift that she has acquired as proof. Not to mention, she has trust in the Wild Hunt and her soulmate which has allowed her to draw strength from us. Lastly, he has forgotten all about the blue moon.

"Therefore, I say this battle is set in your favour Penny but always remember that a Betrayer has earned their spot in hell for reason and he will try just about anything to safe himself. Also Lenox, Lulu, do what you do best my grandchildren, for that will be key to winning this fight, if you understand my meaning."

"Sounds like a plan and I for one, am not about to bow down and sacrifice myself to fuel that idiot. We will win this fight our own way and to hell with him," Penny declared pissed off at the demon's previous actions.

Midir smiled even more saying nothing as the other hounds vehemently agreed with her.

Lenox, my grandson I leave things to you now, though I do ask a favour, Midir mentally whispered.

Anything grandad, Lenox immediately responded.

I wish to take some of these cupcakes with me, I think you Granny will appreciate them.

Take as many as you want grandad, Lenox said with a small laugh.

Midir nodded slightly before teleporting away with an entire plate.

"Where'd he go?" Ally demanded.

"To spend time with my mum; my father is not one to say goodbyes for he believes goodbye is only said to those on their final journey. Though I'm just glad I baked extra cupcakes for I believe he'll be wanting more when he returns tomorrow, for a visit," Lenox's mum said.

Ally picked up a cupcake and bit into it, "Well I can see why. Gosh darn it Mina, these are pure delicious."

"Gosh darn it?" Alfie echoed.

"Mina's a Ritana, swearing in front of her is like kicking a puppy which I hope to Light doesn't sound offensive Mina but still... is what it is."

Mina shrugged, "I am truly not bothered by swearing, words are just words, for it's the feeling behind them that makes them venomous or not. Though I promise there will be more cupcakes than you can shake a stick at once this..."

Mina broke off and let out a litany of colourful swear words, which caused every hounds eyes to nearly bug out of their face. Then she finished with, "... needs to dealt with permanently and I hope my sentiment on the subject was quite clear. Though don't you mollycoddle my children or my dear daughter-in-law during this fight, for that will get them killed. Just let them do what they must, while you prepare to kill any evil drawn to the battle, for even though this demon will not have minions as my father has said, it will draw evil to it. Mark my words. Now eat up, you have training this afternoon I'm sure."

"Wow Mina... you are scarily awesome... teach me your secrets," Ally murmured in awe.

"No secrets, I am a woman blessed with a wonderful family

and I feel the need to see to it, that we will never be crossed again by any evil fool ever again."

"That's for sure," Ally agreed readily enough while munching on another cupcake. Soon her twin joined in and they began their normal bickering over food.

Penny reached in and grabbed four cupcakes before handing them off to her dad, Lenox and Lulu,

Leaning back, she smiled at her dad who was looking at her not eyeing up the pending twin melee.

We've got this, dad.

We damn well do, sweetie. We damn well do, he echoed, looking more at peace than he had in a long time.

Chapter Thirty- Two

The final battle was upon them and from the moment she woke up, Penny knew exactly where to find the last Betrayer, Triton, without being told where to look. For she could feel the location deep within her bones.

Grabbing a basket of food for breakfast from the kitchen, Lenox and Penny headed out and sat on a picnic blanket on a rocky outcrop in the middle of Yorkshire Moors. They ate their breakfast , in companionable silence while watching, a stone circle slowly emerge from a muddy bog at the bottom of a hill

"Hey, Penny. Hi, Lenox," Lulu greeted them as she and Freya joined them about five minutes after Penny and Lenox had arrived.

"Why aren't you at home prepping for battle?" Freya demanded not even bothering to greet them properly.

"I could feel this dirt bag miles away and it was annoying me, so I want to watch the circle emerge," Penny muttered, eating a piece of banana toast.

"Ooh, banana toast! Can I have a slice?" Lulu asked in delight.

"Help yourself, Lou, we brought enough food for you and the rest of the Wild Hunt who are bound to find us here soon enough," Penny replied as she wrapped an arm around Lenox's back.

"Penny! Penny! What are you doing here?" Penny's mum cried out, she arrived with Penny's dad, uncle, and the rest of the elite hounds, proving Penny's comment.

"Eating and watching the dirt bag's portal emerge from the muddy bog at the bottom of the hill," Penny replied, offering her mum a muffin.

Penny's mum growled softly at the sight below them. Though afterwards, she promptly sat down on the rocky outcrop and ate.

"So dirt bag is what we're calling him now, sweetie?" Penny's dad asked as he sat down.

"Yup! I went over other titles and names that we could have called him but since he is a bag of demon garbage emerging from a muddy bog, dirt bag seemed pretty apt."

"I can agree with that," Penny's dad said.

"So, when did he start annoying you with his presence, Pen? It was the crack of dawn, wasn't it?" Lucy asked.

"It was after eight, Luce but I guess in hellhound terms eight is the crack of dawn," Penny admitted.

"Light, he tried that horrible dream thing with me," Lucy cussed out.

"You mean the *you're gonna watch everyone you ever love die before I kill you,* dream thing? Yeah, same here but he didn't seem to realize that Lenox's family are dream protectors, which is why the dream ended with him being run over by a green space cow driving a technicolour spaceship. Which was a nice touch, by the way, Lenox love."

"You got a space cow in a spaceship? Nice. My dream ended with a giant pretty butterfly the size of Mothra hitting him with the force of a supersonic jet."

"Mine ended with him being run over by the Batmobile," Alfie added.

"I saw a huge pony that you couldn't see more than its hind leg and hoof, stomp on him flat," Ally declared happily, making a splat noise.

"Okay, the spaceship and the Batmobile was me," Lenox admitted.

"And the butterfly and the pony was me," Lulu also admitted before adding, "We would never invade your dreams on purpose without just cause though."

"Nah, Lulu, don't start apologizing for that. We know why you did it and we happily understand. He was trying to psych us out, which would have totally worked if not for your dream intervention. Also, I think I'm getting your love of bananas, Lou. I find banana toast is becoming part of my daily breakfast routine. Have to say I have no regrets there either," Ally said.

"Are you seriously discussing banana toast when the final

battle is upon you?" A new male voice demanded.

"Yes, whiny minotaur, I am. Callie, come have a piece of banana toast while your husband stands over there and whines some more about how unhealthy the food I'm eating is, like he always does."

"Why would I whine about it being unhealthy when it's the healthiest thing I've seen you eat?"

"Meat is also healthy, you vegan."

"I'm not a vegan. I still eat cheese on occasion and meat does clog your arteries."

"Says you, whereas the benefits of meat are widely known, including it's higher iron content."

"Not getting into that with you today, Ally," Memphis said before asking for a piece of banana toast.

"Since I feel magnanimous today, sure."

"Hey, I can be magnanimous, too. Have some barbecue tofu jerky," Lucy said as she opened a brown paper bag.

"Where'd you get that?" Memphis asked her as he cautiously took a piece.

"Lenox and Lulu's mum makes it and I'm not a fan of tofu but this tofu jerky is delicious. She fries it up in light olive oil with barbecue spices and words can't even begin to describe how awesome it is."

"Isn't that called tempeh not tofu jerky?" Memphis asked as he bit into it and let out a moan. "It's so good!"

"Yeah, now that I think about it, I believe she did call it tempeh but to me, it's still barbecue tofu jerky."

"I can live with that description," Memphis replied as he ate a few more pieces of tempeh.

For the next few hours, everyone sat in comfortable silence as they waited for the rest of the Wild Hunt to arrive, which they did over the next few hours.

Then as the sun began to set, Penny felt the demon grown in strength and she began to see its evil actions.

"Dear Light," she murmured, shaking her head sadly.

"Hmm," Lenox murmured as he stroked Penny's shoulder and

the taint of evil that tried to infect her.

"Hey, Lenox, don't take this the wrong way," Sebastian said as he suddenly hugged Lenox.

"What are you doing?" Ally asked curiously, cocking her head.

"He's a null, Ally and a hell of a strong one. Which means he can cleanse evil energy," Sebastian said when he let go of Lenox.

"And so can Lulu since she's his symbiotic twin. Sorry, Lulu sweetie but I need you to get rid of the icky evil the dirt bag is trying to infect us with. Ugh, I hate when demons spread their filthy evil all over the place," Ally said as she hugged Lulu.

"It's okay, I don't mind. Free hugs for everybody," Lulu replied cheerfully.

"Thanks, Lou," Reggie said as the hellhound elite all chose to hug Lulu.

"No offence, Lenox," Alfie said.

"I'm not offended that you'd rather hug Lulu than me, Lulu loves hugging people and it doesn't bother me one way or the other," Lenox replied.

"Oh I totally do love hugging!"

"Yes, and you sometimes get in trouble because you hug random strangers like motorcycle gang members, without warning," Freya said.

"Hey, if they look like they need a hug, I'm gonna hug," Lulu said in an almost cheerful belligerent tone.

"Lulu!" Conalai called out in a scolding tone, though to Penny it really didn't seem like he had it in him to scold his daughter over hugging.

"I thought when you used to hug the street urchins in Victorian London and they would rob you blind, that you learned your lesson!" Freya scolded, not suffering the same affliction that Conalai did.

"Not at all," Lulu admitted. "Besides, they didn't rob me. I purposely brought heavy coin pouches with me so the wee mites would be able to have enough coin to eat. I mean, what do I need money for?"

"I dunno to live?" Phoenix offered.

Lulu waved at him with a small hand as she hugged Winston. "Nah, that's what magic is for or Freya, since Freya buys everything for me."

"Not true. You buy what you like and I pay the bills which is much easier with the advent of a credit card. Good Light above, I never thought that I would advocate for the credit card industry but it does keep tracking Lulu's expenses so much easier. So... it looks like he's about to break free."

Lenox stood up and pulled Penny up and swept her into his embrace and kissed her.

"There's no time for that!" Sebastian hissed in the background when Penny wrapped her arms around Lenox's neck.

"Sure there is! Plant one on me!" Ally laughed.

Lenox and Penny ignored them as the focused on each other.

Do you trust me, Penniah? Lenox asked her.

With my very soul, Lenox, Penny replied instantly knowing that the feeling was reciprocated.

Lenox let his feelings do the talking as he wrapped Penny's soul in love before whispering, *I believe I have one last trick up my sleeve. Well, mine and Lulu's.*

Penny realized then what was about to occur and felt pure happiness bubble up in her.

Go for it love, Penny replied.

Lenox smiled before he released Penny with one arm and grabbed Lulu's hand as she stood right behind him.

With time being of the essence, Penny unleashed her powers and felt the hell-link chains spread out and wrap around both twins. However there was no intent to do them any harm, as instead, the chains bestowed them new magical powers.

Then, just as the demon burst free from his prison, a blinding flash of light erupted suddenly, stunning everyone.

"What the hell!" Sebastian hissed as he blinked rapidly, trying to take in both what had happened and the massive demon that seemed to be trying to shake off his daze and head towards them.

"No, hon, you got that wrong again. Not what but who and the answer is there are two new very special hellhounds among us now."

Penny couldn't help but agree when she saw the two large vivid dark purple hellhounds burn with a smoky ethereal fire.

Ha, I knew it! We're totally immortal mongooses, Lenox! Nice! Lulu laughed.

Yes, dear sister, now don't forget we have our roles to play and I leave this part to you. Lenox said letting Lulu, seemingly take the lead.

I'm in it to win it! Lulu replied as she let out a howl and took off, with Lenox close behind her.

Dashing across the plains, Lenox and Lulu could hear the others shouting at them.

"What are you doing?"

"No stop! It's suicide!"

"Lenox! Lulu! Don't!"

Suddenly Penny's voice rang clear across the plane, "Relax everyone, just watch, you'll see."

Lenox smiled as he bore down towards the demon, heading right at the last minute as Lulu went left. The demon swiped at them with its ghostly claws but it went right through them, leaving none of the residual evil that it would have with another hellhound.

Suddenly the demon spoke, unlike the last three who had only screamed, growled and howled. ***"What are you!"***

Your worst nightmare, Lulu cheerfully replied, drawing the demon's focus away from Lenox.

"Lulu, you can't say that in a cheerful tone, add a growl for Light sake!" Ally scolded.

Can't sorry, Ally, I'm a seriously cheerful person.

"But it's not the time to be cheerful!"

Sure it is, you'll see. Lulu said before she added in their deep twin link. *Go for it Lenox, I'll keep this blighter chasing his tail for a bit.*

Lenox quietly agreed, and secretly generated an imitation of himself, using the wisps that joined Lulu in toying with the demon, by darting around him in a confusing pattern.

"I will kill you!" the demon howled in rage.

Nope, Lulu said cheerfully, as she dodged his latest attack, her tail wagging happily.

"I will see you dead!"

Ha ha, nope, Lulu laughed softly.

"What do you mean? You are hellhounds. You will absorb my evil and become weak as babies."

Does it seem like that's happening? Lulu asked as she cocked her head at him.

"Sure it is!"

Is it? Lulu asked again.

"It is!"

Lulu laughed again as she dodged away from his latest attack.

"Stop moving so fast!"

Lulu giggled this time as if she was having a ball.

"Stop laughing at me! Are you crazy?"

Hmm... as far as I'm aware, I'm sane but then what is sanity really?

Frustrated, the demon turned his attention to Lenox. ***"Why aren't you talking? Is it because you know I'll be murdering your girlfriend and sister soon while you watch?"***

Lenox secretly snorted and shook his head at the weak attempt to raise his anger. Though Lenox was also really kind of amused by Lulu's responses.

"Ah, but I will!"

Ha, ha, are you high? Lulu asked.

"You again! Pesky annoying fly!"

I'm a mongoose hellhound, actually, Lulu replied.

"There is no such thing, and I should know. I created the hellhounds."

Last I checked, your name isn't Fironyi, so I find that statement to be untrue, Lulu stated cocking her head.

The demon snarled. ***"Go away fly!"***

OMG, you're totally bad at this demon thing you know, Lulu goaded.

"I am not! I am the worst demon in all of hell!"

I know, I just said that, duh, Lulu retorted dryly.

"No, I'm am the most terrible."

I know.

"I mean I am the baddest."

At being a demon? I know.

"Killing you will be an utter pleasure!"

I can see why. I'm an utter delight.

"I just threatened your life!"

Yeah but it's much more of an empty threat, so I'm not that bothered, Lulu huffed.

"What is wrong with you?" the demon demanded.

Literally nothing, Lulu replied.

"This is a battle for the ages!"

Is it?

"Yes."

Is it really?

"How can you say that?"

Why thank you for asking, and I say that because you are the dumbest demon there ever lived, I swear. You've been throwing completely weakened attacks, all the while bloating your self-worth when you can't clearly see what's going on around you.

"What are you talking about. Wait! What have you done?" The demon roared.

Me? Nothing. Lenox everything, Lulu replied sweetly as she felt Lenox finish his work.

"What?"

Lenox answered this time as he took he released the imitation and appeared again. *I've sealed your magic with my null powers. You've got nothing left.*

He's all yours now, Penny hon, Lulu called out in a sing-song tone.

Lenox shifted into his normal form, then grabbed his twin's hand and they disappeared into nothingness like the last three times so they set up the stone circle in relative peace.

"This cannot be! No matter. I will end you."

Penny snorted in response as it wasn't worth dignifying the demon with any verbal response. She charged across the plane in her hellhound form, unleashing her hell- link chains as she went. Though her first true move was to summon up light magic to drive back the demon as it attempted to go after Lenox and Lulu.

"Away with you wench, I haven't got time to play with you. I have rats to kill," the demon hissed.

They're not rats. They are hellhounds. Ones I will defend with my dying breath if necessary.

"Here, let me hasten that for you then." The demon snarled as it lunged at Penny, abandoning its hunt.

Penny rebuffed him with her hellhound magic, which was actually surprisingly at first, until she realized that her gifts had been reinforced by Lenox's, which gave her the added ability to instantly null all evil energy that the demon directed at her and fight at full strength.

"What are you?" The demon snarled when he realized he couldn't directly harm Penny.

I'm the Brimstone Huntress.

"You are no huntress. I have known and killed many of those in the past and you are too weak to be one of those."

Speaking of weak, that was a purely weak attempt at knocking down my self-confidence. In fact, you've tried to lay me low with words before, dirt bag but it didn't work. For even thinking the worst of myself, I was still too good for the likes of you, Penny retorted.

The demon cursed at her.

I am a female dog, so I don't see that as an insult, Penny replied with a laugh.

"I will kill you," the demon snarled.

You can try but I will come out on top, Betrayer.

"Weak words. No huntresses have before."

So you say but I will defeat you.

"Such confidence for a dead woman."

Still very much alive, thank you for noticing, Penny retorted.

"Not for very much longer."

Done and we're clear of the portal love, Lenox whispered through their soul link.

Penny made no indication that she heard him as she refused to tip her hand. She instead, continued to fight the demon in back in forth movements, which caused the demon to gain in confidence and completely ignore the standing stones and everyone else.

Perfect, Penny thought to herself.

"What's perfect?" the demon asked.

Feeling more bravado than she ever felt in her life, Penny used the moment of confusion on the demon's part to act. Using her divine fire and chains in a combination that the Light had blessed her with in the last battle, she caught the demon off guard with the magical blast and shoved him back into the centre of the stone circle with one fluid moment.

For a moment, nothing happened and the demon froze before smirking.

"Nothing's gonna—" The demon stopped as the trap triggered and held him in place.

"Wrong," Penny replied as she switched forms.

"Dead wrong," Lenox added as he and Lulu took form on either side of Penny.

The demon suddenly attempted to barter. ***"Here now, I'm a generous demon. Free me and I'll let you live."***

"Drop dead," Lulu huffed out before adding, "Wait, you've already done that. Nevermind."

"He has, Lou, so you're gonna have to settle for him staying bound in hell for eternity," Penny said with a shrug.

"Don't be sorry, I like the sound of that so much more," Lulu said as she hugged Penny at the same time Lenox did, which effectively purified her energy.

Thanks, you two, now time to seal this demon within the circle.

Go on, Pen, we'll watch out for you, Lulu said.

Lenox said nothing as Penny felt his overwhelming love instead.

Closing her eyes, Penny focused on clearing her mind as she heard Lulu let loose what had to be an acid retort at something the demon had said to Penny.

Not focusing on the words since she knew that would break

her concentration, Penny instead completely cleared her mind before she added the landscape back into her mind. Though below her feet the ground glowed red instead of a stony grey or moss green and Penny smiled as she knew what was coming.

Summoning up her violin and taking a deep breath in, Penny began to play the last song that she held within her heart. Though as she did, deep within the ground she felt another group of guardians stir, only these were not earth guardians but fire guardians.

The ground shook and trembled seeming to melt away from everyone's feet leaving large pools of lava.

The demon snapped and snarled at the guardians as they emerged from the ground. He pulled against Penny's hell-link chains, causing her to feel pain. Though suddenly, she felt nothing as Lenox and Lulu used their magic jointly to create a cocoon that protected her from the demon's wicked attacks.

We've got your back love, keep playing, Lenox said.

Penny nodded as she continued to play the song on her violin and in her mind's eye, she saw the fire guardians burst from the ground and head into the sky becoming a beautiful electrical storm full of lightning of every colour.

It was almost dazzling to see, though Penny knew that regardless of how pretty it was, she could not stop playing for the music gave the guardians strength to do what they must.

Suddenly the first lightning bolt hit the first pillar and the demon howled in rage as he tried to pull the pillar down with the chains, but before he could move an inch, the next lightning bolt flashed and the second guardian entered the next pillar. Then in a quick succession of flashes, the rest of the guardians entered the pillars and sealed the demon within.

"Don't think you've won," the demon hissed.

"I know I haven't… yet," Penny said.

Deciding to be pre-emptive, Penny took another deep breath and unleashed a large blast of purifying magic across the landscape that Prometheus, Epimetheus and Phoenix added to, which cleansed the land and kept any evil villain from teleporting to their location.

"Are you a fool? You're weakening yourself for nothing,"

The demon cackled at the large amount of magic Penny used.

However Penny knew that in truth she still had plenty of strength to hold the demon until dawn and his words were just bluster.

"Ah jeez, are you ever a chatty Cathy! Light sake's, I'm actually beginning to miss the other three Betrayers since all they did was grunt, scream, howl and hiss," Lulu said.

"I will kill you first!" The demon snarled at her.

"Me, Lenox, Penny; Wash, rinse, dry, repeat," Lulu replied as she waved her hand dismissively.

"What does that mean? Are you mocking me?"

"Of course," Lulu chirped.

"Lulu!" Freya hissed this time.

"Yes?" Lulu asked sweetly.

"Can you not verbally poke the Betrayer?"

"Nope, I'm a total mongoose, my love. Ergo I poke at cobra demons in order to annoy them. It's what I do."

"What is with you and mongooses? Sorry, I can't hold that question in anymore," Raven asked.

"Isn't it mongeese?" Phoenix interjected.

"It's actually mongooses but Oxford Dictionary does allow the irregular plural of mongeese," Lenox's father stated.

"Shut up!" The Betrayer hissed.

Lulu, of course, ignored him. "Mongooses are adorably cute but also ferociously vicious when they need to be. Like wee adorable rapscallions of the natural world. Who wouldn't want to be a mongoose?"

"You've got us there, Lulu, though I have to say you are the most badass vampyr that I've ever met," Memphis laughed.

"You know I would take offence to that except for the fact that it is true. Well, small modification, since Lenox earns that title too, I saw what you did there nephew, while Lulu goaded him," Phoenix remarked.

"That's fair, we're twins after all," Lulu agreed.

"Your twins?" the demon hissed.

"Jeez, don't tell me you just noticed that now." Lulu snorted.

The demon said nothing.

"How does anyone on this planet not know we're twins?" Lulu asked Lenox with a frown.

"Don't know, sis. I thought it was quite obvious myself but it is clear that this Betrayer never paid attention to us for a single moment, which boded well for us."

"I will kill you both."

"Heard that one before," Lenox replied as he looked to the sky.

The first hint of dawn was upon them and Lenox could feel his hope grow deep within him as he knew that it would over soon. Though he wasn't the only one to notice as the demon seemed to realize that dawn was upon them and fought like a mad fiend against his entrapment, yet Penny used her magic to hold fast and keep the demon bound within.

Suddenly the ground shook as the sun rose higher and higher in the sky and ignited the portal underneath the Betrayer.

Penny nearly collapsed to the ground when the giant bright fiery red hell tentacles wrapped around the demon and started to pull him back down towards hell. Though when Penny pitched forward in tiredness, Lenox caught and swept her up into his arms.

Weary, Penny rested her head against his shoulder as she watched the demon fight to no avail to break free. Though suddenly, the demon changed tactics as he fought to head towards them, intent on taking both Lenox and Penny to hell with him.

"Not today, Betrayer," Lenox said as he shoved the demon back with a wall of null magic, causing the demon to lose footing, allowing the tentacles to drag him down.

Penny watched the ground restore itself before the standing stones sank back below the marsh that they had inhabited for eons

"It's over, isn't it?" Penny asked Lenox as she looked up at him.

Lenox nodded before he broke out into a wide smile. "Oh, yes, my love. It truly is."

With that, Lenox sealed his lips over Penny's and kissed her as the warm rays of the sun pierced the natural gloom around them.

Chapter Thirty- Three

Lenox! Penny squealed with happiness before it bubbled over into outwards laughter. She wrapped her arms around his neck, returning his kiss with an intense passion, feeling both loved and giddy at the same time.

A loud growl erupted behind them but Lenox didn't care as he was willing to chance his father-in-law's fury since he didn't want to let go of Penny. Ever.

"Ah come on, Lenox, we know you love Penny but please let us get a least one celebratory hug," Ally complained.

Lenox sighed before he figured that was reasonable, although he really didn't want to be reasonable at that moment.

It's okay my love, I understand why you don't want to let me go but you know we do have our whole lifetime ahead of us.

And what a lifetime it will be, Penniah, Lenox responded before he finally relented and put Penny down on her feet and released her from their kiss.

"Light, I love you, Penniah Hawksley," Lenox murmured in her ear before she moved away from him.

"Well, good because I love you, too, Lenox Hawksley!" Penny declared before she hugged her mum and dad.

Soon after, Lenox's dad and sister hugged him and Lenox felt the same giddiness Penny felt infect him too, as he realized it was well and truly over.

"Yes, it is, Lenox and I'm truly proud of you both. You worked so hard to make this happen," Conalai murmured in Lenox and Lulu's ears meaning every word.

"I am too and damn me, if I've got to start stepping up my game to catch up with Lenox and Lulu. I mean, did you see that Iona? Jeez oh! Can you believe that they secretly plotted the downfall of each Betrayer demon without any of us being the wiser? I'm stunned, I am. Light! I'm gonna make this even more of an epic story. Let's see, I'll start with flashes of thunder and...."

"I think you mean flashes of lightning, Vampyr king and there had better be more than paltry flashes of lightning to make this story even better. Come on man, where's your sense of drama?" Alfie retorted.

"I need to add drama? Really, Alfie? Me?"

"As the muse and patron behind as many as 7,982 classic works of fiction, I know a good story when I see one and if you are going to make this into a work of fiction, then you're gonna need loads of drama, I tell you," Alfie responded.

"And angst, don't forget that either," his twin piped up.

"What are you going on about now?" Penny's dad asked.

"Phoenix writes novellas and novels about all our immortal exploits. Well, not just ours. I meant every immortal species and we're just giving him pro tips when it comes to this story because we want it to as epic as it can be," Ally responded.

Sebastian growled softly as his ire started to grow. "You know what? On you go, Phoenix, just don't cock it up."

Phoenix snorted. "As if. I've been at this for millennia, my man and if there's one thing I do well, it's spin a good yarn that stands the test of time."

"So what now?" Sebastian asked Lenox and Penny, who had secretly made it back to each other and now held hands.

Penny looked at Lenox and winked before turning back to her dad.

"Well, I'm going to finish my thesis and present it in front of a panel. Meanwhile, Lenox is going to finish a few projects in his warehouse for the next week or so. Though in a few weeks once it's a bit warmer in Moonlight Valley, we're gonna build the most epic amusement park that's going to open on July 1st before we go on a six week holiday before the new school term starts at Cambridge."

"You two are going to build an entire amusement park in about two months' time before going on holiday? That's ambitious," Penny's dad said.

"Well, we are going to need loads of help, Dad, you know anybody?" Penny asked with a hint of amusement in her tone.

"Might do but it's going to cost you," Sebastian replied.

"Oh? What's the going rate?" Penny asked, keeping up the ruse.

"Well, I'm going to need you two to help me speak to the Dean of Cambridge, so we can set up specialty hellhound classes since there have been loads of interest from other hounds in getting degrees there."

"Ah, you don't need to talk to that old fuddy-duddy. I've got you covered Sebastian," Raven stated as she walked over.

"Ah, good deal then," Sebastian.

"Hell yes! You hear that, Alfie! We can get proper mechanical engineer degrees, maybe a couple of maths ones while we're at it! Ooh and don't forget I want to get one in nuclear physics! I love plutonium!"

"The nuclear one is going to have to be negotiable, my mate," Sebastian retorted at once.

"Ah, man! I want to play with plutonium."

"Which is why that degree is going to have to be negotiable, for proper tough safety measures need to be in place first and I mean real tough ones. Which is why I'm getting that degree first, so I can make sure you don't accidentally turn Cambridge into a nuclear waste zone."

"Well, I guess that's reasonable but it sucks that you get to have all the fun first."

"I don't see how I'm going to get to have all the fun first when I have to get a degree and run the hellhound pack at the same time to keep you from causing even more nuclear trouble."

"We'll help," Alfie offered.

"You… help?" Sebastian scoffed immediately.

"Yeah, on second thought, nevermind. We'll be too busy to causing trouble for you to be any help to you, so you should probably seek out more responsible hellhound twins."

"More responsible hellhound twins?" Sebastian stopped and smiled before he looked at Lulu and Lenox.

Lenox shrugged, "I have no problem aiding you, Sebastian."

"Count me in, too!" Lulu cried out in delight.

"I might not be a hellhound but where my children go, so do I, so you can count my wife in and me, too," Conalai offered.

"Good deal and now I'm not concerned because I know with you four and Freya, you'll have everything set, and for once I might get a chance of having a wee bit of peace."

"Good luck with that," Ally called out.

It'll be fine, Penny said to Lenox, trying not to scare him.

Lenox still took it in stride. *Sure it will, my love. After all, we took down four Betrayers, ergo, surely we can handle a bit of hellhound mayhem.*

Sure we can, Lulu agreed.

The four of them (Freya included) laughed at the absurdly happy future ahead of them.

*****

A year and half later...

Lenox sat quietly outside the room where Penny was defending her thesis in front of an academic panel. To his left sat his twin Lulu who held his hand as Penny's mum sat to his right. Beside her was Penny's dad, Alfie, Rika, Lucy, Tyr, all the hellhound elite, Lenox's parents, Freya, Lore and Bryn.

No one said anything as they all used their supernatural hearing to listen to Penny's presentation since they weren't allowed to be in the room.

Suddenly they heard nothing more and all of them looked at each other, bewildered until they caught sight of Reggie, who just looked at them all with a sardonic look. It became apparent to Lenox then, that Reggie had blocked them from hearing the results so that Penny could tell them. Holding his breath, Lenox waited for what seemed like forever until he saw his lovely wife exit the room with a neutral expression on her face.

Immediately Lenox stood up and inquired, "Penny love, how'd it go?"

Penny's face broke into a wide grin. "I got it! I got my dual doctorate!"

Lenox smiled in relief before he swiftly swept Penny into his arms and hugged her tightly.

"Congratulations, love, I knew you could do it," Lenox murmured in her ear.

"Ha! You were a bit worried. I saw it," Penny returned with a laugh.

"No, not worried, just excited for you and wanting for you to share your news. Honest I truly knew you had it as soon as I heard you speak. You nailed it," Lenox said.

"You totally did, Penny sweetie, I'm so proud," Ally squealed before she wrapped her arms around the couple.

Lenox gently let go of Penny allowing Ally to muscle in and hug Penny before everyone else got a turn.

"Lunch is on me, sweetie, what do you feel like?" Sebastian said after a moment.

"I could do with a curry. Can we go to Vikram's Cafe? He said he was making Carolina reaper curry again today," Penny replied.

"Um, love is that... wise?" Lenox asked automatically in concern before biting his lips wondering if he had said too much.

Ah, love, don't be alarmed. This is a perfect place to tell them, though can I do the honours?

Lenox nodded as his hand found Penny's and held onto it.

The couple shared a loving look before Penny spoke.

"Uh... you know the question that Mum tries to keep asking? Well..." Penny started as she rested a hand on her flat stomach.

Instantly everyone zeroed in on her hand moment and looked back at her in stunned awe.

"You're pregnant? Really?" Penny's mum blurted out in pure shock.

"Yeah mum, Lenox and I went and saw a healer a few days ago to confirm it. I'm about six weeks along right now and true to other Animalia cycles, I've got about another ten and a half months to go."

"So soon?" Ally asked.

"Mum—" Penny started to say, but again, Ally hugged her,

this time carefully.

"This is truly one of the best days of my life, oh sweetie, congratulations. You two are going to be wonderful parents."

"Yeah, you will and congratulations, too, Lenox," Sebastian said as he clapped Lenox on the back and shook his hand.

"Yes, congratulations, Lenox and Penny! Light, Mina, we've got to make some expansions to our cottage so we have more room for our growing family." Lenox's dad laughed as he congratulated them both.

"Oh, I'm so very, very, happy for both of you," Lenox's mum cried, bursting into happy tears.

Penny wiped a happy tear that slipped down her own cheek before her stomach suddenly growled. "Gosh, I'm hungry. Do you truly think curry is a bad idea, Lenox?"

"Carolina reaper curry? Yes; Another less spicy curry? No."

"He's right, sweetie, having a less spicy curry is best when you're a pregnant hellhound, though not because it will harm your baby but it will give you indigestion like no one's business and you really can't take anything for it. Light, when I was pregnant with you and I found that I craved meat like no one's business, too."

"I want it but I've actually been craving cheese and tomato sandwiches of late. We were going through two loaves of bread a day before I sought out the healer and I do remember her saying that I might crave more vegetables and dairy than a normal hellhound since she believed that our children might be—"

"Hold on," Sebastian said raising up his hand, "Did you say children, sweetie?"

Penny laughed as she realized she hadn't mentioned that part.

"Oh, sorry dad but despite it being the early days, the healer was pretty clear that I was carrying twins. So… er… surprise! There will be another set of twins born to the hellhounds, though the healer believes these twins will possibly not be full hounds but will carry a more even split of Lenox's power and mine," Penny admitted, wondering how all the hounds would take the fact that her twins might not be full hound.

Her dad just smiled. "That's wonderful news, my dear one,

though I can guarantee with *Frick and Frack* here, they'll be taught to give me no peace."

"Damn straight. Got to teach the babies how to be a true Baskerville twin!" Alfie declared.

"Hey, hey, they're Hawksley twins. They're gonna be wise like they're mama, papa and grandpa," Sebastian argued.

"As if! They will still be wee hell-raisers."

Conalai snorted. "As if. Lenox and Lulu were the sweetest children ever. I can see them inheriting that."

"Well, I say they're gonna be sweet, wise hell-raisers. After all, nothing says that they can't be all three. Though above all they are going to be happy well-loved wee mites," Penny said as she and Lenox rubbed her stomach.

"They sure are. Though we're going to need to make them a proper wagon! How do you two feel about the colour blue? I mean I know your favourite colours are green and pink but..." Lulu offered.

"But a blue wagon sounds absolutely lovely. Ah! I can picture our two wee mites pulling their blue wagon full to the brim with blankets, teddies and toys just like Lulu's kids do now with their own red wagon."

"Don't forget cart snacks," Alfie pointed out, "What? We hounds like snacks and don't worry about it sweetheart, for no matter what. In our eyes, they're gonna be hellhounds. Mark my words."

Penny smiled at her uncle's words knowing what he truly meant. For even if her children turned out to be full Ritana, the hounds would still see them as hounds, for they would always be part of the pack. Penny felt very content then, that all of her dreams were coming true.

You know what that means, love? Lenox asked.

What's that?

You've got to create more dreams to aspire to.

Penny shook her head. *No, I'm good for the moment, though the Nobel peace prize is still on the table, albeit years from now. Besides, I've pretty much hit the jackpot here so I am more than content to happily spend the rest of my life with you and our family just being together.*

Lenox nodded. *Yeah that does sound pretty amazing. I love you, Penniah Hawksley.*

As I love you, Lenox Hawksley, forever and forever.

With that, the couple teleported everyone to Vikram's as their family gently bickered amoungst themselves about what they were going to order. Though Penny and Lenox wouldn't change them for the world.

For now the future looked bright, and Penny couldn't wait to face every new challenge with Lenox by her side.

Life is going to be awesome little ones, just you wait and see, Penny whispered said to her babies.

And indeed, for the Brimstone Huntress and her Sage mate, life was going to be amazing, for it was now going to be what they made it.

Epilogue

Three years later…

Lenox and Penny walked hand in hand as twin toddlers pulled a shiny blue wagon filled to the brim with stuff.

"Mama!" The little girl, Mori called out.

"Yes, sweetie?"

"Today is market day," Mori's twin, Bask answered excitedly.

Penny smiled at their children, Moregan and Baskerville Hawksley, who had become the little darlings of the hellhound Compound, being the first children born for the last two hundred years. Though very much like their serious yet sweet father, the little ones didn't know how beloved they were as they instead were happy just bringing joy to others in the disguise of adventures.

"There's granny, Mori," Bask stated before he and his twin waved eagerly at Lenox's mother.

Mina stopped setting up a low table and moved towards them.

"Good afternoon, my sweet ones," she said greeting the eager twins with a hug before moving on to hug Lenox and Penny warmly.

"Where's my mum, dad and Lenox's dad?" Penny asked since it was highly unusual not to see all three when Mori and Bask were out and about in the Compound.

"Just inside the fight club discussing table cloths. Your mum wants the wee clown one. Your dad wants the unicorn one, and Lenox's dad wants the cloud one. Though, we all know that Alfie will bring over a Batman one in a moment."

Mori looked at the table and back at her twin. Bask nodded in full agreement with what his twin was thinking.

"Granny, it's a big table. How about we use all four?"

Mina looked at the table and hummed as she reached out mentally to her mate.

Conalai, Sebastian and Allie came bursting out of the fight

club with the table cloths in hand moments later.

"How is this going to work exactly?" Sebastian asked, rubbing the back of his neck.

"Granny? Our table is eight feet long, right?" Mori asked.

Mina nodded.

"Then there we will use two feet of clown cloth, two feet of cloud cloth, two feet of unicorn cloth and two feet for Batman cloth that Unca Alfie will bring soon," the twins said in unison.

"Ah! Look at you two! Little mathematicians at two years old. I'm so proud!" Ally cried out as she hugged the little toddlers.

"Thank you, granny, but of course we are math magicians, our mummy and daddy are math magicians and you are a math magician and Unca Alfie is a math magician," Bask pointed out.

"Well, true," Ally agreed not bothering to point out that she and Alfie were actually mechanical engineers according to the spiffy new degrees that they had obtained in recent months since she knew her grandchildren equated engineers and quantum physicians with being 'math magicians'.

Sebastian bent down and asked Mori and Bask, "You two ready for market day?"

"Oh yes, grandpa, we gathered our wares to sell," the twins answered as they hugged him in unison before showing off their loaded cart.

"So much stuff! Whatever will you buy with the money you get from market day?" Sebastian asked them.

"We put most in our piggy bank for rainy days grandpa," Mori answered shyly.

"Uh huh, except we buy one Lego set each and we're gonna buy a Batmobile and pony stable one."

"So you're gonna park your Batmobile in the pony stable?" Alfie asked as he arrived with his wife Rika.

"Uh huh, Uncle Alfie. That way the Batmobile is not lonely when he's not crime-fighting, 'cause he's got Lego ponies to talk to," Bask explained.

"That seems fair, wee nephew," Alfie said fondly as he handed Ally the Batman table cloth and began unloading the twins' blue wagon.

Penny and Lenox helped their children set up wares in happy

harmony and quiet peace as they listened to Mori and Bask chat with their grandparents, aunt and uncle.

"Mori, Bask, you're all set, sweeties," Penny declared happily with a clap.

Lenox wrapped an arm around her shoulders and smiled at his two happy children.

"Thanks, mummy and daddy, we're open for business. You buying anything?" They asked their parents.

"Absolutely! Hold on. mum get the camera," Penny called but her mum and Lenox's mum were already filming or taking pictures of everything on their phones.

Penny laughed as she knelt to her children's wares table and picked up a mug that she knew Lenox and the kids had made for her specially. "This one, please and I shall take a bag of jerky, too," Penny said as she handed her son the money and took the mug and the jerky.

Mori opened the money box and Conalai pointed out a five-pound note to hand back as change. Mori dutifully handed her mum the note as her brother put the twenty-pound note in with the rest.

"My turn. I shall take this mug and this bag of chocolate almonds," Lenox said as he knelt next to Penny and paid for his purchase.

"Thank you for your business, mummy and daddy," the twin called out in unison before they ran around the table so they could hug their parents.

"Hey, don't abandon your posts," Sebastian called out with a laugh.

"We're not abandoning posts, grandpa. We're just appreciating mummy and daddy. Though can you please hold down our fort?" Bask asked.

Sebastian laughed as he looked up at his wife. "Yes, grandson, I will. They are totally your grandchildren, Ally."

"Oh yes. When shall you be back at business, Mori and Bask? Since granny and grammy would like to buy some things, too." Ally said after blowing them a kiss.

The twins looked at each other then there parents, before returning to their post. "We open now."

Lenox and Penny laughed as they stood up.

"Oh, Mum, by the way, Lenox and I have talked at length. We know that this little endeavour of the twins was so they could put some money away until they could buy a games console," Penny stated.

"What? They are so little." Penny's mum declared.

Mina clapped happily. "Oh, good!"

Penny felt bewildered for a moment as she could have sworn it was her mum's idea.

Lenox grinned and said, "We're okay with a Nintendo one because we know our wee ones want to play Lego Batman and Mario Kart. So once they close up shop in a few hours, we're okay with you lot taking them to the toy store and buying one. We'll even have a family games night tonight, how about it?"

Lenox's mum made a small fist bump with Lenox's dad before saying, "Yes!"

Penny felt out of her depth for a moment.

"It was not your mum but mine who suggested it, love," Lenox said with a chuckle. "In fact, my mum's got a couple of gaming consoles hidden under the couch that she and dad play all the time with Mori, Bask, Lore and Bryn when they go over to their house. Our kids wanted to add to their granny's game collection, hence 'market day' but I know they'll be okay to have a game system of their own instead."

"But they're so young, though," Ally replied again.

"Doesn't stop them from being the best wee Mario Go Kart players. They've got awesome skills throwing the blue turtle shell," Mina said with pride.

"At me!" Conalai retorted, mock scowling at Mina who just smiled.

"Is it still okay to go to the store with the kids?" Mina asked Lenox one last time.

"Absolutely, Mum," Lenox agreed at once.

"Yes, and it looks loads of gaming will be occurring as both Ally and Alfie try to reach Mina's level," Sebastian said with a sigh.

"Good luck with that," Mina said serenely.

"True story. She's been playing video games since the first console came out and Mina could play professionally if she wanted to," Conalai admitted.

"Wow, really?" Alfie asked.

Conalai nodded.

Suddenly Lulu, Freya and their children arrived.

"Hey, sorry we're late! I just got out of a mood," Lulu said as she hugged everyone.

"Lore, Bryn, come join us! Come, join us! Mummy and daddy said yes to our very own game console and games, so we've got to raise big money now!"

"We're on it!" The older twins called out as they pulled their red wagon over and added to the wares table to help out their younger cousins.

Reggie popped his head out of the fight club. "The wee ones open fully for business now?"

"Yup, yup, we're open for business. Come one, and come all, no discounts!" Bask and Mori cried out happily.

"Yeah, no discounts!" Bryn and Lore declared, too.

Reggie snorted as he looked at Ally and Alfie, who linked arms and grinned.

"They do us so proud," Ally said with a happy, contented sigh.

"They truly do. Now—" Alfie said as he started moving towards the table.

His twin beat him to it.

"Me first!" Ally declared as she whipped out Sebastian's wallet from his back pocket.

"Ally!" Sebastian hissed, though it soon turned into laughter.

"What? You can have it back in a moment but I need to buy stuff right now," Ally returned as she and Mina started making a small pile of things they wanted to buy.

Penny and Lenox stepped aside as they saw the hounds start to pour out of the club and attempt to look uninterested in the kids' wares even though they were quite eager to buy something.

Though they weren't the only ones as Lenox's family arrived and immediately started looking over the wares.

Lenox was quick to notice that Falcon and Anya looked a little strained and it was then he realized that Skull and Reagan weren't there.

Falcon, uh, where's Skull? Lenox asked wondering if he was committing a huge faux pas.

Reagan's been hurt and is healing, though Skull's not taking it well, to say the least and all we can do is wait for now, Falcon mentally replied with a sigh.

Lenox accepted the explanation knowing full well that something else was going on. However, usually, when things were going bad, his family got quieter and pulled ranks closer together.

Can you tell Skull something for me later? Lenox asked.

Falcon gave a short half nod.

We'll go to war for him any day. Just tell us when, Lenox replied as Penny nodded in full agreement.

Both Falcon and Anya fully smiled, looking a bit relieved.

We know that Lenox but it does the heart good to hear it, Anya finally said before adding, *Light, though I hope it doesn't come down to an epic quest or hellhound intervention. For once, I just want Skull and Reagan to be happy without all the nonsense we've suffered.*

Lenox nodded in full understanding, though he knew the truth.

"They'll have to fight for what they want one more time, Anya. I know that's not what you want to hear but know this, the villain who's forcing their hand is going to rue the day he met them, mark my words," Lenox said quietly.

"I'm also not supposed to say more than this, however, I will tell you that hellhounds aren't just landlubbers," Penny offered.

"What the hell does that mean?" Anya asked with a snort.

"It means that as a species, we don't keep our fights limited to land. We will take on any evil villain on the high seas, too," Penny said with a smile, leaving it at that as she nodded good day to a stunned Falcon and Anya before heading towards her children's table.

I'm learning, Penny said to Lenox as she wrapped an arm around her mate's waist.

Lenox smiled and nodded, knowing full well what Penny truly meant. After all, in the years since they defeated the Last Betrayer, Lenox had become a full seer just like his mum and sister, and in response, Penny had learned how to become a proper seer's mate under the tutelage of Freya and Conalai. Which really just consisted of her learning to dodge questions about what Lenox was seeing when he was in a mood or more pointedly, redirecting her mother and uncle from constantly asking Lenox what the winning lotto numbers were going to be.

Though that hadn't been the only change in their lives, for Penny was no longer the hidden Brimstone Huntress but a full-on Animalia Rare, an exalted status among all shifters, for having abilities that could change the fate of the world. Which meant that many Animalia came to her, seeking her guidance and aid. This was something that had taken some getting used to but Penny was glad to be accepted by everything though she was also equally glad that the hellhounds had accepted Lenox, Lulu, Freya, Bryn and Lore as hellhounds and had given them their own ranks.

I like my new hellhound rank as a Mongoose Protector, Lenox said.

Ooh, me too! Lulu eagerly agreed, since she still often claimed to be an immortal mongoose and that the twins' title had been endorsed by Penny's mum who had given a whole host of reasons why the title was apt for them.

Yeah, I can handle you two being hellhounds now, and I must admit, it makes my own twin jealous from time to time, which amuses me, Freya acknowledged.

So you worried? Freya asked after a moment knowing what battle was to come next for the vampyr royals.

Lenox shook her head, *Nah, they've got this.*

That's confident, Freya said.

No, it's not Freya. I meant what I said earlier about the villains going to rue the day he met them, and I can't wait to be a fly on the wall when it happens.

Lenox also knew that now was the time for his family to lift themselves out of the bloody treacherous world that they lived in for so long and finally live their lives the way they wanted to, not only for themselves but for future generations of their family.

Smiling softly at his children who waved cheerfully at him, Lenox waved back, feeling very hopeful for their future.

You've got this Skull. Give him absolute hell, Lenox thought, wishing his cousin all the best before focusing on the now and enjoying his very own happy ever after.

About the Author

I live in Courtice, ON, a place even Google can't find on the map. I spend most of my time driving those nearest and dearest absolutely crazy, and procrastinating on numerous schemes before freaking when a deadline happens.

On a more serious note, I'm really an open book. I like to seeing the lighter side in life, and though sometimes what I write might be on the darker side, I like to think that even at the darkest point in one's lives, there's always hope.

You can check out more on facebook at www.facebook.com/halsinchronicles or my webpage http://www.clairmcintyre.com

Made in the USA
Middletown, DE
15 February 2020

84415845R00255